A BLESSING
or
A CURSE

a novel by Pat McGauley

AUTHOR'S NOTE
This is a work of fiction. Names, characters, places, and incidents either are the product of the author's imagination or are used ficticiously, and any resemblance to actual persons, living or dead, events, or locales is entirely coincidental.

Copyright 2003 by Patrick McGauley (Number pending)

For information concerning this title, please contact:
    Patrick McGauley
    2808 Fifth Avenue West
    Hibbing, MN 55746
    (218-262-3935)
    e-mail: shatiferin@aol.com

Manufactured in the United States of America through Stanton Publication Services, Inc., St. Paul, MN. Published by Pat McGauley Publishing (Hibbing, MN. 55746).

Without limiting the rights under copyright, no part of this publication may be reproduced in whole or in part in any form without the prior written permission of both the copyright owner and the publisher of this book.

ISBN: 0-9724209-1-6

Library of Congress Control Number: 2003093745

First edition, Summer of 2003

DEDICATION

In memory of David Johnsrud

And the tear that we shed,
though in secret it rolls,
Shall long keep his memory
green in our souls.'

—Thomas Moore

In Appreciation

ALL STORIES BEGIN somewhere within the creative thoughts of an author. Were it not for help, however, the story might never go beyond the writer's tablet. I am, therefore, truly indebted to my friends and their thoughtful dedication to my project. After every chapter, I discussed the story with my dear friend, Ed Beckers. Ed helped keep the characters consistent and the plot lines tight. Being far more a 'storyteller' that a writer, my original manuscript required considerable editing work. My recently retired friend, Dan Bergan, offered his expertise on an original draft. As with my first book, I turned to another retired English teacher for further review and polish. Kathy Serrano, like Dan, is a perfectionist. When the 'writing process' has gone through a few rewrites, a final review is required. My friend Nancy Erickson was willing to give this story her editing touches, while Norma Grant spent hours editing the final proofs.

Some will "judge a book by it's cover . . . " I was so pleased with the cover artwork of my neighbor, Dave Wirkkula, that I asked him to do another design for me.

I thank these friends for their many hours of work, and for helping to embue this story, *A Blessing or a Curse,* with the vitality and texture its characters deserve. And, I thank all of those who have worked diligently to preserve the marvelous history of Hibbing and of the Mesaba Iron Range. I have drawn extensively from the research of many, and the assistance of the staffs at the Hibbing Public Library, the Hibbing Historical Society, and the Iron Range Research Center in Chisholm.

Prologue

Through the passage of a decade's time, the writer waited for a second invitation to visit Northern Minnesota's Mesabi Iron Range. His first novel, now out of print, had been inspired by stories the old Hibbing sage shared with him when he first traveled to Hibbing. Sales of the self-published book were modest and mostly regional. But, those who read the novel hoped there might be a sequel some day.

On more than one occasion, the author wondered whether the newsman had enjoyed his effort. But Claude Atkinson wrote to him only once since their long conversation on that frigid January afternoon ten years before. A 'thank you' note arrived from Claude's Hibbing address several months after he had received his complimentary copy of the story. Although puzzled, the writer had other projects in the works and years passed much too rapidly as they always seem to do.

Then one August afternoon, the author received an unexpected letter, a letter that might inspire the second book he dreamed of writing. The penmanship on the envelope was not Claude's, but . . .

> *Dear Old Friend,*
>   *My father asked me to write to you and offer his invitation to visit him in Hibbing before summer's end. His health is failing rapidly these days. He hopes to be able to tell you more of the story he began so many years ago.*

Kindly let me know if you can accommodate my dad's wishes.
Sincerely,
Marc Atkinson

A visit to Northern Minnesota in August presents an opportunity to experience nature's finest handiworks. Shades of green cover the forested landscape, lakes reflect majestic blue skies, and wild flowers in an array of color dance across the hillsides. The sun is pleasantly warm through the long days, while the star bright evenings offer refreshing coolness. Residents of Hibbing enjoy picnicking and watching ball games in spacious Bennett Park, or strolling along tree-lined avenues in the quiet evenings or even driving the few miles East to Dupont Lake for hiking and swimming. Daily life in the Iron Range community maintains a relatively slow pace despite the aggressive mining operations which have always provided the city with its cyclic economic base. Evidence of a mining heritage surrounds the community. Huge mountains of overburden resemble mesas to the east and west, while canyon-like gorges create deep red scars across the landscape. There is both majesty and ugliness in the massive excavations. Mesabi offers severe contradictions. Erstwhile politicians campaign on the 'jobs issue' year after year. Economic development and diversification have become legitimate political themes as Rangers watch countless trainloads of rich hematite head south. But things don't really change much in Hibbing or Virginia or any of the some twenty communities along the long, narrow Mesabi Range. The region has lived and died on the unfortunate fates of 'too much supply' or 'too little demand'.

In years to come, Range demographics will evidence the fatal trend of population decline. In 1956, however, the main streets are still busy commercial strips, new subdivisions spring to life, and most people who want jobs can find them. Graduates of the majestic Hibbing High School remain inclined to continue their education and matriculate to college degrees. But more often than ever before, the children of this mining culture are choosing to relocate in larger, more diverse communities. When the vitality of youth leaves a town, death begins knocking on the door.

The writer remembered Claude's living room as if every detail had been etched in his mind. Heavy oak bookshelves covered two walls from floor to ceiling. A collage of photographs—some of recent vintage—hung in a haphazard clutter on an opposite wall. Claude's guest stared for a long minute at the yellowed print of the former Hotel Moran. An abstract drawing of the magnificent structure had been featured on the cover of his earlier novel. The writer felt that arcane chill of an old memory come to life and crawl down his spine.

One of the newer photos caught the visitor's attention as he paused before taking his chair. A handsome young man in a Minnesota 'Gopher' baseball uniform. Next to that picture was another of the same man. In the second photo, the man was posed with a beautiful dark-haired woman—presumably his wife—and an infant son. The woman vaguely reminded him of Mary, the lovely heroine of his first novel. Memories!

Realizing his rudeness of the moment, the visitor turned and smiled at his host. "I'm sorry. These pictures bring me back to when we first . . ."

Returning his smile, the old man informed, "I call the little one in that snapshot, Claude. But that's not his real name. And that's the boy's mom and dad, Kevin and Angela. I'll be telling you more about all of them presently. Now, please make yourself comfortable," he spoke in a voice weakened by years. Like an old professor, he gave a stern reminder—"I'll expect you to take lots of notes, young man—there's a lot of this story left for me to tell."

Claude Atkinson sat in the same overstuffed chair near the corner of converging bookshelves, hands folded loosely on a blanket draped across his spindly legs. Resting in his lap was *the book*. The former newsman was in his eighties now, but his angular and deeply furrowed face seemed unchanged from years before. Claude's piercing blue eyes still held the glint of younger years when he ranked among Minnesota's most respected editors. The town sage had published countless thousands of *Mesaba Ore* newspapers before passing the reins to his son in the early Thirties.

A wide smile creased his face. "I enjoyed your book. I think you captured the essence of Peter Moran quite well. I was worried that after I told you the story of Hibbing's old-timers—Tony Zoretek and Mary Samora, along with Senia Arola and Steven Skorich—well, I worried that you might have told my story differently than I hoped you would. Any one of them might have been a story in himself—or herself." Claude shifted in his chair. "But, it was Peter Moran's story after all. Thanks for capturing the true spirit of that complicated man and the times he lived in. Such incredible times they were!"

The guest nodded at the compliment without responding. As before, he allowed Claude to do most of the talking, while he took detailed notes on everything the newsman had to say. Regarding the old man, then his notebook, he felt a sudden stir of anticipation.

Claude picked up his copy of *To Bless or To Blame* and thumbed through the nearly three hundred fifty pages of text. "Your portrayal of *this* old newspaper editor was quite flattering," he said in reference to himself and how the story had characterized his role in Peter Moran's life. "And, I quite enjoyed the ending. You left the reader with some serious doubts, but . . . we're here to finish what we started, aren't we?"

Claude adjusted his spectacles on a narrow nose while finding the place he was looking for near the end of the book. The last chapter had been titled *The Fire and the Fall*. "When my son and I discussed your ending, Marc considered a clever sequel for the story. Like myself, he'd formed a strange affection for Peter Moran."

"Dad," Marc asked me, "couldn't Peter and his brother, Denis, have taken off together and started a new life for themselves? They were both in deep trouble with the law at the time. Why couldn't the Moran brothers leave Hibbing that night and head West where nobody would ever find them? They had enough money—at least a thousand dollars—to cover their tracks."

"Well, you see, Marc had trouble with the idea of Denis actually killing his own blood. So did I, of course."

Claude put his finger on the line he was looking for. "Here it is. I thought it was in the last chapter, but it's not. The line is something you had Peter say to himself on the afternoon before the fire, and just shortly after my visit with him in the library at the old mansion. I think your few words here have captured the essence of that tormented man . . . *'I've got everything . . . and I've got nothing.'*" Claude looked up from the book and leveled a stare at his guest. "Perhaps, no truer expression could be written of

Peter Moran. In a few choice words you've effectively summarized his life's story."

Claude put the book aside. "You didn't want to tell your readers what happened to Peter that night, even though I thought you should have." His tone held a tinge of reprimand, "But it was your story, and your prerogative as its author to save the *real* ending for your next book. Clever of you, I guess . . . but, now we've got to pick up from there."

Claude removed his spectacles, leaned back in his chair, and folded his large hands in his lap. His thoughts drifted back to that fateful night in August, 1908. He began the story on an unexpected note, "Years later, I got to know Peter's son, Kevin . . ."

His narrative lasted for almost three hours and spanned nearly twenty-five incredible years! From Claude's reminiscences came this story about what happened after Peter's death. Mostly, it's the story of a boy becoming a man. Kevin, of course, is the character around whom most of this story revolves. Something Claude had told Kevin some years before seemed profound to the listener. The old Hibbing sage was talking with the young man, and contemplating the name *Moran* at the time . . .

"Your name might be *a blessing,* or it might be *a curse. . .*"

BOOK ONE

In a Place Called Hibbing

'THE CAUSE OF DEATH?'

August, 1908

The death of Peter Moran at only thirty-three sent waves of disbelief over the iron mining hub of Hibbing, Minnesota. Flamboyant and driven, Moran had become the community's most powerful entrepreneur in the years following the turn of the century.

"I can't believe it, Clay. What you're telling me is just too damn bizarre. Murder! Who? . . . Why? I know Pete had some enemies. But this makes no sense at all." Claude Atkinson shook his head. "Suicide maybe. Not this though. You're going out on a limb . . ."

Claude, editor and owner of Hibbing's *Mesaba Ore,* was pacing the hardwood floor in his office at the Pine Street building where his daily newspaper was published. Clayton Argir stood in the doorway. The chief of police had spent the previous hour surveying the crime scene in the Moran mansion's library. "None of this is for the record, Claude. I'm just tellin you what I *think* happened. We've still got a lot of loose ends here." The squat officer ran thick fingers through his scruffy beard, staring self-consciously at his unpolished black boots and feeling nervous about the observations he had already divulged. Atkinson, he knew, would get to the bottom of this story and report it with unmitigated honesty to his many readers. The editor's integrity had earned him a statewide reputation as the voice of the Mesaba Iron Range. "It looked like suicide when we got there, Claude. But then we saw those things I told ya about. The tracks at the back door . . . the missing money . . . the stolen car. Someone was in that house. No doubt in my mind 'bout that."

"I won't argue the point, Clay. But that someone might have come along *after* Peter shot himself. He might have heard the gunshot and gone in to see what happened . . . then saw the open safe with the cash." Claude peered out the window at the Thursday morning bustle on Hibbing's main street. "How can you be sure it wasn't a robbery after the fact?"

Claude had been a close friend of Peter Moran for years. He knew the businessman had been seriously depressed over a terrible fire that had totally destroyed his majestic hotel earlier in the week. Moran had also been drinking heavily in recent months. "I might agree that Pete was too damn full of himself to do such a cowardly thing as suicide, but I just can't imagine him putting a pistol in his mouth. Not Pete!" Turning toward Chief Argir at the door, Claude gestured, "Pull up a chair, Clay. Let me get my note pad. Go through the facts one more time for me. I'm going to be writing the toughest obituary in recent memory for today's paper. I dread the thought, but . . ." The strain of his emotion brought deep furrows to his long, angular face. He scribbled the name Pete Moran on the top of the page. For the first time the loss of his friend cut him like a knife in the stomach. Claude pulled his handkerchief from the side pocket of his worn gray suit, then dabbed at the corner of his eyes. "Start again with the phone call you got from Moran's housekeeper at, what was it . . . six forty this morning?"

~

Peter Moran, along with his timber baron father Daly and brother Denis, arrived in the small mining village of Hibbing in 1891. Within ten years the Morans built an empire with their sawmill and lumber operations. When the century turned, they diversified their business to include coal distribution for the burgeoning region of mines and boom towns. Peter was a visionary. He pressed his will upon an aging father and weak brother, wresting control of the vast Moran enterprises while still in his twenties. Using his share of the family wealth, his uncanny sense of timing, and his ruthless resolve, he used his expanding influence to every advantage. Anything and everybody that stood in his way were cleverly dispatched. Over the past several years Peter had added greatly to his fortune through liquor distribution and real estate.

Driven by his insatiable ambitions, Peter built an European-style, luxury hotel. The Hotel Moran was testimony to his persistent desire to be acknowledged as Hibbing's most influential citizen. When his hotel opened amid gala celebration in June of 1908, Peter Moran had reached his pinnacle of celebrity. For every success, however, Peter paid a price. Local politicians whom he had befriended and then manipulated gradually turned against him. Recent business reversals brought a financial strain with which he seemed unable to cope. Peter's invincible demeanor changed in pathetic ways. He estranged himself from friends, began drinking in excess, and conducted his business affairs reclusively in the library of his mansion. The loss of his majestic hotel in an horrific fire pushed Peter Moran to an edge from which he could not see any hope.

Claude looked down at his scrawl of penciled notes. Chief Argir's descriptions were concise and his answers to the editor's many questions consistent. "How much of this can I print?" Claude met the policeman's eyes. "I've got to get a story to the pressroom before eleven, Clay."

"Don't do anything speculative, Claude. Leastwise not yet."

Claude chose not to comment at this lack of an answer. He always preferred listening to talking. Keeping his stare, dangling a pencil from his fingers, Claude waited—noticing perspiration beginning to bead on Argir's brow.

"Probably no more than that Peter Moran was found dead from a gunshot wound at about seven this morning. You could mention the housekeeper found him in the library of his house on Washington Street. And, of course, that police are investigating the matter."

"That's not much."

"Sorry 'bout that, Claude. But you can't say anything about the note we found or my suspicions about robbery and murder. We'll be working on this all day I'm sure. You'll be the first one to know if we find anything more than what I've already told you." Argir was apologetic.

"You found footprints in the backyard garden and dirt near the back entry door. The black dirt in the house was the same manured dirt as Moran used in his garden. No signs of a forced entry to the house. So, someone came through the garden and into his residence last night. These are facts, Clay!" Claude leaned back in his chair. "May I read the note you found in the library again?"

Argir handed the crumpled paper across the desk. "The contents are confidential, Claude. Like I said, we haven't talked to this Senia woman yet. She once worked for Moran and lived upstairs in his house. She moved out and got her own place a few weeks ago. Mrs. Arola's the next person I gotta talk with. I'm going over to her apartment down the street when I leave your office."

Claude pressed the wrinkles from the note on his desktop, adjusted his reading glasses to the center of his straight nose. Cupping his jaw in large, slender hands, he reread Peter Moran's last wishes. "The money he mentions was not found in the safe—or anywhere in the room. That's another fact I can't print, right, Clay?"

"Not until we've verified there really was money. Senia might know more about that, Claude." Argir was respectful of Claude's dilemma. "And nothing about the missing automobile yet. We've called all the police in the area to be on the lookout for a 1908 black Buick. It's the only one in these parts, so it should be easy to locate."

"Why is the note all wrinkled? You said it was found on the floor toward a corner of the room. Why wouldn't he just leave it on the desktop for someone to read?"

"Don't know. Maybe someone threw it away."

Claude shook his head. "I'll sit on this for twenty-four hours, Clay. But I owe my readers the whole story, and I'm gonna tell them it will be in the paper tomorrow. That okay with you?"

"I think that's fair. This time tomorrow we'll know where the car is and maybe even have the guy who took it in police custody. Should know about the thousand dollars, too."

"Fine. Thanks for everything, Clay. And, good luck with your investigation. I know this is a tough job for you. Did you know Peter well?"

"Met 'im a few times, that's all. My wife worked at his hotel before the fire. She thought he was a decent fella, I guess. He paid the folks top dollar that's for sure. We're gonna miss the extra money Esther brought in from being a waitress there, I can tell you that for a fact."

Claude escorted the police chief to the open door to his office and shook hands. "Keep me informed."

Argir turned right on the wooden walkway at the corner of Second Avenue and Pine Street. The buildings lining the south side of Hibbing's main street cast narrow shadows across the red dirt off the ledge of board planking. Up and down the busy street merchants were opening doors toward the anticipated Thursday morning shopping activity. Although legally an unincorporated village, Hibbing was a prospering *city* to its nearly ten thousand residents. Already nationally recognized for its iron ore production, it was the undisputed hub of the rapidly expanding Mesaba Iron Range in northeastern Minnesota. Gigantic open pits, among the largest in the world, surrounded the town on three sides. Every day the encroachment of mining posed a significant concern to local officials. Yet they allowed the stripping activities to continue unabated. In Hibbing, the Oliver Mining Company was king! The community owed its livelihood to the gigantic subsidiary of United States Steel.

The backbone of the community was its population base of immigrants including some forty different nationalities. Most of the first generation settlers had traveled to America with the hope of making enough money to return to their homelands of Finland, Yugoslavia, Italy and every reach of Europe to purchase land. Few ever returned. Mining wages were low. Modest prosperity was all they could ever hope to achieve from their arduous labor. Jobs in the open pits and undergrounds were plentiful, dangerous—backbreaking! Miners did not get rich on the Mesaba. Wealth was in the deep pockets of those few owners and managers of the more than one hundred mine operations, most of whom lived some seventy miles south in the more sophisticated port city of Duluth. Hibbing, they believed, lacked culture, refinement.

Over time, many miners saved enough money to send back to the 'old country' so that their wives and families could join them in America. In 1908, however, Mesabi was an enclave of masculinity. Across its stretch of nearly eighty miles, raucous boom towns sprouted haphazardly along the edges of the pits and underground shafts where the men grubbed in twelve-hour shifts. There were twenty bars for every church and twenty brothels for every schoolhouse. Cultural change would occur only gradually. It would be those courageous women who braved the voyage to this new world who would gradually soften the harsh fabric of life here.

From Aurora to the east and Grand Rapids to the west, tens of thousands of miners toiled daily to extract the millions of tons of rich hematite ore, the iron rock that would become steel—steel that the American economy consumed with the hunger of a starving child. And, in the Hibbing mining region, buried just below the surface of a once pristine pine-covered landscape, were enormous pockets of this red gold. The immense ore body that brought life and vitality to the city would one day take its life away. The 'North Forty' of the city was situated atop the richest deposit of hematite in the world!

~

Clayton Argir tipped his black police cap at passersby as he rushed east along Pine Street. At the corner of Third Avenue he paused in front of the Itasca Bazaar, an impressive women's finery store, and glanced at the window display. Fancy women's clothing seemed almost a contradiction to the masculine texture of the mining city. He contemplated the woman he would interview as his investigation sharpened its focus on those who knew the deceased. Across the street, above Fay's Furniture Store, was the apartment where Senia Arola lived. Argir waited as a horse-drawn ice wagon slowly lumbered through the intersection. He waved at drayman Larry Beckers who was struggling to keep his wheels out of the muddy ruts in the center of the street.

Argir crossed Pine, opened the sidewalk entry door, and climbed the flight of stairs to a short hallway which smelled of fresh paint. Before knocking, he listened for any early morning stirrings inside. His pocket watch read eight twelve.

Senia Arola applied a light touch of rouge to accentuate her high cheek bones and bright blue eyes. Still distraught over the stress of these past two days, her face seemed unnaturally pallid. The tall blonde woman, however, was strikingly attractive. Stepping away from the mirror, she appraised her appearance. The soft yellow dress was new. She smiled approvingly as she smoothed a wrinkle below her waistline. Senia would get to the Merchants and Miners Bank where she worked early this morning. She had missed work the day before and wanted to catch up on some investment option plans she was preparing for her employer.

Senia Arola had been Peter Moran's secretary and financial advisor for several months before taking her job at the bank. She came to Hibbing from Vaasa Province in Finland in the fall of 1907 searching for her husband, Timo, a socialist reformer of wide reputation. Timo became deeply involved in that summer's miners' union strike against the powerful Oliver and other mining companies across the Mesabi Range. In a late night demonstration against a group of strikebreakers, Timo was shot and killed on a shadowed street by a company thug. His murder was kept secret for many months. Only recently had Senia been able to unravel the mystery surrounding his untimely death.

The sharp knocking at her door startled her. She glanced at her foyer clock. Who could be here at this early hour she wondered. "Just a minute." Senia quickly surveyed the apartment. She was a meticulous woman. Everything appeared in order.

The stout man in the doorway was wearing a black, woolen police uniform. In one hand he held his hat loosely at his side. His thumb was hooked under his wide gun belt. In his other hand was a large envelope stuffed with papers. His expression was glum.

Senia tried to mask her apprehension with a tight smile. "Good morning, officer."

"You Senia? A friend of Mr. Moran?" Argir asked brusquely, stepping half a pace closer toward the small foyer inside. Without waiting for her response, he blurted, "Got some bad news I'm afraid."

"Is Mr. Moran in some kind of trouble?"

"Mr. Moran is dead!"

Senia felt her knees buckle. She gasped for breath, feeling faint. "My God . . . No!" She sucked in air, as much as her lungs could hold, stepping back for something to grab onto. Her head swung away from the police officer. "No . . . No . . . Oh, Peter!" She felt an acrid bile rise in her throat, a wave of nausea. In stunned disbelief, she gasped for air as if all had been sucked from the room.

Argir, realizing she might fall, stepped forward to grasp her shoulders. "Let's sit down for a minute, ma'am." Nearby was a dining room table and chairs. Leading her by the elbow, Argir helped her sit down.

Senia dropped her head on her arms splayed across the table top and began to cry. Deep, throaty sobs. Her fingernails scraped at the oak veneer. "Peter . . . Peter. You can't be . . ."

"Can I get you something?" Argir was not good at dealing with grief, even less adept with women.

Senia did not answer, trying to get a grip on her drain of emotion. Her thoughts swept back to the day before when she had been talking with Peter, trying to assuage his depression. He was struggling to reconcile his purpose in life in the wake of the loss of his beloved hotel. Senia fought to recall their last words. Her grief was a mental block. She lifted her head, rubbed a sleeve over her red eyes. "What happened?" Her words choked from a dry, tight throat, were hardly audible.

"You okay?" Argir wanted to touch her arm and console, thought better of the gesture, and withdrew his hand, placing it awkwardly atop the envelope resting on the table in front of him. "Ya wanna talk, Mrs. Arola? I mean help me put this thing together. He wanted you, I mean, Mr. Moran, wanted you to take care of some affairs of his."

"I'm sorry. I . . . I just can't. I mean, this is unbelievable. Peter dead? I was with him yesterday. And the night before . . ." She tried to focus on something to clear her cluttered thoughts. On her wall was a Matisse print that Mr. Moran had given her. The artwork had been for her office when she worked as his personal secretary only months before. Senia riveted her eyes on the splash of color. But her thoughts only drifted back sweeping aimlessly to that earlier time when her every day was spent with Peter.

While in Peter's employ, Senia became his most trusted confidante. In his diverse and complex business dealings he relied on her advice. Her insights were valuable. By training, Senia was an accountant. Her intelligence immediately impressed Moran, but her loyalty bonded them even closer. In his final hours after the fire, it was Senia with whom he chose to share his innermost feelings of despair. Only the day before she stood in the street at Peter's side while he surveyed the charred ruins of his hotel. *"Good bye, my lady,"* he had said. His voice strained. Then he removed his hat, holding it over his heart, his tears already spent . . . *"You've left me with nothing to live for."*

Her office and the comfortable apartment he provided were in an upstairs area of his mansion. He was insistent that she be close to his daily business operations, to be available for him at any time of the day. It seemed like only yesterday. But after less than a year, she had quit his employ and established a new life for herself needing to get away from the complications, manipulations, and dark moods that seemed always to surround Peter's precarious lifestyle. No one could be more frustrating than her boss. At the same time, no one could make her feel so important, so needed. Peter Moran was a walking contradiction!

"Are you feeling all right, ma'am?"

Senia pulled out of her tormenting reverie. "What was that? I'm sorry." She regarded the uniformed man. "Did I get your name?"

"I'm Clayton Argir, ma'am, chief of police here in town. We haven't ever met. I hardly knew Mr. Moran. It's pretty sad. I mean his being dead and all. I've never worked a case where someone so important was . . ." Argir caught himself in mid-sentence. He almost said *murdered*.

Senia was perceptive. "Someone was what, Mr. Argir?"

"We don't have it all figgered out yet. That's what I'm tryin to do, get this matter cleared up some." Argir fidgeted with his cap on the table then took out a pencil from his shirt pocket. He slipped a notepad from the envelope along with a wrinkled sheet of paper then set both off to the side.

"Let me tell you what I know at this stage of our . . . it's what us police call a preliminary investigation. I was just over at his house you see, and saw some stuff. But it's too early to figger out what might have happened there last night."

Thoroughly disconcerted, Senia realized she would miss another day at the bank. She thought of calling her employer. Argir, however, was beginning his 'crime scene' explanation. "So I got this call from Mrs. Graham, Moran's housekeeper, just before seven. She's the one who found the body in the library."

Argir was careful not to express any of his personal speculations but mentioned the dirt tracked into the rear hallway. "Probably from the gardens out back," he said. "And the open safe was empty. Sure looked like a burglary but then there's this note we found. It's got your name on it, Mrs. Arola—wrote out to 'Senia', and that's gotta be you." He slid the page in her direction. "It looks to me like a suicide note."

Senia read Peter's familiar handwriting. The emotions she had checked only moments before came unloosed again. She sobbed as she finally remembered what Peter had asked her the day before . . . "a favor to ask . . ." he'd said, "some business things—a little side job," were the words he used. Senia had been walking away from him on the street near the ruins of his hotel at the time. She strained her memory. Peter had mumbled something else. He said "a note." Yes. She remembered it clearly now. But she was too tired from a sleepless night at the time to have given it a second thought. "He told me he'd leave me a note, Mr. Argir."

She finished reading the words then reread them once more. Peter's note spoke with a sting of finality. She was the one person in his troubled life he had reached for. The last person! The pain of this reality pierced like a dagger to her heart. She cleared her throat, looked into the dark, beady eyes of Clayton Argir. "He just couldn't face life anymore, could he? I didn't think he could ever do something like this. He was a tough man, you know. Anyone would tell you that." She was wrong and she knew it.

Peter's facade was deceptive. Always deceptive! He was on the edge, estranged from the world, and his life seemed an incredible illusion. His ambitions were his failing. He was recognizing that reality. He believed he had nothing more to achieve, no one he wanted to live for. Ambitions realized were his consuming emptiness. All of this settled like a black cloud on her thoughts of the moment.

"Can ya identify the writing, ma'am?"

"Yes . . . it's in Peter's hand."

"He wrote it? You're sure about that?" Argir scribbled something in his notepad. "Can you tell me anythin' about the money he mentions there near the end of the note? Says he's left the wall safe open and wanted you to have the thousand dollars."

Senia nodded, stared at the paper again. "Can I keep his note, sir?"

"Not yet. You can write down what he says on your own paper if you wanna do that. I know you need to do some of those things he asks." Argir was uncomfortable but needed a few more answers. "Did Mr. Moran have that kind of money in his safe?"

"Yes. He always kept that amount on hand. I know that for a fact. Why do you ask?"

"Well, like I said. We don't know what happened to the money. And we don't know what happened to Mr. Moran's automobile neither. The car's gone." Argir's forehead wrinkled in puffy rolls, traces of perspiration shown along the sides of his wide face.

"What are you suggesting, Mr. Argir?"

"All I can tell you right now is that this whole thing looks kinda fishy to me."

"May I ask you, Mr. Argir, is there some doubt about this being a suicide? The dirt in the hallway, the missing money, the car? Do you think there was foul play of some kind?"

"Things just aren't adding up is all I can tell you." Argir had no more questions of Senia Arola and was anxious to return to Moran's house to see if anything further had been uncovered there. The note also mentioned a Father Foley in Duluth. And, a son named Kevin. He had some phone calls to make. He'd talk more with the Arola woman later—when he had more information. Information generated questions in an investigation. "Why don't you write the stuff down from the note? I gotta get going pretty soon."

Senia copied Peter's note word for word. "Are you going to talk to Father Foley?"

"Later on today," Argir mumbled impatiently as she wrote neat lines across her paper. "Gotta find out about this boy, Kevin Schmitz, too."

"I'm going to talk with the priest myself," Senia said firmly.

"Rather you didn't do that. Least not until I've had a chance. This is police business, you know."

"Mr. Argir, I intend to do exactly as Peter has asked. I'll not wait for you to get done with what you have to do. I'm sorry, but this has become *my* business!" Senia had not been impressed with the officer's level of competence. "I'm quite capable of getting to the bottom of this terrible . . ." She looked away from the policeman.

"You do what you have to." Argir tried to be assertive in the presence of the intimidating blonde woman. "But don't forget this is *my* investigation. I don't want you telling Foley or anybody what we've talked about here. Do you understand that? It's gotta be confidential."

Senia fixed her sharp blue eyes on the overweight man across her table. "Mr. Moran asked me to take care of his affairs. I will do exactly that! And in the process," she glared, "I intend to find out what happened to Peter . . . and *why!*"

When Argir left her apartment, Senia cried from the depths of her heart. Unabashed tears ran down the palms of her slender hands covering her eyes, smudging the penciled transcription on the table below her face. It was as if Peter's voice had called up from the page. She saw his handsomely featured face. She visualized his wide smile and sparkling eyes, a face remembered from the good times they shared. Then an image transformed her thoughts. The Peter of yesterday flooded into her memory. His sadness was etched in tired lines on his face. His dull, melancholic eyes stared absently. The man was devastated by the loss of *his lady,* a reference often made to the hotel that proudly bore his name.

She read the words welling from the depths of his depression.

Senia,

When I am gone, I will be leaving many loose ends. You are the only person who can take care of them for me, and I thank you for doing so. When you dispose of whatever is left of my properties, please be generous to my friends and my associates. Give something to Tony for his new business. Pay off Mary Samora's mortgage even if she protests. I'd like you to give something to Lars Udahl, Norman Dinter, and Mr. Pender from the hotel. Take good care of yourself as well.

As I told you earlier today, there is nothing left for me here. I have a son in Duluth. I have not told anybody in Hibbing about him and would like you to keep the matter confidential. His name is Kevin Schmitz. Please talk to Father Foley at St. James Church about Kevin's future financial security and do whatever the priest and the Schmitz family deem best for my sole heir.

Thank you Senia, for this and everything else you have done for me. You will see that the wall safe is open. The thousand dollars inside is for you as a small expression of my gratitude.

Peter

Senia would do everything that Peter requested in his final note to her. Peter's instructions were vague but his good intentions clear enough for her to follow. She would take care of those he named, especially the boy, Kevin. She wondered about the boy, the boy's mother, and the many secrets of Peter's personal life. What he concealed inside must have been some measure of the torment that pushed him to the edge. She felt a swell of flattery that Peter had chosen her to confide in, a twinge of remorse that she had failed to understand the depths of his depression. She reread the line . . . *"You are the only person . . ."*

It was after nine. Senia was already late for work. Mr. Goldberg, her employer at the bank, was a good and understanding man. She must tell him about Peter's death. Who else should she call? She ran her fingers through her long hair, massaged the throb in her temples.

The phone rang eerily from the living room behind her. She let it ring, decided not to answer. After countless rings, the apartment was swallowed in ghostly silence again. She could hear only her ragged breathing. She must call the funeral home to make arrangements. The church . . . which Catholic church would Peter want her to . . . ? And Foley in Duluth. Maybe he could help with all of this. Jim McIntosh, Peter's oldest friend. And Steven. Tony. Mary. How would they cope with this tragedy? Senia must keep her composure. For Peter's sake, she must stay in control . . . keep his abandoned ship afloat.

The phone began to ring again. Confused and feeling overwhelmed concerning the many details screaming for her attention, she moved to her living room, plopped on the sofa and answered the phone.

"Mrs. Arola . . ." a long pause on the other end. "This is Claude Atkinson." The editor swallowed hard, "Has Mr. Argir talked with you?" Claude cursed himself under his breath, "What a stupid question . . . I ought to know better . . ." He was feeling the strain of the morning's events and felt like a cub reporter. "About Mr. Moran?" He tried to recover.

"Yes, Claude. It's so terrible . . ." she sniffled. "I take it you have heard the news as well."

"I have. I don't quite know what to think, or say. But I've got a very difficult job to do and I'd appreciate your help . . . if you will."

"An obituary?"

"Yes, Senia . . . may I call you . . . ?"

"By all means, Claude. I know Peter had great respect for you. He liked you a lot. I'm really out of sorts, but if I can be of some help I'd want to do so." She lost her train of thought, "Do you know what happened?"

"I've talked with Argir, too, and probably know about the same as you do. I'm going to avoid any conjecture, however. I'll just want to highlight some of Peter's contributions to our city, his surviving family, pending arrangements . . . you know, that kind of thing."

"Did Argir say anything about the note Peter left?"

Claude was an honest journalist. "Yes, Senia. I read it."

"Then you know about Kevin."

"I do. I will respect Peter's wish to keep that matter confidential. I only hope Argir will do the same. Just between us, I don't have a lot of confidence in our police chief."

"I'd appreciate that. The boy's identity should be protected. And I share your feelings about Argir. I don't think he believes Peter took his own life." Senia pondered a difficult question, chose to ask: "Do you, Claude?"

"I'll be candid, Senia. I don't think Peter could so such a thing—but the note, his drinking, the state of mind he was in. It's hard to say. We both know someone else was in the house last night. I don't know what connections to make. There was a burglary. Until we've learned a lot more, I can only allude to Peter's death as a self-inflicted gunshot wound. Any suggestion of a possible homicide would turn this town on its ear. I don't want to be a party to that. Not yet anyhow. This is going to be tough enough for everybody to come to grips with."

"I agree. Claude, I've got a thousand things to do right now and hope we can talk more later." Senia was apologetic. The weight of her responsibilities settled heavily like a ceiling caving in on her. "What can I help you with?"

Senia realized how little she knew about her former employer. His mother lived in Warren, Pennsylvania, and was still alive, she believed. She had sent cards to her on occasion but Peter never talked about the woman. "Her name is Katherine, I'm quite certain. And there is a sister in Warren named Emily. She's married and has a family, so there are nieces or nephews. He had two brothers. Terrance was the oldest. He teaches at some college in Philadelphia if I remember correctly. And Denis." A bitter taste came to her mouth.

"Denis was in town for Peter's hotel opening . He created quite a scene. You might remember, Claude." Senia had witnessed the episode. Denis was drunk and obnoxious. He had to be restrained by the security police and evicted from the gala celebration. Peter was outraged over the incident and had his brother on a train out of town the next morning. "I have no idea where Denis is. And there was his deceased father, Daly . . . died out in Oregon a few years ago."

"I knew Daly quite well, Senia. A hellava man."

"There's not much else I can tell you." As she scoured her memory, another thought shot across the clutter in her mind. Pallbearers. "Perhaps you could help me with something, Claude. You were in Peter's circle of friends. Was there anyone besides McIntosh who was really close to Peter? I'll have to arrange for the funeral and pallbearers."

Claude remembered a recent party at Moran's house and wondered if the guests attending were really friends of his. "Luigi Anselmo, the tailor. He might have been a friend of Pete's. Lars Udahl at the lumberyard." As the president of Hibbing's Commercial Club, Peter had many contacts within the mining and business communities. But friends? "Tom Brady. Pete was a huge baseball fan as you know, Senia." Judge Brady was the manager of Hibbing's Colts. The local nine had a passionate following. "Let me think some more and get back to you later. I'll help you with anything as best I can. This is going to swamp you, I'm afraid."

"I'll need all the help I can get. Thanks for your kind offer, Claude."

Hanging up the phone, Senia looked again at the note she clutched in her hand. Before calling the Ryder Funeral Parlor, she would have to talk with Father Foley. She remembered the tall priest from his earlier visits to Peter's mansion. He always came unannounced and late in the evening. She guessed the priest was involved in Kevin's affairs.

The local operator connected her with St. James Catholic Church in Duluth. She recognized the deep voice through the static of a long distance call. "Father Foley, Saint James parish rectory, here."

"Father, this is Senia, Peter Moran's secretary. We've met briefly . . ."

"Yes, Senia. I remember." What was Moran up to, he wondered. His relationship with Peter had been strained. "What can I do for you this morning?" Foley had just returned to the rectory from morning mass.

"I'm afraid I have some bad news, Father. Very bad! Mr. Moran has died."

Foley's gasp was audible. After what seemed like minutes, Foley cleared his throat. "What happened?"

Senia explained in sketchy detail, finishing with the content of the note Peter had left for her. "The police are investigating, Father. I'm in a tizzy, I'm afraid. I can't think straight right now. You're the first person I've called about this. The first of many calls I'll have to make. Will you talk to the Schmitz family for me? I'll want to meet them some time soon, probably after the funeral if you can arrange it."

Foley took a minute to explain that Art and Sarah Schmitz were in the process of adopting Peter's son, Kevin. The boy was two and a half years old and the Schmitzes were his closest parish friends. "I will talk to them and call Jim McIntosh if you'd like. If I can help with the funeral in Hibbing, I'll do that as well. I know Monsignor Potocnik at Blessed Sacrament Church." Foley realized there would be a major issue about a Catholic burial if Moran's death was deemed a suicide. Perhaps there was enough doubt. "Are you familiar with our church, Mrs. Arola?"

"I'm afraid not, Father. And Peter was not a churchgoer to my knowledge."

"If his death was a suicide, the Catholic church will not allow the body to be brought into the church. Give me all the details as you know them, Senia."

She explained why she was convinced that Peter had not taken his own life. "Just too many things that don't add up, Father," Senia concluded.

Foley would make inquiries with the Bishop for her and promised to call tomorrow. "I hate to say this, Senia, but if you could offer a contribution to the church in Peter's name . . . it might help a great deal."

Senia hung up, called her bank, and retold the story to Mr. Goldberg. Expressing his heartfelt condolences, he insisted she take as much time as she needed. "I'll do anything I can, Senia. This is going to really shake up the town. Peter was a pillar here. You know that better than most. We had our differences for sure, but I truly respected the man and all that he did for Hibbing. He'll be greatly missed." The bank president had overseen Peter Moran's business accounts for several years.

She wondered whom to call next. Her dear friend, Steven, was working on the railroad line between Hibbing and Duluth. He would be away until the weekend. She needed his strength and comfort more than ever.

Steven Skorich had been her husband's closest friend in those turbulent days of the miners' strike. It was Steven who had told her about Timo's death. It was Steven who had supported her through that time of grief. But, somehow the loss of Peter struck at Senia's heart in a more profound way than Timo's death. She and Timo had been separated by years and miles . . . she and Peter by only hours.

At one time Steven's nephew, Tony Zoretek, had been like a son to Peter. Tony would be devastated by the tragedy. Senia scribbled a short list. Tony might already be on some job and not likely to be reached at his new carpentry shop. Her closest friend, Mary Samora, would probably be at Anselmo's tailor shop by this time of the morning. Senia felt isolated and frozen by the confusion. What would she do next?

Senia could not help slipping into a reverie of guilt. She could have done nothing to save Peter from self destruction. She must not allow her thoughts to punish her for leaving him alone that day. Senia became angry with herself, angry with Peter. He left her holding a bag, a bag filled with all the 'loose ends' he considered his enterprises and personal relationships to have been. "Damn you, Peter!" Senia shouted into the empty room. "Why? What do you expect me to do?" Then, when the wave of resentment passed, "May God in all his mercy bless your soul. You were my friend and I never quite understood that. I'm sorry, sorry from the bottom of my heart." Senia didn't know any prayers. "Dear God, like Peter, I haven't known you very well. Please look beyond that and help us both. Forgive him for things only you know about . . . and give me the strength I'll need to take care of what he's left behind." She had a penetrating thought as she contemplated what Peter left behind. "God bless that boy who is Peter's blood. Be a part of his life so he can have a greater strength than his father. That's my prayer, however unworthy I may be in your almighty presence. My prayer is for Kevin. And, for guidance in whatever I do in the affairs of his life. Amen."

Senia's next call would be to an attorney. She knew Peter's business interests better than anybody else but would need legal expertise in providing for those named in Peter's final requests. There were several lawyers in Hibbing but none with whom she was personally familiar. Elwood Trembart had been a friend of Peter's for years, but she did not trust him. She knew Trembart as a vindictive man, a wolf in sheep's clothes. No, she would contact the young attorney that Peter had once complimented as being someone who was really "on the ball!" Senia asked the operator to connect her with Victor Power's law office.

"... He was an Ambitious Man..."

CLAUDE ATKINSON WOULD FOLLOW UP the finest news story he had ever written with his most difficult obituary. On Wednesday, the *Mesaba Ore*, Hibbing's widely-read daily newspaper, carried a full front page spread on the Hotel Moran fire. The editor had included a spectacular photograph of the blaze on the front page and included several interviews with firefighters, police officials, hotel guests, and spectators. In an historical perspective, Claude suggested, *"The destruction of our beautiful new hotel is the darkest hour in the short life of our fine city..."*

Claude stared at the blank page wound on the platen of his Adler typewriter. Struggling for the first words of the first sentence, he glanced at the open notepad at his elbow. He sighed his dismay. "Damn it, Pete, why'd you have to leave us this way?"

Claude reflected on his relationship with the flamboyant Hibbing entrepreneur. Peter Moran had always treated him well. Always. Whenever Pete had wind of a story, an insight on some business deal or commercial club information, his first call was to Claude. Pete had given the editor lots of timely stories over the years. Their connection went well beyond the business activity in the booming community. The two men were friends, sharing both mutual respect and common interests. Both were strong supporters of everything that might make Hibbing a better place to live. Pete loved this city almost as much as he did. But Moran had the money to make an indelible mark on the economic fabric of this town. When Peter boasted that "Hibbing's my town!" he was not exaggerating the claim. His fingerprints were on everything that was Hibbing, Minnesota, in 1908.

Only weeks before, on Independence Day, Claude and his wife, Dora, were guests at the Moran mansion for an afternoon barbecue party. When Pete had his gala grand opening at the hotel, Claude was seated at the head table along with other local dignitaries. Peter gave the editor the first tour of his majestic hotel, "I want you to see my place before anyone else . . ." he'd told Claude.

But there were problems, too. Peter had a ruthless streak. When he wanted something to happen, he would stop at nothing to achieve his ambitions. He wanted to build a fine European-style hotel. It would be his landmark—for *his* city. That building became his obsession. He was driven! In order to build his hotel on the site he coveted—near Hibbing's baseball park—he felt compelled to undermine a project already started on that location. (A St. Paul contractor had already inititated construction of a hotel on the corner of Third Avenue and South Street. And, the out-of-town investors would not sell the property to Moran). Toward his end, Peter hired people to disrupt the construction activity of the St. Paul contractor. In the process of sabotaging the project, he implicated himself in an 'accident' that might have been grounds for a manslaughter conviction. The case against him would be strong. The St. Louis County grand jury had subpoenaed Moran in an inquiry into the death of a bricklayer on the project site. Claude had been instrumental in bringing this story to light. Earlier in the week he broke the news of a grand jury hearing to Peter in Moran's library at the mansion. Only four days ago! Claude remembered how devastated Peter was about the allegations.

The death of Hibbing's most influential citizen was a news story as well as an obituary. Claude would mix his commentary with the facts he could use from Chief Argir's report an hour before. He broke his stare at the blank page, looking at a wall clock that spelled *deadline*!

"Why'd you go and do this, Pete?" Claude mused again as he bit at his lower lip and hit the first key to his headline:

LOCAL CIVIC LEADER DIES

Hibbing has been twice saddened in as many days. The tragic loss of the landmark HOTEL MORAN in Tuesday's horrific fire will chal-

lenge Hibbing's city fathers to recover from disaster. In the wake of the fire is an even more tragic episode in the history of our fair community. Peter Moran, local business and community leader, has died in his home on Washington Street. Police Chief Clayton Argir was called to Moran's residence early this morning. He identified Peter Moran at the scene. An investigation is being conducted, but the Mesaba Ore cannot report even preliminary findings at this time.

This editor is reminded of a Shakespearian tragedy he studied while in college. The play, 'Julius Caesar', contained a poignant eulogy from Caesar's nephew, Marc Anthony. I had to memorize that famous speech in an English Literature class. (I realize that I am both stretching my memory and taking great liberty in borrowing from the Bard). In his tribute to a man that many had come to despise for alleged misdeeds, Marc Anthony profoundly observed: 'the evil that men do lives long after them, the good is oft interred with their bones . . . so let it be with Caesar for he was an ambitious man.'

I had come to know Pete quite well over the years. What bound the two of us together as friends was the fact that we cared mightily about this town. Whatever seemed best for Hibbing was worth fighting for to the mind of Peter Moran. He was a fighter, make no mistake about that. Yes, 'he was an ambitious man . . . ' and because of his ambition we have benefited. Let us not bury the good. Each of us who claim this town as our home owes a debt of gratitude to the work of his hands. Peter Joseph Moran was thirty-three. He was preceded in death by his father, Daly Moran. The Morans were pioneer loggers in the Hibbing area and responsible for supplying lumber for the growing Mesabi Range. Kathleen Moran, his mother, lives with his sister Emily in Warren, Pennsylvania. Brother Terrance is a college professor in Philadelphia. Another brother, Denis, last resided in the Eugene, Oregon, area.

Funeral arrangements are pending at this time.

～

Senia was feeling overwhelmed. Since her early morning meeting with Chief Argir, the conversation with Claude Atkinson, and a call to Father

Foley in Duluth, she had wandered aimlessly about her apartment. Still in disbelief, the list of things to do seemed to bring a mental paralysis. The stark black phone seemed to scream for her attention and repulse her at the same time. She didn't know what to do, whom to call next, what initiative to take. She prayed that some voice might shout from an invisible realm and tell her: *"Do this next, and then that . . ."*

The telephone rang.

News of Peter Moran's death spread rapidly as is always the case in a small town. Mildred Graham, Moran's housekeeper, called her widow friend Clara Solberg at Luigi Anselmo's tailor shop after Chief Argir left the house. Clara relayed the shocking news to Luigi, who called Mary Bellani Samora. Luigi reached his seamstress before she left for work.

Mary was saddened by the news. "Tony must be told of this tragedy. It will hit him hard . . . and Senia, too. Oh, my God in heaven, help us all get through this." She said a quick prayer before calling her beloved Tony Zoretek at his carpentry shop. "Eternal rest grant unto him, O Lord, and may Your perpetual light shine upon him . . ."

Mary Samora was not fond of Peter Moran. She mistrusted his intentions. Thought him to be dishonest, manipulative. Yet there was a generosity and goodness below that arrogant exterior that she could not forget. She fought back her tears at the many memories Peter would leave with her. "May he rest in peace . . ."

Harvey Goldberg at the bank told his employees about Hibbing's loss of the civic leader after hearing the news from Senia that morning. Moran, he realized, had shaped the city more than any other person in the fifteen years of its life. Moran's lumber framed the bricks of his Merchants and Miners bank and had built the majority of the structures up and down the streets of Hibbing. Harvey made a few calls, further spreading the news.

Claude Atkinson called Elwood Trembart of the village council, who called fellow attorneys Walt and Vic Powers. Fred Bennet, the Oliver Mining Company manager, heard about Moran's death from businessman Tom Godfrey. Godfrey talked with Mayor Weirick over coffee at Fay's Cafe and their conversation was passed among the others having breakfast. Moran was the president of the local Commercial Club and the driving force behind Hibbing's economic development efforts. By nine o'clock on that Thursday morning, only two hours after the local police arrived at the death scene, half of the town had heard about the apparent suicide. Most agreed that the hotel fire of two days before had depressed Peter Moran beyond his ability to cope. Despite his well known strength of character, Moran was always unpredictable and impulsive. Suicide, although a cowardly act, seemed to many almost honorable under the circumstances.

Senia let the phone ring several times before picking up the receiver.

"Senia . . ." There was a long pause at the other end of the line. "Have you heard?"

Senia recognized the voice of Tony Zoretek. She breathed deeply, summoning every ounce of composure. Her tears were already spent. She must be strong. If she could not handle this, who else could?

"Yes, Tony. It's . . . what can I say? Tragic."

"Lars called me from the lumber yard. I guess he heard from one of the policemen who saw Peter's body at the mansion. Then Mary called me. She was pretty broken up. Lars heard it was . . . suicide. How could he do such a thing, Senia? The guy was tough as nails. Invincible!"

Senia did not reply at first. Her mind was awhirl with the possibility that Peter Moran could not do what rumors were claiming. She knew Tony was a man who could share her confidences. The two of them shared a trust bond with each other, and had close relationships with Peter. "I don't think he could . . . or did, Tony. There are some things I've learned from talking with Argir when he was here less than an hour ago." She mentioned that someone was in Peter's house last night, stole money—"Can you come over later? Have a cup of coffee? Bring Mary with you. Peter left me a note and it says a lot. I'm going to need some help with sorting all this out. And, more than anyone—even Steven—I need you, Tony."

"I'll wrap up a few things here, swing by Mary's, and be over in an hour, Senia. Anything, anything I can do to help. I'll let you go now. Make a strong pot of coffee. We're going to need it."

Tony Zoretek hung up the phone, dropped his tall, strapping frame into the chair behind his desk. In an earlier time the ruggedly handsome carpenter had been closer to Peter Moran than anybody else in Hibbing. That was until something ruptured that relationship only months before. That *something* remained elusive. Tony remembered Peter with mixed emotions.

Tony was a Slovenian immigrant who arrived in the mining hub of Hibbing more than a year before. His arrival was under the worst possible circumstances. A miners' strike had just erupted across the Mesabi Iron Range. Tony, along with hundreds of other immigrants, were unknowingly hired as strikebreakers. 'Scabs!' While laid off from the iron ore mine last winter, he had had a bizarre experience. Peter had been run over by an out-of-control carriage just before last Christmas and was seriously injured. Tony was walking nearby when the accident happened and carried the unconscious man to the Rood Hospital, where Moran recovered from his injuries. Later the wealthy businessman invited Tony to his Washington Street mansion to extend his gratitude.

Everything in Tony's life changed dramatically after that meeting with Moran. Peter gave him a job at his lumber warehouse, encouraged his training in carpentry, took him under his wing like a son. Peter had much to do with Tony's becoming a local baseball celebrity as well.

"You gave me a life, Mr. Moran. Treated me like a prince in your castle. Without you . . . I don't know where I'd be today!" Tony felt the well of tears, rested his face on powerful arms folded on the desktop. He could not imagine a Hibbing without Peter Moran. "Whatever it was that came between us . . . I loved ya, sir." Tony prayed silently for the soul of a man who might need a lot of prayers. He knew Peter had always been too self absorbed to ever ask God for any help. Peter Moran believed in his own power and influence and, Tony believed, invincibility as well. "You'll always be a part of who I am, sir. I'll remember you every day of my life."

Senia's next call was to Victor Power, Peter's lawyer. She placed her scrawled copy of Peter's note on the table beside her cup of tepid black coffee.

"Mr. Power, this is Senia Arola calling. We haven't met but I know that you were a friend of Peter's—his attorney, if I'm not mistaken."

"Yes, Mrs. Arola. I've heard about . . . my condolences. He was very fond of you, I know. He told me so. This is all very . . . very unbelievable.

Hellava guy Pete was. We'll all miss him more than we can possibly realize right now."

Victor Power and Peter had become fast friends in recent months. When Vic left the law practice of his older brother, Walter, Moran was among his first clients. Power helped Peter close quickly on a 120 acre tract of land south of Hibbing in Alice Location. In many respects the two men had become confidantes. Both were ambitious, headstrong, and community-focused. Both shared a dislike of Elwood Trembart, a local attorney and village council president. In one regard they had a major difference of opinion. And on this matter the two argued vehemently over whiskeys at Moran's Shamrock Saloon. Peter was pro-mining company. He believed that the city should cater to their needs. Give the Oliver and other companies sizable tax concessions and privileges. "They're our life's blood," Pete would argue. Vic Power disagreed. "The people are always right. And the people are the mine workers—not the company owners!" He believed this credo with an ardor that would become a political platform for him in the years ahead.

And, politics was in the blood of twenty-seven year old Victor Leon Power. The stocky lawyer, only five-four in thick-heeled shoes, had been in Hibbing for less than ten years. His brother Walter had been mayor for a single term and the fascination of political activism rubbed off on the younger brother. Both Powers boys might acknowledge that law and government were inherited. Their father was a criminal lawyer and elected public official well known in Calumet, Escanaba, and across the Upper Peninsula of Michigan where the Powers boys grew up.

Senia would use discretion in her conversation with the attorney. "Peter left me a note, sir. He asked me to take care of his affairs, mostly financial . . . but, I think, some legal things as well." She was uncertain about revealing the confidence Peter had divulged regarding his son, Kevin. Chief Argir had read the note. So had Claude Atkinson.

Power's question, however, gave her no alternative. "Pete was a bachelor, no children. The disposition of his estate should be relatively easy. Do you know of his survivors, Mrs. Arola?"

"Yes, sir." Senia's head throbbed. She put her hand over the mouthpiece and whispered to herself. "Peter, I've got to tell this man about your son. I'll do whatever I can to keep this as . . . as private as I can. But I'm going to take care of your son. Kevin will be my greatest priority."

"Mrs. Arola? Survivors? I've got a pen and paper here. I'll write down everything you can tell me and advise you as to how you might proceed with Pete's affairs. Everything is between the two of us, as you know. Strictest confidentiality! I've got a pretty good file of things Pete had going on. His business affairs, real estate, and the like. There's no last will and testament, I'm afraid. So his wishes expressed to you in the letter will be what we're going to have to follow. You are what we call an 'executor' and we'll have to go through some probate proceedings soon. Understand?"

Vic Power spoke in rapid staccato with voice always pitched high. Senia was distracted by the lawyer's 'matter of fact' commentary. "Yes. I understand. I will be the executor. I have access to all of Mr. Moran's records—financial and otherwise. They remain in my former office at his mansion. And, sir, I understand probate quite well," she replied indignantly, then added a footnote to her response. "I am an accountant."

"Good. I'm sure this will all go quite smoothly. As you know, however, we're talking about an awful lot of business decisions. That's why it's important to have a list of surviving family. Have you tried to make contact . . . . ?"

"No, Mr. Power, I haven't." Senia gave the attorney the names and locations of Peter's mother and sister. "His two brothers are another matter. Terrance is somewhere in the Philadelphia area and Denis . . . you might want to talk with Mr. Argir about Denis. I think he is in some kind of trouble with the law."

Denis Moran was, indeed, a fugitive in "trouble with the law." As they spoke, Denis was on the run. Duluth police had tentatively identified Denis Moran as a collaborator in the bungled kidnapping scheme of Peter's son only days ago. Although their search for his whereabouts had proven fruitless, two suspects—a man named Sam Lavalle and a woman named Lily Brown—were in the St. Louis County jail in Duluth. Hibbing police had been alerted to keep an eye out for Peter's brother. (The conspiracy had been quickly thwarted. Too many people had witnessed the inept break-in, and the flight of the kidnappers through the West Duluth neighborhoods. Within an hour two arrests were made at a Raleigh Street address. Fortunately, Denis had been able to escape the scene unnoticed by the police.)

The robust, bearded, unkempt brother had a vendetta. He had fled Duluth and taken the train to Hibbing intent upon killing Peter. Denis blamed all his personal misfortunes on his wealthy younger brother. Soon the local police would learn that the footprints in Peter's garden and the dirt tracks on the floor of the mansion's back were made by a man of Denis' size. Soon the Grand Rapids police would find Peter's stolen Buick in Lake Pokegama south of that city.

As Senia and Vic Power conversed this Thursday morning, Denis Moran, traveling as John Jones, was on a train headed for Minneapolis. 'Mr. Jones' had a thousand dollars in his satchel. Jones became 'Johnson,' a passenger traveling from St. Paul to Kansas City. (Denis' plan was to get to Denver, hang out there for a while, then head out to Eugene, Oregon where his former wife still lived.) 'Johnson' became 'Olsen' after K.C. He would take his time and cover his tracks. Denis was not a smart man—but learning to be careful.

Senia wrapped up her conversation with Power. "Let's talk more about all of this later, Mr. Power. I've got so many things to do I'm feeling overwhelmed."

The August morning embellished its finest sunshine upon the turbulent mining town. The spreading rays crept over the massive ore dumps surrounding the sprawling open pits, capturing the thick film of red dust, and creating an amber glow across the eastern sky. The clank and creak and hiss of ore trains hauling their rich lodes of hematite echoed across the landscape. Mining and the tumultuous activity it engaged were what defined the character of Hibbing, Minnesota. Within a radius of five miles of the hub city, nearly a hundred mines bustled with the diverse daily enterprises of drilling, digging, and hauling the thousands of tons of rich iron ore. The blasting of earth to shatter the buried veins made an incessant reverberation. Like earthquakes the tremors rumbled underfoot of the boom town. As the mining encroached on all sides, fragments of dirt and rock flew in every direction, often pelting the houses clinging to the edges of the crater-like pits. Along the Mesabi, human life was compromised by the ambitions of mining interests. The Iron Range fed the steel mills of the East and spurred the expanding American economy.

Tony Zoretek left his shop on Center Street, turned down Third Avenue, passing Fay's Cafe. Painted across the glass front was an inscription that gave him pause: "We Feed the Hungry." On a cold December afternoon the previous winter he had passed the popular local eatery without enough money to buy so much as a cup of coffee. He remembered feeling hunger pangs from days without a decent meal. An unemployed mine worker at the time, Tony's future looked bleaker than that raw afternoon. Now he had a small carpentry business of his own. A savings account of more than three hundred dollars. How dramatically his life had changed in those short months. The memory of that difficult time in his young life brought Peter Moran back into his thoughts. Moran had given him a job at his lumber yards and provided the training that now would be his livelihood. Peter had touched his life in many ways.

"Tony! Did ya hear about Pete Moran . . . ?" called Mr. Olander from the doorway of his shop. Olander sold fine wines, liquors, and cigars on the busy commercial strip of Third Avenue. Like most of the merchants in Hibbing, Nils was a member of Moran's commercial club.

"Yes, I have, Nils. Only an hour or so ago. Terrible . . ." was all he could say to the merchant.

"My condolences, lad. I know the two of ya were good friends."

"We *were* great friends. I was just thinking about that. We all owe him a lot, don't we? Me especially."

Down the street on his left the ruins of the Hotel Moran still smoldered from the blaze that had brought the four story landmark to the ground. Tony remembered working on the building's construction while a novice carpenter. "Mr. Moran . . . thanks for all you did for me. I'll never forget," he mumbled hoarsely to no one but himself. As he passed alongside the charred walkway into the street alongside the remains of the hotel, a putrid odor—the lingering aftermath—stung his nostrils. The stench of once plush carpets, fine draperies, bedding and furniture combined with the kitchen's storage of foods and every other imaginable content of the palatial hotel. Nothing survived the blaze. He paused for a moment to regard the rubble and made a sign of the cross.

Tony's fiancé, Mary, had called him at his carpentry shop. She would not be going to work that day. She was devastated and asked if he could come over to her house. "I need you, Tony. This all hurts so much." The thought of Mary Samora brought the crease of a smile to his face. He needed her, too.

Walking past Khort's Grocery store he saw his friend, Tommy Pell, stocking produce for the large wooden table on the walkway. Tommy was a teammate on Brady's Colts baseball team and a roommate in the house he shared with several of his buddies.

Tommy put down the basket of tomatoes and stepped out to console his friend. "We've lost our biggest fan, ain't we, Zee?" The nickname was a baseball monicker among the guys. "Sorry 'bout that. Gonna be kinda strange without ole Pete Moran in the grandstand."

Tony explained that he would not be able to travel with the team on their weekend trip to Ironwood and Bessemer. The Michigan trip was a windup for the playoffs and the Colts needed some wins. Tony had become the most valuable pitcher on the staff and would be sorely missed. "I'm going to have to help out with all the arrangements, Tommy. I'm on my way to Mary's right now. We'll want to get over and see Senia this morning."

The two men shook hands, "Good luck in the games, Tommy," Tony said in parting. He walked three blocks south in an oblivious funk. Memories were flooding his thoughts. Where would he be today if he had not befriended Peter Moran? Without realizing how far he had walked, Tony found himself stepping toward the porch at Mary's Garfield Street home. He paused to collect himself, realizing that there were tears in his deep-set blue eyes. "So what? I'm crying like a kid . . . but . . . I've never lost a friend before." He rubbed a sleeve at his eyes, knocked at the door.

"Tony!" Mary fell into his arms, clutching his shirt. "How could he?" Her eyes were red from crying, her hair disheveled. "I'm an absolute mess, Tony. An emotional wreck . . ." She looked into his face seeking to lighten her melancholy. "Messed up in every sense of the word, I'm afraid. Just look at me. Have you ever seen such a wretched woman in your life?"

Mary was beautiful—even in her state of anguish. Her creamy complexion, wide-set oval eyes, and long, dark tresses had inspired the nickname of 'bella' in her childhood homeland of Italy. She possessed inner beauty as well. She worked in the tailor shop of Luigi Anselmo, her countryman. Mary was a seamstress. Her fashionable dresses were among the most exquisite in Hibbing. Mary Bellani Samora was also a woman in love. Tony was her man.

There was a time when Peter Moran courted her. On one occasion he had given her a lovely gold-chained cameo necklace, a gift that was a torment for her on this morning. She clutched the jewelry in her small hand as she held Tony. "He was a good man—wasn't he, Tony? I mean, even all the bad things he did were . . . were misunderstandings. Don't you think? I know he was so good to you. And that makes up for everything else."

Tony did not reply. Holding her close, kissing her softly, and stroking her hair, he wanted to give her time to vent her emotion.

"I was mean to him. I think he must have hated me, Tony."

"Now . . . now, don't think that. He loved you Mary. He loved me, too. I know that. And it gives me some kind of comfort. Despite everything that came between us—all of us, including Senia—he cared as deeply as he could. Maybe Peter couldn't really love anybody. Maybe he could only take care of them, give them the things they couldn't get themselves. He was generous to all of us. I'll give him that, really generous!"

"Did you ever feel close, *truly close* to him?"

Tony contemplated Mary's question, held her away so he could meet her eyes. "Many times. I think I found a father figure in Mr. Moran. He certainly treated me like a son—even spoiled me with all the things he gave me. Yes, truly close." He smiled for the first time, a wide, contagious smile.

"He took me to my first baseball game back in April. During the game I felt his arm across my shoulders. "One day you're going to be out there playing, son." He called me *son*. More than once, I think. And, I knew his feelings were honest. I think he would have been a good father if he had kids of his own."

Mary returned his smile. When Tony smiled, and he did so very often, she melted into his good humor and positive disposition. Tony's goodness attracted her more than any other quality. "Peter's feelings for you more than make up for anything else. Anyone who loved my Tony is worthy of my love." She laughed at what she had said. "I guess I must love the whole world then. I can't think of a person who doesn't think you are a wonderful man. And, I thank God every day that you are mine, Tony. I really do!"

They kissed and clung to each other for what seemed like minutes. The room was sun-splashed and quiet. "Senia! Tony, we must get over and see Senia. She must be . . . she needs us. Steven is away. She's probably struggling with this all by herself."

"Let's go right now. I talked with her earlier, and she is hurting. I promised we'd be there for her." Tony was always anxious to help a friend during a difficult time.

Mary brushed her hair from her face, rubbed at her eyes. "Just give me a few minutes to get ready. Give her a call, sweetheart, tell her we're on our way. And see if I've got any cinnamon rolls left in the pantry."

JAGGED TONGUES OF FIRE

PETER MORAN'S FUNERAL swelled the Blessed Sacrament Church to its capacity. In addition to those packed inside, nearly a hundred local mourners gathered in the Saturday morning drizzle outside of the church. The funeral service was brief and subdued. Because of the lingering controversy surrounding Peter's untimely death, a mass was not conducted.

Father Patrick Foley, a priest from St. James Church in West Duluth, assisted the parish prelate in the unusual ceremony. Monsignor Potocnik gave a carefully worded eulogy extolling the contributions of Mr. Moran to the community. "He loved Hibbing with a passion and served with a progressive spirit." The organist was permitted two musical interludes, *'How Great Thou Art'* as the opening hymn, and *'Ave Maria'* as the recessional. Following the memorial service, the funeral procession traveled south of Hibbing to a hillside cemetery. At the gravesite final prayers were offered. Peter Moran was laid to eternal rest.

Claude Atkinson served as a pallbearer. The newspaper man returned to his Pine Street office to work on the Sunday issue of his beloved *Mesaba Ore*. He sat slumped at his desk contemplating the story that he would place in the upper right corner of the front page. His article would be brief. The obituary in yesterday's issue profiled the deceased and his commentary was spent. Often Claude would read his words aloud as he wrote them with pencil on paper.

Peter Moran was buried on Saturday, August 29. Many close friends and business associates attended the funeral service at the Blessed Sacrament Church, although none of Moran's family was able to travel to Hibbing for the ceremony. Monsignor Potocnik acknowledged each of them in his inspired eulogy.

Claude paused, raised his pencil, and decided not to mention family members by name.

Attending to the casket were pallbearers Lars Udahl, Norman Dinter, Thomas Brady, Tony Zoretek, James McIntosh, and Claude Atkinson. McIntosh, a former Hibbing businessman and close family friend, traveled from Duluth for the service.

Claude reviewed his words and found them sufficient. In his 'From Out of Town' column, a regular Sunday feature detailing visitors to Hibbing and locals traveling to other destinations, he would identify other Duluthians in town for the funeral. Among these were a Mr. and Mrs. Arthur Schmitz and their son Kevin.

The news all week had been tragic. Moran's hotel fire was the biggest story Claude had ever done and Peter's death . . . ? The editor shook his head, "Damned if I won't get to the bottom of all this!" He rarely cursed, but emotion churned inside him. "There was foul play. I can feel it in my bones."

Atkinson's front page stories were in his 'out basket' ready for the print shop. His staff designed the layouts. He picked up a piece that had arrived in Friday's mail and browsed the syndicated copyright from G. P. Putnam & Sons in New York. The article was titled 'Hunting the Wapiti.' Its author was the highly popular Theodore Roosevelt. The American President, a widely acknowledged sportsman, related his hunting recollections which appealed to millions. In this particular expedition, Roosevelt had been hunting in the southwest corner of the Bitter Root Range. "The Wapiti is, next to the moose, the most quarrelsome and pugnacious of American deer," the President observed as he detailed his account of the hunt. The story featured several illustrations which always caught the eyes of newspaper readers. In one of these a hunter was aiming at a Wapiti from the edge of a clearing with the caption below: "He plunged wildly forward!"

Claude amused over the story and decided it was an appropriate levity from the hard stories that had consumed the thoughts of Hibbingites for several days. "Thanks for something lighthearted, Mr. President. We can all appreciate the break," Claude said as he pushed away from his desk. He could go home now and have an early evening whiskey and, perhaps, a couple of aspirin to ease his headache.

After the burial, Senia Arola sought out the tall priest from Duluth. "Father Foley, it was so nice of you to make these arrangements. I know it was a difficult task in such a short time. Thank you . . ."

Foley nodded offering a wan smile. "The Bishop had sufficient doubt about 'suicide', but your promised contribution to the church probably made it all possible, Senia. Thank you."

"Would it be possible for me to meet the Schmitzes, Father? I know you traveled here with them. Perhaps all of us could talk briefly about Peter's final note to me."

"They are anticipating a meeting. Where would you suggest?"

The four of them met in the rectory of the Blessed Sacrament Church in mid-afternoon. Kevin was put down for a nap, while the adults found comfortable chairs in the Monsignor's office. Foley made the introductions, poured coffee, then offered a prayer for the soul of Peter Moran. When he finished, an appropriate silence filled the room.

"Senia, we are all familiar with the situation presented us. As I've told you, Art and Sarah have initiated adoption proceedings through the county. It will be just a matter of time. Peter was supportive of the idea and, as you know, has been most generous in providing for Kevin's care in the past."

Art spoke for the first time. "Mrs. Arola, we told Mr. Moran that the child support payments were no longer necessary. I hope you understand. We are, Sarah and I, reasonably well set financially. We'd both feel much better if we took care of all Kevin's expenses by ourselves."

"I can appreciate that, Mr. Schmitz. I will certainly respect your feelings in every regard. But . . ." Senia swallowed hard. "Mr. Moran has left a sizable estate for me to administer. In his note," she took the folded paper from her handbag, "he made it clear that he wanted to assure your son's—*and his*—financial security." With discretion, she emphasized *his*. "He asked that I do so with the guidance of Father Foley and both of you."

"What do you suggest?" Foley leaned forward in his chair. "I know that Peter set up a trust fund for Kevin with Jim McIntosh. It was for twenty thousand dollars when he reaches eighteen, if my memory serves me. That's an incredible amount of money for a young man to come into, don't you think?"

"Father, with all due respect, that amount is quite insignificant. Mr. Moran's assets will liquidate in the hundreds of thousands. I will be meeting with his attorney and some of his business associates on Monday. I'm afraid Mr. Moran was quite estranged from his immediate family."

"And, quite estranged from his son as well," interrupted Sarah indignantly from her husband's side. Art gave her hand a gentle squeeze. "Is it right for a boy of eighteen to wake up one morning and learn he's got a fortune in his hand? I just don't know."

"My wife has a legitimate concern. Don't you agree? We want Kevin to face life on his own. That's the way it should be. We are opposed to any arrangements, trusts or otherwise, that might compromise our son's opportunity to make a life for himself."

Foley felt the role of mediator settle heavily upon his shoulders. The priest sat back in the chair, massaged his temples, looked at each of the people about him. His eyes met Senia's. "Mrs. Arola, what do you propose to do?"

Senia gathered her fragmented thoughts and spoke from her heart. "We are all born into a different world, Father. Circumstances we must learn to live with. We have very few choices. Decisions are made for our well-being by those who love us. I was born into a wealthy family in Finland. Father, I might guess that your family in Ireland was not so well off. What I mean to say is simply that each of us finds our own way by following our hearts, our spirits. My parents did not want me to come to America. I'm here because I chose to be. I have every belief that one day Kevin will make his own life choices. As we all have. And, I pray that they will be good decisions." Senia smiled toward the Schmitzes. "I know that you both will teach him sound values. He will be, when he reaches adulthood, a work of your hands. If he is blessed with a large inheritance, he will be challenged to do good things with it."

Senia's observations made good sense to the priest. "May I suggest that we support Mrs. Arola in what she must do. God knows it will be a difficult task. It might be wrong for us to make any decisions this afternoon that we might regret down the road." He looked at Art Schmitz, spread his hands before him in a gesture of appeal. "Art, I am more than willing to work with Mrs. Arola in this regard. What do you think?"

"You have been with us through everything, Father. We trust in your judgment." Art smiled at his wife. "All of us want what's best for the boy. He's lucky to have . . ." He let the thought drop, lacking the words to fully express his sentiment.

"I want to be as involved in Kevin's life as you will allow," Senia proposed. "Perhaps I could be a surrogate 'aunt' or something. It would be a blessing in my life if I could have some small role . . . some connection as the boy grows up."

Art and Sarah nodded their agreement.

Foley stood, summoned Senia and the Schmitzes to join him in the center of the room. "Let us join hands together in prayer." The priest bowed his head and asked his God to bless all of them in their shared responsibilities in guiding the life of Peter's son.

That night, Senia found comfort in her man, Steven Skorich. The large, bearded Slovenian brought a bottle of wine to her apartment along with a bouquet of flowers. Steven was an intelligent and sensitive man behind the misleading appearance of being a simple 'working stiff.' Despite the two different worlds they lived in, they had an almost spiritual bond. Their strongest connection was an ability to communicate at a depth that allowed each to be themselves—open, honest, and accepting of their differences.

Steven was unusually subdued. "I never knew the man, Senia. During the 'troubles' (Steven had been an activist during last summer's miners strike against the powerful iron ore companies). He was on the other side, a zealous adversary. Moran spoke against our cause, always supporting the Oliver against our union's efforts." Then he smiled, dropping his arm around

Senia's shoulders and pulling her closer to his side. "We've been through this before haven't we, my dear? He was good to you and that's really all that matters to me now. I've forgiven him every time I've held your hand."

On Sunday, Senia and Steven spent the day with their dearest friends, Tony and Mary Zoretek. The four of them took a carriage into the countryside south of Hibbing, enjoyed a hiking excursion into the woods and, later in the afternoon, a picnic together. Senia was relaxing after the stress of the previous days and laughing at Tony's good humor. Tony related a time when he and Peter were playing catch behind the stacks of lumber in Moran's yards. Tony was demonstrating a new pitch he had learned from Tommy Pell. "Watch the ball drop!" Tony warned Peter who was crouched in a catcher's stance behind the improvised plate used for practicing. "Keep your eye on it, sir. It's going to be hard to catch if you don't follow it right into your mitt."

"I can catch anything you can throw at me, Tony." Peter boasted in typical bravado. "Let'er fly!"

Tony explained how his pitch cut sharply downward about two feet in front of Moran. Peter turned his head away at the last instant and the ball hit the dirt before he could react. "It bounced up and caught him right in. . . ." Tony laughed at the memory, "Right in the place where no man ever wants to get hit!"

Steven almost rolled to the ground in his laughter. Tony's story put a different frame on the man he had disliked for so many years.

On Sunday evening, Senia was alone again in her Pine Street apartment, sitting at the oak table in her small dining room. Steven had returned to Chisholm where he lived, leaving his promise to call every day and see how she was doing with the final affairs of Peter Moran. "I wish there was more I could do to help you with all this. All I can do is keep you in my prayers and support the decisions you have to make. I'd like to be an 'uncle' to little Kevin. Let's both of us make an effort to be as involved as the Schmitzs will allow. They seem like wonderful people."

Senia's thoughts were consumed by the boy she would provide for. She could understand Art and Sarah's concerns about the inevitable wealth

Kevin stood to inherit. But, it was Peter's wish that his son be provided for and Senia had been entrusted with that responsibility.

She made a list of Peter's business interests and their approximate market value.

–Liquor distribution operations including warehouses, equipment, inventory . . . $250,000;
–Lumber yards: warehouses, equipment, inventory . . . $200,000;
–Local business properties—Liquor establishments:
Shamrock Saloon-$55,000
Red Rock Tavern-$40,000
Lumberjack Bar-$30.000
–Real Estate
Pine Street Consolidated (three commercial buildings)-$75,000
Third Avenue Consolidated (seven commercial properties)-$120,000
Moran Hotel property (Third Ave. at South Street)-$35,000 . . .
Insurance . . . ? $50,000
Alice location land (120 acres)-$25,000
Washington Street home/property-$100,000
–Other assets: $50,000 (est.)

Senia would discuss the estate with Victor Power the following morning at the attorney's office. She realized that her numbers were only preliminary estimates, and that Power would have a better idea of market values and a strategy for their prompt liquidation. She had to trust her judgment and the integrity of Vic Power. She was comfortable with the lawyer. Steven had told her that the miners trusted Vic. "He's not like the other businessmen in Hibbing. He's not pro-company," Steven believed.

Senia would get as much done on this Monday as possible. She told Goldberg at the bank that she would return to work on the following day. Her employer encouraged her to take the week off but she needed to get back into a routine. Vic Power could resolve most of the legal affairs and get Peter's estate on the market.

The pugnacious attorney greeted Senia with a genuine smile and firm handshake. The short, stocky lawyer wore a gray suit that fit tightly across his barrel-like chest. His shirt was unbuttoned at the neck and his tie dangled loosely. "It was a nice funeral service, Mrs. Arola. Peter was highly respected."

Like his friend, Peter Moran, Vic was not much at small talk when there was business at hand. "Let's see what you've got there, Mrs. Arola. Make that Senia. I think that's a lovely name." Power did not wait for permission to use her first name as he regarded the folder she had placed before him on his cluttered desk. He scanned the numbers. "Well done, Senia. You've got a good head for finances. That's obvious to me. But . . . I think you might have undervalued the lumber business. That was Pete's 'bread and butter' over the years. There's going to be lots of building construction . . ." Power looked up from the pages as if caught in a thought. His pudgy finger found an item that brought a chuckle.

"What is it, Mr. Power? Is something wrong?"

"No, not at all. Speaking of building, I can't help amusing over the Alice Location property. I worked with Pete on that. We stole it from under Elwood Trembart's nose. Really pissed him . . . .excuse me, ma'am . . . really upset El. I don't think Trembart ever forgave Pete for that. Tough luck. I've never cared much for Elwood anyhow. And the feeling's quite mutual I assure you. Politics in Hibbing are messy! No one ever forgets and no one ever forgives."

Senia was confused by the humor. "I don't get it, sir. I thought . . ."

Power interrupted, "We kept it quiet. Even Claude Atkinson didn't know about it, and Claude knows everything that goes on in this town. There was some bad blood going on. Anyhow, that Alice property is going to be priceless some day." He scratched his head while leaning back in his chair. "If Peter had lived, he was going to buy all the land south of town that he could get his hands on. That was his plan, and I was in complete agreement. You see, Senia, a few of us know that Hibbing is going to have to move one of these days."

"Move? What do you mean? Move?"

"We're sitting on the richest lode of iron ore in the world. Right here on Pine Street! There's more value in that ore than there is in this city. We're already surrounded by open pits growing by the day. I've got a handful of pending law suits against the mining companies over the damages that their blasting is causing to residents whose houses have been pelted by flying rocks. Hibbing is a doomed peninsula! That's all there is to it. Mark my words. The land south of town is worth investing in."

The two reviewed the estate and value estimates for more than an hour. It was decided between them that the liquor distribution business and taverns were highly marketable. "Peter was getting squeezed by his distributor in Duluth—the Fitger's Beer guy, John Allison. His territory was being cut by the new operations in Virginia and Grand Rapids."

"I know about that, Vic." Senia realized her disrespect in using the attorney's first name but before she could apologize, Power smiled easily.

"Thanks, Senia. All my friends call me Vic."

Power would work on the matters they discussed and get back to Senia by the end of the week. "I'd like you to talk with Mrs. Samora about her mortgage. Peter seemed quite insistent on that. And, Mr. Zoretek? Find out if Tony has any interest in getting involved in the Moran lumber operation. Maybe he and Lars Udahl can work something out."

"I'll do that. What else?"

"I'm going to talk with a few people I know about the properties. I think the market is good right now. Keep the 'Hibbing is doomed' comment to yourself. Word gets out that I said that and everything will be tough to sell. I move quickly, Senia. Don't be surprised if I find some buyers in the next few days." Power stood from his desk, removed his gray suit coat and paced to the window looking out at busy Pine Street. "Something else, Senia. The hotel. God, I still can't believe it. What a magnificent building it was—only operational for a few months. Sure must have been a blow to Peter. He was so proud of that place. Everybody was. I see you question the amount of insurance. What's that about?"

"I didn't handle the hotel financial accounts. His manager Sweeny did those numbers. Now Sweeny's gone. I think he was pocketing some premiums and manipulating the books. He was not someone I trusted. I think . . . maybe fifty thousand in insurance is all he carried. The hotel was worth five times that amount." Senia frowned over the memory of warning Peter about his bank manager's greed.

"We'll check that out. Anything else?"

"What about Kevin?" Senia was more concerned about the boy than anything else. "Peter's son. How do you propose we go about putting everything in a trust."

"No problem. When he's eighteen he's going to own this town! Not really this town as we know it today, but the next one for sure."

That prediction troubled Senia.

The following week, on a hot and blustery September Saturday afternoon, Steven Skorich was returning to Chisholm after spending the gorgeous day with Senia. The air was unseasonably dry and the road was dusty. His old roan pulled the wagon easily. Ahead, and off to the right, Steven saw a rising billow of smoke. A grass fire he thought. But the smoke gathered quickly, blocking the eastern sky. Then fingers of flame! A wall of fire was racing across the landscape, aroused by strong winds. Spurring the horse forward, Steven turned onto the road toward Pillsbury Location, a small mining community on the edge of the open pit mine. Before going a hundred yards he saw people, mostly women and children, rushing toward him on the narrow road. Panicked people. Screaming in their alarm!

"Don't go in there!" Warned a woman with an infant in her arms. "It's all gone . . . our home, the whole town is burning down." Her face streaked with tears. "All gone," she lamented.

Following the first deserters were the men, haggard from their futile attempts to contain the blaze. "It's out of control," shouted a man Steven recognized from when he worked in the Glenn mine nearby. "Steven, we're heading ta Chisum. Can't stop the damned thing no more. We tried. But its a fire from hell fer sure."

Steven packed as many women and children as were possible in his small wagon and turned back to the main road. After a few minutes he pulled his horse to a stop on the hilltop several blocks above Longyear Lake. The sky was black now. The milling townsfolk were unnerved by the ominous threat rapidly sweeping around the community on three sides. It appeared as if the eastern wind would push the fire to the north beyond the town. As Steven looked down Lake Street, he recognized terror in the frantic scramble of people. They were carrying their belongings and hurrying toward the Longyear bridge below the hill.

Then, something startling happened. Steven sensed it immediately. The wind shifted powerfully to the west. The path of the deadly blaze had changed. Chisholm was going to be swallowed in the inferno!

"Where are you going?" Steven shouted at a group of women pulling several children along behind them. "Get down to the lake!" Steven hollered above what had become a roar in the background.

"The schoolhouse! We're takin the kids to the school. Its safe there. That's what everyone's sayin'. Get the chillen off ta the school." A tall, slender women called back as she shepherded her straggling flock down the street to Steven's right.

Steven gave the reins to a teenage boy sitting wide-eyed at his elbow. "Take the wagon down to the lake and stay there until this blows over. Will you do that for me?"

"Yessir. I done this with my pa's wagon lots a times," he beamed proudly over the responsibility rendered by the large man. "Doncha worry none, sir."

Steven leaped from the wagon and headed for the Monroe school. He judged that in minutes the fire would be upon them. He sensed the school was not the safest place to be. The wall of flames was sweeping at hurricane speed across the western spread of the city, devouring everything in a half mile swath. By the time Steven reached the packed building the fire was nearly on his heels. Breaking through the heavy door he shouted above the frightened murmur of voices. "You can't stay here! We've gotta run for our lives to the lake."

The panic-stricken group, needing someone to take charge, recognized authority in Steven's imposing size and strong voice. Quickly the group moved out of the structure and began running down the street toward the lake, only a few blocks away. Before rushing off to join the evacuees, Steven hastened down the hallway to check every room. Within precious minutes the fire would at the door. Perhaps only seconds! Steven heard the cry of a baby to his left. He pushed into the room. A heavy set woman, clutching a cane in her hand began to cry . . . " I can't run. M'legs are gone bad." Huddled in the corner at her side were her three children, one yet an infant, but a few months old. Steven could feel the searing heat at the back of his neck. Flames were crawling across the floorboards. "You kids follow me." He loosened his leather belt so that it hung from his trousers nearly to the floor. "Don't either one of you let go of the belt. Keep your eyes closed and heads up. We've gotta try to run through the hall and out the door. Don't let the fire scare ya." He ripped off his plaid shirt, wrapped it over the woman's head to protect her and the child in her arms, then slung the heavy woman over his broad shoulders. "Hang on to the baby for dear life. We're gonna get all of you out of here."

Racing through the jagged tongues of fire with the two children at his heels, Steven found the entry and charged through it into the school yard beyond. The small open space of the Monroe school's playground was surrounded by fire on three sides. But to the west lay a narrow opening for escape. Although terrified at the moment, the children would be okay. "Yer pants . . . !" the little girl let go of his belt pushing her brother away from Steven. "Yer burnin!"

Steven felt the sear of heat at his ankles. He set the woman and baby down to douse the flames crawling up his trousers. He felt the raw scorch on his bare back. He hit the ground, rolling over in the gravel, and slapping at his blistering shoulders. The pain was excruciating, but the fire was gone from his clothing. Steven had no time to worry about his own injuries. Grabbing the woman again and shouldering her weight, Steven led the family to safety beyond the school yard.

Claude Atkinson was at his desk when the phone rang. "Claude, thank God I caught you at the paper. Our town's on fire!" Claude recognized the shaken voice of his friend, Bill Talboys, the proprietor of the *Chisholm Herald* newspaper. "We can't stop it. All the water's gone, and we're in retreat, Claude."

"Holy Jesus, what can I do, Bill?" Claude no more than got his question out and he heard the fzzzzt. The line from Chisholm was dead!

Thinking quickly, he tried the Hibbing operator. The familiar voice of Tessie Maras asked, "Number please?" Calmly, Claude instructed. "Tess there's a big problem over in Chisholm. A fire. I think the phone line is out, so we've gotta act quickly. I want you to place a call to St. Paul. Get Governor Johnson's residence. This is an emergency! Then I want you to contact Captain Healy at the armory. I think Johnson will want to call up the national guard." He paused in his thoughts. He knew the governor well, but did not want to usurp any of his prerogatives in an emergency situation. "Get Chief Welch at the fire department. Tell him to get as many volunteers as possible on the road to Chisholm. Let Chief Argir at the police department know as well. And, Vic Power. He can get the word out everywhere in Hibbing. Our neighbors are going to need all the help we can give them. Got that, Tess?"

By two in the morning, the state militia, under Captain Healy's leadership, was in Chisholm and martial law had been established. Bleary-eyed, Claude Atkinson stood at the top of Lake Street at sunrise on Sunday morning. The main street lay devastated. Looking north down the five blocks toward the lake, only two brick structures remained from what had been a thriving business community. At his side stood two of Chisholm's valiant fire fighters, Henry Fugere and Ed LaFrance. "Couldn't handle it, Mr. Atkinson," said Fugere. "The winds were from hell."

LaFrance put his arm across the shoulder of his colleague. "We gave'er a fight though, din't we?" He offered a wan smile. "We might'a lost our little town but we ain't lost none of our folks. Thank God fer that."

Steven Skorich spent the night lying on his back in the cool mud along the east shore of Longyear Lake. Lingering on the edges of consciousness, he fought against the pain that raked his back and legs. Despite his incredible strength, Steven could not lift himself from the mire. The burns were deep in his flesh. He'd need to get to a hospital soon . . . or . . ? After an hour, he gave in to the pain. Closing his eyes on the shadowy world about him.

Martin Alto found Steven's wagon near the bridge. Alto was one of several men who lived in Steven's apartment above Nolan's store on what had been Lake Street. He searched for his friend in the early Sunday light. Along with one-armed Lefty Graff and three other men, Alto led the search party along the lake shore.

"Steven . . . Steven." Martin bent over the huge frame of the man he loved and respected more than any other. Korenjack, as he was called by his friends, lay unconscious in the black muck. Alto hailed the others. "Over here! Quick! Steven's badly burned. We gotta get him over to the

Rood Hospital in Hibbing. I don't think he's conscious. We're gonna hafta be careful not to do him no more damage."

The five men laid a thick cushion of blankets in the back of the wagon and gently laid Steven on his stomach. In two hours they had him in the hospital, under the careful attention of Doctor Ambrose Hane.

A Letter to the 'Old Country'

February, 1909

It had been nearly six months since Peter's funeral, yet the memory of him kept a lock on Senia's thoughts. She found everyday activities draining. The past months were a blurry nightmare she could not escape. She plunged into her work at the bank as if her job were the only calm water to anchor her troubled ship. Peter's death. Then Steven's tragedy. Her own lingering grief over her deceased husband, Timo. It was as if the world were in a conspiracy with Hades to burden her with the weight of all human suffering. But she was a strong woman before all these troubling events. Even stronger because of them! Senia recognized, however, that her strength of character often isolated her, engendering in her a spirit of independence. More often than not, she preferred solitude to the company of others. Yet, even those closest to her could not discern changes in her personality. Senia was good at hiding her innermost feelings.

She spent most of Saturday at the Rood Hospital visiting Steven, where recovery from massive third degree burns was incredibly slow. His spirits, however, seemed elevated by her presence. In another two weeks he would be released into her care while convalescing. He had nowhere else to go. "I'll be living with you, my dear . . . and we're not married. What will people think?" Steven's good humor was not diminished by his tragedy. "Maybe we ought to get Judge Brady over to the hospital before I'm discharged and have him do some nuptials. If we don't we're sure to get ourselves in the gossip grapevines of Hibbing," he teased.

"For better or for worse," Senia rejoined. "Which is it, my man? You look pretty good to me but . . . I think we ought to wait a while. I'm going to want a totally functional husband in my bed, Mr. Skorich." Senia ran her fingers across his smoothly shaven face. "I always knew there was a handsome face under that thick beard. I can see something of your nephew in your mouth and jaw, now that all that hair has been shaved. And, let me assure you, Steven, that is a compliment." Senia laughed deeply. "I love you . . . and don't think I'm not tempted by your proposal."

Inside, however, Senia knew she was not ready for marriage. She had become too self-absorbed to offer the companionship this decent man deserved. Steven had put his life on the line for complete strangers. He would do anything in the world for her. She knew she loved him deeply, but . . .

On Sunday, Tony and Mary joined her on a trip to Duluth to celebrate Kevin's third birthday. Art and Sarah Schmitz hosted a wonderful afternoon affair. Senia saw Peter's features in the lad's wavy brown hair, pug nose, large ears. She often wondered about the boy's mother. What did Barbara look like? What kind of woman was she? Father Foley was unable to give Senia much information in that regard, and even Peter's closest friend, Jim McIntosh, had never met Peter's lover of years past. Peter's private life was a mystery. Perhaps some of Peter Moran would unravel over the years in this boy who had his father's blood pulsing in his veins. She would watch him grow and come to know him as intimately as circumstances would allow.

Senia was 'aunty' to the spirited lad. Mary was regarded as an aunt as well. And Tony an adoring uncle. Art, being an only child, grew up without many social contacts beyond his own parents. Sarah had an unmarried sister she was not close to. They both believed having an extended family would be good for the boy. The relatives from Hibbing were always welcome visitors and the feeling of *family* grew among them. Tony held a special, almost profound attraction to Kevin. It was hard to separate the two of them whenever they got together. Senia watched as they played on the floor. Tony softly tossing a rubber ball to Kevin and the boy gleefully rolling it back, giggling as his uncle congratulated . . . "Atta boy, Kev!

You're gonna be a baseball player one of these days. Uncle Tony's gonna teach you how to pitch."

Being with Mary and Tony always pleased Senia. The two of them were so much in love. Their very presence could light up a room. Senia knew of their engagement and plans to get married this summer. But no specific date had yet been mentioned. On the trip to Duluth, Mary was especially ebullient and whispered to Senia that Kevin's birthday was going to be "more than just a birthday party" for her and Tony. She said the two of them had an announcement to make. Senia remembered wondering if Mary were pregnant, then dismissed the notion. That would be a secret best kept to themselves. Yet, she wondered if they made love.

In the living room eating chocolate cake with freshly made ice cream, Tony caught the eye of Father Foley across the table. The St. James pastor was as much a part of the family as any of them. Even more so. Father Pat, as Art called him, spent nearly as much time at their home as he did at the rectory.

"Father, friends . . ." Tony cleared his throat. "We've got some news, Mary and me. You already know we're going to get married, but now Mary's picked out a date." He beamed toward his lovely fiancé, squeezed her hand under the table.

Mary gave him a peck on the cheek. "We both wanted all of you to be the first to know." She looked toward Senia, "We'll tell Steven tomorrow when we visit the hospital. I wish he could be here this afternoon, but it won't be too much longer and he'll be up and about," she said, thoughtful of her closest friend's feelings.

Sarah smiled from her place next to her husband, excitement in her soft voice, "Congratulations to both of you! When will it be?"

"July twenty-fourth at the Immaculate Conception Church. We will be talking to Father Dougherty next week," Mary bubbled. "And, Father Pat, we want you to perform our marriage vows. Can you do that in a Hibbing parish?"

Foley crossed his long arms on the table, leaned forward in his chair, "I would be most honored. And, can I do that? Well, I wouldn't allow even the Vatican to stand in the way of such a wonderful privilege! I'm going to put a circle around that Saturday on my calendar as soon as I get back to the rectory."

Vic Power had proven true to his word. The disposition of the Peter Moran estate went smoothly through the probate process. In close consultation with Senia, Power had liquidated most of Moran's real estate holdings within six weeks. A consortium of Chisholm businessmen, anxious to recover from fire losses, joined with J.J. Le Bonious and Carl Thiel of Hibbing in purchasing a block of Third Avenue properties. For the Chisholm merchants the deal was an investment while they were rebuilding their former establishments in their swiftly recovering community.

Con O'Gara, an old friend of Peter's, purchased all three taverns. The Clark Fisk Corey Insurance firm was quick to close on the Pine Street properties. Fred Bennett, the Oliver superintendent, paid top dollar for the Moran mansion on Washington Street.

From her new position as vice president at the Merchants and Miners Bank, Senia arranged loans for Lars Udahl to purchase the Moran lumber operation. Lars and Tony Zoretek forged a profitable arrangement by starting a branch location in Chisholm where lumber was in great demand. Senia also helped Norman Dinter gather several investors to purchase Moran's liquor distribution network. Dinter was a bright and ambitious young man with some innovative business ideas for expansion.

Having completed her analysis of all of Peter's hotel accounts, Senia discovered thousands of missing dollars. Jerry Sweeny, who managed the hotel, had been skimming and shifting funds. Senia had warned her employer on several occasions about Sweeny's practices but to no avail. When Sweeny left Hibbing before the hotel fire, he absconded with nearly fifty thousand dollars. No one had heard anything of his whereabouts. When presented with the figures, Power promised to initiate embezzlement proceedings on behalf of the Moran estate. If Sweeny were alive, Vic Power would find him and see that he was put behind bars.

At Power's suggestion, Senia invested a portion of the estate profits in an additional 120 acre tract of land in Alice Location. (Power believed that the Larrabee Forty south of Hibbing would become the next major building site.) Everything else was placed in trust for Peter's heir, Kevin Schmitz.

Tony Zoretek's carpentry shop had been in existence for only a few weeks before the tragic Chisholm fire. The rebuilding effort in the neighboring community was a phenomenal undertaking, and Tony moved swiftly to become involved. Sensitive to the misfortune of so many, Tony bid on jobs at only slightly over his own costs. He hired a capable team of carpenters and masons so that his projects could be completed in minimal time. His first major contract was to rebuild the O'Neil Hotel, which had been a Chisholm landmark. By February, Zoretek was building a new hardware store and furniture outlet on Lake Street, and thirty homes in the residential district to the west of the downtown area. Lars Udahl opened a lumber warehouse near Longyear Lake and supplied Tony's crews with building materials at a fraction over cost.

At the same time, Tony was busy in Hibbing. The mining hub was continuing to grow rapidly into the area known as the 'South Forty.' He was especially attentive to a house that he and Mary had designed in the Brooklyn neighborhood to the southwest of town. On a nearby property, he was building a house for Senia as well. With all the activity going on, Tony worked long hours, finding little time to do the actual carpentry himself. Most of his efforts involved supervising his growing operations in both Hibbing and Chisholm. He also had crews doing various jobs in Keewatin to the west and Buhl a few miles to the east.

∼

Claude Atkinson was frustrated. Since Peter Moran's death nearly six months ago, he had pursued every possible lead the police could give him. The editor did not like unfinished business—and the Moran case was unfinished business! Claude was of the conviction that Peter had been murdered. He would bet his newspaper on it. Further, he believed the murder was fratricide. Denis Moran was on the top of his list of suspects.

When Peter's Buick was discovered underwater in Lake Pokegama near Grand Rapids, the police there questioned railroad officials and confiscated departure records. The Friday train to the Twin Cities had twenty-eight passengers, twenty-four of whom were men. Of the twenty-four men, all but four were well known Grand Rapids residents. None of the four others matched the description of Denis Moran. Police were seeking a man believed to be "large-framed, red-bearded, and roughish-looking." No one fit those vague criteria. The 'Mr. Jones' on the passenger list was well-built, neatly dressed and business-looking. Minneapolis records did not show any 'Jones' traveling out of that city.

"He probably stole one of Peter's suits, shaved his beard, and used the most obvious alias imaginable. That's all it would take. He's wanted for kidnapping but nobody seems to give a damn." Claude was venting his frustration to Vic Power over the telephone. "Sorry to harp on that theme all the time. What have you turned up, Vic?"

"We found Sweeny in Winona. Only took a few weeks. He'll be doing about ten years at the Stillwater prison. Just be patient, Claude. Let the Feds do their job. They tracked Sweeny down, and they'll find Denis Moran, too. They've got agents in Pennsylvania and out in Oregon. His days are numbered."

"I wish I had your optimism," Claude mumbled.

"So what's new on the local political scene, Claude? I hate to change the subject, but you know me. One of these days I'm going to run against Doc Weirick for mayor. He's just a mining company crony, and people are going realize that things have got to change. I think I'll be the guy they'll want to make that change." Vic Power had ambitions that Claude was well aware of.

"I'm sure you will run, Vic. Get your base established before going after Weirick. He's got lots of money, my friend. And money talks! Keep working on your Roosevelt ties," Claude advised, smiling to himself.

Tony sat at his desk in the Center Street office on this bitterly cold February afternoon. Spirals of chimney smoke danced from every rooftop. The wind whisked snow into sizable drifts along the walkways. Winter in Northern Minnesota was a shroud of depressing gray. It was nearly five o'clock and Mary would be home from her seamstress job at Luigi Anselmo's tailor shop. Tessie Maras connected his call.

Although tired, Mary was still brimming with the excitement of the weekend trip to Duluth, Kevin's birthday and their announcement of a wedding date. She had promised Tony supper on this Monday but looked despairingly at the shelves of her pantry. She hadn't gotten to Khort's grocery store over the weekend and the contents of her icebox were as meager as the pantry. She sighed over the prospect of preparing a meal. Mary's fatigue of the moment dulled her appetite. Hearing the ring of her phone, she pondered an apology. Surely it was Tony and just as surely he would be famished.

Without waiting for Tony to say a word, she picked up the receiver and breathed in a husky, teasing voice, "Tony, my love, I cannot wait to be in your arms, to kiss you passionately, and take you to my bed."

Tony allowed a pause, changed his voice to a higher pitch. "I'm sorry . . . this is Father Dougherty from the church," his words perfectly disguised. "What is this talk of passionate kisses?"

Dumbfounded, Mary tried to recover. Had Tony asked the Catholic priest to call her and arrange a meeting to set their wedding on the church calendar? The color in her face drained as she struggled for words to cover her fatal blunder. "Father . . . I am so sorry. Truly I didn't mean . . ."

Tony could not contain his laughter. "Hello, Mary," he said in a husky voice of his own. "Such talk from the woman I will marry. Have you no shame whatsoever?"

"You terrible man . . . you! How could you? I nearly had a heart attack."

Tony was thoroughly amused. "I am terrible, my dear. But I couldn't resist the opportunity. Are you recovered?"

"Just for that, Mr. Zoretek, you will not be given any dinner at my house tonight. I can be a spiteful and unforgiving woman."

"Spiteful, unforgiving, and so very lovable, Mary. I wish I could have seen your face."

Mary loved his humor. More than anything, Tony could make her laugh. All too often at her own foibles. "My face dropped to the floor, young man. And, calling me lovable will not earn you a meal tonight."

"That's just perfect. I wanted to take you out to supper anyway. I know you must be awfully tired from the weekend and long day at work. I've got us a table at the Aspenwood for six-thirty. Senia says their food is fantastic.

And I'm craving something Italian!" His suggestive comment passed Mary's usually quick attention without a rejoinder. "Afterwards we can go over to the hospital and visit Steven. Then, maybe . . . those passionate kisses you promised to give to Father Dougherty?"

July 1909

It had been two years since Tony's arrival in Hibbing. In that time he had written home to his family in Churile, Slovenia, only four times—letters at Christmas and Easter. In two weeks he would be married.

On this gorgeous Sunday morning, he was awakened early by the singing of grosbeaks and warbling of wrens from the trees outside his bedroom window. His roommates were sleeping off hangovers from a late night on the town. The house was unusually quiet. Tony would pick up Mary in a few hours. The two of them would join her friends, the Depelos, from Mahoning Location, and go to Mass at the Italian Catholic church.

The sun sat low in the eastern sky when he roused himself out of bed. Pulling on his trousers, he headed downstairs to the kitchen and started a pot of coffee on the cast iron stove. Splashing cold water on his face, he regarded himself in the small mirror hanging over the sink. He smiled easily at the face reflecting back. "You're one lucky man, Tony Zoretek," he said to himself. What had he done, he wondered, to have been blessed with such good fortune in this wonderful new country. Having recently achieved his American citizenship, he was brimming with self-pride and a consuming gratitude. As he did most mornings, Tony bowed his head and said a prayer. His words were always a mix of praise and thanksgiving for his wonderful life. He always remembered his betrothed Mary, his family in the Old Country, his uncle Steven, and his friend Peter Moran in those impromptu prayers.

In the kitchen table drawer he found a tablet and some sharpened pencils. Words tumbled from his thoughts to the paper with ease.

Dear Father, Mother, and brothers Jakob and Rudolph,
    It is with great joy that I write my loving family on this beautiful

Sunday morning in Minnesota. Since my last letter at Easter time, your son and brother has enjoyed continued happiness and success.

Mother, your brother Steven has almost completely recovered from the serious burns I told you about. He is living again in Chisholm where the people regard him as the hero of the terrible fire that destroyed their town. He would want me to send his love to all of you.

Tony paused from his letter reflecting on the uncle he so loved and respected. Since his recovery, Steven had made some changes in his life. He wanted to be in Chisholm where he felt a sense of being rooted. And he wanted to work with the miners who were his closest friends. With Senia's help, he had set up a small office in one of the new buildings on Lake Street. His business was the fulfillment of his dream to help mineworkers build a future for themselves and their families through an investment program. Nearly three hundred miners were contributing two dollars a month from their wages into a fund that Steven invested through the local bank. Senia provided her expertise, and the returns were consistently coming in well above the market in general. The American economy was recovering from the '07 slump, and Steven was learning the intricacies of stock and bond activity.

In two weeks I will have the happiest day of my twenty years. Mary Samora and your son will be united in marriage and begin our lives together. I do not have the words to describe my feelings of love for Mary. She is the most wonderful person I have ever met and she loves me as much as I do her.

Tony reread his last two lines. "Does this seem foolish?" he wondered. How else might he express the happiness he felt inside? There were no words . . . "I love her and she loves me. What else can be said?" But even the word love seemed inadequate. Over the past year she had become the very center of his existence. Her easy smile, her caressing touch, her bright eyes, her full mouth, her lilting voice, and her throaty laugh. Her indescribable beauty . . . the looks she gave him, the words she spoke, the taste of her kisses, and the smell of her hair. The quiet times, the tears of sad moments they shared and the radiance of joyful times together. She was his everything! How could he ever communicate the depth of his emotions with anyone but her?

> *I will soon be finished with a house we planned together and we both will pray for many children to fill the rooms. And, I will keep one room for my brother Rudolph in the hope he may come to this great country and join the Zoretek family here. Please tell my brother to study hard in school and to learn the language of English so he can advance his education in our schools.*

Tony had been sending money home to help his parents—a portion of which he encouraged them to save for his youngest brother. Rudy, now a boy of twelve, had no future in Slovenia. The oldest son, Jakob, would inherit his father's small tract of land. Such was the timeworn tradition of his homeland. This reality had been the motivation for Tony to make his way to America two years ago.

> *My little carpentry business has grown. The city of Hibbing needs more and more houses for the many immigrants who come to this area in search of jobs. Even my old friend from Ljubljana, Lud Jaksa, has come back here from Chicago and works for me now as a carpenter.*

Tony was always mindful of his simple roots. Both he and Mary often talked about the values they had brought from their rural villages. It was an integral part of the bond between them. Tony's eyes moistened as he looked up from his letter. In such a short time he had experienced so many blessings. It almost overwhelmed him. How could his family relate to what he was telling them about starting his own business, giving jobs to people, building a new house? How could they possibly imagine this America of his? They could not, he realized. It struck him that he could hardly understand this marvelous country himself. He must never, however, give his family an impression of self-importance. Nor should he ever appear boastful of his accomplishments.

> *I know, father, that you had great hopes for your son when you gave me your permission to come to this country. I know that you and mother have kept me in your prayers every day that I have been gone from your home. I thank our Father in heaven for my parents and ask Him to bless your lives as he has mine. The only sadness I will have on my wedding day is that you will not be here to share it all with me. Mary's parents in Italy will also be unable to join us in our happiness.*

Tony thought of Mary's family in Piedimonte of the Campania in southern Italy. Like himself, she had been sending small amounts of money back to them and her six younger brothers and sisters. Angelo and Justina Bellani were too old to travel such a distance. But maybe, some day, one of Mary's family would make their journey to this country.

Pouring the last cup of coffee from the pot, Tony wandered over to the kitchen window and looked out at the blooming morning. It was after seven and he would take a bath in the large metal tub stored in a closet off the kitchen. In a few days he would be leaving his buddies and getting settled in the nearly-finished house in Brooklyn Addition. He would miss the guys and all the shenanigans going on in the house they all shared. They were a fun-loving lot.

Back at the table, Tony would write the last lines of his brief letter.

> *I am enclosing a bank draft with my letter. I hope that the money will bring you as much pleasure as it gives me to be able to send it. I will keep each of you in my prayers and light a candle for the Zoretek family in our church this morning at Mass.*
>
> Your loving son and brother,
Anton

Tony Zoretek wed Mary Bellani Samora in the Immaculate Conception Catholic Church on July 24, 1909. The wedding was a simple affair including only the couple's closest friends. Steven Skorich, walking proudly up the aisle in front of his nephew, was Tony's best man. Senia Arola was Mary's maid of honor. Kevin Schmitz, dressed in a suit and tie, presented the bride and groom with their rings. Showing more emotion than was usual for him, Father Foley said their vows. A reception following the wedding that Saturday night was held at the Italian Lodge.

'THE PEOPLE'S POWER'

November 1913

Victor Power and the Progressives scored an impressive win in the Hibbing mayoral election. Power's political ambitions were deep-rooted and his coalition of voters had developed over three years of careful organizing. The promise of vast public improvements combined with the spirit of 'rugged individualism'—a theme of Roosevelt's Progressive Party—served as an inspiration to the voters in this bustling mining town. His was a party of miners and other working men who wanted the ironclad grip of mine owners to finally end. Another critical element in the Power strategy involved cultivating the support of the powerful saloon keepers of Hibbing. In that regard, Con O'Gara was an important ally. Power defeated incumbent Doc H.R. Weirick by nearly two to one in the final vote tallies. The victory was a mandate for change!

At the Tuesday night campaign celebration in Power's law office, Victor embraced Steven Skorich. "Couldn't have done this without you, Steven. I can't thank you enough for all the work you did with the miners in town. And, they turned out to vote just like you promised they would."

Although Steven lived in Chisholm, he was a frequent visitor to Hibbing. His friend, Senia, and a growing investment business brought him to Hibbing several days a week. Steven had liked Vic Power from their first meeting years before. Power had the heart and spirit of a miner. He gave voice to their issues and had the courage to fight the battles with the powerful companies in a war that needed to be fought.

"It was you they wanted to go to the polls for, Vic. They listened to what you were saying and liked it. What's more, for the first time in my memory the miners feel some sense of power." He paused for the effect of his pun . . . "Did you get that my friend?"

Power was too self-absorbed in his moment of success to catch his friend's humor. "I'm going to do what I said I would, Steven. As God is my witness. I'm going to take this town where it has never been before." The line was a favorite during Power's campaign. The implication was subtle. He knew the town was going to go somewhere. And, that somewhere was south to Alice. His long range plans would include a water system project in tiny Alice along with everything else necessary to ensure an easy transition. He even planned to push for consolidation of the two communities as soon as he was sworn in.

"You get those streets paved, improve the town's municipal services, and get more people on the public payrolls. Then our people will give you another mandate next year." Steven smiled, clasped his hand on the smaller man's shoulders. Vic Power was a little giant, he realized.

"The mining companies are going to have to pay for a lot of what I need to get done. So are these fine people." He gestured a short arm in a sweeping motion at the assembled crowd. "I'm planning to raise the city's levy and that's not going to be popular." Power frowned at the prospect.

"Nothing's free. We'll pay what we've got to without complaining. So long as you make it clear that what you're doing is right. Maybe the days of company rule have ended today. I sure hope so."

"So do I. Steven, where's your lovely lady friend? I haven't seen Senia in the crowd." Power looked about the crowded office. The space was too small for the gathering, and several people were congregated on the walkway outside the door. "We need more room, Steven. There must be a hundred people here already."

"It's a pleasant evening. Let's carry the celebration right out into the street. This is a night for the people after all. Reminds me of ole Andy Jackson's party when he got elected."

"A student of history are you, my friend?" Power laughed at the reference.

Power's petite wife, Percy, joined the men. She beamed at her husband,

"We have so many friends. Victor, you must get outside and mingle, my dear. Everybody wants to offer their good wishes."

"I'm going to head outside myself." Steven looked over the heads of the crowd. Over six feet tall, it was easy for him to see everything around him. "There's Senia now. Out on the sidewalk talking with Mary and Tony Zoretek. Let's go out and join them. Percy, Senia is anxious to meet you."

The murmur of many voices became a discernible chant rapidly swelling through the room. "Victor . . . Victor . . . Victor . . ." The scene was becoming increasingly boisterous. "Victor . . ." The new mayor was expected to give a thank you speech at eight, and the clock was sweeping toward that time. "Victor Power . . . he's our man . . . if he can't do it—no one can!" The Power refrain caught on quickly and was repeated over and over. Soon the slogan was being hollered out on Pine Street.

Claude Atkinson moved through the throng and found Power at Steven's side. "Congratulations, Victor. It's a great day for Hibbing," the newsman declared over the din. "I'm here for your speech. Going to give it a big front page spread in the *Mesaba Ore* tomorrow. Make it another fiery one, Vic. The town needs a wake up call."

Atkinson had broken ranks with many in the business community by openly supporting Power. Lately Claude's newspaper had not been as promining company as in the past. There was still a lingering unrest from the miner's strike in '07. Labor issues had not been resolved, and Claude believed conditions in many mines were even worse than they had been during that walkout. Claude could handle the heat that his recent editorial commentaries evoked. He was a righteous man, and his readers held him in high respect. Vic Power knew that and had always been candid with Claude when issues developed. The two men did not always agree, but both were highly tolerant of their differences. Claude had encouraged Vic to be more conciliatory in dealing with mine management issues and not to "pick fights you can't win."

"The town's had a wake-up call, Claude. Two to one is the way I count the votes. A landslide over that corrupt regime that Weirick had going here. Let's go out and give our folks the congratulations they deserve. I serve them after all. It's not the other way around—never will be!"

Vic Power did not disappoint Claude Atkinson nor any of the nearly three hundred Hibbing citizens that night. His speech was rousing and inspiring. He finished his twenty minute staccato delivery with the words, "My name's Victor Power, friends. You all know that by now. But 'power' is a frightening concept to me. I promise all of you here tonight that we have a scored a *victory for people's power . . . I will be the people's power!*"

Claude loved the clever phraseology of those last words as he scribbled them down in his notebook. "I truly hope that you mean what you say," he mumbled under his breath.

Back in his office, Claude contemplated the historical significance of this election. The newsman framed everything within his personal concept of regional history—Mesabi Iron Range history. As he thought about Vic Power his eyes narrowed on a thick red-covered book resting by itself on his shelf.

Since his arrival in Hibbing nearly fifteen years ago, Claude had taken deep interest in the sweep of mining. At first he merely kept a journal. The journal grew over the years. In 1906 he began writing a history of the Mesabi. The project remained a secret kept in an old wooden file cabinet behind the desk in his office. Not even his wife or son knew about the project. He had worked on polishing the manuscript in the early mornings and late evenings for five years. In every detail, the history was meticulously portrayed. Claude titled the book *The Red Country* and sent it off to a St. Paul publishing house. In March of the previous year, twenty-five copies came off the press. The Minnesota Historical Society called his work "the masterpiece of the Mesabi." Claude, however, was disappointed with the nearly six hundred page tome. "I didn't really capture the people here well enough," he told a friend after the publication. "I'd like to tell the story over again. Maybe someday I will. The next time, if there ever is one, I'll tell more about the people who made this town what it really is."

∼

Seven year old Kevin Schmitz sat on the hard wooden bench outside the office of principal of St. James Catholic school. Sister Paula had sent him out of the second grade classroom again. This time Father Foley would be called to the office of Mr. Lyons, the school administrator. Kevin sat with hands folded in his lap, feet swinging loosely inches above the floor. The boy had been sent to see Mr. Lyons several times before. This was not something that frightened him. Even the presence of Father Foley failed to intimidate the youth. He hummed under his breath to relax himself, picked at some playground dirt under his fingernails.

Kevin had carried a skirmish from morning recess back into the school. Inside the classroom he shoved Gerald Garden, causing the boy to fall against a desk and bang his head. Gerald screamed for Sister Paula's intervention. The nun stepped quickly between the two boys, grabbing Kevin by an ear and pulling him into the hallway. "To the office with you, young man. I'm going to get Father Foley this time. I've had about enough of your misbehavior!" Sister Paula's patience with Kevin's rowdiness had been spent. Still clinging to the boy's ear, turning his head painfully downward, she led Kevin up the stairs to Mr. Lyons' office.

"What was that all about, Kevin? I'm sick and tired of your bullying the other children. I will have no more of that. Now you sit here while I get Father to come over here. Do you understand?"

Kevin was large for his age and physically stronger than many of the older boys in third and fourth grade. Since kindergarten, however, he had been the target of teasings he could neither understand nor tolerate. When he was five, in his second day at the St. James school, a girl named Sally McDougal called him the 'kidnapped kid.' He ignored the comment because he had no idea what she was talking about. Later, other kids gave him the same ribbing and taunting.

After school one day, Kevin asked his mother what it all meant. Sarah Schmitz was comforting but unwilling to explain anything to the boy. "I'll have daddy talk to you when he gets home from work. Now you just forget about it and run off and play. I just saw Mikey out in the back yard. You two can play until I call you in for supper."

Later that evening, Art Schmitz talked with his son. He tried to explain what was a very complicated story as delicately as he knew how.

Kevin had indeed been kidnapped as a child of eighteen months. Three men had broken into their home on a Monday morning after Art had left for his job at the ship yards. The abductors tied Sarah to a kitchen chair and fled with the boy to the alleyway behind the house. He was loaded into a wagon and carried off to the kidnappers' hideout on Raleigh Street several blocks away. Inept and careless in their crime, a man and a woman were quickly discovered in a coal bin at the West Duluth house where both were hiding. They were arrested and jailed. Two of the conspirators, however, escaped. One of the men, named Ducette, was later arrested in Hibbing on arson charges. He claimed credit for the devastating HOTEL MORAN fire. While in their custody he also admitted his involvement in the Duluth kidnapping.

The other fugitive was Denis Moran.

Art Schmitz described the episode in guarded words. "When you were just a baby, some very mean men took you from the house. Your mom called the police and they found you in a few minutes. You were not hurt at all by the bad men and came home just like nothing even happened."

"I was kidnapped then, wasn't I, Dad?"

"Well . . . I suppose you could use that word, son. But, like I just said, nothing bad happened. Me and mom were just awfully scared, that's all."

Kevin was frustrated by his father's description of those events. "Is there a better word than 'kidnapped', dad? I mean that's what the kids at school called it. Said I was the 'kidnapped kid.' Made me mad. Kidnapped is kinda scary to me."

Art searched for another way to characterize what was troubling the boy. "Kidnapped only means that you were taken without permission from me or mom. Do you understand, Kevin? If Father Pat or Uncle Tony came by to take you somewhere—like to a circus or something—we would say that's just fine. They could take you away because we know them and trust them."

"Jeeze, dad, I know that." Deflated by his father's feeble explanation, Kevin became even more frustrated. "So I was kidnapped by some strangers? I still don't like other kids saying it. It makes me mad. Really mad! And you didn't tell me why it happened. How come these people wanted to take me? What did I do?"

Art lost some color, his eyes narrowed. The boy was only seven. Too young to understand anything about that dreadful episode and the complex circumstances surrounding the crime. Local newspapers sensationalized the kidnapping and trial that followed. The fact that Kevin was the son of the late Peter Moran managed to surface at one point in courtroom testimony. Secrets revealed during the trial, however, were carefully swept under the rug in the Schmitz household.

The boy's innocent questions stirred the nightmare that haunted Art and Sarah like an odious secret hidden in a dark closet of their life. Both had hoped and prayed there would be a right time to explain these things. A right time to tell him that he was an adopted child. Maybe when the boy was in high school.

"I don't know what to say, son. I guess these men wanted money. They thought we were rich or something. It was a mistake on their part. We just can't understand some things. That was one of those things." Art was not pleased with his deception. He would try to recover from the awkwardness of the moment and deal with the issue more indirectly. "Kids are just mean sometimes. They like to tease and if you get mad they just tease all the more. If you ignore it, pretty soon they just forget about it. Goes away all by itself."

Kevin didn't like the advice from his father that night, but he couldn't simply ignore it. And forgetting it was something he was never going to do. The taunting only made him become belligerent and contentious. In time the teasing about his kidnapping did pass, but his aggressive behavior toward his classmates continued. Kevin Schmitz gained a reputation at school as being an indignant and obstinate child.

The only person Kevin could really talk with about things that bothered him in school or at home was eight year old Gary Zench, a public school kid who lived north of Fifty-Seventh Street on the rocky hillsides. Gary came from a poor family and his clothes were always worn and dirty. The boy was small for his age. Skinny, thick-lipped, with short, curly dark hair, and deep brown eyes. His father was a heavy drinker. Sometimes Gary wore the bruises of his dad's bad temper about his eyes. Often Gary Zench skipped school because of the shame he felt about his family's problems. The attraction of the two boys was that of opposites. On more than one occasion, Kevin's parents forbade him from playing with the Zench boy. Gary's family had a bad reputation. And, they were Protestants. "There are enough good Catholic kids to play with in the neighborhood," his father told him.

Father Foley summoned Kevin into the office with a stern look in his deep-set eyes. The tall clergyman was an intimidating figure in his black attire.

The St. James school children both loved and feared the amiable parish pastor. His presence in the principal's office would strike fear into their hearts. But Kevin knew Father Pat more as an uncle than a figure of authority. Foley, he was certain, would not discipline his misbehavior. Despite the scolding he would surely get from Mr. Lyons, Foley would seek to understand the reasons for this latest incident. Kevin smiled weakly, hung his head, wrung his hands. He would be apologetic, promise to reform, and use his most contrite behavior. He might even conjure some tears of remorse. At seven, Kevin was already a manipulator and well aware of his ability to wriggle out of uncomfortable situations.

After directing the boy to a straight-backed wooden chair in front of his desk, Mr. Lyons cleared his throat, nodded toward Foley, and folded his thick arms across his chest. "Will you please explain to Father Foley and myself what happened this morning? Sister Paula is at her wit's end about your bullying the other children. This is what? The third time you have been sent to my office already this year?"

Kevin sniffled into the handkerchief gripped in his small hands for proper effect. His first four words were, "I'm very sorry, sir." From there he went on to explain how Gerald Garden had teased him on the playground. Shifting the blame for instigating the incident to the other boy he told how the badgering just "caused me to lose my temper again." Kevin was quite articulate in expressing how badly he felt about his problem with a nasty temper. "It just gets out of control sometimes. I like Gerald, and I've tried to ignore his teasing, but . . ."

Foley asked Mr. Lyons to allow him to speak alone with the boy for a few minutes. The principal respectfully excused himself from the room. The priest had talked with Kevin's father about the kidnapping issue on other occasions. Art Schmitz shared his frustration about his inability to explain what had happened to his son in a way that the boy could understand it.

"This kidnapping business still bothers you a lot doesn't it, Kevin? I know that your father has talked to you about it. He feels bad . . ."

Kevin interrupted the priest. "Father Pat, I know that happened when I was a baby. It's not something my dad should worry about. I've just got to learn to ignore the teasing. And, I will sir. Honest to God, I will. Is it wrong to say that, Father? I mean, *honest to God*? Is that like swearing? I sure don't want to say it again if it's a sin." Kevin would steer the conversation from his behavior issue to the Catechism studies in class. "Sister Paula has told us about taking the Lord's name in vain. I don't want to do that. And, I've had straight A's in my religion lessons, Father. Did you know that? I take my school classes seriously because dad says he wants me to go to college when I'm older. I think I might want to be a priest like you some day, Father Pat. A priest is a very important person, isn't he, Father?"

Father Patrick Foley could not help being charmed by the boy he had known so intimately from the day he was born more than seven years ago. He recognized Kevin's deliberate avoidance of issues that churned inside. Foley was beginning to see the personality of Kevin's father in the boy's cleverness. Perhaps it was inevitable. Foley was concerned. He sensed that this boy was going to be a challenge to him and to his parents in the years to come.

Giving Kevin a hard stare, however, Foley could not let the lad off the hook that easily. "We are not here this morning to discuss your grades in school, nor your thoughts on the priesthood, Kevin. Your misbehavior will not be tolerated. I will instruct Mr. Lyons to keep you after school for an hour every day for the next week. And, I will expect you to explain all of this to your parents. Do you understand that?"

"Yes, Father. I deserve the punishment . . . and, I'll tell my parents that you gave me a good scolding about what I did."

The late autumn afternoon was unseasonably cold. The steel gray skies foretold an early winter. Fallen leaves from trees stripped of their color and vitality by autumnal northerlies whisked about the yard, clinging to bordering shrubbery. The landscape appeared lifeless except for the scurry of ambitious squirrels creating their stash for the white months ahead. The robins, along with their warm weather friends—purple martins, chickadees, and wrens—had long since flown to more hospitable climates. Unyielding asters offered the last resistance to the inevitable.

The Brooklyn neighborhood where Tony and Mary Zoretek lived was a mile south of the turbulent mining activity. Although still a prospering city, Hibbing's dilemma was becoming more apparent. The open pit mines had an insatiable appetite gnawing away on three sides of what was becoming a peninsula of land jutting out into a colossal canyon. Merging operations formed one continuous excavation. Increasingly, people were building and settling away from the downtown commercial areas along a corridor toward Alice Location. The Zoreteks were among the evacuees.

Mary was putting two and a half year old Angela to bed while Tony bounced Marco, his chubby toddler, playfully in his lap. Early evening was a favorite time for the young couple. When the children were down, the two of them would spend hours together. Talking about their workdays, common friends, local events, and their lives in general. There was never a lack of something to share with each other. Their love grew daily.

After feeding Marco and putting him in his crib, Mary joined her husband on the living room sofa. "They grow so fast. I can't believe our son is already sixteen months. How time has flown."

Angela, named after Mary's father, Angelo, was born on March 12, 1911. Having come from a family of three boys himself, Tony was delighted to have a daughter. "I'll give you a son next time, Mary," he winked, and promised, when he first held Angela. "And I've already picked a name for him." The name he had chosen, Marco, was bestowed on the boy born June 6, 1912.

In addition to their two children, Tony's fifteen year old brother, Rudolph, was a member of the Zoretek household. Rudy had arrived in Hibbing the past August and was attending the impressive new Lincoln High School. A freshman, Rudy loved the school routine and was doing well with his new language. Excelling in all his classes, his favorite was American history. The teenager was in his bedroom studying his English lessons as Tony and Mary visited downstairs. When away from his school activities, however, Rudy spent most of his time with his beloved Uncle Steven. Steven took him on long walks in the forest and helped him with his English as they combined nature walks with education. There was a lake to the east of town which Steven called 'Timo's Lake' where the two of them would fish for northern pike by the hour.

It was hoped that Mary's younger sister, Theresa, might be able to make the passage to Minnesota early next year. Theresa would be eighteen. Mary wrote to her sister often and encouraged her to "Work extra hard on your

English so that you will be able to find a good job here." Theresa, Mary knew, enjoyed boys more than her studies at school.

Busy with the children and their large house, Mary was finding less time to devote to her dress shop just down the street from where they lived. Mary's skills as a seamstress had gained her a wide reputation and her dresses were the most stylish fashions in town. She had trained three young women in her craft and was becoming more confident in their ability to run the business in her frequent absences. Mary would usually spend two or three hours in the afternoon with her employees while Sadie Baratto watched the children.

Tony's carpentry business thrived. He had a crew of twenty-four carpenters and masons working jobs throughout the central Mesabi district. Lud Jaksa was his right arm in keeping atop the many projects. Tony spent most of his time preparing bids, ordering materials, and going to meetings. Real estate was becoming a major preoccupation. He was the vice president of the Hibbing Commercial Club, parish council treasurer at the Immaculate Conception Church, and active in the Fraternal Brotherhood of Elks.

In the summer, Tony played baseball for the Honorable Judge Tom Brady's baseball team, the Colts. Tony had learned the game shortly after his arrival in Hibbing from his friends at the Moran Lumberyards where he had worked. It did not take him long to perfect the art of pitching and, once given an opportunity to show his talents, became almost legendary in the highly competitive Northern League. A natural athlete, 'Zee' as he was nicknamed, mastered a variety of pitches and the skill of placing each of them exactly where he wanted. In a 1910 shutout against the visiting Duluth White Sox, Tony struck out twenty-one batters over nine innings without giving up a hit. That season Tony won twelve games without a loss. He was equally dominating through the next two seasons. But his interest in the game was waning with his growing family responsibilities. Mary was a great baseball fan but also tiring of the time demands of the popular sport.

This past season, Tony only pitched every other home game. When he did pitch, however, it was a community event with the grandstands filled to capacity.

"I talked with Mayor Power today at the Club meeting," Tony mentioned to Mary as she sat beside him crocheting a pink blanket for Angela's bed. "What a fireball that man is! Mary, I think one day he will want to run for governor of Minnesota."

"I think he will serve us well, honey. I got goose-bumps listening to his speech the other night at the victory party. Everybody was so excited!" Mary would use Tony's observations about the new mayor as a springboard for one of her favorite issues. "It won't be long before we women will have the vote. Our local suffrage group has been getting more vocal on the matter." Mary pouted, put down her needles, and tugged at Tony's sleeve. "It's just not fair that we can't vote! Do you want to argue that with me, Mr. Zoretek?" Her tone was provocative. "What do you think about the matter?"

Tony only smiled at her questions. They had argued before and Mary always won. How could he disagree with her logic? "I've told you a thousand times that I agree. I just don't want to go around town shouting 'women's rights' at the top of my lungs. Vic thinks an amendment to the federal Constitution will be coming in the next couple of years."

"That won't be soon enough." Her tone of voice was playful. "I'm going to start marching down the street one of these days, waving an American flag. Senia will be at my side. We'll make enough noise to be heard as far away as Washington."

"I'm sure the two of you would love to do just that, my dear." Tony would steer their conversation in another direction, away from the politics that so inspired his wife. "I talked to Tommy Pell this afternoon. You won't believe what he's gone and done, Mary."

Tommy Pell and Tony had been close friends for years. Pell was his catcher on the Colts' team, a former roommate when he lived with the guys in his bachelor days, and always someone Tony enjoyed being around. Tony had offered Tommy a job with his company many times but Pell was happy with his employment at Khort's Grocery.

At a party several years ago, Tommy had met Molly Trembart, the daughter of a prominent Hibbing attorney and city council member. Molly had returned from college at Saint Scholastica in Duluth and was teaching English at the Lincoln High School. Molly's father did not approve of his only child seeing the uneducated, seemingly unmotivated, and carefree ballplayer. "That kid's no good for you, Molly. He's going to be a grocery boy all his life. When I forbid you to see him I'm only looking out for your best interest. Believe me about that." Elwood Trembart was a sour man. He cultivated friendships among those whom he perceived to be the elite within the community he despised. To him, Hibbing had a contemptible lack of culture, too many filthy immigrants, and the unsavory reputation of having more bars and brothels than the rest of the Mesabi Range combined.

But Molly would disregard her father's advice. Handsome, good-natured, Tommy Pell would be her man, despite her parents' objections. Her friend, Albert Bennett, would come to the door to take her on a date whenever she was home from college. Albert was a young man her father approved of. Albert was studying law and came from a prominent family. But after leaving the Trembart home, Albert would take Molly to her secret meetings with Tommy Pell and spend a few hours at a local brothel while they spent their time together. On one occasion, Albert saw Mr. Trembart leave a prostitute's room and sneak out the back door of the Northern Hotel. He never told a soul about it.

"What's new with Tommy?" Mary returned to her knitting, leaning her head on Tony's chest as she made herself comfortable on the sofa. "I'll bet it has something to do with Molly and their secret affairs."

Many times Tom and Molly stopped by to spend an evening with the Zoreteks. It was always a fun time for the four of them. Molly was bright and always brought along a popular novel for Mary to read. Tom and Tony had a thousand things to talk about. Often they would have wine and cheese snacks until nearly midnight when Albert came to the door to take Molly home.

"They got married," Tony said softly and without emotion, seeking a reaction from his wife.

"They what?" Mary dropped her needles, punching Tony lightly in the ribs. "And you've been talking about politics all this while. How can you do this to me? What did he tell you?" She pulled at his shirt, forcing his face to hers. "Tell me everything, or I'll pull your hair!"

Tony could not conceal a laugh. "That's all. They got hitched."

"Don't you dare make fun of me, Tony Zoretek."

Tony gave her a light kiss on her full lips. "Every detail?" Then he told her everything he'd learned. Tommy and Molly were married the previous weekend in Duluth. Molly lied to her parents about a reunion with college classmates. Tommy's friend, Walt Spragg, was living in the port city and arranged for the local judge to do the small ceremony at the county courthouse. The two of them planned to live apart for a while. How long they didn't know. Molly would tell her parents at Christmastime. She feared they might disown her. "Tommy wanted to talk to me about building a house in this neighborhood. I've built a little two bedroom place over on Sixteenth and told him I'd hold it."

"I've got to call Molly." Mary brimmed with her excitement, then wrinkled her nose as was a habit of hers when she teased with Tony. "You men just don't get the details. Didn't Tom tell you about when he proposed? What she said? Any of his feelings? Why do guys always give only a brief report of things that are . . . so essential? I'll find out from Molly what really happened. I'm so happy for them."

Tony pulled her close, shifted on the sofa so he could hold her in his arms. The happy news brought his affections to the surface. "And I'm so happy for you . . . having you, I mean. I don't tell you how much I love you often enough." He met her wide oval eyes. "You are more beautiful at this moment than when I first laid eyes on you. I really mean that, Mary." He paused and cupped her face in his strong hands. "And, there's something else that's even more important—you're the best friend I've ever had. What would I ever do without you?" The thought was profoundly scary to him.

Mary smiled, knowing that his words were from the heart. She was so happy with their life together and their consuming love. Sometimes her deepest emotions got all caught up inside. She couldn't express feelings the way she would like to. When this happened, Mary would revert to her good humor to relax herself and release the knot of sentiments. She couldn't find the right words to respond to Tony's emotion of the moment. She chose to tease, "I'm your pal, huh. That's great. And, what would you do without your pal? I'm not going anywhere. I don't dare to, you handsome bloke. Don't think I'm blind at other women looking at you, lust in their secret glances." She was amusing herself at Tony's expense. "Even Molly. She thinks I've got the best looking man in Hibbing in my bed every night. She's told me that. Girl talk can be so . . . so obscene." She wriggled her nose again, wondering at the word obscene. "I'm ashamed to admit it, but it's the truth. Anyhow, our vow said 'for better or worse' and sometimes I'm ashamed of how I talk. Like now . . . '

Tony looked confused. "What do you mean . . . like now?"

"I mean—I've been teasing you again. What you told me was so beautiful I couldn't respond to it."

Tony shook his head, chose not to reply.

"I mean . . . what I really mean, and can say now . . . is . . . I love you. More than life itself, I love you. Remember once I called you my prince—you are that, Tony. I love you . . ." she breathed into his face, kissed him deeply. "Let's go up to our bed, my handsome man."

A New Doctor in Town

May 1916

Rebecca Kaner said goodbye to her mother on the porch of their Highland Park home in St. Paul. The two women stood awkwardly, mother wiping away her tears, holding her daughter at arm's length for a final appraising moment. Becca reflected her mother's dark-complected features: deep brown eyes, straight nose, and full mouth. The widow cleared her throat, "Father would be proud of what you are doing, sweetheart. It's something he often talked about doing himself. But I guess I was always less than enthusiastic about relocating. Your mom has never been the adventuresome sort. Anyhow, he'll be watching you from his place up there. You know that. But I'll worry about my little girl."

"Mom, as I've told you, I'm not doing this for Dad or Doctor Hane or anyone but myself. I need to leave St. Paul. The Cities just aren't the same for me anymore. You know that. And, please don't worry. I'll be just fine. The Hanes will meet my train tomorrow, and I'll be going to work next Monday. It's really quite exciting, don't you agree?"

Becca, as her father had always called her, was twenty-eight and finished with her medical internship at the Ramsey County Medical Center in St. Paul. Ramsey made her a lucrative offer to stay, but she had declined. She also declined a similar offer from St. Mary's Hospital in Duluth. Young physicians were in great demand everywhere.

Paul Kaner, Becca's father, had passed away in February. Before he died the two of them had talked at length about her future. Paul had studied medicine at the University of Minnesota and while there had been a roommate of Ambrose Hane. The two of them forged a lifelong friendship. While Paul chose to practice in familiar St. Paul, Ambrose went to Duluth. Hane's fiancé, Ethel, was a Morgan Park girl. Ambrose wanted to be nearby while the two of them planned their wedding. Ten years ago, Ambrose and his wife left Duluth for an opportunity in Hibbing's new Rood Hospital. Ambrose would be the assistant chief of staff there, while Ethel worked at the bank of their old friend, Harvey Goldberg.

Paul told his daughter to talk to Ambrose before making a decision on where to practice. He knew his daughter was still hurting from her broken relationship of five years and wanted to get away from St. Paul. "There's no place on earth quite like the Iron Range," Paul had said. "Ambrose loves it there," speaking of the mining hub of Hibbing. "You would be breaking new ground, Becca. No women doctors are up there. And, being Jewish . . ." He let the thought drop. "It's still like a frontier in many respects. Mostly men, immigrants from all over the world. If you want a challenge . . . there's no better place to hang your sign."

Rebecca Kaner had visited Hibbing eight years before with her boyfriend, Mel Hartman, a reporter for the *St. Paul Dispatch,* who had been assigned to cover the grand opening of the new Hotel Moran. The hotel was magnificent. The two of them spent the weekend there along with a few of her friends from college. It was the first time Mel had kissed her. Becca's memory of Hibbing was deeply etched in her memory. She was fascinated by the vitality of the mining city. It was like no place she had ever been before. While there, she and Mel saw a wonderful vaudeville show from Chicago at the Power Theater. She also bought a new yellow dress at a small tailor shop and wore it for the hotel reception. The dress was timelessly fashionable and still a favorite in her wardrobe. The lovely seamstress at the shop explained how she had made the dress, a Paris pattern with no others like it anywhere to be found.

After her father's funeral, Becca called Doctor Ambrose. From that conversation her mind was made up. She was going to Hibbing. She had talked with 'Amby,' as he preferred to be called, only two nights ago. The doctor and his wife would meet her arriving train from Duluth. "I've found you a nice little two bedroom house and offered the contractor a down payment. We'll look at it after you're settled in. Ethel thinks it's just perfect."

Following her father's unexpected heart attack came another terrible blow. Melvin wanted some space from their relationship. He had interviewed for a sportswriter position with a Chicago newspaper. "It's something I need to do for myself," he told her. Mel's brother, however, told her the truth. Her fiancé had another woman. She was already living in Chicago.

The May Thursday afternoon was drizzly and cool. From the window of the train car, Becca watched Hibbing come into view. The gray shroud seemed to steal any early summer color. The trees and buildings and landscape presented a discouraging bleakness. On her trip, she had wondered about her decision to practice medicine in such a remote location. But, Becca was an optimist at heart. She thought of her father and how supportive he was about her determination to always challenge herself. This was what she had to do and where she had to be. And, she thought of Melvin, too. His deceit still pained her deeply. Maybe there would be someone else, maybe even in this unlikely place.

She laughed to herself as she rose from the upholstered seat to make her way down the congested aisle toward the doorway. "What kind of people live in this place? Are they all miners?" Then she remembered that visit years before. How impressed she had been with the dashing and confident owner of the new hotel!

Ambrose Hane spotted the tall brunette who possessed her mother's striking features. Rebecca had long hair, parted and combed straight over her delicate shoulders. Her dress was a finely tailored black a-line style that accentuated her slender figure. Although he'd seen the lovely girl only months before at her father's funeral, Ambrose thought Becca looked older than he had remembered. She moved with the bearing of a confident woman.

"Over here, my dear!" Ethel Hane called, waving her hand and taking a few steps toward Becca who was retrieving her satchel from the porter. "How was the trip?" Ethel embraced the taller woman affectionately. "We're so delighted to have you here, my dear," she added before Becca could breathe a word.

Ambrose stepped forward, offered his hand and a wide smile. "You look more beautiful than ever, Becca. The picture of your mother I must say. Welcome to Hibbing."

"I'm delighted to be here. Thank you both for coming out to meet me." She bent over and gave Ambrose a light kiss on the cheek. "I'm exhausted as you might imagine. I thought the ride would never end."

"And you must be famished as well. We've got a wonderful supper waiting for you back at the house," said Ethel. "Some wonderful Northern Minnesota walleye and wild rice."

Off to the side, a few feet behind Ethel, stood another woman. She was tall, blonde and had striking blue eyes. It seemed apparent that the woman was with the Hanes. "Oh, let me introduce Senia. Senia Arola." Ethel exclaimed. "She is a dear friend of ours and a fellow employee of mine at the bank."

Senia stepped forward, smiled, "I've heard so much about you, Doctor Kaner. I'm delighted to finally meet you."

"It's my pleasure. Becca, please." She regarded the other woman, smiling warmly and extending her hand. "And, Senia . . . what a lovely name. I don't think I've heard it before."

"It's Finnish, Becca. My grandmother was Senia."

"Will you be joining us at the Hanes? I'd love to make a new friend on my first day in Hibbing."

"I've been invited and wouldn't miss the opportunity." Senia offered her arm to Becca and the two of them began walking down the platform together while Ambrose looked after the luggage being unloaded.

While loading the baggage into the back of the small truck he'd borrowed from the hospital, Ambrose sidled up to the three women. "I think we've got everything packed in. I'm starved. We'll have lots to catch up on back at the house. And, Becca, I think your next few days are going to be busier than you might imagine."

"Tomorrow morning you'll meet our friend, Tony, about the house I told you about. Then Ambrose wants to give you a hospital tour in the afternoon," Ethel added to her husband's comment.

"And, we're planning to see a musical at the Power Theater on Saturday," Senia said. "Becca, I think you'll find our town has more to offer than meets the eye. I so wish we had better weather for your arrival. The place does look kind of gloomy at the moment."

"I'm so excited. I can't wait to get involved in everything. My dad is surely smiling in heaven." Becca sighed at the thought. "And, Amby . . . I'm starved too."

~

Tony looked up from the desk in the far corner of his new real estate office on the corner of Pine Street and Second Avenue. Mary had done the decorating and given the room a masculine but comfortable appearance. His secretary occupied a desk near the entry door in front of an oak railing that separated her space from the oak furniture in Tony's section of the spacious room. Three comfortable leather-backed captain's chairs were arranged in a half circle in front of his desk and a rich Persian rug covered the floor space. Leafy rhododendrons were placed in corners throughout the room. On his wall hung a large van Gogh print of sunflowers in a vase.

Ambrose Hane and the attractive new physician had just come in from the sun splashed street. A shaft of light spread across the floor. Doctor Kaner was, as Ambrose had told him earlier, a strikingly lovely woman. Tony was on his feet, opening the gate of the railing. "Come in please, I've been expecting you." His smile was natural, showing fine straight teeth, and a dimple on the cheek of his smoothly-shaven face.

Becca was struck by his handsome features, tall and trim frame, and a firm but comfortable handshake. His suit was finely tailored she could tell.

Ambrose made the introductions and complimented the lovely morning. "Becca would like to see the house we've talked about, Tony. I've told her something about it, but I'm at a loss for the kind of details that a woman would want to know."

"I can appreciate that. I'm not much good at that myself. Most men want to know about the construction specifications and per square foot costs, I'm afraid. Women take what we build and make a home out of it. I guess that's as it should be. I've often wished that I were more creative. Fortunately for me, Mary has an eye for the feeling a room should have."

Becca smiled inwardly. "He's obviously married," she thought, noticing the gold ring. "Some lucky woman."

"I was telling Ambrose earlier that I'd like to find a place away from the city's downtown area. Senia's told me that she lives in Brooklyn and loves the location." Becca could not help fixing on Tony's deep-set blue eyes.

"Well, so does Tony. I must not have mentioned that," Ambrose said. "He's been building most of the new houses down there."

The three of them talked for several minutes. "I'll bet that Mary will be one of your first new patients, Doctor Kaner. She's really excited about having a woman doctor in Hibbing. Before too long you're going to be swamped, I can assure you."

Becca's thoughts wandered. Would all her patients be women? She felt a pang of guilt about wondering if a man like Tony might one day be a patient of hers. "I'll look forward to meeting your wife, Mr. Zoretek," was all she could say.

Becca loved the little two-bedroom stucco and brick house. Explaining the construction, Tony walked them through the rooms. The shiny linoleum-floored kitchen was spacious. A new Monarch stove was set near the north wall. Finely crafted cabinets lined the wall. The sink was porcelain with an eight gallon tank for used soap water. A sizable ice box occupied another corner of the room. A mirror was built into the woodwork near the sink countertop. The ample dining room was connected to the kitchen through a wide plastered archway. The living room looked out over a small front yard to the newly paved street. She could imagine the furnishings, accessories, and color schemes. Most importantly, she could afford the house. Her father's estate had provided her with a sizable inheritance. Enough to purchase her own medical equipment as well as the furniture she was imagining at the moment.

"That's Senia's house over there." Tony pointed at a similar house across the street and down near the corner. "She's been there for nearly three years. The bus from Alice Location swings by here so getting to the hospital in the morning will be quite convenient."

"I'm sold, Mr. Zoretek. If we can get back to your office I'll sign the papers and take them to Mr. Goldberg at the bank. I've got to set up an account there later this afternoon anyhow."

Tony met her eyes. "May I ask a favor of you, Doctor Kaner?"

Becca felt a flutter, "Why, most certainly."

"If you please, I'm Tony. And I've heard Ambrose call you Becca. May I use your first name as well? I'd be much more comfortable . . ."

"As would I . . . Tony." Becca smiled.

"Once you've settled in a bit, I'll want to bring my wife over to meet you, Becca. Mary's a wonderful seamstress and might be helpful in making some custom curtains or drapes for the windows. I'll leave that to the two of you." Tony returned her smile and escorted his two guests out the door and across the green front lawn.

Becca Kaner's first week at the Rood Hospital was mostly an orientation period. Word of her practice was becoming widely known in Hibbing. The *Mesaba Ore* editor, Mr. Atkinson, had written a fine article about her in his popular local newspaper. She found the reporter to be highly intelligent and insightful. He also had the warm typically small-town, congeniality. She was amused by a humorous observation in the story Claude wrote. *"Having met Doctor Kaner and having learned of her excellent credentials, I have a feeling that I will be going to the hospital more frequently with my minor aches and pains. I've long believed that whenever a man ails, it's a woman who can make him feel better . . . and sooner."*

But in her first week, Doctor Kaner did not have any male patients. She saw several women about female issues, had a dozen children's colds, a few cases of measles and mumps. Becca made three house calls—a boy with a severe case of tonsillitis, a girl with a mastoid ear infection, and a toddler with a serious poison oak infection. She also delivered two new babies at the Rood Hospital. "It'll take some time, Becca," Doctor Hane consoled. "And I for one don't care if you see a single man. At the same time, I think every man in town is delighted that their wives are able to have a woman doctor."

"If that's the way it's going to be, so be it. I'll take whoever comes my way." She embraced the small doctor. And, let me assure you, I am truly delighted to be of help in any way I can, Amby."

In her second week, a miner named Ollie Kochevar had been rushed to the hospital with a badly broken leg. The sturdy man suffered his injury when some railroad ties had slipped from a flatbed car, pinning him to the ground. Becca was working by herself on the floor at the time as the other doctors were in a meeting.

"You'll have to wait while I get one of the doctors from the meeting, Mr. Kochevar," the nurse said.

"Ain't no doctors here right now?" Ollie was in pain. "All yer docs havin a meetin?"

"Well, Doctor Kaner's on duty," the nurse paused, "but she's a woman doctor, you know."

Becca overheard the comment and swallowed her anger. She rushed into the room where the miner lay on a stretcher, while two tall men stood over him wondering what to do. Seeing the doctor, the men quickly removed their hats in respect. "I'm Doctor Kaner. I fix broken legs and broken arms and everything else that's broken. Do you want me to take care of you, or do you want to wait a few minutes?"

Ollie smiled. "You're my doc, ma'am. Let's get me offa this stretcher." He pushed himself up on his elbows, anxious to get himself off the floor. His pain was excruciating. "You otta be able to fix me up as well as anyone else in this place."

Becca laughed. "I'll guarantee it, Mister . . . ."

"Just call me Ollie."

As Becca set the break with splints and heavy gauze tape, she asked the miner what had happened. Ollie Kochevar explained what the track gang had been doing that morning. "When da shovel moves to new ore diggins, we gotta get the tracks changed fer da ore cars. Gotta get'em laid fast cuz time's money ta da company."

Becca had a thousand questions about open pit mining, and Ollie enjoyed talking about the work. The two of them, along with the men who had brought Ollie to the hospital, talked for nearly an hour. She learned how dangerous the jobs were and developed a deep respect for the men who worked in the mines.

"You wanna be my reguler doc, Miss Kaner? I'd like for ya ta be. If ya can do it, I mean. Can a woman . . . ?"

"Yes, a woman can, Mr. Kochevar. And, I'd be delighted."

∼

Steven Skorich was troubled. His small investment business was struggling in the sluggish economy, his relationship with Senia seemed unusually strained, and the Iron Range seemed like a powder keg waiting for a spark. It was the latter concern, however, that caused the inner knot in his stomach.

As he waited for his old friend, Martin Alto, to join him at Conley's Cafe, a favorite early morning coffee stop on Chisholm's Lake Street, he stewed over news of another accident in the mines. One of his few clients, Joe Phillipich, had been killed by a blasting misfire at the Agnew Mine. It was the seventh mine fatality in the Hibbing district this year. He would visit the widow that afternoon.

Steven had been an activist in the unsuccessful 1907 miners' strike. The memory of that failure still left a bitter taste in his mouth. The Western Mine Federation organizers had fled—some of the leaders with strike funds—and left a leadership void that troubled him. Grievances regarding unresolved issues aggravated his ulcers. Not only did his stomach ache, but tension and stress seemed to heighten the pain from his burns of years before. Yet, it seemed to Steven, his miner friends chose to suffer their continued exploitation in silence.

"Korenjack, my dear friend, I can read your face like a book. What's the matter?" Martin Alto said cheerily, as he took a chair opposite the tall Slovenian. Martin offered his hand in greeting. "Too bad about Joe."

Steven gave a wan smile, running his long fingers down the stubble on his unshaven face. "We've got to talk, Martin. I guess I'm not good at concealing my emotions, am I? Yes, Joe's accident bothers me greatly but there is so much more on my mind this morning. It's like I'm carrying a bag of ore on my shoulders, and it's wearing me down, my friend."

Martin met his eyes and sipped his hot coffee. "Unload some of that bag, Korenjack. What can I do to help you?" Alto used Steven's nickname, 'Korenjack,' affectionately. The two men had been through many difficult times together and knew each other well.

"You're someone I can be perfectly honest with, Martin," Steven said. "Since the eight hour day came along a few years ago, things have gotten worse for the miners, not better as we imagined it might. You know that. The bosses are pushing harder for production, and the men are taking it all with hardly any protest. Joe was killed by that very push to blast more ore. I said *killed,* Martin! Work conditions are getting more dangerous by the day."

"We don't have any leadership, Steven. There's no organization any more. It's like we've been abandoned. Nobody seems to care about us or what the companies are doing."

"There is some organizing going on." Steven frowned. "And that really scares me. Over on the East Range. The Wobblies are mustering up a following. They're mixing their socialism with mine grievances. And people are listening, too. I'm concerned about what's happening in Aurora and Biwabik." Steven leaned forward over the table. "Your folks are getting into that bullshit, Martin. Pardon my choice of words, but it won't work. We both have been through it before." Steven rarely used profanities, but he was agitated.

Martin agreed with Steven. The Industrial Workers of the World—the 'Wobblies' as they were known—did have some solid roots in the Finnish community. The Finns were *his folks,* as Steven had intimated.

"I've tried to discourage my friends," Martin said defensively. "I've been to the Finn halls over there a number of times. But with things so darned bad . . . nobody's listening to my arguments."

Many of the blacklisted Finns who were trying to survive by farming on marginal cutover lands were still very active in the miners' affairs. After the '07 strike, those of Finnish ancestry experienced the greatest discrimination. A few of them were ardent advocates of socialism—all of them paid the consequences. Few Finns were reemployed after that strike. "I'll keep preaching, of course, but I'm not very optimistic. Something's going to happen one of these days; I can feel it in my bones." Martin's face expressed his feelings more convincingly than his words.

"That's what concerns me, Martin. When it does, that something you feel is going to be worse than back in '07. There's a world war going on now and . . . how can miners expect to get much public support? It would be almost unpatriotic to walk off the job when the whole free world needs American steel." That reality was troublesome to the large Slovenian.

"And, there's something else, Martin. There's so much dissension among our people out there." Steven's eyes narrowed. "It breaks my heart that miners are becoming fragmented along ethnic lines. Finns don't trust the

Slovenes and vice versa," he sighed. "Everybody hates the Montenegrins. The Italians keep to themselves and so do the Swedes. We are not at all unified. Nothing like it was in the past. How can we hope to resolve that?"

The spark that would ignite the powder keg happened at a mine site near Aurora in early June. A distraught Italian miner had been cheated by the company on his monthly pay check. The miner threw his pick in the air and shouted, "I quit! I'd rather burn in hell than take this crap any more." With that he walked off the job. Everybody on his shift followed, and the mine was paralyzed. Almost overnight there was marching in the streets of East Mesabi Range towns. In Biwabik, McKinley, Gilbert, Sparta and Eveleth. Parades of protesters. As word spread, the numbers of miners supporting the walkout mushroomed. The echo of 'strike' reverberated throughout the canyon-like open pits and deep into the recesses of the underground tunnels. Soon mines were closing everywhere.

Virginia's mining district shut down as the wave of discontent spread west to Mt. Iron, Buhl, and Chisholm. In one week Hibbing's vast operations were at a standstill. Across the Mesabi nearly twenty thousand miners had joined in the anti-company strike effort. The line between factions was clearly drawn and tensions frightfully escalating.

Steven was on the phone with Vic Power this Thursday morning. The Hibbing mayor was not surprised about how rapidly the strike had swept the Mesabi. "We've talked about this on many occasions, Steven. It had to happen. My sympathies are with the miners more than ever before. It's going to get very ugly. The Oliver won't take this lying down. I've learned that they've already had a thousand goons deputized in Duluth." When Vic Power talked, he hardly took a breath. Words rolled off his tongue like rain off a rooftop. "With that damnable contract system of paying underground miners . . . I can't believe that the business community will side with the companies this time. And the wages. Good God! How can the Oliver justify what they are paying workers in light of the profits they're making on every ton of iron ore?"

Steven sensed that the mayor had more on his mind and did not comment. In his heart he knew Power to be a noble advocate.

"I've talked with Claude Atkinson about all this several times this week. He's been running articles in his paper raising serious concerns about working conditions. He's even been to some of the mines and talked with the workers. Claude's not going to roll over and be a mouthpiece for the Oliver." Vic Power's voice was as high pitched as his emotions of the moment.

"It will get ugly!" Steven agreed. "The Wobblies are sending in some big guns as we sit here talking. They see this as an opportunity for some national attention. And the Wobblie folks are great organizers. Believe me about that. I've heard Carlo Treska and Sam Scarlett are already in Virginia. Liz Gurley Flynn gave a rousing speech in Eveleth yesterday. Big Bill Haywood is supposed to be in Hibbing next week."

"What are they saying—the Wobblies? Are they sticking with the miners' issues or preaching their socialist crap? I won't tolerate any red flags and socialism rhetoric, Steven. I'll chase them up and down the streets of Hibbing if they try to undermine our American values. Gonna fight them tooth and nail if they try that!"

Steven met his eyes. "They are promoting their socialist ideas. What's worse, though, is the violence they're talking about. Flynn told the Eveleth rally to arm and defend themselves and their jobs. She got a huge ovation for that."

"I hadn't heard about her speech. Bad news for everybody." Power looked from Steven to the window. "She ought to have been arrested. That woman would be in the Hibbing jail right now if she'd encouraged violence in this town."

Victor pushed away from his desk as if ready to get busy with something. "I'm going to get the village council together this afternoon. We can't sit back and watch things happen. We'll need some kind of plan. All of us will. I mean mayors and elected officials across the Range. That will take some organizing for sure."

"That's what you're best at doing, Vic. Getting people together to make something happen," Steven complimented.

"Steven, can you help me with that? You're pretty well known, and let me say respected as well, across the Range. People remember you from the last strike. They'll listen to you as a private citizen and humanitarian more than me as an elected politician."

Vic Power leaned back in his chair, chewed on an unlit cigar, and ran his thick fingers through his combed-back hair. A grand council of all the Range mayors would have some leverage in mediating between the miners and companies. He would push this idea through his own aldermen today.

"I'll make some appointments right away!" Steven said with enthusiasm. "I know some people on the East Range but not so many west of Hibbing. Norm Dinter at Moran's liquor warehouse was born in Grand Rapids and grew up in Nashwauk. I'll see if he can get the word out over there. He's a good speaker and one of your biggest supporters, Mayor. Let's keep in touch on this."

Violence was inevitable. Deputized company thugs, many of whom came from Duluth or the Twin Cities, were ruthless in their zeal to wreak havoc across the Range. Breaking into houses without warrants, disrupting meetings, and instigating fights in the streets—the goons and their guns were setting an ugly tone. A Slovenian miner was killed while defending himself against an intrusion in his home. Later a gun battle erupted in which a deputy was slain along with two innocent bystanders. Within a month the Mesabi was paralyzed. Union organizers Treska and Scarlett had been arrested and shipped to the county jail house in Duluth. Holding them on the Range would be too dangerous.

Claude Atkinson could not be impartial. His Mesaba Ore ran an article in July condemning those in the business community.

> *The business people in the affected towns have called mass meetings and have damned the strike leaders up one side and down the other, just as the mining companies wanted them to do, but no attempt has been made to save anything out of the wreck for the laboring man.*

In Hibbing, however, mineworkers found a groundswell of support from the merchant community. This had not been the case in the 1907 strike when workers were denied any credit and their homes were foreclosed. Too many had suffered unfairly under the tight fisted control of the 'Steel Trust' who pulled the strings of local company officials. Atkinson and Power were tireless in their efforts at getting the two sides to communicate. State officials, led by Governor Burnquist, were in opposition to the strikers' position. Burnquist regarded the popular Hibbing mayor as a potential political threat if the workers prevailed. Already Power had achieved a statewide reputation as a fighter for the working man. With the help of Steven Skorich and Norm Dinter, Power developed a Range Council of mayors to pressure the companies and send their support of miners' demands to the media in Minneapolis and St. Paul. As the governor received heated criticism from the big city press, he became even more enraged and threatened.

The miners fought a spirited fight, but a hopeless one as well. The everyday needs of the miners and their families became more acute as the strike dragged throughout the summer. Slowly they began to return to work, and by September more than half of the mines were operating at normal production levels. Quietly the strike was called off and the leadership dispersed. Some talked openly about rekindling the issues the following spring. The promise of more violence hung in the air as the mines began preparations for the winter's seasonal shutdown. The companies made it clear that any resumption of labor hostilities would cost jobs for good. And, the sentiment of patriotism was growing rapidly as the United States moved closer to involvement in the World War. Labor agitation would be considered treasonous in the eyes of public opinion.

Throughout the strike, Steven Skorich maintained a middle ground between the miners and the companies. His allegiance to the workers was well established, his disputes with the Wobblie leadership equally well known. Tirelessly he met with both sides, discussing grievances in rational tones, offering compromises whenever appropriate.

In November, the Oliver Mining Company issued a ten percent raise in pay for all mineworkers, a seemingly unsolicited gesture that helped mightily in diminishing the hangover tensions from the strike. Those closest to the Oliver decision, however, knew that Steven Skorich had been the catalyst for the company's unlikely concession.

Meanwhile, Vic Power pushed his Hibbing agenda with vigor. His campaign promises were realized at considerable expense. His street-paving program was initiated and municipal services expanded. The increasing public payroll had become an important factor in the town's economic life. Nothing Power accomplished, however, came without controversy. Yet, his bid for a second term went without opposition. The reelection theme, *Victory and Power,* spread the mayor's reputation beyond the boundaries of Hibbing.

~

The previous year, in 1915, the local levy was pushed beyond a million dollars. In protest, the mining companies who were assessed for most of the taxes refused to pay. They took the city to court for overspending Minnesota's per capita tax limits. Irate, Power took his arguments to the state capitol in St. Paul. While there ostensibly to meet with state legislators, Power sought out the state auditor. He convinced the official to deny the issuance of any additional leases on state lands. His rhetoric and tactics gave him the leverage he needed. A mining official was believed to have told the national media, "Grass will grow on the streets of Hibbing before we pay those taxes!"

In an interview the following day, Power retorted. "Then we'll put our men to work cutting the grass!" The exchange was reported across the country. Power and Hibbing made national news for a brief time. Becoming widely hailed as the 'Fighting Mayor', Power was able to reach a compromise with the companies late in 1915. Hibbing would place some limits on its spending and the companies would pay their back taxes of nearly a million dollars.

Demonstrating an unflagging energy to every battle, the political future of Hibbing's colorful mayor was guaranteed for years to come. But the strike had drained the seemingly tireless thirty-five year old. In the fall of 1916, he and Percy purchased a small home on Swan Lake a few miles west of Hibbing. The pristine setting became a favorite retreat. When there on weekends, his love of hunting and fishing were satisfied, enabling him to enjoy a needed relaxation away from the bustling life in his city.

BOOK TWO

'Don't Push the River'

Portents in Dreams

March 1918

Marc Atkinson had his father's blood. Working daily with his father at the *Mesaba Ore,* the young journalist learned the news business from a true professional. Hibbing had two newspapers. The *News Tribune* was cutting into Claude's circulation. Marc had the numbers in front of him.

"Dad, we're down twenty from last week and nearly a hundred since the first of the year. Advertisers are using Hitchcock's paper more than ours these days. He just got a huge contract from the Oliver to do their Liberty Bond promotions. They're running a full front page spread."

Claude smiled as he usually did when Marc was frustrated. "You read their rag every day, son. What are they running?"

"All the war releases. They must have fifteen stories in yesterday's paper. We had two. Our front page had a story about the Range Building Contractors Association and coal shortages. Even a story about the high school declamation contest. People want the war front news." Marc gave his father a wry smile, a smile much like his father's. He was taller than his dad, combed his blond hair back from his forehead, and wore smartly tailored suits. His narrow frame, long legs, and shuffling stride clearly marked him as an Atkinson.

Since the strike nearly five years ago, the *Ore* had suffered advertising losses. Claude alienated some businessmen by supporting the mine workers. He had also been a Vic Power supporter during the so-called 'Tax War' with the Oliver Mining Company. Although Power was widely popular in the community, many of the merchants opposed his policies.

"I headlined a story about the Dutch government accepting the Allies' demands. That's a positive step toward peace over there. And, I used the story about the German defensive strategy in France. Both were newsworthy. The *Trib,* on the other hand, ran something like, 'Huns advance toward Moscow.' They used that story about the use of those terrible gas shells. If what they're doing works, let them beat me up. I have no tolerance for calling the Germans 'Huns' even if they are the enemy. We've got lots of solid German families living in our town. How do you think they feel about being called 'Huns'? They get enough discrimination as it is from small-minded people. I've heard enough ethnic labels in my day, son. I'll never promote stereotypes in my newspaper."

Claude was not a pacifist. Patriotism ran deep in his marrow. His paper promoted the 'Thrift Stamp' program in every issue. Claude's editorial comments encouraged everyone to do their fair share in the war effort. "We're not on the front line," he once wrote. "We're the 'linebackers.' Winning teams have great linebackers."

Claude's values, however, were not the same as those of his son. Nor were his views of journalism. "God willing, the war's going to be over soon. We'll be living in the same world as the Germans when that happens."

"You might be right about that, dad. But don't you think stories about German atrocities are good for morale at home? Don't you think?" Claude sat back in his chair, regarded Marc. "Atrocities are what war is all about. On both sides. And morale? Well, I guess I don't know much about that. We're out to win this war. Don't need to pump up people's resolve about that fact. People aren't tires."

Marc did not reply. He never won an argument with his father.

As Marc turned toward the door, Claude said. "Our boys will be coming back to Hibbing one of these days soon. I can't be shortsighted, son. This paper will be what they'll read when they're home. They always have."

Marc's discouragement passed with an easy smile. The *Ore* was a community journal. What was happening in Hibbing held priority over national news. It had always been that way. He knew that most of the boys overseas wanted their parents to send them the *Ore*—not the *Trib*. Maybe his father was right. "So, what are we running in today's issue, dad? The Frank Kleffman rink winning the Curling Club trophy in an extra head?" He was trying to be facetious.

"Yes, Marc. I like the curling story. The sport has a big following in town. Going to take it up myself one of these days. When I've got the time that is. Then your mom will divorce me for sure. And find something about the hockey game with Eveleth last weekend. Another thing, Mr. Sheehy at the D. M. & N. depot has a new schedule for trains to Duluth. Three a day—seven, noon, and four. That's great news, don't you think?"

Alone at his desk, Claude pondered what his son had told him. American involvement in the world war was clearly the shaper of history in 1918. Several hundred of Hibbing's boys were already fighting in the trenches of Europe. Hibbing's mines were producing record levels of iron ore to make the steel necessary for the war effort, millions of tons! Life in Hibbing *was* about the war. Claude acknowledged that fact and reported what was happening with clarity and conviction. He included short 'side bars' on local boys serving in the armed forces in every issue. He wrote about Larry Seymore, Sam Hopke and Tommy Pell with the Marine Corps' Third Division near the Marne River in France only three days ago.

But, Claude's news was also about sixteen year old Emily Hardy. The high school speech student had won the declamation tournament against Grand Rapids and would participate in the state meet in Minneapolis. How proud her family must be about her accomplishments. Doctor Kaner delivered a baby in below zero weather last week when the mother had fallen on an icy street on her run toward the hospital. Both mother and baby girl were doing well at the hospital. Countless hundreds of miners were toiling every day through the harsh winter to keep tonnage levels high, even with a shortage of men due to the war effort. Tom Huber was working with a broken arm because, "My crew needs me, or even half of me . . ." Tony Zoretek had been chosen as the new president of the Range Building Contractors. Luigi Anselmo was sending scarves and mittens to the boys overseas.

Claude would chronicle daily life in the mining hub as he had done for nearly twenty years. Hibbing's people would continue to be his stories. The editor smiled to himself. "I'd better write some letters before I forget." He'd congratulate Emily, Rebecca, Tom, Tony, and Luigi. "Keep up the good work," he would tell them. "Hibbing's a better place to live because you're a part of this fine community."

The editor's eyes scanned the cluttered office. His furnishings were inexpensive, his walls needed paint. Above the door hung a framed, handwritten transcription he read every day. The Thomas Carlyle quotation always appealed to his sense of history.

> *Nothing that was worthy in the past departs, no truth or goodness realized by man ever dies or can die; but is all still here, and recognized or not, lives and works through endless changes.*

June 1918

Tommy Pell hunched next to Lester Brooks in the muddy trench south of a wooded area near Chateau-Thierry. For countless hours the two marines had been pinned down without rounds for their trench mortars, not knowing where the front line was, nor where the enemy lurked inside the dark forest. "Cap'n Rask says the Huns are gonna counterattack our position. Thinks it might be tonight. I'm scared, Tommy. Seen too many of the guys blown to bits."

"We've made it this far, Les. Can't see much worse than we seen already. Don't worry about it, buddy. Rask's been wrong most of the time. He gets his info from Bundy and Bundy gets his from the French. Damn Frogs don't have no idea what's goin' on here."

In the quiet hours of the late afternoon, Tommy Pell thought of home. Thought of Molly. The reverie pushed this horrific war out of his mind.

Their marriage had started off on a miserable note. Molly Trembart's parents hated him, were unforgiving of the elopement. At first their love for each other was all that mattered. Love was not enough. In their second year, Molly started encouraging him to find a 'respectable job'—told him he was wasting his potential. "Quit your job as a grocery clerk and start working for Tony. He's doing so well with his construction business. He'd give you a good position, maybe even an office job." One day she said, "You're too lazy." On another, "You're no fun anymore." She began spending more time at the Trembart home, less at their apartment.

Tommy became uncommunicative. Depression consumed him. Even his job at Khort's Grocery suffered from his stress. Some mornings he slept in and missed work. Molly was a school teacher. Tommy a stock boy at the store. Molly enjoyed going out to eat, to dances, the theater. Tommy enjoyed staying home. So Molly dined out and went to the theater with her parents and their friends. Tommy stayed home. When he started drinking, things got much worse. He quit the baseball team, avoided his friends. Everything in his life was going downhill.

It was no surprise when Tommy was among the first Hibbing men to sign up for the draft. Rather than wait, he joined the Marines. When he waited for the train to take him to his basic training, he waited alone. He hadn't told anyone about his decision. One day he was having a beer at the Red Rock Tavern, the next day gone from Hibbing. Tommy had not been back since November of 1916—nearly two years ago.

But he was resolved that afternoon to make amends with Molly. He still loved her. The two letters from her were worn from a hundred readings. He would go back to Hibbing when this was over and take a job with Tony's company, maybe even some college classes to help him learn business. He was smart enough to be anything he wanted. Given time, even the Trembarts might come to respect him. The thought of being with Molly again brought a smile to his parched lips. "Just wait for me, Molly. We're gonna make it next time, sweetheart. I ain't gonna be lazy ever again. You just wait and see."

The German counterattack hit with a thunderous barrage of artillery shelling. Tommy looked for Les who had been beside him only minutes before. Les was gone. Then came the nauseous wave of gas.

"Tommy! Over here! I ain't got no mask with me." Les was huddled near a large stump some fifteen feet from the trench where he had gone to take a crap. When the shelling had started, he'd hit the ground, machine gun fire whistling over his head. "I can't breathe! Throw me my mask! Tommy!"

Tommy could not locate his buddy's mask near his rifle and helmet. There was no time to look. " Where are ya? I'll toss ya mine, Les. Can ya hear me?" The noise was deafening. "Can ya hear?"

"Over here, Tommy," Les was choking.

Tommy Pell stood to hear where the voice was coming from, raised his eyes above the lip of the trench. Spotting his friend to the right he heaved the mask in Lester's direction. Two bullets split his neck as his arm arced and released. He toppled backwards, grasping at his severed wind pipe, gargling blood.

Tommy Pell was one among the 1,811 fatalities in the battle at Chateau-Thierry in June of 1918. Nobody would ever know that he gave his life for a friend and died an heroic death.

Steven remembered Tommy Pell as he read the obituary in the Sunday issue of the *Mesaba Ore*. He was sitting in Senia's living room while she prepared an early afternoon meal in the kitchen. Claude had characterized the young man as an American hero. Surely he was that. There were so many young 'heroes' in the world war. Heroes of every color and nationality and nation. Steven thought of President Wilson's 'Fourteen Points' plan for world peace, remembered a widely quoted comment that this was . . . "A war to end all wars!" His homeland of Slovenia had been ravaged by war for centuries. Such was the human condition he believed. Those who have power use it for their profit. Those that do not, seek it at any cost. The cost was always the loss of human lives and the untold sufferings of the poor and innocent. Steven despised war of any kind in any place.

"Tommy Pell was killed in France, Senia." Steven called the news toward the kitchen in a flat voice. "Chateau-Thierry. Sam Hopke died near there as well. And the Markovich's son, Freddy, from Chisholm. He was killed last week." Steven sighed deeply. "When will it all end?"

Senia heard Steven's comment over the rumble of boiling potatoes on her stove. She chose not to reply. Lately her conversations with Steven had been strained. Their differing philosophies on so many issues of the day had caused their close relationship of the past to suffer. Senia was a Republican, an investment banker, a capitalist. Steven was a humanist, a champion of the downtrodden of the world. Knowing he was reading the Sunday paper, she anticipated his next observation would be about the Eugene Debs' story. Steven read the paper from back to front, bottom to top. The habit annoyed her. Tommy Pell's obituary was on the left front page she remembered. The Debs' story was page one's headliner. She waited for some comment from the living room. All she heard was silence. Then a sniffle.

Steven read about the Debs' trial. Tears welled in his eyes. The socialist leader, four-time presidential candidate and union activist had been given a ten-year sentence in a federal prison. Treason! Debs had given a stirring antiwar speech in early June. The colorful orator from Indiana had always been a thorn in the side of the political establishment. "They can't tolerate dissent, opposing political views. Nobody loves this country more than Eugene. But he loves the people . . . not the government." Steven mumbled under his breath. He would not discuss his torment with Senia. She didn't really understand the gravity of these things.

Steven remembered a handwritten letter he had received from Debs in August of '16, after the mineworkers' unsuccessful strike on the Mesabi. The three-page letter was addressed to Steven personally. Debs spoke of the injustices in the mines as if he worked there. "Don't give up the fight, Steven. Have the courage to stand for what is right . . . regardless of the suffering you may be forced to endure . . ." He had signed the long letter, "Fraternally . . . your brother, Eugene."

Steven had read the controversial Debs' speech. Everything he said was consistent with the life he led, the causes close to his heart. "While there is a lower class, I am in it . . . while there is a soul in prison, I am not free . . ." These words rang like gospel to Steven Skorich. His friend would be living his famous words.

"Dinner's ready, Steven," Senia called from the dining room where she had set the table.

Later that evening, after Steven had caught the train to Chisholm, Senia crossed the street to visit the Zoretek home. She had called Mary a few minutes before and been invited for coffee. Mary was distraught. Tony had gone over to the Trembarts to give Molly their condolences. Tony cried over the paper that morning and remained out of sorts all day. Tommy Pell had been like a brother to him. Many of the baseball guys were meeting Tom Brady at the Blessed Sacrament Church at five. After their private memorial prayers, Tony would walk over to console Molly. He told Mary how much he dreaded the visit. "I really don't know if she still loved him. What can I say to her? That Tommy always loved her . . . even when he left for the marines? I know he did."

"Just speak from your heart, Tony. That's all you can do." Mary gave him a long hug before he left for the church. She could feel her husband's hurt as if it were her own.

~

Senia seemed distracted as the two women talked about Tom and Molly, and their marital issues. "The Trembarts could never accept Tommy," Mary observed. "As much as I love her, Molly was terribly spoiled. She's admitted as much to me several times. Tony thinks they would have gotten back together. Despite the Trembarts."

Mary sensed that there was something heavy in Senia's thoughts of the moment. It wasn't the Pells. "What's bothering you so, Senia? I can tell you're not yourself tonight."

Senia's smile was forced, unnatural. "Nothing really. Just Sunday, I guess. Sundays have a melancholy air about them for me. I don't go to church as you know. What is it about a Sunday?"

"Is it Sunday . . . or Steven?" Mary was perceptive. She knew that on Sunday Steven always visited. It was their day together, their niche from a busy week. In the past the four of them spent Sunday afternoons together, often at the new Bennett Park a few blocks away. Lately they had not been doing much of anything with each other.

"You know me too well, Mary. Yes, Steven is . . ." Senia did not have the words to finish her thought. How might she frame the question she wanted to ask her friend? It seemed so personal. And it seemed like a mother asking a daughter for advice. Senia was ten years older than Mary, but their difference in age never bothered either of them before. Mary had something that Senia did not. That was the crux of the matter. Senia struggled with her emotions, her question. But Mary had the insight she needed and Mary was her closest friend. She had talked about her 'issue' to Becca on several occasions. Becca was a single woman like Senia and their feelings often jibed.'

"How do you love a man, Mary?" Senia finally blurted, feeling a sense of shame over how trite the question sounded as it left her mouth. Words cannot be retrieved. Senia attempted to recover, "I mean . . . you and Tony are so much in love. Have been from the very first . . . It's always been like some kind of magic."

"And you and Steven struggle with your feelings." Mary sensed Senia's discomfort. "I know. The two of you are so different, yet that's what always attracted you to each other, differences and the ability to talk about them. Always."

"That's changed. I've changed. Since Peter died . . . what, almost nine years now—August of '08. The world Steven lives in . . . and mine . . . we're both about different things. Do you know what I mean? I've built walls around myself. I know that. I've become selfish in so many ways. Independent."

Mary let Senia vent her feelings.

"Steven is such a righteous man, so good and decent and caring. Mary, I almost resent him for that, for his concern for others more than himself. He's put his life on the line—many times. I'm not that way. I'm so into myself that I hate it. My job, my house, my activities, my . . . everything! Steven is into people. People I don't know. And quite honestly, people I don't really care about. Isn't that terrible? I can't seem to love that lovable man, Mary. There's been nothing . . . nothing 'physical' between us for two years. I'm ashamed to admit that, but . . ." She took her hankie from the sleeve of her dress, dabbed at her eyes.

"How do you love a man? Senia, it's not easy." Mary got up from the table, poured more coffee as she thought about what she might say. Senia was hurting. Feeling vulnerable. She sensed the pain was deeper than Senia would admit. She would not pry.

Mary sat, took Senia's hand in hers. "I guess you just let them be who they are. I'm selfish too, Senia. I think about my things more than I do about Tony . . . or even the children. Maybe it's our nature. I feel that if I'm growing and comfortable with myself . . . that's attractive. Tony's never told me what to do, and I've never told him what he should do. If something concerns both of us, or the kids, surely we talk about it. Nobody makes a decision—it just kinda happens. Nothing to argue about. We both want the other to be happy. Always. Tony's a brooder sometimes. I let him brood until he gets over it. And that handsome man of mine snores. Sometimes it drives me from our bed." She laughed at the thought.

"I know. Steven and I are the same way. We don't interfere with each other's lives. We don't really argue much either. Steven is so tolerant." Senia laughed. "And I don't mind that he snores. Maybe all Slovenian men snore."

"I don't think I answered your question very well," Mary said. "Love? I don't think it can be defined. There are so many dimensions. Some of it is physical for sure. It's commitment and shared responsibilities. Mostly, it's a spiritual thing. How do I describe the feeling of love? I just need Tony . . . need him so that I can be who I am."

"I had that 'spiritual' thing once, Mary. And I'm ashamed to say that it was not with my husband, Timo. I loved Timo dearly. I love Steven, too. With all my heart I do."

"But you were not *in love*. There is a difference I think. It's hard to bring the two feelings together. Most people probably never do."

Senia swallowed hard against her emotions. She had to get something out. Something buried deep. Something frightfully knotted in her stomach. Maybe if she said it, then she could deal with it. "I was in love once. *Spiritually in love.*"

Mary knew before Senia finished her thought. How could she have missed it all these years? The two of them had shared almost everything, like sisters. Yet this secret was always there. Below the surface. Like a sin that could not be confessed. Senia had been in love with Peter. *She still was!* That love would haunt her the rest of her days.

~

"Trembarts' house was full," Tony said sitting at Mary's side on their living room sofa. "But it was strange. Really strange. More like a party. Molly flittered about like a hostess. I hardly talked with her. She said we *must* get together later. *Must* she said. I'm sure she meant the three of us, but somehow I didn't get that impression. All the men were talking business or Vic Power's politics. The mayor was getting nailed by most of the businessmen there. It was like a commercial club meeting. I felt really uncomfortable, Mary."

Mary was unusually quiet.

Tony continued, "Brady said the baseball team will serve as the pallbearers for the funeral next Wednesday. Wants the players to wear their uniforms. The guys were a somber lot. Tommy was well liked. Never saw Brady cry before. Lots of tears at the church. I didn't see any at the Trembarts."

Tony left the topic, asked about the kids. Angela, a lovely seven year old, was feeling fluish when he left that afternoon. "Did you call Dr. Kaner?"

"No, I didn't. She seemed better and ate her supper after you left. She said she had an oral report for her class tomorrow. She read it to me. Our daughter is already quite the orator, my dear. Her report was about our patriotic duty to purchase 'U.S. Thrift Stamps.' She's bringing her booklet of sixteen stamps to class with her. (The twenty-five cent stamps were sold at local banks and the post office. Sixteen were required to fill a booklet. The government would redeem the booklets for five dollars in five years.) You'd have been so proud. Maybe you can get her to practice one more time in the morning before school."

"And Marco? Did he pull the weeds in the garden as I asked him to do before I left? He said he needed to earn a nickel for something. I think he has his eye on a bicycle at Gambucci's hardware store."

"Oh, he got the weeds all right. And my petunias as well. I had to replant them when he was done." Mary laughed. Soon to be six, little Marco was an ambitious lad. "It's the red Schwin, my love. He's saved more than a dollar. Wants to negotiate the bike purchase with you. Says he'd be willing to pay half. A businessman in the making."

"Or a con man. And, Rudy?"

"Like every afternoon. Playing baseball with the neighborhood boys. He lives and dies that game."

Tony's brother Rudy was almost twenty, taking classes at the junior college, and working part-time with Tony's carpenter crew. "He's becoming quite a pitcher. We were playing catch in the back yard this morning. He stung my hand a couple of times. And Lud says the boy is a hard worker on the job. We've got lots to be proud of with our kids, don't we?" Tony dropped his arm around Mary's shoulders. Tony's brother always made Mary think of her own sister, Theresa. He was sensitive to that feeling. Theresa chose to marry a landless young man from the village in Italy. Her decision came only weeks before she was to leave for America and Hibbing.

Mary was not thinking of Theresa at the moment. Her conversation with Senia was still troubling her. There were few secrets that she kept from Tony. This would be one of them. Tony was too close to his Uncle Steven.

And, women's confidences were best kept to themselves. "Senia stopped by for coffee while you were gone."

"How's Senia been? I haven't seen much of her lately. I think she lives at the bank. Was Steven over today?"

"It's Sunday, my dear."

"I haven't seen much of my uncle either. I'll have to give him a call tomorrow. We were planning a fishing outing together next weekend."

Mary was tired, and Tony sensed it. "You go to bed, dear. I've got some book work to get done. I'll be up in an hour or so."

"Do you think Senia and Steven are happy?" Mary rose from the sofa. She couldn't keep the question from slipping out.

"Will they ever get married? Is that what you mean?"

"No. Just happy together. Sometimes I wonder."

"They're more like best friends, I think. In the ten years they've been together, I don't think marriage has ever come up. That is kinda unusual these days. Two very busy people with two very different lives." Tony knew their relationship had always puzzled Mary. They had talked about it many times. "I think they are happiest when they are apart. But they're awfully lonely, too. Neither one of them wants to be alone. That's the attraction."

As was usually the case, Mary realized her husband had an uncanny perception of things. "Maybe you're right about that." Mary gave Tony a light kiss and turned toward the stairway.

"I love you, Mary Zoretek." Tony never forgot to say those words before she went to bed, nor in the morning when she got up.

That night Tony fell asleep on the sofa. He had a terrible dream, a nightmare he would not remember the following morning. But a dream that would strike clearly at some future time. It was a death dream. He saw Tommy Pell trying to make it home. His friend was bloodied, gasping for breath as he swam against the waves. Enormous waves. Ocean waves. He seemed to be calling Tony's name. But his speech was garbled. Something about a job. Was it a job he wanted Tony to do? Then a woman without clothing. Her image was framed by flames. She was looking away from Tony as if ashamed of her nakedness. Her skin was a dazzling white, her waist slender, hips well-rounded. Water and fire were everywhere about her bare feet. Then she turned, looking upward at him. Meeting his eyes, smiling suggestively with lips pursed, inviting a kiss. Tony felt passions swelling. Lustful desires consuming him.

He was standing on a high place watching them both. Indecision. Both wanted him, needed him. But Tommy began swimming away. His face expressionless. The nude was Molly. Tommy waved a final goodbye, slipped under the water. Molly walked into a fiery wall, disappearing from his sight. Both were gone, the fire was gone, the sea was quiet. Tony was left alone with a feeling of empty confusion over his paralysis.

Mary came to his side. She smiled. "Let them go." Then she disappeared.

Then everything became an Eden-like serenity, with azure blue skies spreading over calm water. One perfectly white cloud rose over the golden horizon far away. Mary was somewhere in that cloud. Tony sensed her presence but could not see her. He reached his arms as far as he could, seeking her hand and knowing her hand was there for him.

Then Angela was at his side. A knowing smile creased her round face. Marco was crying from some place below. Steven was walking toward him. "Nephew, I've been looking everywhere for you. Let me take you home."

Tony cried, "I'm not lost. I'm looking for Mary."

Steven took his hand, led him down a path. Tony looked back over his shoulder. The cloud was gone. In its place a snow-white dove was flying off into the endless blue sky. A golden ring encircled its neck. The ring was familiar.

"Tony, you're having a bad dream." Mary shook his shoulder, kissed him lightly on this damp forehead. "Come up to bed." She frowned, "Have you been crying, my love? What's the matter?"

Tony sat up on the sofa, rubbing his eyes. He reached for Mary's hand. Her left hand. The golden ring on her finger startled him. "I was scared, Mary. The dream I had . . ." He strained his memory but his mind was a blank. "I wish I could remember."

∼

Kevin Schmitz also had a bad dream that night. In the nightmare his dog was barking loudly at the back door. When he went to let the dog into the kitchen, his father was sitting at the table in his tattered bathrobe. It was quiet outside, so Kevin imagined the dog was already in the house. "The dog's gone," was all that his father said as he turned off the kitchen light and told Kevin to go back to bed.

But Kevin climbed out of his window and went searching the neighborhood. He found his friend Gary Zench sitting on a rock. Gary had a bag with some old clothing and newspaper-wrapped sandwiches stuffed inside. He was going to run away from home.

Kevin was startled from his dream by his mother's call from the kitchen. He mumbled to himself, "Poor Gary, he's had things so tough. I'll have to find him another dog."

Earlier the day before, Kevin met Gary at their meeting place on the West Duluth hillside a few blocks north of Kevin's house. Kevin could tell that Gary had been crying. When he asked his friend what was bothering him, Gary told his tragic story.

"My pa killed Sport!" Then he broke down in tears. Sport was Gary's black Labrador. His affection for the animal was absolute. Gary told Kevin that Sport had been barking that morning while his father was trying to sleep off another hangover. In a volatile rage, Gary's dad took a pistol out of a dresser drawer and stomped through the house. Sport was at the back door barking to go outside and Gary was about to let the dog into the yard to do his business. Mr. Zench put the pistol to the dog's head and fired two shots.

Gary watched Sport die on the floor in a pool of blood. "Clean up this mess and get the fucking dog outta the house!" was all Gary's pa said as he lurched away and went back to his bed.

JUMPING A TRAIN

June 1918

When Sister Anne de Poris entered the St. James classroom at precisely eight o'clock, as she did every morning, the children immediately became silent. The sixth graders held the nun in the highest respect. Sister Anne loved her students and loved teaching. This was the last day of the school term and containing their enthusiasm for the anticipated class picnic would be a challenge.

The Catholic sister strode to the front of the room, her long black gown flowing from her tall, slender frame. Facing the even rows of desks as she had every morning for nine months, Anne gave her class a warm smile. "I know how excited you are for the trip to the zoo, but I must take care of a few matters before we proceed out to the bus." She cleared her throat, "And, I know that some of you are nervous this morning, wondering if your grades will allow me to give you a promotion to the seventh grade next fall."

Kevin Schmitz sat straight in his desk, the third seat in row four near the window looking out over the small playground behind the school building. Kevin was tall for his twelve years, and sturdily built. His wavy auburn hair was always neatly combed, his bright blue eyes were, as always, focused on his beloved teacher. Incredibly bright, the boy was often bored with the routine assignments required in subjects which held little interest for him. These assignments, however, were always completed in his finest penmanship and turned in on time.

Most importantly, Kevin's behavior had improved markedly since third grade. In situations that once caused him to be confrontational and assertive, he had learned to be a compromiser—a negotiator. Kevin had a remarkable gift for talking. Whenever an opportunity to give an oral report arose, he was the first volunteer. He loved being in front of the class or standing by his desk while his classmates sat below his eye-level. It always gave him a feeling of importance.

On the previous day, Sister de Poris had divided the class into groups of boys and girls for their final spelling contest. The weekly competition was always a favorite for Kevin and his classmates. The boys lined up along the wall by the windows, while the girls stood in their line in front of the chalkboard. Words were presented alternately, and a student who misspelled a word was required to return to his or her desk to sit while the contest continued. Kevin was usually the last one standing. Twice during the school term, Kathleen Murphy had won.

The day before had been a tense affair. Kevin and Kathleen were into their fourth word as the other children watched the contest from their desks. Clapping or cheering was not allowed, but sentiments clearly followed gender lines.

"Kathleen, please spell the word *vacuum*. A 'vacuum' is a space without air. A 'vacuum cleaner' is used by mothers to remove dirt from the floor. Spell *vacuum*."

Kathleen bit her lower lip. "Vacuum." She paused. A frown crossed her pretty face. Her slender hands squeezed nervously at the side of her long, green dress. She closed her eyes in total concentration, repeated the word, "vacuum." Somehow she mistrusted the logical phonetics of the word. Were there two 'c's'? Did the word end in an 'e'? She took a deep breath, smiled at Sister Anne with confidence, and recited: "The word vacuum is spelled v . . . a . . . c . . . c . . . u . . . m . . . e . . . !"

She knew immediately that she was wrong. Sister Anne's anguish over the error was obvious. "I'm sorry, Kathleen. The same word goes to Kevin. Vacuum."

Huddy Tusken, Kevin's neighbor and friend, heaved an audible sigh of relief. Heads turned toward him. "Hudson, we will have none of that in the classroom," Sister Anne reprimanded. Contrite, Huddy apologized, "I'm sorry, Sister. I was hoping Kathleen would get it right," he lied.

"Now, Kevin."

Kevin's eyes caught those of Kathleen across the room. She was the cutest girl in class. And the brightest by far. Enjoying the competition, he was tempted to purposely misspell the word he knew. An error would prolong the contest. Kathleen glared back, a challenging expression that seemed to say 'go ahead smarty-pants! I'll bet you can't spell it either.' She had called him just that—'smarty-pants'—on more than one occasion. But Kevin could not let victory escape him this day. It was their last showdown and he wanted badly to win.

"Vacuum. V . . . a . . . c . . . u . . . u . . . m . . ." He spelled the word, looking directly at Kathleen rather than at Sister Anne.

"That is correct, Kevin. Everybody can clap for our winner now." The boys were overly rambunctious in their applause. The girls subdued.

Kevin walked across the room, offering Kathleen his hand in congratulations for a well-contested match. His gesture was sincere. He would like to feel her hand in his own just one time. "You did well."

But Kathleen turned away in a huff and returned to her desk. She felt as if she had let down every girl in the world that morning. Shaking hands with 'smarty pants' was not going to happen. Never!

Kevin shook the memory of the day before from his thoughts. His eyes were now riveted on Kathleen Murphy at the front of row two.

"I want to congratulate all of you for doing an excellent job this year. I have given Mr. Lyons my promotion reports, and all of you will go on to the seventh grade next year." All of the children hooted their elation at the news. Huddy Tusken more than most. Next, Sister Anne would announce the 'top student award.' Every year the student with the highest overall grades, daily mass attendance, and most exemplary deportment was presented with a rosary. She held a black string of beads in one hand and a blue string in the other. Everybody knew that winning the award was between Kevin and Kathleen.

"I have compiled all the grades and subtracted demerits for misbehaviors and masses missed." She looked from Kevin to Kathleen. Kevin's heart sank.

"My decision has been more difficult than I can remember. We have two most deserving students this year." The nun's gaze remained on Kathleen sitting in the front desk only a few feet away.

Then, Sister Anne took a step toward the center of the room. As she did so, she slipped the blue rosary into the pocket of a long fold in her garment. "This year's award will go to Kevin Schmitz."

Summer vacation. Endless, idyllic days of playing outside until dark. Fun and games like kick the can, hide and seek, and captain may I. Sleeping later in the mornings. Baseball in the afternoons. Kevin loved baseball! And, this July day was special. Uncle Tony was taking him to a Duluth White Sox game at the Wade—West Duluth's new stadium. Tony's former team, the Hibbing Colts, were in town. Just Uncle Tony and Kevin would be going. He wasn't disappointed that his dad didn't want to join them for the ball game, but he was perplexed. Kevin had been disturbed by his father for several months—maybe even longer. His dad was a brooder who spent too much time with his newspaper in the living room and never cared to play catch in the long, narrow back yard.

As he sat on the front porch waiting for Tony, he remembered his birthday party the previous February. Birthdays . . . always his favorite day of the year. They were more fun than the Christmas celebration. Christmas was mom and dad, grampa and gramma. Mom's parents were not pleasant to be around. They just sat on the couch like the old folks they were. And, his presents from them were always Sears catalog clothes.

But on his birthday the whole 'family' was at their house. Auntie Senia, Auntie Mary, Uncle Tony and his cousins. Rudy was so much older and almost as tall as Kevin's uncle. Angela was seven. Girls of seven were not much fun to be around. Six year old Marco, on the other hand, he thoroughly enjoyed. Marco always liked to play and always sat next to Kevin at the dinner table.

Kevin remembered the day vividly. Beautiful Auntie Mary gave him the Mark Twain book he wanted. He'd read *Tom Sawyer* last winter and was anxious to learn about the adventures of Tom's friend, *Huckleberry Finn*. Mary was the nicest woman in the world in his eyes, even nicer than his own mom. Mary was a hugger and a kisser. He liked that. And she was so pretty—easily the prettiest woman he'd ever seen!

Auntie Senia was more quiet. He often caught her staring at him. It made him feel uncomfortable. She was nice enough, but he couldn't quite figure out what bothered him. Senia gave him lots of presents that day. A baseball magazine, a Duncan yo-yo with a bag of extra strings, a green sweater (something he would wear to school without protest), and a new five-dollar bill for his savings. Auntie Senia always liked to run her fingers through his hair.

But his favorite present by far was the baseball glove from Uncle Tony. The leather mitt was one that Tony had used when he played. Kevin's hand was too small, but he would use the glove anyhow. With the glove came the promise to see a baseball game the next summer. "I'm going to drive down to Duluth when the Colts play here. You and me are going to sit on the bench with the Hibbing players, and I'm going to get you a baseball bat to go with the glove." Tony was the greatest! And, he had baseball stories that made Kevin's eyes grow wide. Auntie Mary would call him a braggart when he told about some of the games he'd pitched. "I was pretty good back in those days, Kev. I think that's why Auntie Mary fell for me. It wasn't because I was a carpenter. No, she wanted a tall right-hander." Kevin saw him wink at Mary as he described her attraction.

Father Pat was always at the house. Every weekend the priest joined them for Sunday dinner. Most Wednesday nights he came to play canasta. Father Pat gave him a box of new pencils and a leather-covered diary. "I think you should keep a daily journal of things going on in your life, my son. Some day you'll look back on these days and be grateful for the memories." Kevin enjoyed writing and thanked the priest.

Mom and Dad didn't have much to say about his presents. They both liked the green sweater and approved of the book. But the old glove brought a frown to his dad's face. "Kinda big for you, isn't it, son?" was all he said. Dad didn't care much for baseball. Sports were a waste of time in his manner of thinking. Mom did not seem pleased with the gift of money from

Auntie Senia. "How will the boy ever spend five dollars?" she said. He couldn't help thinking that Senia was upset with mom's comment. "The boy's got to learn the value of money," was his aunt's quick reply.

Sometimes Kevin became agitated by his parents. They seemed so different from his relatives. And he often wondered about his relatives. Who were they? His dad was an only child. Kevin knew that. His mother had a sister who lived in Florida. Kevin had only seen his Aunt Cecilia once in his entire life. His aunt was not married. So many things just didn't make sense. He knew what relatives were supposed to be—and his were not. He'd never thought about these things until the past year. What made him think about his aunts and uncles was something churning deep inside that felt unnatural.

Art Schmitz was a small-boned man with wispy blond hair combed back from a high forehead. His nose was narrow, features sharply defined. Sarah was short and heavyset. At twelve, Kevin was taller than his mother and already only an inch or two shorter than his father. His parents were quiet people, had few friends, and rarely left the house except for something at the church. Kevin was outgoing, easily bored, and anxious to be anywhere but at home. He often found himself staring at their features and wondering, contrasting their behaviors with his own. It was confusing—sometimes troubling. The first entry in his secret diary might be, "Who am I?"

From his perch on the porch he could see the shiny new car approaching up the hill. Uncle Tony had written to him about the new Oldsmobile he had just purchased. His letter said, "I'll be taking my first road trip in the Olds when I come down for the baseball game. I'm looking forward to our special time together, Kev. If I don't have any car problems, and if the new Highway 53 is smooth, I should be at your house in the late afternoon. Your uncle is usually on time, so count on it."

It was late afternoon. True to his word, Uncle Tony was on time. The two of them would go for a ride in the car, have something to eat (but save room for hot dogs at the ball game!), and then be off to see the Colts and White Sox play.

As Tony pulled to a stop in front of the house and waved, the front door opened. Racing across the front lawn to hug his tall uncle, Kevin did not see his dad come onto the porch. Art stood awkwardly, watching his son embrace Tony. The scene was affectionate. How Kevin loved that uncle of his! Art could not remember the last time Kevin had hugged him nor when he'd hugged the boy. He troubled over his relationship with his son, wondering if his son thought about the same things. One day the secret would be revealed. Art Schmitz knew that. And he had a sinking feeling that that "one day" would not be too far away.

"What do you think of this machine, Kev?" Uncle Tony always called him 'Kev.' The boy liked the sound of Kev. It had a masculine ring to it. "She's got six cylinders and nineteen-horsepower under the hood. And she drives like a dream."

Stepping away from his uncle, Kevin gave the machine an appraisal. The automobile was a deep maroon color with the collapsible roof cranked down to the back and inside were black leathered seats. "It's a beauty, Uncle Tony. A real beaut! Can we go for a ride right now?"

"Let me say hello to your dad first, Kev." Tony looked toward the front porch. Art wore a sad, strangely melancholy expression. "How are ya, Art?" Tony called as he approached. "What do you think of the Olds?"

Art smiled wanly. "Pretty sharp, Tony. What did it set you back? The price I mean?"

The question seemed inappropriate, unlike Art. Something was bothering the man. "Business up in Hibbing's been good, Art. It's kinda been the company car for me. I use it a lot doing the real estate part of my job. I'm lucky to be able to afford such a fine machine." Tony did not tell Art that the car cost nearly twelve hundred dollars.

Sarah joined her husband on the porch. Offering her hello, she regarded the car out front. "Kevin has been waiting all day for this. All week. He's quite excited about the game."

"Are you sure that the two of you don't want to join us? I've got lots of room and would love to have you come along."

"We don't much care for baseball, Tony. I haven't read the evening paper yet, and it looks like the grass could use some cutting," Art said.

"No, you two run along and have a good time. Would you like something to eat before you go? I've done some baking today. The cinnamon rolls are still hot." Sarah saw Kevin's head shaking 'no!' The boy was tugging at Tony's sleeve to get going on their excursion.

Tony declined the rolls, put his hand on the boy's shoulder. "Kevin, run in and get your ball glove so we can play some catch before the game."

While the boy ran inside ahead of the slamming screened door, Tony chatted with Art and Sarah. Both of them were unusually cool and distant, offering one word answers in response to his questions.

When Tony and Kevin were in the car, Tony hit the electric start button. The engine responded with a sudden roar. Looking up to wave goodbye to the Schmitzes, Tony noticed that they had already retreated inside the house. "Well, Kev, we're off. I'm going to show you the time of your life . . . just wait and see."

~

Gary Zench, Kevin's closest friend, had moved from the neighborhood to a place called Riverside to the west. Gary's father had a job in the nearby shipyards and rented a duplex on Cato Street. The three miles, however, did not separate the two companions. On summer days they would meet at various places along the railroad tracks that ran east to west on the south side of Grand Avenue. Gary hitched rides on the trains passing by Riverside along the St. Louis River. Usually they met near the ore docks where columns of trains dumped their loads of iron ore into waiting ships. The noise there was incredible. Billows of thick dust hung heavily in the air, and a southern wind would carry the red soot across the rocky outcropping rising sharply from the bay. But the scene was exciting when viewed from their hillside perch on the sunny south side of a grassy knoll. The Wade ball park was within sight of their special place and, off in the distance, lay the shores of Wisconsin.

"Ya know, Gary, I've never had so much fun. My uncle is the greatest guy in the world."

Like Kevin, Gary loved baseball and was full of questions. "Did ya really sit on the bench with the players? Did yer uncle know the guys?"

"Gosh, even the Duluth players. The Sox manager and a coupl'a other guys came over before the game to say hi to Tony. The manager sez to me, 'son, this guy was the greatest pitcher I ever seen in this league' when they were shaking hands. I guess what my uncle told me was really true. He can still throw the ball a hunnerd miles an hour. I'll bet ya on that."

"I'll be damned." Gary was wide-eyed.

The two boys talked about the game and several other episodes related to Kevin's wonderful night. Gary puffed a cigarette he'd stolen from his dad's pack that morning. Kevin declined having a drag.

"On the way home after the game, Tony told me he'd like to have me come up to Hibbing and spend a few days before the end of the summer. Golly, that would be swell! He said that he'd ask my parents about it."

"Did he? What did they say?"

"They were in bed when we got back to the house. So Tony said I should ask them in the morning. Said he'd call and talk to them, too." Kevin's face told of his disappointment. He fought back tears of confusion. "My dad said that was not a good idea. Told me Hibbing was too far away. Not to bring it up again."

"It's not that far." Gary sensed Kevin's frustration. "Ya could take one of those trains and be up there in a few hours." He gestured toward a long line of empty ore cars chugging up the hillside to the east.

"He don't want me to go to Hibbing. That's what bothers me. I don't think it's Tony and Mary or my cousins. It's Hibbing. Ma said maybe we could go up there together when I'm older. I don't understand it."

"What's wrong with Hibbing? That's where most of this here ore's comin' from." Pointing his finger, Gary looked out toward the enormous docks which supported hundreds of cars. "I think it'd be kinda interesting ta see the place."

"I'm gonna, Gary! One way or another I'm gonna go up there and see it for myself. My folks aren't going to take me up there. I'd bet on that."

"Way to talk, Kevin. Hell, I'll go with ya. We can hitch a ride on one of them trains out there. Wouldn't be hard ta do."

Kevin was late for supper. His parents were already seated at the table. "Where have you been all day?" Art's face was sternly disapproving.

"And your clothes are filthy again," Sarah chided. "That's ore dirt. I'm sure of it. Gets the wash water so filthy it takes an extra hour to get it all out. Answer your father, son."

"Down by the ore docks," Kevin admitted. He met his father's eyes in a defiant stare. "I didn't do anything wrong. I was just watching the trains and ships. Lots of the trains come from up in Hibbing."

"Were you with that Zench boy?" Sarah's voice was tight, her tone reprimanding. "We've told you not to see him."

Kevin turned his glare to his mother across the dinner table. "You don't like him because he's not Catholic. I don't think that makes any difference. And, you don't like that his family's poor. There's lots of poor Catholics, too. Some of the St. James kids . . ."

Art cut off his son. "Listen, it's not that, son." He considered what he would say. "Have you met the boy's family?"

"No. Gary doesn't talk much about them. His pa's kinda mean to him. I know that. He's given Gary a black eye or two. His mother's nice to him, though. What does that have to do with anything?"

"Well, son, there's something . . ." Art struggled for a word, "Something 'unnatural' about the Zenches. The boy's mother is a 'colored' woman. Do you know what that means?"

"Colored?"

"She's a nigger, son." Art swallowed hard on the word he had just used. He was angry and didn't mean to be so blunt. "Colored means that she's a black person. It's just not right that the races mix like that. Do you understand what I'm saying? People don't like for whites and blacks to get married. It's always been that way."

Kevin was astonished. "No. I don't understand that at all."

"I'm not saying that I'm . . ."

Kevin pushed his plate away. "I'm not feeling so well. Excuse me please."

~

Hearing the rap on the open door to his rectory office, Patrick Foley looked up from his parish budget work. "Well, I'll be . . . Kevin! What brings you here on this beautiful summer afternoon?" But the priest could read the boy's face instinctively. Something was wrong.

"We've gotta talk, Father Pat," the boy said from the doorway. He had been trying to get up the courage to see the priest for almost a month. In two weeks the new school term would be starting.

"Come in and sit down." Standing, Foley gestured toward the chair in front of his desk. His first thought was the secret shared between the priest and Kevin's parents. One day this conversation would have to happen. He knew that dreaded day would come, but . . . Kevin was only twelve. All of them hoped that Kevin's adoption would not become an 'issue' in their lives for another several years.

"I've got lots of things inside, Father. It's been giving me a stomach ache—like I'm all twisted up inside or something. I can't talk to Art or Sarah about it."

"Art and Sarah? That's very disrespectful, Kevin. Children do not call their parents by their first names. I've never heard you say . . ."

"I know what disrespecting is, Father." He said indignantly, "Maybe I'm wrong to do that. If I am . . . I'll be going to confession next Saturday. But they've been disrespecting me, I think."

"How is that?"

"Do you know the Zenches, Father?"

The priest remembered the family from up the hill. He knew they had moved away, but didn't know where. "Only a little. I never met them. They used to live in the house where the Leary's live now. Am I right about that?"

"Yes. They live out in Riverside now. Gary is my friend. But Art . . . I mean, my parents won't let me play with him any more. They told me I'd be grounded for the rest of the summer if I did."

"Why is that, Kevin?"

Kevin tried to explain. "Gary's mom is a nigger. My dad used that word. Mom said I should say 'darkie' or 'colored.' Anyhow, they both think that Gary is bad because of that and because he's not Catholic. I don't think that's right."

Patrick Foley recognized a dilemma when he saw one. He could not side with the boy nor could he contradict the parents' judgments about their son's playmates. The priest could not believe that Kevin's adoptive parents were prejudiced. Foley was not. Duluth's labor shortages during the war brought hundreds of new families to fill the jobs in the shipyards. And a new steel plant was being constructed near Morgan Park in the west end. The priest had seen a growing racism within the community, even in his own parish. Only two weeks before he'd spoken from the pulpit on that very issue. His homily stressed the tolerance of differences.

"We should not judge people by the color of their skin, Kevin. Colored people are no different . . ."

"Art does!"

Foley shot a dark scowl. "Please don't interrupt me."

"I heard your sermon, Father. I thought it was pretty good. We both think the same."

"Will you let me continue, Kevin?" Foley sat back in his chair, ran his long fingers through his dark hair. How might he continue? He looked dolefully at the boy, felt a pain in his own stomach. Kevin would be facing many difficult questions in the years ahead. This was only the beginning.

"There's more, Father. I want to go to Hibbing."

Kevin's candor caught the priest by surprise. His mouth dropped.

Hibbing was where the boy's biological father had lived. "What do you mean?"

Kevin explained about his Uncle Tony's invitation and his parents quick refusal. "Let me talk to them about that, Kevin. Maybe something can be arranged. Maybe all of us could take the train up for a day. I was a pastor at Blessed Sacrament Church there many years ago. It might be a fun thing to do. I'll talk to them next time I'm over at your house. How's that? Maybe the two of us together can change their minds."

"Why don't they like Hibbing?"

"I can't imagine that they 'don't like' Hibbing. Maybe you're just imagining that. And, if I remember correctly, you were there once years ago. You were just a little tyke at the time. Only two or so."

"For a man's funeral?"

"Yes, that was it? You've got quite a memory, young man."

"Who was the man, Father?"

"You didn't know him. He was a friend of your family."

Kevin noticed a slight quiver in the priest's hand, saw Foley's eyes narrow. "What kinda friend did my family have in Hibbing? Was it a relative like Tony or Mary or Auntie Senia?"

"Yes, it was. A very close friend of Senia's as a matter of fact." The priest wanted to steer away from this conversation in the worst way. But Kevin was so blunt with his questions. What did the boy suspect? He would have a long talk with Art and Sarah. Maybe even tonight.

"How's your summer vacation been, Kevin? That ball game with your uncle must have been just about the greatest thing. Did you know that I go to ball games now and then? I'm quite a White Sox fan. As a matter of fact, they're at home next Saturday. How would you like to join me for the game?"

Kevin recognized the diversion. Sensed the priest's discomfort with their conversation. He would let Father Pat off the hook. "That would be swell."

"Maybe your folks would like to join us. We could all go together."

"They don't like baseball, Father. They don't like any of the same things that I do. We're so different them and me. Sometimes I just can't understand it. It's like we're totally different people."

The following morning Kevin met Gary at their favorite spot on the railroad line near the ore docks. Kevin left the house as soon as his father had gone off to work. His mother was still sleeping.

"I gotta do it, Gary. Were ya just jawing me, or would ya hitch a train up to Hibbing? I dare ya."

"Can we get back tonight? D'ya think? If I ain't home before dark, my ole man will kick the shit outta me," Gary said.

"I didn't think your folks cared about what you did."

"Ma does. If she tells my dad I been bad—he just loses it. That's why my ma don't say much. She knows his temper. Sometimes when he's mad at me he hits ma in the face, too."

Kevin winced at that reality. "We'll get back before it's too late. I've got a fiver in my pocket. Saved it from my birthday. The paper has a schedule in it. Says we can take the train one way for two bucks each. So if we hitch a ride up there we can take the passenger train back. Least that's my thinkin', Gary. Ya wanna do it?"

The two boys jumped from the empty ore car as the long train slowed down somewhere south of Hibbing. Kevin lost his balance as he landed, badly scraping his knees and elbows on the rough, rocky rail bed. Gary landed on his rump, tearing his already ragged trousers. Brushing himself off and dabbing at his bloodied arms, Kevin helped Gary to his feet. "You all right, Gary?"

"Ya. I done this lotsa times before. What about you?"

"Just some scratches, that's all." Kevin looked ahead down the line of tracks. "Let's go have us some fun, Gary."

The boys made their way the half mile into town, taking Third Avenue north toward Pine Street. For most of the early afternoon they just wandered about, looking in store windows, feeling the adventure of it all to their bones. "All my relatives live here, Gary. We gotta be careful that they don't see us. I'd get in big trouble."

Gary was wide-eyed over the city. He'd never been away from West Duluth before. "Place is lots bigger than Duluth, I'll betcha. All the stores and stuff. And back up there . . ." Gary gestured widely toward the huge dumps to the west, "them's mountains. I swear it. Din't know about mountains bein' up here. An all them trains too. Must be a hunnerd."

"That's what mining's all about. I learned that those mountains you're talkin about are called 'dumps'. That's what I heard in school. We had a guy from the Range at St. James last year. He talked to the class about mining. I really thought it was interesting."

"Dumps?"

"Yah. They just dump the earth that's on top of the iron ore in those big piles. Just dump it so it's not in the way of the mining, I guess. Then they dig those big holes to get the ore out. Or, something like that."

"Jeeze." Gary shook his head in wonderment.

As they neared Canelake's Candy Store, the chocolate aroma was arresting. Kevin felt for the crisp fiver in his pocket. "You hungry?"

"Starvin'! We don't have no breakfast at home most days. Unless there's somthin' left from supper."

Kevin bought a small bag of rich chocolates for thirty cents. Together they walked down Third from Center to South Street. "There's the ball field where my uncle Tony played!" Kevin said excitedly. The boys found the gate open, wandered across the lush green grass, then ran around the bases. Across the street was Mesaba Park. In the park were gardens, fountains, benches. The boys, tired from their running about at the ball field, found a bench facing a large, spouting fountain. "This thing must have a name," Gary said as he approached the gurgling spray. "There's a name on this thing here." Shading his eyes from the sun, he read the inscription to Kevin who was sprawled across the bench. "Donated to the city of Hibbing by Peter Moran—that's what it says here. 1906."

Kevin did not respond. His thoughts were on baseball. Imaginations of his uncle pitching from the mound where they had just been. How much he'd like to tell Tony that he'd visited the field where the Colts played their games.

In late afternoon, the boys found the railroad depot. There was a five o'clock passenger train back to Duluth. "I'd like to purchase me two tickets to Duluth," Kevin told the ticket master at his window.

"Where's yer parents, young man? Can't be selling tickets to no kids without their parents. Ya otta know that." Ingram Staver frowned at the two boys. The taller of the two lads had blood on his shirt and torn trousers. The darker complected boy looked like a runaway in his tattered clothing. "Ya got yer parents here somewheres?"

"No sir, we're just by ourselves. Our folks live in Duluth. They sent us up here on the morning train. I went to see my gramma. She's really sick," Kevin fabricated.

"Who might your gramma be, son? I know most of the folks 'round here. Maybe she'd tell me if'n it's okay to let ya on this here train." Staver narrowed his eyes at the youth. "Who's yer gramma?"

Kevin's expression did not betray his fear at being caught in a lie. Without hesitation he replied, "My gramma's name is Johnson. Ruth Johnson." He pulled the name out of nowhere. Johnson was a common name in West Duluth. Ruth? Ruth was just a woman's name.

"Don't know no Ruth Johnson. Maybe I'll just give Mister Argir a quick call, he's our police chief here. I'm sure he'll be able to help you boys out. Maybe he knows yer gramma."

Tasting defeat, Kevin feared the worst of all possible outcomes. He did not want to get arrested and go to jail. If that happened he'd really be in big trouble. Thinking quickly, however, an idea popped in his mind. "If you'd just call my uncle, he'll tell ya who we are."

"And who's yer uncle, lad? A Mister Johnson?" The ticket man smiled. By now he was convinced these were runaway kids. He'd let the police handle it.

"Zoretek. My uncle's name is Tony Zoretek. You can call him if you'd like."

"Mr. Zoretek? The contractor?"

"Yessir."

"Who might I tell Mr. Zoretek that I'm talkin with?"

"Just tell him, Kevin."

Tony was amused by the situation, but he did not show it. Boys! Tony, hands on his hips, stood with Kevin off to the side of the ticket window. "What is this all about, Kevin? And what happened to your clothes? You look like you jumped off a train or something."

Kevin apologized for everything. "I just had to see where you played baseball." Pleading with his uncle not to tell his parents, he promised never to do such a foolish thing again.

Tony would keep the secret. The boys made it home safely that night. Kevin was grounded until school started for ruining his clothing.

But, Art and Sarah would never learn of Kevin's adventure in Hibbing that day.

INFLUENZA

July 4, 1918

The three women waited on the depot platform for the early evening train from Duluth. Their disappointment had turned to outrage. For the first time in their memory the dependable Duluth, Mesaba and Iron Range schedule had been disrupted. Both the morning and noon trains did not leave Duluth.

"We've been sabotaged!" Becca Kaner said vehemently. "All our planning for nothing. And, I think we all know who's behind it."

Becca, Senia and Mary had worked for months on their Independence Day Parade procession. The nearly fifty Hibbing women involved in their local suffrage club had organized a protest march for that morning's annual Fourth of July parade. They had arranged for the prominent daughter of Elizabeth Cady Stanton to join their march and rally set for the Tapio Hall in the afternoon. But, Harriot Blatch did not arrive.

"It's that damnable, Elwood Trembart. I'd bet on that," Senia said. "He was the Grand Marshall and we all know where he stands on women's rights."

"He probably had his political cronies in Duluth shut down the daytime train service," Mary agreed. "Tony offered to drive all the way down there and pick her up, but it was already too late. What are we going to do now?"

"He's a big shareholder in the railroad. But you wouldn't think one man could stop the trains. I think more than a few others are in on his conspiracy against us," Becca enjoined.

"We've only lost a battle, ladies. We're going to win the war." Senia was easily more agitated than her two friends. She had done most of the planning, contacted Mrs. Blatch on several occasions, and made the arrangements at the Tapio Hall. "Tomorrow's Friday. Lots of the locals have the long weekend off from work. The banks are closed, Vic Power's given all public employees an extra vacation day, and the weekend will have several ethnic picnics going on."

"We'll have our parade then, won't we? Tomorrow, or maybe Saturday. Senia, you know Vic better than we do. He's one of Steven's best friends. Maybe you can get him to reissue our permit to march on Pine Street, down Third Avenue." Becca was excited over the prospect. "And we won't be just a small part of a big parade—we'll have everything to ourselves."

"And our new car would be just perfect for Harriot. I'll ask Tony to give it a good polishing in the morning." Mary shared the enthusiasm. "And how about having our rally at the fairgrounds instead of the Tapio Hall? The grandstand there holds hundreds of people."

The three women were best of friends. For the past two years they had met monthly as the 'Hibbing Women's Book Club.' Each month a popular book was discussed among the three of them and four other local women. Molly Pell, the newly widowed school teacher, was one of their members. So was Percy Power, the mayor's wife and Esther Hane. In March they all read the controversial new book, *Mobilizing Woman Power*, by Harriot Blatch, a leader in the National Women's Party and a renowned activist in New York state. Her efforts had helped bring about a revolutionary suffrage rights constitutional referendum in her home state. Now the path was paved for the Nineteenth Amendment—full suffrage for women. After reading the book, Senia took the initiative to arrange for Mrs. Blatch to travel to Hibbing. In her first letter to Blatch, Senia emphasized, "With so many women taking the jobs left vacant by military conscription, those old slogans about a 'woman's place' have become obsolete."

Blatch responded with enthusiasm, "The Iron Range has long been known as fertile ground for protest against established patterns of discrimination. Your mine workers have fought for their rights on several occasions. Now it's our turn to fight for our rights."

The three women watched as the night train from Duluth slowly crawled into the depot. The coaches were packed with travelers who had been delayed throughout the day. They recognized Harriot Blatch immediately.

Harriot would stay with Senia while in Hibbing for the weekend. On that Independence Day Thursday evening the women were up late discussing their plans. Senia invited Vic and Percy Power to join them. Tony and Steven along with Ambrose Hane were also visiting Senia's crowded house. Power promised to get a parade permit the first thing in the morning. "I'm with you ladies one hundred per cent. Always have been and I think all of you know that. Percy would kick me out of the house if I didn't give you women every opportunity to express your views." Vic always loved an opportunity to orate. Large groups or small. "And it's my great pleasure to meet you, Mrs. Blatch. I have long admired your personal courage, and that of your mother as well. Elizabeth Cady Stanton was a soldier. And, your father, Henry, one of the great abolitionists. I read once . . ."

Percy nudged her husband in the ribs, "Victor, dear, please let the women speak," she whispered behind her hand.

"Yes, Mrs. Blatch, we're all very honored to have you with us in Hibbing. Now, I've done enough talking. What are your plans, ladies?"

Harriot Blatch was an engaging speaker. The nationally known suffrage leader expressed her positive thoughts on the future of the movement, and the widely discussed constitutional amendment. "I've traveled widely, although this is my first trip to Northern Minnesota. You must show me your mines while I'm here," she suggested with a sparkle in her eyes. "Your iron ore has been so very critical to our war efforts. It's an honor for me to be in this historic place. Indeed, I shall have something to share with my friends back in New York when I return."

Their meeting lasted to nearly midnight. All agreed that Saturday would be best for their suffrage parade. Steven would arrange to have a few hundred mine workers join the women. "Many of our men are supportive—not the majority yet, I'm sorry to admit—and they'll be happy to march at your side, Mrs. Blatch. Our women folk always stood at our side when we fought the companies. Now it's our turn."

"I will walk with you as well," Mayor Power said emphatically. "I'll stand up for what's right regardless of how popular the cause. So will many of our public employees."

The August morning graced Northern Minnesota with all her late summer radiance. Becca Kaner gazed at her back yard flower garden through the kitchen window as she sipped a cup of coffee. It was already her third summer in Hibbing. Realizing how swiftly that time had passed, she wondered about her future here. There were no men in her life. At thirty-one she often thought about that fact. "Why isn't there another Tony Zoretek out there?" she said to herself. Mary was her dear friend but being around her sometimes brought a guilt she found troubling. Tony often flirted with Becca when they were all together. Good-natured flirtations. The 'Miss America Doctor' he called her. But as a female doctor, and Jewish as well, she was almost beyond approach to the few eligible bachelors in Hibbing. She had dated Marc Atkinson a few times and found him to be pleasant company. Yet there was no physical attraction. Their relationship was strictly platonic. Marc was someone to go to the theater with when a good play was in town or for an occasional dinner date. Matthew Baraga was a single doctor on the Rood staff but a devout Catholic as well. There were barriers in that regard. Hibbing had a sizable Jewish community and an active synagogue, but Becca was not orthodox. If things did not change one day soon, she might move to Duluth. St. Mary's Hospital was an option. Becca was familiar with the attractive port city. On weekends she often traveled to the Lake Superior shores. She might spend hours basking in the sun on the wide sandy beaches of Park Point or sitting on the granite rocks of the harbor.

"But, how would my friend, Ollie, handle it?" She laughed to herself. On the counter top was a birthday card her miner friend and patient had sent her two weeks before. Inside the card was a note, "For my favrit gurlfriend, Docter Kaner. From Oliver Kochevar with the best fixed-up leg in all Hibbing."

She put down her cup, rubbed the remnants of sleep from her eyes. She had slept late on this Saturday morning. She planned to work in the yard for an hour before doing her weekend grocery shopping. Later in the afternoon she had a fitting at Mary's dress shop. That evening it was dinner with Senia and Steven at the Zoretek's house down the block and across the street.

Her blooms were perfectly segregated and arranged by size and color. Both Mary and Senia had helped her get a garden started one June weekend three years before. Her friends were avid gardeners. In the east corner of the plot she had a cluster of blue-colored flowers: Joe Pye weed toward the back, catmint shrubs toward the front with some phlox and bellflowers. The center section was a striking array of white blossoms: potentilla, yarrow, coneflower. To the left were her favorites—red beebalm. The beebalm attracted humming birds and butterflies. The wide spread of red blooms included some speedwell spears, lupin, iris, and daylilies. Weeding and watering the garden gave her a sense of peace in the early mornings and evenings after a hectic day at the hospital.

Becca heard the ring of her telephone. It was Marge Dowling, a nurse at the hospital, and her voice was high-pitched with concern. "Bad mine accident, Doctor Kaner. I can't reach Weirick or Hane . . . you gotta get down here!"

Becca did not get to the Rood Hospital in time. It wouldn't, however, have made any difference if she had. "He hasn't been breathing for twenty minutes, doctor. We tried respiration. Everything. The poor man got crushed at the Utica Mine . . . about an hour ago. Timbers collapsed at the fifth level of the south tunnel the foreman who brought him in told us. The guy was working by himself when it happened." Nurse Dowling explained the details as she understood them.

Becca concealed her emotion. Mine work was so terribly dangerous. The push for wartime production made safety a secondary consideration. Her remorse for the dead man was tinged with an anger. She looked at the note pad the nurse had handed her. Bruno Moscatelli was the man's name. "Give the Oliver office a call. They will want to notify the family. I'll sign the death certificate when it's ready." Becca pulled the white sheet over the man's iron ore red-creased face. As she did so she thought once more about looking for a job in Duluth away from these kinds of human tragedy.

~

Claude Atkinson had a knack for spotting newsworthy stories from the wires that crossed his desk every day. Certainly the world war was what preoccupied most of his readers. The *Ore* continued to chronicle major battles and strategies. Those who wanted more war news would pay the five cents for a rival *Tribune* issue. In July, Claude spotted a story dated from Fort Riley, Kansas. The army base reported a 'considerable outbreak' of the flu. In one week more than five hundred troops had been through the camp's hospital. The story reminded him of the serious outbreaks in Europe—something being labeled as the 'Spanish Flu' that was causing untold misery across the Atlantic. Some military analysts were suggesting that the Germans were spreading a bacteria.

In July, public health officials in Philadelphia issued a bulletin about the 'Three Day Flu.' In August came a story from the Chelsea Naval Hospital where flu sufferers had overwhelmed the facility. One sailor described feeling like he had "been beaten all over with a club." In September, sixty-three men died in a single day at Camp Devens near Boston.

Claude ran an unusual headline on September 5, *'See Your Doctor!'* The U.S. Surgeon General, Rupert Blue, warned of a 'serious influenza' and issued a press release on how to recognize the influenza symptoms. Blue prescribed bed rest, good food, salts of quinine, and aspirin for the sick. In his commentary, Claude was emphatic.

> *For several months I have followed the spread of this 'Flu' and reported stories from Brussels to Boston. State officials have sent the message that there is no danger of an epidemic and cautioned our citizens not to worry. I'll be blunt. I'm scared!*

By October America was seized by an epidemic of monstrous proportions. Nearly a thousand died in a single day in New York. The contagious virus was heading westward with Chicago reporting a death rate of staggering proportions.

Samuel Novak woke up on Monday morning, October 14, with a splitting headache. He told his wife he wasn't going to work. By noon his temperature had spiked to 104.

Leo Erickson was a broad-framed Swede who had not been sick a day of his life. But while working in the Hull-Rust Mine, he began to sweat profusely. He sat down. Couldn't gather the strength to get back on his feet.

He told his foreman, "I can't understand it. I feel weak all over . . . no energy. And I got lotsa pain in my joints." Leo was taken to the hospital.

Martha Bates complained to Doctor Hane, "My throat is so sore I can't hardly swallow. Even chicken broth didn't help me none."

Helen Weber's symptoms went from a lower backache to a throb in her temples. She left her three children with her neighbor and walked to the hospital. Helen asked to see Doctor Kaner and was told that she'd have to wait. "We've got ten new patients and are running out of beds, Mrs. Weber," Nurse Dowling said. "Lots of flu going around."

Hibbing had an outbreak! Most of the cases seemed to come from the section of town between Railroad Street and Lincoln in the west side. Doctor Hane told Chief Argir to issue a quarantine. Both the Rood and Adams Hospitals were overcrowded in four days. Nine of the flu victims had already died.

The Oliver Mining Company brought all of the cots they could muster from their infirmaries to help the hospital staffs with shortages, and made a substantial financial contribution to assist in the purchase of any supplies which were needed in the hospital's effort. In a time of grave crisis the area's major employer was compelled to render all and every possible assistance. The company feared for its work force.

But the contagious influenza was spreading citywide with every passing day. The southwest section of Hibbing was quarantined, then part of Brooklyn. Nearby Mahoning Location and Kerr and Kitzville all had reported shocking numbers of new cases.

Molly Trembart and her fellow teachers did neighborhood canvassing, visiting every house to inquire about family members who might be sick. At every stop they informed residents of preventative measures which had been published by the Colgate Company. Among the instructions were chew food carefully, drink fluids, and avoid tight clothing and shoes.

Mary Zoretek and Senia were Red Cross volunteers working in their Brooklyn neighborhood. More than twenty families had sick members. In two weeks the number of identified cases neared four hundred. Forty-seven people had already been delivered to the local coroner for an autopsy exam.

Claude called the virus a 'homicidal maniac!' in one issue of his newspaper. The editor passed along all of the information at his disposal to his community as Hibbing tried to ward off the invisible killer. He was in constant contact with Ambrose Hane at the hospital and Vic Power at city hall.

Becca was working twenty hour days catching a few hours of sleep at her chair in the office when totally exhausted. The hospital was like a mad house. On Thursday, October 24, she was attending to thirty-five patients in her overcrowded ward. When a lucky person was released to go home for complete rest, two more stood in line for the available bed.

It was six-thirty in the evening when Becca stepped out of the ward into the hallway. Famished and drained to the last ounce of her energy, she needed a break. Heading to her office for a sandwich and some much needed coffee, she heard an unmistakable voice calling her name from the confusion somewhere in the congested corridor behind. She stopped without turning around, seized with a sudden panic. "My good God, no! It can't be." She screamed silently, feeling a sharp pain gripping in her chest.

"Becca! Becca!" It was Tony's voice. A voice charged with unbelievable fear. "Becca! Mary's sick!" He was trying to explain in strained, impatient words as he rushed down the hallway in her direction. "She was feeling poorly last night. But thought she was getting better this morning." Tony gasped. "She didn't call all day. I had no idea until I got home an hour ago."

Spinning around, she saw the tall form only feet away. Tony's face was drained of color. Mary was stooped at his side, clutching his loose jacket with fingers sapped of strength, coughing into the woolen shawl draped over her head and shoulders. Her color was almost bluish, dark circles ringed under her wide, ovaline eyes, her full lower lip hanging agape as she gasped in labored breaths.

"What can you do? I've tried to bring down her fever . . . she's giving up on me. Becca, she's got that flu really bad—I know it. You've gotta do something. I can't lose her. I just can't lose her, Becca. She's everything . . ." He was crying now. Mary fell against his side, losing her balance. Tony caught her, lifted her limp body into his arms. "Where can I take her? I'll help you. Just tell me what to do."

"Tony . . . I'm going to die. I can't make it . . ." Mary's voice was almost a whisper. She mumbled again, "I don't want to . . . the children, Tony . . . I'm going to die," she repeated her consuming dread. Her swollen eyes closed on the fight she was conceding. "Let me go, Tony . . ."

There were no beds in the ward. Becca's mind raced. "My office, Tony. Follow me quickly." As she raced down the hallway she fought her own tears. Becca had come to recognize the face of death these past weeks and knew Mary was in desperate condition. In minutes she would be delirious.

In the small office she swept everything from her desktop in one swoop of an arm, grabbing a fresh, white gown from a hanger, spreading it across the flat surface. "Lay her down here, Tony. It's the best I can do right now. Talk to her. Keep her spirits up as best you can. I'll run and get some ice for her fever, some aspirin . . ."

Becca returned in minutes with everything she could get her hands on in the nearby supply room. Swinging open the office door she saw him cowering in the corner, sobbing uncontrollably, his strong fingers wrenched behind his head. Tony was on the edge of shock. Looking from him to the desk, she dropped the bowl of ice onto the floor, felt her knees begin to buckle, and screamed!

Tony's devastation was absolute. In the days following Mary's death he shut himself in their bedroom for hours at a time. The pain would not abate despite the well-intentioned efforts of his dearest friends. Nothing would console him, not even his family. Losing Mary was worse than losing his arms and legs. It was paralysis, emptiness, despair! Everything around him brought back a cherished memory and with each memory, more tears. Private tears. In the presence of others he wept inside. For nearly a month, Tony let his business take care of itself. His interests were as dead as his spirit for living.

In those first few days he had to be strong. The funeral arrangements, the wake and burial, receptions held at the Immaculate Conception Church, gatherings at the homes of Mary's closest friends—hundreds of people, many he had never met before. People whose lives Mary had touched in some small way. Their stories of his wife, their condolences, their laments over one so precious. It was so busy, so absorbing that Tony hardly had time to grieve. Someone was always there to lift his spirit with their heartfelt sympathy. God had blessed them both with so many friends—All of Hibbing seemed to grieve along with Tony, even as other deaths from the horrible flu shrouded the community like a winter blanket.

Then the celebration of her wonderful life was over. The focus of concerned friends became Tony. But Tony felt cheated, cheated of the time alone he needed to deal with his own grief. He felt deprived of precious moments beside her casket without others at his elbow, time at the grave site when no one else was there, time in any place he chose to be privately connected with his love.

Lud Jaksa, his business associate, took charge of everything at the Zoretek operation headquarters. Sadie Baratto cared lovingly for the children. His Uncle Steven did the autumn yard work, raking leaves, mulching gardens. He was always at the house to help Sadie and comfort his nephew's kids. Senia and Becca stopped by often, did the shopping, helped with the housework.

Angela Zoretek was the most vulnerable. Her confusion became her anger. She could not put things together in her mind. The *why* of her mother's death drained the child to her soul. Mary's daughter was seized by an inability to grasp the ever elusive *why*. "God needed a perfect angel" . . . "Only those specially loved and blessed are taken to heaven so young" . . . "We were given her as a gift from a loving God . . ." None of this pacified the seven year old. Sadly, the one person who might help her cope with her questions was not there for her. He was not sharing his own innermost feelings with those who needed him most.

Angela somehow sensed that reality and left him alone. One night she crept into her father's bedroom and found him lying awake, staring at the ceiling. She found his hand, held it to her mouth and softly kissed it. Not a word was spoken for nearly an hour. The two of them lay at each other's sides holding hands. There were no tears. Finally Tony turned his head to meet the brown eyes of his daughter. They were her mother's dark oval eyes. "We will talk about this soon, sweetheart. Thank you for being with me . . ." was all that he said. Angela left him and went to bed to cry herself to sleep. She would give her father more time—perhaps another week. Then they would talk. She would get better answers to her questions from him. She would learn *why*?

Tony slipped into retrospective thoughts . . . remembering how it had been.

For nearly a month only one person was able to break the ice that gripped the soul of Tony Zoretek. That one person was Becca Kaner. Becca had been there. Becca had seen him at his worst in that small office room at the hospital. It was Becca who saved his life. In the minutes following Mary's last breath, Tony wanted to go with his wife into her journey beyond. In that terrible moment he had a surreal recollection of a dream. The vague memory crept from some unconscious level into his thoughts. A dream of being alone while Mary's spirit floated away. He needed to hold her hand on that incredible flight to some mystical, eternal realm. "I can't let her go without me. Becca, please . . . she is my everything." Tony sobbed. "I don't want life without her . . ."

Recognizing the depths of Tony's anguish, Becca held him. Becca's words brought him back to reality. "You can't go there, Tony. Let her go—it's her new life. She will wait . . ." Becca felt the tall man's tears on her neck as she let him hold her tightly. "Let it all out, Tony. Say good-bye." Then she gently pushed herself away, stepping out into the corridor, shutting the door behind her. For several minutes she listened to the deep, sorrow-filled weeping. Tony's last professions of love, prayers for her soul, "Wait for me, Mary my love. One day I will hold you in my arms again." Then it was quiet in the room. "Becca . . . Becca, I'm okay now . . ."

Becca came back inside, took Tony's hands in hers. "Love is eternal," was all she could say. Delicately covering Mary's body with a clean sheet, she offered Tony some laudanum, a strong sedative, along with a cup of ice water. "Let me drive you home now, Tony. There is nothing you can do here. Your family will need you. They'll need your strength to get through this . . . this terrible loss." And, she drove him home. Nothing was spoken between them during the fifteen minute ride. At his house, Tony smiled weakly, "Thanks, Becca . . . for everything. Pray for her, will you please?"

Upon returning to the hospital that night, Becca learned that a child had been born. The time of birth was listed at 6:42. The eight pound four ounce boy was the fourth son of Anna and Edgar Bourgoyne. The couple had named him, Richard. Becca realized something profound as she looked at the report on her desk. A new life had entered this world at precisely the same moment as Mary Zoretek gasped her last breath of life. She left her office for the maternity room and found the mother asleep. In a crib nearby, baby Richard gurgled his delight of life. Becca held his small hand in her own, smiled. "Praise God," she said.

November slammed the door on the mild days of October. Autumnal winds wailed in the trees, stripping the branches of their last few leaves. Nearly a month had passed since Mary's death. The horrific flu virus had passed through Hibbing, leaving forty-two human tragedies in its wake. Seven of those deaths were people that Tony knew personally. Florence Udahl, the wife of his dear friend Lars, was among them. Lars, he realized, was grieving just as deeply as he was. The Udahls had five children at home. Five kids without a mother.

"Damn it anyhow!" Tony was standing at his bedroom window watching the bluster outside. "Enough self-pity! Get on with your life, Zoretek." Mary would be ashamed of her husband wallowing like a weakling in his misery. Mary who so loved every day of her short life. He turned away, regarded the closed door, muttered to himself again. "I'm letting go of this nonsense, Mary. I'm ready to get on with my life. Pray always for me. I'll need that more than ever before."

A confident smile creased the face looking back at him from the dresser mirror. At that moment he felt a transformation. A new man would leave that room this morning. A man who would let the ink dry upon the happiest chapter of his life and begin writing the next one.

Downstairs, Sadie was in the kitchen serving breakfast to the children. It was a school day for Angela and Marco, and she would not let them out the door without something warm in their stomachs. Oatmeal, with the aroma of added cinnamon, simmered in the large pot on the stove. Toasted bread with a large slab of butter, along with a jar of strawberry jelly, rested on the table along with freshly sliced peaches.

"Good morning, children. Can I pull up a chair and join you?"

Angela leaped from her chair, ran to her father, embracing him as tightly as her little arms could. "Daddy! Daddy . . . sit by me, please." She was beaming. "It's so good to see you before going to school. Just like it used to be before . . ." Angie swallowed hard, "before mom left us. It can be like that again, can't it, Daddy?"

"Yes, it can. And, yes, it will, sweetheart. I'm coming back to the breakfast table every morning. Sadie, a bowl of your oatmeal please. And a cup of that Arco coffee you brew so well." Tony laughed, more deeply than seemed natural. It felt so good. "Marco, did you make your bed like mom said you should in the morning?"

"Yes, I did, daddy. And I said my morning prayers, too. Just like mom wanted me to."

"And, Rudy. How is my brother doing on the job these days? I'll want a complete report on what you've been up to at the supper table this evening."

Rudy smiled widely, "I'll talk your ear off if you'll let me. Work's going just great. We're still building houses in the Larabee Forty."

"All of you at the dinner table tonight? Hallelujah!" Sadie Baratto said jubilantly. "I'm going to put a pot roast in the oven . . . with all the fixins too."

"It's been much too long, Sadie. I'm sorry." Tony replied to her enthusiasm. "And there's something else that's long overdue. Let's talk when the kids are out the door." Tony would ask his housekeeper to strip the bedroom upstairs. Get rid of the drapes, bedspread, furniture. Clean out all the closets and pack Mary's old clothing in cardboard boxes to give away through the church. He'd have the room completely redone.

Tony had a small office next to Mary's sewing room toward the back of their spacious house. It was here he did much of the book work connected with his business operations. He took a cup of coffee into the room and made himself comfortable in the leather chair at the desk. Near his elbow lay the black telephone that he had not touched in weeks. He scribbled a list of people he would call that morning.

First, he would call Lud Jaksa at the Hibbing shop office and catch up on business matters. He'd call Lars Udahl and arrange a meeting. He would suggest having lunch together that day. Tony's condolences to his dear friend were long overdue. And, Senia. Senia had tried to reach him several times in the past weeks and he had not returned her calls. She would be at the bank this morning. Tony would invite her and Steven over tomorrow night for some wine and cheese. Tonight, he remembered, was for his children and brother Rudy.

Tony wrote the name of Father Dougherty on his note pad. He would have to thank the priest for everything he'd done during those difficult days. His Uncle Steven. How could Tony have been so out of touch with those who meant so much to him? He ran his fingers through his long, dark hair in contemplation. "I'm coming back, my friends," he said to himself. "Back to the land of the living. Finally!"

At the bottom of his list he wrote, 'Becca'.

As he was about to pick up the phone and get Tessie, the local operator, Sadie Baratto knocked at the door, entered the room with a pot of coffee and a hot pad to protect the the oak desktop. "Sadie, how many people can you sit at that huge dining room table?"

"I think about twelve, comfortably, sir."

"Will you do me a big favor, Sadie?"

"Anything, Mr. Zoretek. You know that."

"I'd like to have some people over to the house on Sunday. Could you get to the meat market and find a huge turkey? Something big enough to feed an army?"

"Khort's will deliver whatever you'd like. That would be easy."

"And, how many kids could we get around the kitchen table? I've got a lot of catching up to do with my friends."

That afternoon Tony had lunch with Lars Udahl at Fay's Cafe. The two old friends embraced unashamedly when they met outside the restaurant. "We've both got our hands full, don't we Tony?" Lars said. "But we're gonna do what we've gotta do."

"We've got to, don't we?" Tony shrugged. "And we will."

Lars insisted that Tony try Fay's Swedish *lutefisk*. Tony balked at the suggestion. Both of them enjoyed some banter about ethnic foods. "We'll compromise. You try some Slovenian *sarmas* and I'll have a bowl of your lutefisk."

They left the hard conversation of surviving tragedy and talked business. Lars told Tony how well Lud Jaksa was doing with all the building contracts. "I hate ta tell ya that everythins just rollin along without ya, but that's a fact, Tony. Construction's goin great an it's only gonna get better in the next coup'la years." Before leaving Lars at the restaurant, Tony invited him and the kids over for a turkey dinner on Sunday. "I'll invite Lud to join us."

That night, Tony spent precious hours with his two children and with Rudy. With Marco being the first to bed, he excused himself and tucked his son under the fluffy quilt his mother had made. "Is there anything you'd like your dad to tell you about, son?" he asked the six year old. "About mom?"

"Daddy, would read me a story? Like ya usta do? *Brer Rabbit?*"

Tony found the Uncle Remus book where he had left it on the boy's shelf weeks before.

Later, about eight o'clock, he sat on Angela's bed. "Honey, I know that you've got lots of questions. Can your daddy help you figure them out? I've wanted to talk with you . . . but . . . I haven't known what to say."

"You miss her lots, don't you, daddy? I do too. Maybe more than you think a little girl can. I know she's an angel and all that stuff. But . . . I still don't know why God would do that to us."

Tony anticipated the question that had no answer. He took Angela's hands in his. "What do you think? If someone asked you that question, what would you tell them?"

Angela turned from her father's gaze. Shaking her head she began to sniffle. "I don't know. I can't know . . . can I? Did you ask me that because you don't know either?"

"Yes I did, Angela. You took the words from my mouth. We can't know, can we? We will never know."

"Oh yes we will, daddy." Angela perked up, looked him straight in the face. "She will tell us herself. Won't she? When we're all together again, she'll tell us."

Tony could not help his smile at his daughter's innocent wisdom. "Yes, she will. I think you've got things pretty well figured out all by yourself. Good night, my punkin head."

"I missed you calling me that, daddy. G'night."

With Rudy it was different. Tony's brother was a young man of twenty. Like all the Zoreteks, the lad was tall, broad-shouldered, ruggedly handsome. After talking about his job and his Americanization classes, Rudy said, "You can't take all the grief upon yourself, Tony. There's enough to go around. Mary was like a mother to me just like she was to her own kids. I loved her . . . more than I can say, but I love you, too. Can I tell you something, brother?"

Tony didn't reply. He only stared at the mature young man sitting across from him. It was like seeing himself years before.

"It's about time you picked yourself up from the floor. Lots of people need you." Rudy's words carried all his emotion of the moment. "It's good to have you back."

About ten o'clock the phone rang. It was Molly Trembart Pell. "Tony, my dear man, how have you been?" A silence crossed the line. Molly added, "I saw you this afternoon, as you were leaving the cafe with Mr. Udahl. Gosh, it's been weeks since the funeral. I just had to call."

Tony did not know how to respond. His friend Tommy had been buried in July and his feelings about Molly were still confused. She had sent a huge bouquet of flowers to the house after Mary's death, attended the funeral, and called his house on several occasions since. "I guess I'm about ready to get on with my life, Molly. I've been at the bottom far too long."

"We've both been grieving, haven't we, Tony? Losing our spouses so tragically . . . gosh, it's so hard to cope with, isn't it? I know Tommy and me were having some difficulties but if he hadn't . . ." Molly let the thought drop. "You know I loved him, don't you, Tony. Not like it was with you and Mary, but in our own way."

Tony pictured the falsely contrite widow on the other end of the phone. Molly was a beautiful woman, bright and educated. Mary had known her much better than he did. And Mary was always her friend—understanding and forgiving. Tony, however, knew how much Tommy loved her. How deeply his friend suffered through her rejection! Before leaving Hibbing, Tommy confided to Tony, "I've gotta get out of this town—get away from her and that damnable family. They ruined everything for us. They always poisoned Molly with their hatred of me." Tommy could show his emotions with Tony. The two of them had been the best of friends and roommates for years. He was near tears on that afternoon, "I ain't no big patriot, Tony. I love my country and all that, but the Marines—that's just a ticket out of this town. Maybe if I'm a hero or somethin' like that; then maybe the Trembarts will have some respect." Tommy was totally distraught, "But I love that woman. Always will, I guess."

Tony swallowed the memory. "What do you mean, 'in your own way'?

There's only one way to love someone, Molly." He held back what he wanted to say. He wanted to call her selfish, cruel, misguided.

"It's just different with everybody, I think." Molly sensed Tony's discomfort with her comparison and decided to try and lighten their conversation. "I'm so glad to see that you're getting out and about again, Tony. It's hard, believe me I know that for a fact, but we find our way. I've always admired your strength . . . you'll make it, I know you will. Everybody's pulling for you." Her words sounded awkward and trite. "If you need someone to talk with, well . . . you know, I'm here for you."

When he hung up his phone, Tony felt strangely violated by Molly's invitation. Her innuendo only provoked bothersome thoughts. What kinds of solicitations would he have to deal with in the years to come? Could he ever love again? Did he want to? These thoughts had no place in his life of the moment. Living tomorrow and the next day were all that mattered.

'DON'T PUSH THE RIVER...'

June 1920

The dramatic changes destined for Hibbing's landscape were in their second year. The downtown commercial area was becoming a skeleton of its former self. The world war had ended in an armistice, but the demand for iron ore remained insatiable as America continued its unparalleled prosperity. As many had predicted, the city was destined to relocate. Hibbing sat upon millions of tons of rich hematite ore, and economics dictated the inevitable—the mining companies would claim their bounty! The Oliver Mining Company, a subsidiary of United States Steel Corporation, owned more than eighty city blocks. The land and mineral rights had been purchased thirty years before at a cost in excess of three million dollars. The 'North Forty,' as it was called, composed the heart of what had developed into downtown Hibbing—from densely built Pine Street south beyond the railroad yards. Gaping open pits encroached the city on three sides. The continual blasting required by mining ventures presented an increasingly grave danger to citizens in the community. A plan for moving the city and its nearly twenty thousand people had been on the Oliver's drawing boards for several years. It was no longer advisable to delay the inevitable.

The first building was moved from its northern location in September of 1918. From that time and for many years to come, Hibbing became what one observer called, "A City on Wheels." Wood-framed structures of every size were lifted with jacks and anchored to cribbing of large timbers. Huge wheels were attached below the weight, and the entire assembly attached to Cleveland steam-crawler tractors to be carefully tugged to their new location. Sometimes four or five buildings at a time could be seen along the mile-long Third Avenue corridor south toward Alice location. The moving process was difficult, but for the most part, a smoothly coordinated operation.

Meanwhile, the Oliver was preparing a new business district a mile south of the existing city on land well removed from mining activity. The new Howard Street was already six blocks long. Attractive new stores were being built along paved, well-lighted streets. As a gift to the *new* city, the mining giant was building three major edifices: a new city hall patterned after the *Cradle of Liberty* historic Faneuil Hall in Boston, the nearly two hundred room Androy Hotel, and a fabulous new high school. The Hibbing High School would be like no other in all of America. Its dimensions were awesome; its construction and design a marvel to behold. A mining official claimed the building was "a testimony to the importance of education in the new community." Other vital services were also under development. A new public utilities building was nearly completed.

Two hundred forty acres of Alice land had been held in the Peter Moran estate. Senia Arola, the vice-president of the Merchants and Miners Bank and the executor of that valuable property, proved to be a most competent negotiator in her dealings with the Oliver and others seeking to purchase parcels of the land. "How ironic!" Senia confided to Harvey Goldberg as she signed the final papers on the sale of a large tract of property along the Howard Street corridor. "The magnificent Androy Hotel is being built on Peter's property. He must be rolling in his grave."

"The hotel and half of the city, Senia. I'm told that Elwood Trembart is seething over that reality. Old Pete knew what he was doing back then. What was it—fifteen years ago already?"

Her memories of Peter were with her every day. A photograph of the two of them together at one of Moran's garden parties was her most treasured possession. "Eleven years in August, Harvey." Senia could have given the time in days. On Wednesday of every month, regardless of weather, Senia brought flowers to the Moran grave site. "Elwood will never forget that Peter bought that land from under his nose. Sometimes I think that old hatred keeps the man going. It's a big part of the reason he hates Vic Power."

With her signature on the papers, the trust fund for Peter's son, Kevin Schmitz, would grow by more than two million dollars. When the boy was eighteen, Senia would have her meeting with Kevin. She was counting the years, the months, and the days. Kevin was born on February 13, 1907. In less than five years the young man and Senia would begin a most interesting relationship.

Ever popular, Victor Power was in his eighth consecutive one-year term as mayor. His leadership during these difficult days was of critical importance. Often extravagant in his building and improvement programs, he continued to have problems with the mining companies and citizens over his taxing proposals. His agenda was an expensive one, and everyone paid the price. He was becoming as well known in St. Paul for his battles in the state legislature as he was on the Iron Range. The colorful 'Little Giant,' as he was often called, had already built a national reputation in the mining hub of America. After the war, returning veterans were promised a bonus for their service to country. Power himself paid the first installment out of his own pocket so that the men would have spending money for their Christmas shopping. The story made the front pages of newspapers from New York to San Francisco.

Power had been among the first to relocate his legal business to the new city to the south. On this gray, June afternoon, Victor Power was chatting with Claude Atkinson in the editor's office of the new *Mesaba Ore* building on First Avenue, south of expanding Howard Street. "You've got a swell-looking place here, Claude. All new printing presses humming back there; I love the smell of the ink when you walk in the side door," the mayor commented as he reclined in a leather chair.

"I've put myself in debt so deep they're gonna bury me right here before I'm paid up. Wouldn't have it any other way though," the newsman smiled. "It's like I'm starting life all over again in this new building. Maybe I'll do a better job with my reporting from down here." Down here was a reference to the southern location of the relocating city.

"The paper's going to look pretty fancy with the new formatting Andy Zdon's doing in the shop. We're going to have a sports' page and even run a daily comic strip. Our new city's getting a forward-looking newspaper out of all this—as fancy as anything in the state."

Victor smiled his agreement. "When we're done, Claude, this is going to be one fine looking city. Hibbing's going to be as fancy—as you so aptly put it—as any town in Minnesota." From the back window of Claude's building the new Rood Hospital construction was visible. "This town's going to have it all. That's if the damn politicians in St. Paul don't pass that new tax law." The mayor's thoughts were always consumed by politics.

"Victor, you're going to lose that battle. The legislature is going to set a new taxing system for the mining companies, no matter how hard you fight against it. And, they're going to tie your hands with property tax levy limits as well." The editor looked his friend in the eyes. "Aren't you getting tired of all this, Vic? Running down to the state capitol every week, endless testimony before committees, wheeling and dealing . . . you're going to wear yourself out before you're fifty."

"You think I've got fifty years in me, Claude?" The small man plopped in a chair, loosened his tie, and lit a cigar. "Fifty! That gives me ten more years of this 'wheeling and dealing' as you call it. Let me assure you, my old friend, I'd be damn happy with that."

The two men enjoyed their almost daily banter about the people and the daily life in the city they both loved. Changing from the topic of politics, Victor exhaled a puff of cigar smoke, "Percy's all worked-up about moving the house. Worried is probably a better way to put it. Like everybody in town, she saw the Colonia disaster last week." He laughed at the widely discussed misfortune. En route to a new site in South Hibbing, the wood-framed Colonia Hotel had slipped from its rigging and collapsed onto First Avenue. Such accidents were uncommon, but when one did happen, public concern was heightened.

"I wrote an article on that just this morning," Claude recounted. "I told the folks there would be tons of fire wood out there for winter burning. So there's always some good with the bad."

Victor picked up a copy of yesterday's paper from the desk, rifled to the fifth page—across from the popular society column—and found the advertisement he was looking for. "I promised Percy I'd take her to the movie tonight. *Evangeline* is playing at the Princess Theater." The William Fox film starring Miss Miriam Cooper was getting rave reviews. Longfellow's immortal love epic was one of his wife's favorites. "Why don't you and the missus join us?"

"I'm going to have to decline the invitation, Vic. I'm going to be here late again tonight. Don't tell Percy you invited us to join you . . . if that got back to my wife I'd be in hot water."

~

Kevin Schmitz sat at the desk in his bedroom with his diary open in front of him. The thirteen year old was tormented. Angry. He scrawled the date—June 16—across the top of the white page. He would let his feelings flow from troubled thoughts to penciled words. He began his entry with five capitalized words centered on the top of the page, then underlined them boldly:

TODAY IS A BLACK DAY!

On the floor by his feet lay a scrunched copy of the *Duluth News Tribune*. Kevin read the newspaper every day. Starting with the sports page and working backward to the front page. Mr. Barker, a social studies teacher at Denfeld High School, lived down the block. Kevin knew that Barker encouraged all his students keep up with the daily news. It was a part of his Civics class discussions every morning. Kevin would be in his class next year and he would be prepared in advance.

Something terrible had happened the night before. The headline story was accompanied by a large photograph of a ring of men several deep looking toward the camera, as if they were posing proudly. Kevin counted twenty-three faces that could be clearly identified in the horrible picture. He'd counted the faces several times. The sixth face was that of his father. Art Schmitz was looking at the ghastly sight while two other men were leaning forward at the photographer. One of the two was Mr. Meyers, who worked at the ship yards with Art.

Kevin's next line began to express his torment.

My father

He drew a slash line through the two words, 'My father' and wrote Art Schmitz above it.

is a murderer. One of thousands of murderers in this hateful city. I have never been so ashamed as I am now. How can anything so terrible happen? I feel as if on this day I can no longer be a son to this bigoted man. Diary, in all these pages I have not yet discovered who I am.

Kevin had kept a diary for the past two years. He did not write in the book every day, but never missed at least one day each week. His messages were very personal. Troubling. He raised questions that only Gary Zench knew about. Questions about his parents and their behavior. Often his questions expressed inner doubts and fears. At thirteen he was both perceptive and precocious: perceptive beyond his years! His belligerence of youth had long since passed and his attitude noticeably mellowed. Kevin had discovered a spirituality in himself that was both fulfilling and troubling at the same time. At times he thought of the priesthood as an escape into religion and out of the kind of life he had witnessed in his parents and those of his friends. But he wasn't always a good boy. His bouts of anger made him think he had something of the devil inside him. His diary was a chronicle of contradictions he found in himself.

Kevin wrote further.

How can I ever forgive what he has done? God, help me find some way to deal with this. And, God, keep me always from prejudice.

On the bottom of the page he concluded the entry. He could not allow his pen to elaborate the gruesome details in his book. Just as he had started with five words, he concluded with five words.

A lynching happened last night.

The *Duluth News Tribune* story reported and pictured the incident in graphic detail. A West Duluth woman alleged that she had been raped by six workers from a traveling circus that was in town for the week. The "carnival roustabouts," she claimed, were black. The nineteen year-old girl was white. Outrage swept through the city like a fire out of control. Fueled by latent racial hatreds, rumors of the incident became wildly exaggerated as they spread. Towards nightfall, a mob of nearly ten thousand people—women and children among them—assembled outside the city jail. Spurred by their animosity, a group of men armed with clubs and hammers stormed the jail, easily overwhelming the small cadre of police officers. Racing up to the second floor, they found the cell with the black inmates. Smashing down the wall, they dragged three of the protesting men down the stairs and into the street while the crowd madly cheered. The circus workers, stripped of their shirts and bound, were beaten and choked as the mob leaders dragged them across Superior Street and up the hill to the corner of Second Avenue East and First Street.

A hasty mock trial before the throng of cheering spectators was more like a sporting event than a search for any justice. The men, Elias Clayton, Isaac McGhie, and Elmer Jackson professed their innocence to no avail. One by one the mob strung them up, hanging them from a light post at the street corner.

There were voices of reason in the crowd. But their protests against the mob rule were overwhelmed by the mass hysteria. The *Tribune* article mentioned Father Patrick Foley's passionate appeal to allow the accused to stand trial in a court of law. The priest's attempt to administer last rites, however, was thwarted by a solid ring of demonstrators who blocked any effort to interfere with the lynching. Veteran Sergeant Oscar Olson was cited for his valorous efforts to save the prisoners from their inevitable fate.

The front page photo of the shameful episode showed three bound and bruised black bodies hanging from the ropes around their necks. Many of those posing for the picture were well-dressed men. Most were smiling over their sense of righteous vindication.

When he returned from work that Wednesday evening, Art Schmitz was visibly distraught. "Sarah, where is the paper? I've got to have the paper!"

"I left it on the couch like always, dear."

"It's not there!"

"Kevin's probably got it then. He's upstairs in his room."

Art panicked. His face was conspicuous in the horrible photo. He'd seen a copy on the Grand Avenue street car while traveling home from work. Everybody was talking about last night's hanging in downtown Duluth. "God, what am I going to do? Kevin will see the picture . . . !"

"What was that, Art? You're mumbling." Sarah asked from the kitchen. "Where were you last night?" As was often the case in their communication, she was not really seeking an answer. Sarah had no idea where her husband had been the night before; if he wanted her to know, he would tell her. Art's Tuesdays were often spent bowling and playing billiards down the street on Central Avenue. She'd gone to bed early and hadn't heard him come in. "Holler up to Kevin. He'll return your newspaper. He's already had an hour to read his sports page."

Art had learned about the girl's rape while at work the previous day. One of his associates, a warehouse clerk named Harold Greene, cursed. "Damned niggers! We gotta do somethin', guys. I'm goin' downtown tonight. Everybody's goin'. We'll show them no-good bastards they ain't gonna get away with rapin' our women. Art, you comin' with me?"

Most of the time Art was a weak man, a follower always seeking approval from his fellows. He was torn inside about joining Harry. He knew there would be trouble. Harry was a hothead and a bigot. He despised Blacks and Jews and immigrants alike. "Nah, I've got too much to get done at home, Harry." Art declined meekly.

"You ain't got the guts to give them circus scum a taste of Duluth medicine? Ya gotta stand up, Art. We don't do somethin' about it . . . then our town's gonna get overrun by those no-goods. Pretty soon they'll have all the jobs. The steel plant's already smellin' like somethin' outta the Deep South with all those niggers. They work for almost nothin' as it is."

"Ya . . . I'm as concerned about that as the next guy, I guess. But you don't need me, Harry. There'll be lots of folks down there making speeches and all that."

"Speeches? Hell, man. We're gonna do a damn lot more than wag our tongues. I'll pick ya up about seven. I'll get a few more guys to join us."

Art didn't want to be at this scene. He was scared by the vehemence swirling in the air. His stomach was churning. The word *lynching* was being bantered about. What if those circus boys didn't do it? Confusion throbbed in his head. Harold Greene, however, was screaming his hate at the top of his lungs and making Art feel increasingly uncomfortable. Art cowered behind him, trying to disassociate himself from his hulking coworker near the center of protest. When he spotted Father Foley in the massive crowd, he pulled his hat brim down over his eyes and turned away, hoping to avoid the priest's eyes. Foley was trying to calm the storm of angry tirades raging around him, but to no apparent avail. Art wanted to join the priest and be associated with some voices of reason.

At about eight-thirty the crowd began smashing the police station windows with a hail of rocks and bricks. The Mayor was out of town for meetings and Police Chief Murphy was in Virginia. Only courageous Sergeant Olson and a thin core of fifteen officers were left to defend the inmates. Inside the station, Duluth Commissioner Bill Murnian told the officers not to shoot any demonstrator. "I do not want to see the blood of one white person spilled for any blacks," the official told a reporter. The mob learned about Murnian's order and were emboldened by the power they now held. Near nine o'clock, a group of younger men, many of them unemployed war veterans and shipyard workers, stormed the building. As the main Superior Street door was penetrated, hundreds of men armed with hammers and crowbars broke into the south entrance on Michigan Street.

Within minutes the jail house was overwhelmed, the grilled cell doors broken down, and the black men were being dragged out of the building. Art moved with the crowd across Superior Street and up the hill still watching for Foley. There was a frenzied energy in the air that seemed to consume him along with everybody else. Art got caught up in the moment, found himself yelling along with hundreds of others: "Hang 'em!" He hated himself for the words that came out of his mouth, but he shouted again. A tall man next to him gave Art a heavy slap on the back, his eyes ablaze with excitement. "Hang 'em! Hang the niggers! We're gonna have us a real necktie party, fella. Gonna string'em up." His mouth was twisted and drooling in anticipation.

When the lynchings began, Art found himself in the second row of the mob circling about the lamp post. He looked for Harold Greene in the swollen crowd. As he gazed over the head of two men in front of him, a camera flashed in his eyes. He couldn't find Harold anywhere, and the mob was beginning to drift away from the three dangling men. Always searching for Foley's face, Art made his way back toward the jail where Harold had parked his car. It was late when the men made their way through the crowded streets still milling with people, and returned to their quiet West Duluth neighborhood. After he was dropped off, Art Schmitz tried to pray. His night on the sofa was sleepless.

"I'll get the paper later, Sarah. Gonna go out in the yard for a while before supper." He slipped out the back door, sat on the stoop, his small hands covering his face in self-disgust. Tears welled in his eyes. "What have I done? How can I ever explain this to Kevin? To Sarah? It's all so terrible . . . I was there. God help me . . . forgive me." He tried to pray but he was too consumed with his guilt. What if they didn't do it?" Art mumbled over the raspy sobs escaping from his throat. "Oh, God . . . I'm so sorry." His heart ached over his tragic mistake.

When he returned inside, the wrinkled newspaper was on his living room chair. At supper nothing was said about the lynching in downtown Duluth the night before. Art asked Kevin about the standings in the major baseball leagues. Kevin did not reply.

In the weeks following, the incident was never spoken of in the Schmitz household. Kevin became noticeably withdrawn. Art spent more evenings at the bowling alley down on Central Avenue. Sarah never saw the newspaper photograph. Father Foley was transferred to the Sacred Heart Cathedral in downtown Duluth, and his new assignment kept him too busy to visit with the Schmitzes as often as in the past. Even the priest tried to put the episode behind him, praying for the souls of those who incited the hanging as well as for the black victims. Foley, although praised for his efforts, carried a guilt of his own. His protest had been too feeble to make any difference.

Governor Burnquist sent in the state militia the day following the mob lynching, and things gradually quieted down. The killings became national news for a short time, but 1920 was a national election year and politics pushed the story from the news. Several men were arrested for their role in the tragedy. None went to prison!

In the ensuing days and weeks, it became apparent that the girl's story was a fabrication. Doctor's reports and interviews unraveled the truth. Three innocent men had been hanged in Duluth on that twentieth night of June, 1920.

Claude Atkinson followed the Duluth story carefully. The editor was disgusted when the news broke, infuriated as the truth became evident. His outrage was apparent in every story he printed about the murderous episode. With the Fourth of July only days away, Claude voiced his sentiments for the last time.

> *On Sunday our community, along with our great nation, will celebrate the anniversary of its cherished independence. Indeed, all Americans may look with pride upon our many freedoms, our liberties, our brotherhood of diverse people. We are truly a people blessed by a bountiful God. With parades and picnics and gala festivities of many sorts, we will glorify our 'stars and stripes' throughout this weekend. And, rightfully so.*
>
> *Less than a year ago the Great War concluded. With our clearly established leadership in the world, we have an opportunity to ensure that world peace will be everlasting. People everywhere will look toward America as the beacon of hope. No other country has a greater responsibility nor a greater opportunity to ensure a righteous world than we do. Let us celebrate being Americans on this great holiday as never before.*
>
> *But let us remember, too. Let us remember the lives sacrificed in our worthy endeavor to rid the world of German tyranny. Let us remember those patriots who fought for independence so that we may be free of tyranny ourselves. Let us remember all those nationalities and races that have toiled to ensure our greatness. Let us remember*

how far we have come in our short history. Let us remember how far we have yet to go before we earn the self-respect required to be the great society we have yet to achieve.

We have failed mightily in providing a spirit of unity amongst our peoples. We have failed to respect the right of all our citizens-workers, women, and minorities-to enjoy the fruits of our Constitution. We have failed to learn the lessons of a war that tragically divided one America into two countries. We have failed our fellow Americans. Evidence of these failures slapped our faces with that sad reality only weeks ago. An unruly mob of haters blemished the conscience of America only sixty miles from our doorsteps here in Hibbing.

So, I hope you will excuse me from all the Independence Day festivity. I'm going to my Lutheran church for Sunday morning's service. Later I'm going to a Catholic church to light three candles. Then I'm going to visit the Jewish synagogue for the first time in my life. At each stop I will say a prayer for my country and I will thank God for blessing me with the freedom to share these words with you. And, I will say a prayer for the souls of Elias Clayton, Isaac McGhie, and Elmer Jackson.

God bless America!

As he finished his commentary, Claude closed his eyes. What he had written was sure to incite controversy in his community. But he'd done that often enough before. If one person looked at this country through different eyes because of his few words, then the world would be a better place than it was on this day. *"God bless America,"* he repeated the three deeply felt words to himself.

Throughout the happy years of his marriage to Mary Bellani Samora, Tony had made many lasting friendships within Hibbing's Italian community. On this Independence Day he and the children, along with Sadie Baratto, would watch the parade wind down Third Avenue before spending the afternoon at the annual Italian picnic in Mesaba Park. Later that evening they would watch the fireworks at the fair grounds.

The late morning sun was rising above the buildings which lined the avenue. Already the temperature was approaching ninety, and their palace in the shade would not last much longer. It had rained the day before and the humidity added its discomfort to the heat. Nine year old Angela sat on the curb watching the Hibbing band as it marched smartly down the street in colorful blue woolen uniforms. The band was playing a stirring rendition of Sousa's 'Stars and Stripes Forever' for the appreciative throng lining the walkway. Hats were respectfully removed as the flag passed ahead of the strutting majorettes. Following the band's procession was the ever ebullient mayor and his lovely wife Percy, waving from the shiny Buick convertible as they passed. Vic Power knew almost every face in Hibbing. "Tony, Angela, Marco . . ." he shouted above the din of the spirited music. "God Bless America!" Victor had shed his suit coat, loosened his tie, and was perspiring in the sweltering heat. Mrs. Power, as always, looked perfectly cool and composed.

As her father and brother waved back with enthusiasm, Angela only smiled weakly. It wasn't the mayor or the band that caused her funk—she was simply bored. And, troubled. The pretty, brown-eyed girl would have preferred staying home and reading her Louisa May Alcott book, or sewing her quilt on mother's Singer machine that morning. Nothing much excited her on these long summer days.

Angela Zoretek missed her mother more than she would ever talk about. It had been nearly two years since her death, but the emptiness was as real now as it had ever been. Framed on her bed stand was a photograph of her mother, behind it a vase with yellow daylilies from the garden Mary enjoyed during the short summer months. In her closet hung dresses her mother had made, dresses she often wore in the privacy of her room. In her treasured seclusion, she often had quiet conversations with her mother. Last night her mother told her not to worry. In her mind was her mother's voice, telling her things no one else could know about. This communication was another of Angela's many secrets.

Her dad had invited Molly Pell to a small outdoor party at their house the night before. Or, Molly had invited herself. (Angela wasn't quite sure. Molly called the house too often to suit Angela.) Mr. Jaksa was there with a lady friend and Mr. Udahl with his new wife, Tessie. Some other people who worked with her father were present also. She couldn't remember their names. The adults were having a good time—laughing and joking and carrying on until late. Watching from her upstairs window, she saw her father drinking a beer and was disturbed. Her dad never drank beer! She also saw her father talking to Mrs. Pell. She wished she could hear their conversation and strained to eavesdrop to no avail. Whatever Molly might have said made Angela furious. Molly Pell made her father frown and pace. When daddy paced, he was upset. Angela did not like that woman!

But her mother told her not to worry . . .

After the parade they all walked to Mesaba Park, only two blocks from where they watched the parade. At the Italian picnic they were greeted by the Depelos and Anselmos. To Angela, they were almost like relatives. Lucia Depelo had traveled from Italy to America with her mother many years ago. How often Lucia had told her that story. And 'Grampa' Luigi Anselmo, owner of a local tailor shop, was the man her mother worked for after coming to Hibbing. Luigi had wonderful stories about her mother and what a beautiful seamstress she was. Armando Depelo, Lucia's son, and Rudy were best of friends. They were easily the most handsome men at the picnic, and all the girls competed for their attention. Angela hated how girls were always flirting with her brother. (Actually, Rudy was her uncle; but, she could never think of him that way.) And, Armando! If Angela only were a few years older . . .

"Tony Zoretelli!" John Depelo called out as he approached the big food tent on the picnic grounds. Tony's Italian friend had given him an appropriate 'dago' surname years before. "John Depelovich, my Slovenian friend, how are you this beautiful afternoon?" Tony stepped toward the willowy man, embracing him warmly. "It's so good to see my *kum* again." Their tease was a traditional greeting at the ethnic event. The word *kum* was Slovenian for friend, and John always appreciated the reference.

"Luigi, find a cold bottle of milk for Tony," John said, knowing Tony did not drink alcohol.

"Make that a beer, Luigi. It's the Fourth, and I'm celebrating with my friends," Tony said.

Both John and Luigi were surprised but said nothing.

After the Italian reggiano, fettucine, and raviolis along with sweet breads and amaretto cream candies, the men wandered to an open space to place some bocce ball. The women cleaned up and visited while the children played tag, ran races, and filled themselves with ice cream. The afternoon festivities were great fun for everybody. Angela, however, stayed close to the apron strings of Lucia Depelo and had a thousand questions for her. "What was it like in my mother's village in Italy? What was Gramma Justina (Mary's mother) like? Was she as beautiful as mommy told me? Why did mommy come to Hibbing?" Understanding the girl's curiosity, Alicia told her stories of the village of Piedimonte in the Campania of Italy where both girls had grown up. "Yes, your gramma was a lovely woman. Everybody said your mother looked very much like Gramma Justina Bellani." And, why she and Mary came to Minnesota was a familiar story that Angela never tired of hearing.

"What was my mom's favorite food?" Angela's question spurred another round of inquiry. When she returned home, Angela would add all the information to her secret notebook which was brimming with stories, anecdotes and feelings she had about her mother. Along with Mary's dresses, and the framed picture on her bed stand, the small tablet was her most precious treasure.

After saying their good-byes in the early evening, the Zoreteks returned home before traveling to the fairgrounds for the fireworks. Earlier in the day, Tony had invited Becca Kaner to join them. Becca had worked that day at the hospital and was unable to enjoy any of the holiday festivities. Becca had brought over some Jewish *Kichlach* and *Baklava* for the children the day before and found Tony preparing for his small patio party. "Just some friends from work," he had told her about the evening event.

Tony parked his Oldsmobile to the west of the grandstands where they had a clear view of the starry night sky. Sadie had stayed at the house to catch up on ironing and Rudy was with his friends, so Angela and Marco had the back seat to themselves. By ten o'clock, after twenty minutes of sky-lighting explosions, the children had fallen asleep.

"The kids loved the treats you brought over yesterday, Becca. So did I, especially the honey pastry." Tony was nervous in the presence of his lovely neighbor. And he was feeling guilty about the night before. Did she wonder why he hadn't invited her to his party? Did she know that Molly Pell was there?

"Becca, I . . ." The words stuck in his dry throat. He looked from the sky to her face framed in the glow of a nearby lamp post. Becca had the same dark hair and eyes as Mary. For a brief moment he made a comparison—then swallowed a pang of guilt. What had he started to say?

Becca saved him from the discomfort. "I'm glad you liked the *baklava*. It's one of the few things I learned from my mom. I think it's Greek. Mom wasn't the best cook in the world, but neither am I. It was fun to spend a rainy afternoon baking in the kitchen." She put her head back over the seat and gazed into the sky. "How was your party, Tony?"

"I wanted to tell you about that." Tony glanced into the back seat, saw his children asleep, covered them with a blanket he'd brought along. "Awkward." He wondered where that word had come from. "I mean . . . it was a good enough time . . . but—" He looked at her profile as she reclined in the leather seat. Her nose was straight, mouth full, chin sharply defined. "But I felt out of sorts, I guess." He would begin his confession. "I did something I'm not very proud of, Becca. I invited Molly Pell to come over and join us. My guests were all couples and I . . . well, I asked Molly . . ."

Becca turned toward him, saw a trace of torment in his deep-set eyes. "Molly's a good friend of mine, Tony. I think she'd be a fun date for something like you had planned. Molly's quite social and she's so very pretty." Becca smiled. She had thought that maybe Molly and Tony might get together at some point. Both had lost their spouses, both were bright and attractive, and both were Christians. "What do you mean by 'out of sorts'? Didn't you have a good time?"

"No. I honestly didn't, Becca. I really don't have any . . . what should I say . . . 'romantic interest' in Molly. She's called me so often—invitations to a party or a movie or a play. I've always declined with some sort of flimsy excuse. Then she didn't call anymore. For almost two months. I can't understand why I missed her calling. Maybe I felt I wasn't interesting to her any more. So I had a vanity issue of some kind. Stupid, I know, but that's the truth of it." Tony ran his fingers through his long hair. "I called her the other night. Just to say hello, and . . . anyhow, after I asked her to the party, I almost wished I hadn't. It was the strangest feeling. To ask a lady out to a party and then, a minute later, wish you hadn't?"

"I think I can understand. Is it Mary, Tony? Feeling that you somehow betrayed your love for her?" Becca knew how deeply Tony had been in love and how deeply he must still miss her. "One day you will be able to love again." She bit at the side of her mouth. Becca was walking on thin ice whenever she brought up Mary. "Some day, Tony. Just remember, *'Don't push the river . . . it flows by itself.'* The expression was Eastern and a favorite of Becca's. "Just let things happen as they might."

"It wasn't Mary. I think I've been through the valley with all those feelings. I hope so, anyhow. No, it wasn't Mary's memory that made me feel out of sorts. I didn't really want to be with Molly last night. I think I explained that to her in some awkward manner. I told Molly that I wasn't comfortable being with her. She said she understood, but I could tell she wasn't being honest with me. 'Call me again . . . when you feel ready' she told me. And I said I would do that."

Becca put her hand on Tony's. "Don't always be so hard on yourself. Sometimes I think that you're just too honest for your own good."

He smiled, taking her hand into his, gently squeezing. "Maybe you're right. I like your expression, *'Don't push the river . . .'* I haven't heard that before."

Tony had not been totally honest that evening with Becca. He did not tell her that his being 'out of sorts' was because he had asked the wrong woman to his party. He had feelings for Becca that he could neither understand nor communicate. He would let his river flow by itself.

In the back seat, Angela heard every word of their conversation from under the blanket. She would add the information, and her feelings about it, to her tablet. Angela did not like Becca either. She realized that her teeth were gritted from the pain and confusion of her father's words.

A Date in Duluth

November 1923

At sixteen, Kevin Schmitz had added bulk to his six foot frame. The handsome young man turned the heads of most girls in the hallways of Denfeld High School. His broad shoulders, square jaw, and thick chest combined to give Kevin the appearance of a youthful Jack Dempsey. As a sophomore, the sturdy boy was the second string fullback in Denfeld's single-wing offense. On defense, Kevin started the last two games at line backer. But now it was basketball season. Throughout the summer months Kevin spent hours at the makeshift basket mounted on a phone pole in the alley behind his house. He and Huddy Tusken played 'horse' by the hour, practiced long-range set shots, and tested each other with rugged one-on-one competition. Huddy was sure to make the team as a starting guard and, with his size and agility, Kevin was hopeful of a forward position. When spring came, Kevin was certain he would be the school's number two pitcher. Kevin loved sports with a passion.

After two hours of calisthenics, wind sprints, and dribbling drills, Coach Charlie Monson blew his whistle. "Line up along the base line, men," he shouted at the twelve sweat-soaked boys doing lay-up drills under the basket. Kevin stood at the end of the line—only senior Benny Goeden was taller. He knew that Coach Monson was going to announce the starting five for Saturday's opening home game with rival Morgan Park at the Denfeld gym. Looking down the line at Huddy, he sucked in his breath and gave his buddy a wink.

"I know you guys have been waiting for this all week." Monson glanced at the clip board in his hand. "In two days we play the Wildcats and they're gonna be a tough test for us. I've been watching each of you during our scrimmages and taking notes on what you're doing well and what you still need to work on." The coach looked at each of the boys standing in rigid attention before him. "It's a long season and nobody better think they've got a position locked up. Do ya understand that? If you don't produce, you're gonna get bench time."

Monson's eyes focused on the sheet of paper on his clipboard. "When I call your name, I want you to hustle down to the other basket for free throws. The five names I read off will start on Saturday. Okay, now listen up ... Tusken ... Knox ... Udovich ... Strand ... and ... Schmitz. Now, the rest of you get to shower early. See ya tomorrow after school for our final scrimmage."

At the dinner table Kevin shared his exciting news. "I made the starting team!" His blue eyes sparkled.

Art was reading the paper as he forked a dripping piece of roast beef to his mouth. Spots of gravy appeared on the white linen table cloth. "Look what you made me do, son." Frowning, he regarded the stains. "Sorry, Sarah. Kevin disrupted my eating."

Sarah did not reply to her husband's apology.

"I was only kidding you, Kevin. I shouldn't be reading the paper at the table. I'm surprised your mother didn't say something about it before I spilled." He pushed away from the table to get a wet cloth for the stains. "I seem to have a lousy sense of humor these days. I'm sorry."

"May I be excused, please?" Art's apology was not what Kevin needed to hear, and his appetite had disappeared. "I'd like permission to call Uncle Tony, please. I'll pay from my allowance."

"Long distance will cost you a quarter, Kevin," Sarah informed the boy. "You must be careful about your spending. Quarters make dollars, you know."

"Go ahead, son," Art said as Kevin was leaving the kitchen. "And, congratulations on making the basketball team. We'll have to get to a game this season to see you play." The compliment and the promise were ill-timed.

Kevin needed the praise at the dinner table when his enthusiasm was still alive.

Kevin sat on the chair by the telephone table in the corner of the living room. 'Have to get to a game,' he mumbled his frustration. Kevin believed that Art could care less about his ball games. Art and Sarah (they were Art and Sarah—not Mom and Dad—in his thoughts these days) had been to one football game that fall. Only one. Uncle Tony and Aunty Senia had driven the sixty miles from Hibbing twice to see him play and taken him out to eat after the game. Tony was still his favorite person in the world. Senia was nice, but different. She always stared, always tousled his auburn hair. What was it about him that so interested his aunt? In his diary, Kevin had wondered through his carefully written words if she knew something about him that he didn't know himself. But, she was always kind and very generous. Every time they were together she slipped him a five dollar bill when no one could see. "Shhh," she would say as she put her finger across her lips. "Use this money wisely, Kevin."

The operator connected his call to number 104 in Hibbing. Sadie answered the phone and hailed Mr. Zoretek. "Uncle Tony! This is Kevin calling. I've got some great news for you." Kevin went on to explain his exciting achievement. The two of them talked for nearly ten minutes.

"Kev, I'm going to change my plans for Saturday night and get down to the Denfeld gym. I wouldn't miss your first varsity game for the world. I'm so proud of you. Rudy will be excited by the news, too. Maybe he'll come along with me. I'll tell your Aunt Senia about it as well. Maybe you'll have a whole rooting section from Hibbing to cheer you on."

When Kevin hung up, he felt the lump in his throat. In the old days, Aunt Mary would be with his uncle for the trip to Duluth. She would have lit up the gymnasium with her beauty. His friends would have asked him who the good-looking woman in the stands was.

Then Kevin remembered the funeral—over five years ago already. He remembered how badly it hurt him to see his uncle in tears. How he didn't know what to say. All he could do was give Uncle Tony a big hug and cry along with him. He had been to Hibbing three times in his life and two of them were for funerals. Mary's and . . . a man who was a friend of the family. He was only two at that time and could not remember much about that day. Kevin had asked Father Foley who that man was. And, he'd asked his father. Both had simply dismissed the question with . . . "Someone we all knew back then." Back then was probably 1909. His other trip to Hibbing was one of his favorite secret diary entries.

While his parents were still in the kitchen, Kevin decided to sneak a quick call to Gary Zench. The Zenches had a new telephone but Gary never used it to call Kevin's house. Watching the kitchen entry way, he asked the operator to connect the memorized number in hushed voice. Gary answered and the two of them talked for less than a minute. "I'll get over to Denfeld one way or another, Kev. Good luck on Saturday!"

Tony walked through lightly falling snow flakes across the street and down the block of his Brooklyn neighborhood. It was only seven, but the late fall darkness had settled in weeks before. Becca answered his knock on the door and welcomed him into the living room with a wide smile. "Well, what a pleasant surprise. What brings you out on this dreary night, Tony?" Then she frowned, "Not bad news, I hope. Unexpected evening visits always seem to bode of some misfortune."

"No, Becca, not at all. Good news as a matter of fact. My nephew, Kevin—I think I've told you about the boy—well, he's become an aspiring young athlete down in Duluth." Tony said as Becca took his wool jacket and hung it on the coat tree near the door.

"Many times, Tony. I know how much you love that boy. Don't tell me he scored a touchdown."

Tony laughed. "Not this season I'm afraid. He'll get his share next year, I'm sure. And football is over with already, so high school basketball is just getting started."

"Basketball I can understand, Tony. Football, I honestly haven't a clue about all that first down and seven yards to go stuff. It's all so confusing, with players knocking each other down all the time and kicking the ball up and down the field. It's a wonder that the hospitals don't sponsor the teams. I'd guess there are more broken bones in one football game than there are in the mines in two weeks."

Amused by Becca's insight, Tony offered, "I'll have to give you a little coaching some time. Football's a great game."

Becca brought in some leftover coffee. "I won't blame you if you don't drink it. It's my morning's brew and pretty powerful by now." She gave him a wide smile as she handed him the cup. "I am really surprised to see you. I said that already, didn't I?" She laughed at herself. "It's been ages, Tony. But I'm glad you came because I've got some news for you, too. But let's hear your news first." Becca sat on the other end of the sofa from Tony, placing her cup and saucer on the coffee table.

Over the past few years Tony had visited Becca's house only on rare occasion. Since the night of the fireworks, three years before, the two of them had seen little of each other. Aside from a New Year's party, a vaudeville show with the Udahls in May, and dinner once at his house when Marco was down with the mumps this past summer, the two of them had been neighbors more than anything else. There was small talk from the yard, brief 'How are you's?' when passing in the street or shopping at the grocery store, helping with the snow shoveling when a winter storm blew in. His remoteness puzzled even himself.

But Tony found himself in her living room tonight and felt strangely surprised by his spontaneous decision to make the visit. Before asking Rudy or Senia to join him for his trip to Duluth, he'd wanted to ask Becca. Perhaps they could spend the day, watch the ore boats come in at the harbor, have dinner, and just enjoy time away from Hibbing in a place where nobody knew them. He was lonely and in need of a woman's companionship. His few dates with Molly Pell were more like social engagements—lacking in any intimate or meaningful conversation.

"I was wondering if you've made any plans for Saturday—or even if you have the weekend off, I mean . . ." He felt terribly awkward, as if he were speaking with two tongues in his cotton dry mouth. "Are you free to have a date . . . ? Kevin has a basketball game in Duluth," he blurted.

Becca felt a discomfort of her own. This was so totally unexpected.

She had given up on Tony long ago. In her thinking, he was a 'one woman man'—for life! There were many times she wished he'd shown some interest in her. So many times! But, except for that Fourth of July night so long ago, that never happened. She had often wondered if she'd done something wrong and offended him that evening at the fairgrounds.

Becca had recently made a major decision in her life, and only Ambrose Hane knew about that decision. Becca was going to take a position at St. Mary's Hospital in Duluth. Her interviews two weeks before went well, and a position for her would be available on the first of next year, less than two months away. She was going to begin telling her patients about the move next week.

Becca swallowed hard against her emotion of the moment. She wanted to say yes, but felt troubled by the timing of Tony's invitation. What if something started between them? The something romantic she had so wanted years ago and had since given up on because of his apparent indifference. Her puzzlement was etched in her brow. She fidgeted with a doily on her coffee table and looked away from him, trying to focus on the glowing chandelier on the ceiling. She sighed and was about to say something, but the words were stuck in her throat.

Tony sensed discomfort in Becca's hesitation. "I know this is . . . this is really short notice for such a trip. I can understand your reluctance, Becca. Perhaps I should apologize for upsetting you."

"No, not at all, Tony. I am flattered by your invitation. It's just . . ."

Tony smiled. "I think I let too much time pass us by, Becca. It's not that I haven't thought about asking you to go out for dinner or . . . whatever. But, I just thought about it and didn't do anything about it. That's pretty obvious isn't it?" He met her eyes, "I'm sorry about that. These past few years I've been too self-absorbed for my own good. With work and the children and far too many evening meetings, I haven't been a very good friend to you or to more than a few others who deserve a lot more attention than they get from me. I haven't been a very good friend, Becca, and I'm sorry. And my excuses are just as lousy as my friendship."

Becca was aware that Tony had dated Molly Pell but was not inclined to say anything about it right now. Tony had asked her—not Molly—to see his nephew play a basketball game. She wanted to accept in the worst way. "Don't be so hard on yourself, Tony. Being an only parent to those beautiful children and running a business the size of your construction company is more than a handful. And those evening meetings are for the benefit of everyone who lives in Hibbing. You deserve to be commended for all you do."

"I know that, I suppose, but I spread myself so thin that I don't seem to do justice to any one thing . . . I just do an okay job on lots of things."

"You do far more than you give yourself credit for." Becca regarded Tony sitting with his elbows on his knees. He seemed to have found her own earlier attraction to the cut glass chandelier sending its soft glow into the pleasant room. On an impulse she would never quite understand, she reached across the space between them on the sofa and found his hand. "I'd love to go with you on Saturday."

At breakfast that Saturday morning, Tony sat next to Angela and across from Rudy. Marco was already outside playing with his friends in the back yard. "I've asked Doctor Kaner to join me for a trip to Duluth. Kevin's starting in his first basketball game." His comment met with silent stares. "I thought you were seeing Mrs. Pell, Tony." Rudy finally broke the cool spell that hung in the air. "She was one of my favorite teachers when I was in high school. I thought you liked her."

"And you think she's so pretty, too. Don't you, Rudy?" Angela blurted. "Well I don't."

"What do you know about anything, little girl?" Rudy shot back.

"Just a minute, you two." Tony intervened. "Mrs. Pell is a fine lady. I don't believe I brought her into this conversation. I simply told you both that I've asked Doctor Kaner out for the day. Please don't make any more of that than is necessary."

"I don't like your doctor friend either, Dad. You shouldn't be seeing other women, you know." Angela gave her father a sharp look. "Even if mommy thinks you should, I don't!"

Tony regarded his daughter. "What are you talking about, Angela? Where in the world did you get any notion of what your mother thinks?"

"She tells me things, that's all," Angela said in a defensive tone.

Tony was confused by her revelation and, putting down his coffee cup, he inquired further. "Will you kindly explain what this is about to your father?"

"I know what you're thinking. You think that mommy only talks to God and the angels in heaven. So you won't believe what I say anyhow."

"Give me a chance, sweetheart. I'll always listen to what you have to say. And, I don't think you would ever lie to your dad." He regarded his daughter as if she were no longer the child he had come to understand so well. Angela was maturing into adolescence and deserved to be treated with a sensitivity more appropriate to her age. He saw a blossom of Mary in the girl's delicate features. Tony expressed his concern with a different tone, "It's important to your father to be someone you trust with even the most confusing things. I need to be there for you."

Rudy stood up from the table. "Excuse me please. I've got things to do and this matter is none of my business. Uncle Steven asked me to work on our deer stand out by Timo's Lake. We're going hunting again on the weekend. Steven's already got his buck, so it's my turn."

Tony gave his brother a quick smile. "Thanks, Rudy. Have a good day—I'll talk to you later."

When Rudy left the kitchen, Sadie Baratto did the same. The housekeeper would clean up later. "I'll be doin' the laundry, Mr. Zoretek. If'n ya need me for anythin' just give a holler."

"Please talk to me, Angela. I know you are still confused and hurting about your mom. I am too. Even after all this time. But it's not right for either of us to imagine things. We can't talk to your mother any more. Not until we go to heaven to see her again. We've talked about her waiting for us many, many times."

"I know, daddy." Angela hung her head, staring at the table. "I can't help what goes on between me and mommy. It's not all the time . . . only in my room. I'm not imagining that, daddy. She speaks inside my head, not out loud so you could hear it."

Tony had no way of responding to Angela's alleged experiences. He could neither believe nor deny what seemed so real to his daughter. "Can we talk more about this later, honey? I'd like to learn more about what your mommy is telling you."

"I'll ask her about it, daddy."

Tony glanced toward the wall clock and realized he had better get ready for the trip to Duluth. The sixty miles would take nearly three hours and he wanted to enjoy some time at the harbor with Becca.

"There's something else we should talk about, daddy." Angela looked up with a puzzled expression. "Rudy told me once that Doctor Kaner was jewelish. Is that a good thing or not?"

Tony repressed a laugh, reached for Angela's hands, and squeezed them gently in his own. "Becca is Jewish, honey. That mean's she's not Catholic like we are. It's a different religion than ours, that's all."

"How is she different?" Angela searched her father's face and saw that his forehead wrinkled ever so slightly. When her dad did that, Angela knew he was bothered by something.

"I'll tell you what. I'm going to ask Doctor Kaner to talk with you about that. Would you like that?"

"No. I'd like you to tell me, daddy."

∼

Senia had gotten Tony's message on Friday morning. She was in a meeting at the bank when he'd called. The message said, "Kevin wanted me to tell you that he has his first basketball game on Saturday night at Denfeld. Please get back to me." Senia puzzled at first. They had gone to football games together earlier in the fall but this was not an invitation to join him for the trip to Duluth. She wondered if Tony was planning to go or not.

When she talked with Tony later, Senia was hurt. All Tony would say was that he had a date and wondered if she and Steven might want to drive down together and meet them at the gym. Senia's curiosity was piqued, but she chose not to pry. She told him that Steven would be too uncomfortable on such a long drive in her automobile. Senia had few friends and wondered if either Becca or Molly might want to go with her on Saturday, then thought better of the idea. It might not be safe to travel such a distance at night without a man in the car. "I'm afraid I won't be able to make it, Tony. Maybe another time. Will you give my apology to Kevin and give him five dollars from me after the game? I'll pay you back when I see you next."

That night Senia and Steven went out to dinner in a new restaurant on Howard Street in South Hibbing. Senia's mood was unusually somber, and Steven picked up on it immediately. "A long day, Senia?"

Senia tried a weak smile. "I guess so, Steven. I let myself get too wrapped up in the bank and it takes me a while to wind down. I'm sorry if

I'm a bit out of sorts. As seems to be the case most of the time, I look to you to perk me up, Steven." She held her cup of coffee across the table as if to propose a toast. She almost wished it were a glass of wine but Prohibition had made that impossible. As she thought of what to propose, she felt her mind go blank. What had she wanted to say? Her first thought, as always, something to do with Kevin. But a toast to the boy's making the basketball team would be foolish and inappropriate. She paused, considering something pleasant. "To our time together tonight."

Steven clinked his cup against hers. "Always my favorite time," he responded with his wide smile.

Over the past many years Steven had come to accept the reality of their relationship. Senia was never going to commit to another marriage. He'd watched quietly as she changed from the outgoing, conversant, and effervescent woman he knew from when they first met. He remembered their first date, and their kiss afterwards, as if it were yesterday. But that had been almost fifteen years ago. Both had become too involved in their lives apart from each other, Steven in his small investment business, local politics, and miner union activities. Senia was equally absorbed in her job at the bank, her temperance society meetings, and her many women's rights activities.

But there was another aspect of her life that seemed hidden from Steven's perception. Something that stole Senia away from him and the comfortable intimacy they once shared. Maybe it was her deceased husband, Timo, but he doubted that to be an issue. Maybe it was the complicated affairs of her former employer, Peter Moran. Managing his estate had proven to be time consuming, perhaps even stressful for her. And, maybe it was the boy in Duluth with whom she was so preoccupied. He'd only met Kevin twice in all these years but sensed Senia had some nebulous commitment to his affairs. Maybe he should ask her about it, and maybe it was best left alone until she needed to talk about it. He was more open about his life than was Senia. On many occasions he shared with her the delightful times he'd spent with his nephew, Rudy. Rudy had become the son he might never have. Was the same true with Senia and Kevin?

Senia looked over her reading glasses at Steven, who was regarding the menu. Such a wonderfully sensitive and considerate man he was. Not once in these many years had he ever pried into the realms of her privacy. Intelligent and insightful, Steven knew more about her than any other person. Even when she shut him out of her emotional turmoil, he remained devoted to her. He had always been her strength. Her love for him was a paradox she struggled with almost daily. She was ashamed of herself for her lack of trust and her guarded honesty.

"I sometimes wonder why you are always so good to me, Steven. All I seem to give in return for your kindness is small talk and companionship. I wish I could give you so much more."

Putting his menu aside, Steven met her bright blue eyes and placed his large hand upon hers. "You give me what you can, my dear. I know that. Yes, I'd like so much more and you know that, too. I'll enjoy what we have with patience and respect your need for your own life."

Steven gently rubbed the back of her silky smooth hands. "Some people are not meant to be married because the cost of a marriage is giving one's self completely. A huge price to pay." Steven's eyes had a far away look. "Some people get married and soon discover they have lost their self somewhere within the complexities of their union. When that happens, there can no longer be any real love. And, there are some people who cannot be whole without their partner. So, there are as many kinds of relationships as there are couples involved in them."

Senia considered his wisdom. "Tony and Mary had a complete love, didn't they Steven? They were not whole without the other. I always envied that. Do you think Tony can ever find happiness with another woman?" Her question would steer conversation away from their unusual relationship.

"Yes, I do. I pray for that every day. There will never be another Mary, of course, but there will be someone he can love." Steven smiled at something hidden behind her question. "Why do you ask, Senia?"

Senia told him of her conversation with Tony earlier that day. "He has a date for tomorrow, and I'm dying to know who that might be. Could he have met some lady in Duluth that we don't know about? If he were going out with Molly Pell, I'm sure he would have told me. So it must be someone else. I just couldn't bring myself to ask."

Steven had never thought Tony and Molly could have a meaningful relationship. Molly was too full of herself, too much the local social climbing type, and too superficial for his nephew. He'd always kept his feelings to himself, however. But there was a woman he respected highly and considered to be the kind of person who might make Tony happy. A woman that his miner friend Ollie Kochevar often talked about and treasured dearly. He would keep his notion to himself. "If Tony has an interest in someone, I'd have to believe that she is quite a lady. And, I agree, I don't think it is the widow Pell."

Tony had heard good things about *The Flame,* a restaurant near the Lake Superior shoreline where fresh lake trout was the house specialty. He suggested they eat there before heading out to Denfeld in West Duluth that evening.

Arriving in mid-afternoon, he and Becca spent a few hours wandering about the waterfront bundled up in warm clothing against the strong lake winds. Eventually they found a bench where they could sit and watch the ore carriers sail into and out of the busy harbor. Becca talked about the iron mining process that terminated with loading the huge ships bound for steel plants out East. "I'll bet you didn't know that your friend knew so much about the mines."

"And I'll bet you're going to tell me how that all came about." Tony responded with a quick grin.

Becca explained how she'd met her miner friend, Ollie, and about their many conversations about what he did in the Hull-Rust Mine. "I find it all so very fascinating. I guess if you live in Hibbing you'd better learn what drilling and blasting and steam shovels and track gangs are all about."

An occasional grain ship passed in front of their view as well as some smaller fishing boats. Across the lift bridge lay a long, sandy peninsula. "That's Park Point," Becca explained. "I've been to the beaches there many times." She laughed at a memory. "A group of us girls from St. Paul came up to Duluth after graduating from St. Thomas College. I think that was the first time I tasted beer. It was terrible. Oh, Tony, we were quite a bunch. If my parents ever knew about some of my escapades, they would have had a heart attack, especially my mother. But they thought I was 'Miss Perfect.' I always had the highest grades and that was what my mom and dad wanted most. So if my grades were good, then I must be good. At least that was my mother's logic. Somehow I don't think my dad was quite so naive."

"You must have been very close to your father," Tony observed.

"I was. He was so easy-going. And for a doctor, he was quite the liberal, I think. I remember when I was twenty . . ." She told Tony about her trip to Hibbing for the grand opening of the Hotel Moran. She didn't mention her fiancé, Mel Hartman. "You can imagine my surprise eight years later to find that majestic hotel gone. Do you remember the fire that destroyed it, Tony?"

Tony nodded, then shared his excitement as a novice carpenter working on the hotel's construction. "Everything about it was spectacular. Peter was that kind of guy. He wanted elegance and paid top dollar for all the imported woods, glass chandeliers, and exotic furnishings. It was truly an amazing place." He talked of the hotel but not of its owner. His relationship with Peter Moran was something he never quite understood.

While dining afterwards, the two of them talked about their families and different motivations for coming to Hibbing many years ago. And they talked about the dramatic changes they had seen in the past several years as their new city developed to the south of what many were already calling 'Old Hibbing.' Tony explained how the moving of the city had expanded his business, while Becca told about how much she enjoyed working in the new Rood Hospital. "We've both seen a lot of changes and, I'd guess, we'll see many more in the years to come."

At seven o'clock they entered the packed Denfeld gymnasium while the two teams were going through their warmup drills. "That's him, number twelve in the maroon jersey," Tony said with unabashed pride and excitement as they found places to sit in the bleachers. "My gosh, every time I see Kevin I think he's grown another inch."

"What a handsome young man," Becca said. "And, only a sophomore. He must be six feet tall already!"

The game started slowly with both teams unwilling to be too aggressive in moving the ball toward the basket. It was almost all defense and turnovers in the first three minutes. After the first quarter, Morgan Park held a

7-4 lead. Kevin had missed a set shot but had two rebounds. Then Denfeld went on a run. Tusken scored three baskets and Kevin made a lay-up, was fouled, and made the free throw. Kevin's three point play put Denfeld up by five points at half-time. 16-11.

Becca enjoyed the contest and asked Tony many questions. "Why did Kevin dribble the ball all the way down the floor when he caught the rebound right under the basket? He should have jumped up and put the ball in right there rather than run the other way. Don't you agree, Tony?"

Tony could not help but laugh at her observation. "That was the other team's basket, Becca. He would have scored two points for Morgan Park." As he explained various facets of the game, he remembered when Mary first saw him play baseball so many years before. All of Mary's questions about the American game she had never seen before were as humorous as they were endearing. Those distant memories were like life's most precious jewels to him. He remembered how easily he'd laughed back then. He also remembered how easily he'd fallen in love.

But, Becca was not Mary. For the first time, Tony was comfortable with that. Becca had a wonderful sense of humor he was realizing, and she was quick to understand even his more complex explanations of the game. Toward the end of the game Becca said, "They're stalling on purpose. Kevin could have taken an easy shot but he passed to that Tusken boy instead. I don't think Denfeld wants to give the other team any chance at getting the ball and scoring."

Tony was impressed. "That's exactly what Coach Monson wants his kids to do. Keep the ball and use up the remaining time. He's got to be quite content with a four point lead and only a minute to go."

After the game, Tony and Becca waited near the bleachers for Kevin to leave the locker room. "Uncle Tony!" The familiar voice echoed across the large empty space of a nearly emptied gymnasuim. "Thanks for coming. I knew you'd be here." His shower-wet auburn hair glistened under the lights, his blue eyes sparkled with excitement. "We're pretty darn good aren't we? Isn't Huddy a great guard? He's the kid I practice with all summer in the alley."

Tony embraced the tall lad. "You're both pretty darn good if you ask me. You had five points in your first varsity game, that's just wonderful."

Tony congratulated, "And, I agree with you, Kev, Denfeld's got a nice team this year."

Kevin acknowledged the lovely lady standing at his uncle's elbow. Smiling, he didn't wait for his uncle to make an introduction. "I'm Kevin," he said extending his hand to Becca.

Tony recognized his blunder. "I'm sorry, Becca. This is my nephew, Kevin. Kevin, this is my friend, Becca Kaner. She's a doctor up in Hibbing. She was your Aunt Mary's doctor, as a matter of fact, and a good friend of hers as well."

"It's my pleasure to meet you, Kevin." Becca beamed. "I've heard so much about you from your uncle and from Mary, too. I really enjoyed seeing you play."

"Thanks for being here . . . Doctor . . ." Kevin searched for a proper reference to the tall, striking brunette. She was almost as pretty as his Aunt Mary. "It's quite a drive from Hibbing so I'm really honored."

"I'm Becca, Kevin. At the hospital, from eight to five, I'm *Doctor*. On the weekends I'm just a *person* enjoying my other life."

Kevin laughed. "A pretty nice person I'd have to say."

They talked for several minutes before Tony realized the time. He gave Kevin the five dollar bill from Senia and explained his aunt would get down for another game soon. "Tell her to bring along Steven when she comes. He's a swell guy." He looked from Tony to Becca. "And I sure hope my uncle will take you to another game. Maybe we could all go out for lunch or something. I'd enjoy that."

On the long drive up dusty Highway Fifty-three, they talked about the game, but mostly about Kevin. "He's such a mature young man, Tony, so well-mannered and outgoing. I'll bet every girl at Denfeld has a crush on him."

Tony agreed. He wanted to tell Becca the story about Kevin, the adoption, and how he became 'Uncle Tony' to the boy. Becca had not inquired about how they were related to each other. And, what was equally puzzling was that Senia was Kevin's aunt. How did all of this come about? Perhaps it was her tactfulness that kept her from asking a lot of questions that crossed her tired mind.

After stopping briefly for a sandwich and coffee at a small restaurant between Duluth and Eveleth, their conversation ebbed for the first time. The scrub tamarack and balsam lined road seemed endless, the night had clouded over, and little traffic broke the dark monotony. Tony moved his hand from the floor shift toward Becca's lap and found her hand. "I'm really glad you came with me, Becca. I haven't enjoyed myself like this in years." Then he swallowed hard. "Can I ask you something . . . it's kind of personal?"

"That depends, Mr. Zoretek." Becca replied teasingly. "How personal?"

Tony smiled at her remark. Mary often teased him with his surname just as Becca had done. But the coincidence, and her tone of voice, unsettled him for a moment. Why was he unconsciously comparing the two women with each other at every opportunity? Their mannerisms, phrases they used, and their spontaneous humor? Was it fair to Becca to hold her to his imaginary and exaggerated standards?

Tony recovered, "Not too personal, I hope. May I ask why you decided to come with me today? When I asked you for this date on Thursday night . . . well, your expression told me you didn't really want to go. I think I was about ready to excuse myself and apologize when you said you'd be happy to join me. Did I get your messages confused?"

For a long moment, Becca sat quietly. All day she had been holding what she wanted to tell him inside because she was having such a wonderful time. But it wasn't fair to keep her secret—and it wasn't honest. If she didn't say something tonight—when might she have another chance? Tony would learn about it anyhow, and it would be sooner than later. He deserved to hear of her decision now.

"You read my reluctance quite well, Tony." Where should she go with her explanation to him? She could not speak of the attraction she had felt over the past few years. Nor could she ever admit to her jealousy over Molly Pell. "I think I had two good reasons for accepting. First, I really wanted to be with you for Kevin's game and have a chance to meet him. I know you didn't get that impression from me, however, especially the wanting to be with you part." Enough said in that regard. How long she'd waited for this date was best kept to herself. Her feelings for Tony complicated what else she had to say.

"I'm flattered by the first reason, and the second? I think I can make a pretty good guess, Becca. Let me try anyhow. When I came over to your house you said you had some *news* for me. After I left, feeling pretty good I might add, I realized that I didn't give you a chance to tell me what you were hoping to. Another apology I'm afraid. I wasn't very thoughtful. So, I'll bet you wanted to give me your news today."

"How perceptive you are. I did have some news but after you asked me for a date I think I forgot about it myself." She laughed softly. "I must have been pretty flattered myself."

"And, I'd guess that despite all the talking we've done today, you've managed to keep that 'news' pretty well concealed," Tony said.

"You're right again. No wonder you do so well in the business world. You're a mind-reading contractor. How could anybody top that?" Becca was feeling some tension. "I think I told you many times today how much I enjoyed Duluth. What an interesting city it is with so many things to do. Well, that's part of my news, Tony." Becca caught her breath before continuing. She said nothing for what seemed a minute or more.

Tony took his eyes briefly from the road to see a sad expression on Becca's face. She was looking out ahead of the car as if in some distant reverie. What she was about to tell him had some pain attached.

"I've taken a position at St. Mary's in Duluth." Her voice was strained through her dry mouth. "I'm leaving Hibbing, Tony. In less than two months. I'm thirty-five and have no future there. It's selfish of me to be always thinking of myself because I do love my patients, and I'm devoted to Doctor Hane. But . . . I'd like to meet someone one of these days and have a family. In Duluth, maybe there's more opportunity for that to happen. I just don't know. A part of me wants to stay where I am, and another part is pulling me away." Becca was sobbing softly, dabbing at her eyes with a handkerchief. "So, that's my news."

Time for Truth

December 1924

Among the countless thousands of Americans who turned fifty-two in 1924, one of them was Claude Atkinson. On Sunday afternoon, the twenty-eighth day of the month, Claude found himself in his office at the *Mesaba Ore* building. His birthday cake would be shared with his family at dinner time, and he'd insisted on no celebratory party. Claude was in a reflective mood as he considered the unusually large Wednesday issue of his paper which would be published on New Year's Eve. As was the *Ore's* tradition, the last newspaper of the year would be a chronicle of major stories from the previous twelve months.

The week between Christmas and New Years was always a slow time in his community, like a necessary pause in the hectic yule season and a time to reflect on things past as well as a time to contemplate a new calendar. For many, the holidays marked a melancholy time. A time when loved ones who had passed away the year before were remembered by their conspicuous absence around the Christmas tree or at the dinner table. A time when poor families felt a sense of disappointment over what small pleasure Santa Claus was able to provide their children. A time when some were presented with gifts in a measure more than deserved, while others received less than expected. A time of changing traditions as materialism etched new patterns on the American psyche, patterns which seemed contrary to the wholesome values of old. A time of resolution to make changes in lives that were either missing something—or needing something of perceived importance.

A time to redefine oneself. And, in Northern Minnesota, a time when cold winds seeped through loosely fitting window panes, bringing chill to the bones.

In a contemplative mood of the moment, Claude laughed softly to himself at his childhood memory of feeling cheated by having a birthday so close to Christmas. He'd always found fewer presents under the tree than his brothers and sisters because, they were quick to remind him, "You've got a birthday coming in three days!" This year, however, his wife, Dora, got him the one thing he most wanted for Christmas: an attractive, dark brown, felt Stetson hat that matched his topcoat perfectly.

For his birthday he hoped for a new Meerschaum pipe to add to his collection. His son, Marc, had been so informed weeks before. Claude lit his old bowed pipe and sat back to absorb the pleasant Prince Albert tobacco aroma wafting about his desk. In his cluttered office, with no one else in the building, he was as close to heaven as he could imagine.

Glancing toward his notepad centered on the table to his left elbow next to his trusted Adler typewriter, Claude mused to himself: "Twenty-four was not much of a year. What in the world can I highlight as stories really worth writing about?" If momentous news stories were hard to focus upon, the radical changes in American culture were certainly worth some ascerbic commentary. He could begin his annual story with his impressions of traditional values now in crisis. "I like that idea. Where are we going with all this craziness?" Claude began a rough draft of his thoughts.

We are now a nation of more than one hundred million Americans. That is astounding to me. One hundred million individuals. I want to highlight that word 'individuals' because is what we have become. Our cherished culture is being undermined by every imaginable subversion of the ideals I grew up with. To this writer it often seems as if everybody wants what is convenient and comfortable for themselves. I call ours a 'me generation' because that is the attitude of so many of our young people these days. And, the parents of our youth foster this new morality by allowing their children to do pretty much as they please. My parents must be turning in their grave!

> *Our laws are flouted by racketeers and blatant criminal elements, prohibition is proving to be an unenforceable nightmare, 'cultured' Americans in our cities are into 'swing' and 'jazz' music and dancing 'the shimmy' or the 'Charleston' in speakeasies. Our women folk are wearing the most revealing and ludicrous clothing while their escorts cavort about in 'zoot suits'. We adore buxom Fanny Brice, ponder Harry Houdini's alleged omniscience, and seem enamored with Freud's absurd sexual interpretations.*

Frowning, Claude looked over what he had written, pulled the page from his tablet. Was he being too critical of change? Change, as he more than most realized, was inevitable. America was prospering, and this new generation wanted their fair share of material wealth. But the editor worried over free credit to consumers and buying stocks on margin. Were these affluent economic times really based upon sound financial practices? People wanted more comfort, more convenience, and more fun at the same time. And they wanted it the easy way. Had Claude unwittingly become an old fogy while observing only his fifty-second year? Most of these cultural trends, he realized, were not the stuff of his community. Relative isolation had its blessings.

He stuffed the page of commentary in his drawer, "Maybe another time," he muttered. A few days might temper his views and turn his focus on some of the more positive attributes of what many pundits were already labeling as the *Roaring Twenties*. Although he wasn't a fan of swing music, he enjoyed an Al Jolson song and often hummed George Gershwin's 'Rhapsody in Blue' while relaxing at his desk or in his bathtub. He'd thoroughly enjoyed John Ford's epic tale 'The Iron Horse' at the movie theater only weeks before. The story was compellingly presented on the screen. And, truth be admitted, Claude had his own streak of materialism. Life was good. Later that night he might smoke some imported Turkish blend in an expensive new Meerschaum. Truly, Claude enjoyed his pleasures as much as the next fellow. "Always find the positive, Claude! Things are never as bad as they may seem."

He smiled to himself and regarded the pad at his elbow on which he had scribbled a list of several possible items for his feature on the year of 1924.

Of the twelve he'd listed, seven had wide slash marks through them indicating he'd already decided to omit them. Contemplating the remaining five, Claude decided each would be afforded a paragraph of print and, if the *Ore's* files would allow, an appropriate photograph:

-Vladimir Lenin's death in Moscow creates a power struggle between Stalin and Trotsky;
-Teapot Dome scandal further evidences corruption in American government;
-Republican Coolidge defeats Democrat Davis in one-sided presidential election;
-Prohibition gives rise to organized criminal activity and rampant gangland murders;
-Washington's Senators defeat the New York Giants in seven-game World Series.

Of all the stories, the last on his list provided greatest personal interest and amusement to the editor. Claude was a baseball fan, and Walter Johnson of the Senators was his favorite player. Claude listened to every game of the fall classic on his *Motorola* radio. Game seven almost had him biting his fingernails, but Walter pitched four perfect innings of relief in the twelve inning, 4-3 Senators victory.

His local stories might be easier to write than the national events, but one of them still settled hard in his stomach. On a bitterly cold early February afternoon, a human tragedy of momentous proportions consumed the mining town of Crosby, Minnesota. Fifty miners were working in the underground drifts of the Milford Manganese Mine when a blast rocked a shaft two hundred feet below the surface. That blast split open the bottom of a large pond situated near the mine, causing an instant flood from which there seemed no escape. The miners were slammed into the rock walls by the incredible force and buried under countless thousands of tons of water and mud. Only seven had managed to escape!

Claude had traveled along with his friend, Steven Skorich, down to Crosby on the Cuyuna Iron Range some ninety miles from Hibbing the following morning. The two men watched as the men and women of Crosby tried in vain to pump the water from the underground tunnels, listened to the mournful wail of the whistle signaling tragedy at the mine, and talked at length with widows and their fatherless children. It was an experience he would never forget and easily the most terrible mine accident in Minnesota history.

Claude was caught up in the tragic memory. Relighting his pipe, he considered how he might appraise the past year of Hibbing's already color-filled history. The city's almost twenty thousand citizens were nearly equally divided between the gradually disintegrating 'Old Hibbing' and the increasingly bustling 'South Hibbing.' The evacuation, Claude knew, would continue for many years.

Between the old town and new city bloomed luscious Bennett Park with its gardens, fountains, playgrounds, and public zoo. The zoo featuring exotic birds, monkeys, bears, and buffalo was a community favorite. On summer nights band concerts entertained citizens at the pavilions, ball games were held under the lamps at adjacent diamonds, and the ice cream man made his rounds along the curving streets. On weekends, hundreds of families picnicked in the six acres of elegant greenery and broad grassy slopes. The location was advantageous for both sections of the divided community.

Majestic Pine Street was becoming a pleasant memory, while Howard Street was growing into an impressive eight block long commercial hub of prosperous mercantile activity. Banks, theaters, fine clothiers, dime stores, restaurants—the new city had everything one might imagine. The luxurious Androy Hotel towered over the corner of Fifth Avenue, casting long shadows across wide Howard Street. Two blocks to the south and east of the Androy stood Hibbing's most spectacular structure, The Hibbing High School. The red-bricked building, completed two years before on a ten acre plot of land, was monumental in its dimensions. The boldly striking exterior of the five-storied structure created the impression of a "medieval castle outlined against the sky." The nearly $4 million dollar edifice possessed interior hallways resplendent in colorful murals and granite columns. In its every aspect, Hibbing High School inspired a commitment to quality education which was unparalleled in all of Minnesota. The curriculum spanned kindergarten through two years of college preparation. Without question, the high school was the community's greatest source of pride.

Education would define the future in the minds of Hibbing's largely immigrant population.

The era of Victor Power was probably over as the flamboyant politician had retired from public service earlier in the year. Power chose not to run for reelection in 1924. The 'Little Giant' had served Hibbing for nine consecutive one-year terms before being upset in 1922 by attorney John Gannon, a protégé of the Elwood Trembart faction of conservatives. Trembart's political machine was pro mining company, and advocated deep tax cuts along with curtailment of public employment. Trembart had long been Power's nemesis.

Victor had little energy for that '22 campaign as his wife, Percy, had died unexpectedly the year before. Somewhat recovered from the loss of his beloved wife, however, Vic Power stormed back to win the mayor's office once again in 1923. "Let me finish my agenda," he appealed to the electorate. And, as they had so often done before, Hibbing's voters responded overwhelmingly. Claude and Vic still had coffee together every morning at the lawyer's office only a block from Claude's newspaper building. His friend, however, was still consumed with lofty political aspirations and was often mentioned as a viable candidate for governor or state senator. But the energetic fire no longer burned. At only forty-four, Vic Power was a tired man.

Always near the center of activity as the community spread southward into new neighborhoods was Tony Zoretek. Few people held Claude's utmost respect more than Tony. When anything in Hibbing needed to be done—be it money raised for some local charity, or some booster needing to step forward for a cause—Tony volunteered his time and seemingly inexhaustible energy. If the handsome contractor ever decided to run for mayor, Claude had no doubts that Tony would win by a landslide. Who would even want to run against the popular community stalwart?

When the Volstead Act had spawned the Eighteenth Amendment and ushered in the widely despised Prohibition five years before, Claude remembered that Tony was the first to come to the aid of Norman Dinter, who had built a prosperous liquor distributorship with hard work and resolve only to see his operations forced to come to a halt. Dinter stared at financial ruination. Claude recalled a conversation he had a been part of when

Norman, Tony, Vic and Claude were gathered at Dinter's liquor warehouse on a subzero January night.

"It's the law I'm sad to say, Norm. I've gotta have the police shut you down along with sixty taverns in town. This damnable law is idiocy, but it must be enforced." Orders from the governor's office were folded in an envelope stuffed in the mayor's topcoat pocket. Later, Power would have to meet with Con O'Gara and the saloon keepers' union people. Con, along with Norm, had been staunch supporters of Vic Power through many campaigns. "Maybe I can get some of your people some public jobs. I'll do the best I can for them all."

"I've been expecting it for weeks, Vic. I've been straightforward with my men about this Volstead business and given them all bonuses so they can get by for a few months." Dinter's face wore a solemn, defeated expression. "Well, I'll just have to wait this prohibition nightmare out, and find me another job in the meantime. That's all there is to it."

"You've got another job, Norm. You start as soon as you get your place shut down," Tony said. "I'd be honored to have you working with me."

Claude remembered Tony's offer. He'd deliberately said *"working with me"*—not *working for me*. Within two weeks Norm Dinter was handling much of Tony's expanding real estate business. And Tony had worked out something at Senia's bank to ensure that the lease on Dinter's liquor warehouse was kept current.

Claude inserted a page in his Adler and began his story on 1924. He'd pick up the report the following morning and work more on the texture of his New Year's issue of the *Ore*. It was already dark outside and he'd promised his wife to be home before six.

∼

Denis Moran also turned fifty-two in 1924. The felon was already sixteen years removed from the scene of his brother's death. Denis had fled Hibbing that night in the car stolen from Peter's garage, then ditched the Buick in Pokegama Lake near Grand Rapids and fled the Iron Range on the morning train to St. Paul. Over the years he had been 'Jones,' 'Olson,' and 'Johnson' as he made his way across the western United States—to Denver, Portland, San Francisco, and back again to midwestern St. Louis.

For the past several years, Denis was *Danny Morgan*. Danny Morgan felt at home in East St. Loo's notorious underworld where he'd befriended a flamboyant gambler named Charlie Birger. Morgan's first impression of Birger was expressed when they first met in Charlie's busy speakeasy on State Street and North 13th. "God damn, man! Thought ya waz Tom Mix," Morgan commented with wide eyes. While staring at Charlie Birger across the smoke-filled room, he thought he was seeing his favorite movie hero. When introduced, Morgan said, "Heard a lot about ya, Mr. Birger. If'n ya ever need some muscle in yer place, I been a bouncer before. Lots'a different taverns out west."

Birger was impressed with the wide shoulders, good looks, and fine clothes of Danny Morgan and pleasantly affected by the Tom Mix compliment. Birger liked to dress in outrageous costume and favored a beige cowboy hat and finely crafted, western leather boots. Birger was making a reputation for himself in gambling, prostitution, and bootlegging in St. Loo and throughout southwestern Illinois, a reputation that intimidated folks as far away as Chicago. Birger killed people who got in his way.

Birger reminded Morgan of a Duluth hood named Sam Lavalle, whom he'd worked with years before when he was Denis Moran. Lavalle was the culprit behind a kidnapping debacle that almost put him in prison. As it turned out, Lavalle got ten years at the Stillwater Penitentiary and another accomplice, Lucy Brown, got four years at the woman's reformatory. Denis Moran escaped arrest along with the other two that day in Duluth and fled to Hibbing with his mind set on killing his despised brother. Every misfortune in Denis' troubled life found root in Peter. The hatred was irrational, but Denis needed a scapegoat. From the night of the murder, running was the substance of his transient life.

Over the years since, the federally wanted fugitive lived on the edges of society. As Danny Morgan he'd become a high-roller with lots of money in his pockets, fancy women at his side, and respect as one of Birger's trusted lieutenants. Prohibition had proven a perilous but profitable career for the likes of Danny.

In 1924, Birger's rising career hit a temporary bump in the road. The gangster ended up with a one-year sentence in a Danville, Illinois, prison when convicted on bootlegging charges in Williamson County. Morgan helped run Birger's affairs while the boss did his time. Part of the Birger booze-running operation transported Canadian whiskey across the Manitoba border into northern Minnesota. Danny Morgan was living on the edge of the law again. Minnesota was a dangerous place for him to be operating, but he could not repress the challenge of visiting his old haunts in Duluth and Hibbing. The only description the police in those parts had of 'Denis Moran' was that of a red-bearded, heavy set man, with the appearance of a 'swarthy lumber jack.' Since then, he'd kept himself clean-shaven, lost forty pounds, and dyed his red hair black. Often he wore fashionable eye glasses and always dressed impeccably.

When his work brought him anywhere near Duluth, he'd often park his car on Fifty-Seventh Street a few blocks down the street from the Schmitz house. From there he could spend an hour or two hoping to catch sight of his nephew, Peter's son. In the morning the lad usually left for school about seven-thirty; in the afternoon he got home around six. Sometimes he was lucky and caught a glimpse of his brother's son. What a good looking boy Kevin Schmitz had become!

Sitting in the seat beside him on this chilly December night was Carlo Berducci, one of Birger's men. Having closed a sizable deal the night before, they left the border town of International Falls earlier that morning. The inconspicuous truck with cases of whiskey they purchased was on its way through Superior on a journey to an East St. Louis warehouse.

Denfeld High School was on Christmas vacation, but Kevin had basketball practice every afternoon. Filled with thoughts of a new full-court press Coach Monson was teaching the team, Kevin paid no attention to the nondescript black automobile as he passed beside it on the snow covered street. While walking the cold asphalt street, he deftly dribbled his basketball with hands encumbered by bulky wool-lined choppers.

"There he is now." Danny Morgan whispered, pointing through the frosted windshield of the Ford sedan. "That's my nephew, Kevin. Ain't he a tall fella, Carlo? Saw in the paper he's playin' basketball. Must be comin' back from practice now."

Carlo watched the boy go in the front door, but didn't reply.

"He ain't got a clue I'm his uncle, ya know. Better that way for now. I'd like to meet'im some day though. He's got good ole Moran blood in him, that's for sure."

"What'cha mean, Danny? Moran blood? Ya said his name's Schmit or somthin like that, din't ya? Ain't he a Morgan like you, or is the kid's ma yer sister?"

Danny was tempted to tell the story. Decided against it. "Ya, somthin' like that. Relatives get complicated, ya know. But, he's the spittin' image of my brother. My brother was a sonofabitch, though. Had lots'a money that guy. Money that shoudda been my pa's." Danny pressed the starter, flipped the light switch, and pulled his hat down over his eyes, "Let's get the fuck outta here. Just wanted to see the kid, that's all. Ain't nobody's business but mine."

~

Fifty-two year old Patrick Foley sat in his office at the rectory of the Sacred Heart Cathedral in East Duluth on that cold Sunday afternoon. His four years in the administrative center of the diocese had passed swiftly and pleasantly. The large parish was more impersonal, but being a colleague among the resident priests was always stimulating. Monsignor Bill Bauer was a noted orator, Shakespearean authority, and baseball fan. The two of them spent hours arguing about sports, playing canasta, and listening to Gershwin music on their Victrola phonograph. Father Maloney from Dun County, Limerick, was someone with whom Foley could share both good humor and memories of Ireland. Foley and Maloney had enjoyed a wonderful trip back to the 'old sod' together the previous summer.

There were days, however, when Foley missed his flock at St. James Church. Kevin Schmitz called him every week, usually on Wednesdays, to catch up on things and talk sports. But the two of them often went weeks without seeing each other. Two nights before, however, Foley had attended the Denfeld and Duluth East basketball game and visited with the tall youth afterwards. Kevin was a senior in high school already. How the years had swept past, Foley realized. And, with the passing of years, Kevin's long-delayed revelation was an approaching reality the priest thought about almost daily. Although Art and Sarah had remained distant friends with whom he communicated far less often than in the past, Senia Arola remained in frequent contact with the Sacred Heart pastor.

Within minutes, the Hibbing woman would be visiting him at the rectory, and Foley knew there were serious matters that needed to be discussed. Senia was the executor of the Peter Moran estate—most of which was being held in trust for Moran's son, Kevin. In less than two months, Kevin would turn eighteen and inherit a fortune.

Senia had traveled to Duluth on Saturday with her friend, Becca Kaner. The doctor was busy with the moving of furniture from Hibbing to her rental house on London Road in the fashionable East Side of the long, narrow harbor city. On the trip down, the two women talked about Becca's reasons for moving. "It's a one-year arrangement, Senia. That's why I'm renting this place rather than buying. I may find that I miss Hibbing too much . . . but, maybe I'll fall in love with Duluth."

Senia had already heard about Tony and Becca's date of weeks before. "I don't think you'll fall in love with Duluth, Becca. I think you're already in love and not with anything so abstract as a city, for heaven's sakes. I think Tony will stay in touch with you."

"I've got a lot of thinking to do about that. Tony is just about the most wonderful man I've ever met. But, I'm not Mary . . . and, he's not Jewish. So, we've each got our mountains to climb before we can ever hope to have anything more than a casual friendship."

Senia wondered if Becca was running away from something too difficult for her to live with. She knew her friend's feelings well but not her motivations. "Absence makes the heart grow fonder, Becca." Senia offered the familiar cliché.

"And, out of sight . . ." Becca grinned. "Who can tell? I am going to talk with a rabbi down here once I'm settled. And, I'm going to visit with a Catholic priest, too. If that is the major issue I'll want to do my homework. I'm surely not orthodox . . . but, my roots are deep."

"If you don't mind, Becca, I'll mention that to Father Foley when I see him later. He's a wonderful man—very broad-minded, and intelligent."

Becca knew that Senia's friend, Steven, was Catholic. She wondered if that was an issue that strained their unusual relationship. Senia, Becca knew, was very closemouthed about anything relating to her and Steven. What was it that had kept them from being married over all these years? "Speaking of your priest friend, you'd better be getting over there, don't you think? I've got enough to keep me busy for a couple of hours with arranging, picture-hanging, house cleaning, and a thousand other things."

"Don't wear yourself out, Becca. We've got a long drive back to Hibbing tonight." Senia borrowed Becca's Chevrolet for the short trip over to the Sacred Heart Church.

After a brief wait in the rectory corridor, Senia was escorted by a secretary to Foley's office for her appointment. Senia was apprehensive.

The tall priest met her at the door with his engaging smile, putting Senia somewhat at ease. "So good to see you, Mrs. Arola. Senia. It's been nearly a year, I think." He gestured toward a comfortable upholstered chair near his desk, "Please do sit down, I've got some coffee coming in a few minutes. You use cream if I remember correctly."

"That would be just fine, Father. And, thank you for seeing me on such short notice. When arranging this trip to Duluth with a friend of mine, I realized it would allow us an opportunity to talk face-to-face about Kevin for a change. Heaven knows we've spent hours on the telephone. I'm anxious to resolve Kevin's issue in the most convenient manner possible." Senia would get directly to the point of her visit.

Foley regarded the attractive woman. She had traces of gray in her long blonde hair, more wrinkles about her eyes than he remembered and wore a more serious expression than he'd seen before. Knowing that Kevin's well-being weighed heavily on her shoulders, Foley would lighten the atmosphere before getting to the matter they would need to consider.

The coffee arrived. Foley sat back in his chair. "My friend, Father Maloney, asked me a good question this afternoon, Senia. 'What's the difference between an Irish wedding and an Irish wake?' Well, I thought about that and gave a few wrong answers. Then Maloney told me. 'There's one less drunk!'" Foley guffawed at his retelling of the Irish joke. "Maybe you have to be Irish to appreciate the humor."

Senia's laugh was tight, but she understood the priest's attempt to put her more at ease. "I think Peter would have enjoyed that story, Father. He was quite the Irishman and known to imbibe some Irish whiskey on occasion. Frequent occasion—I might add!"

Foley sipped his coffee, then met Senia's eyes. "We've got some difficult business ahead of us, don't we? I know we've talked about this over the phone on countless occasions, but this afternoon . . ."

"This afternoon we have to make some crucial decisions," Senia finished Foley's comment for him.

Foley nodded. "We'll need to set up a meeting with Art and Sarah soon. As you know they have never said a word about any of this to Kevin—despite my constant encouragement to break the ice that's built up between them. And, as I've shared with you before, I would not be surprised if Kevin hasn't harbored some justifiable suspicions about his parentage for several years. I think we all should have cleared this matter up long ago . . . but the Schmitzes would have no part of any such thing." Foley ran his long fingers through his silver streaked hair. "But I think they are about ready to let go now. It's been so very hard on the two of them. Perhaps even more so than it's been for the boy."

"You may be right about that, Father. You know the family better than anyone and have given Kevin remarkable guidance over the years. I'm so grateful for all that you've done." Senia spoke from her heart. "You have been the most important person in Kevin's life . . . even more so than his adoptive parents."

But, deep inside, Senia had been waiting for her turn to become an influence in the young man's life. As meaningful as Foley had been in the past, she would soon become even more critically involved in framing the young man's future. Peter's 'death wish' had consumed her life for more than sixteen years. On February 12th, Kevin might finally learn who he really was! "Have you considered what we are going to do in February, Father?"

"It's been a constant torment for me. I'll be candid about that. With so many things going on in his high school life—baseball season around the corner, senior prom in May, then graduation—I wish we could wait."

Senia expected Foley's suggestion. It made good sense to her as well. "I hate to think that we are negotiating, Father. We have always put Kevin's welfare before anything else." Having rehearsed this very scenario in her mind many times, Senia knew where she was amenable to compromise. "I am willing to let you and the Schmitzes work something out among yourselves without my interference. If the three of you believe the best time to broach the issue is in June, after Kevin has graduated, I can accept that. But to be honest with you, Father Foley, I have waited patiently for my time with Kevin. The two of us, Kevin and I, have many difficult bridges to cross. He is going to have to deal with some serious decisions, and I want to be a part of all that."

Senia fought against her emotion of the moment. "I know that his father would want me to be involved. It was his last request." Senia reached for her handkerchief tucked away in the purse on her lap. She could recite the note Peter had left her word-for-word from her memory. "You know my feelings about this, Father."

"And your business with Kevin is best taken care of in Hibbing. Am I right about that?" Foley asked.

"Yes, Father. Art and Sarah will have to let go of the boy when he graduates. I want Kevin to know who his natural father is by the time he comes to Hibbing in June. That might sound cold and callous, but . . ." Senia let her sentence drop incomplete.

"I agree with you. Let me propose this. After graduation, Kevin and I will travel up to Hibbing together. I can stay with Monsignor Potocnik and Kevin could spend a few days with his Uncle Tony if you can arrange it. He'd love that, I'm sure." Foley smiled at the thought. Kevin, he knew, was devoted to his uncle. "While visiting the Zoreteks, you and Kevin can spend as much time together as you need. Perhaps Mr. Power can be involved in explaining the estate business."

Foley had been in the middle of this dilemma from that February day when Kevin was born nearly eighteen years ago. It was he who had placed Kevin in the Schmitz home after the death of his mother, and it was he who'd been through the contentious battles with the boy's father when the adoption process began several months later. Kevin was as close to him as a son might have been. Painfully, he realized that he would have to 'let go' of Kevin as well.

Senia smiled naturally for the first time. "A workable solution, Father. As always, you seem to have a good perspective on what needs to be done and how best to do it. If you were serving a parish in Hibbing, I might consider becoming a Roman Catholic." She laughed easily. "That's the truth, Father."

Foley was inspired by Senia's gracious attitude and unexpected compliment. "I'm flattered. Maybe when Kevin is visiting you folks in Hibbing, he'll get you to go to Mass with him one Sunday. He never misses Mass, as you will learn. And we've got some wonderful priests up there—better sermonizers than this old Irishman, I'm willing to bet."

Senia laughed. "I'd enjoy going to Mass with Kevin. My friend Steven is a Catholic, you know, and he's invited me to his church in Chisholm many times. Oh, and lest I forget, I have a Jewish friend who's moved down here from Hibbing and she'd like to talk over some of her issues with you. She is a friend of Tony's. Can I leave her name and phone number with you?"

Foley scribbled Becca's name on his desk calendar and promised to call early next month after the woman had settled. He glanced toward the clock and realized he had another meeting in fifteen minutes. He steered their conversation toward conclusion. "The more I think about it, Senia, the more comfortable I become." On his desk was a framed photograph of Kevin in his baseball uniform that the boy had given him last spring. He picked it up and passed it to Senia. "Quite a boy, isn't he?" Foley watched the woman's eyes as she regarded the picture. She was obviously impressed.

Foley began to rise from his chair, "I have every confidence that Kevin will handle what's down the road for him. He's mature beyond his years, with a very good head on his shoulders. I've watched him grow from a somewhat belligerent seven year old to a responsible and personable young man. I'm really proud of him."

"Do you think he's anything like his father? Peter, I mean?"

"Not any more. There was a time when I worried about the lad having that temper . . ." The priest paused in the memory. "No, I don't think so. Time will tell, of course, but Kevin has his own personality. Of that I am quite certain, Senia."

Senia seemed disappointed by the priest's observation but said nothing at first. She believed that Foley and Peter Moran had not seen eye-to-eye on the issues surrounding Kevin's adoption years ago. She bit her tongue, "Time will most certainly tell!" She repeated Foley's comment with her own peculiar emphasis on *time*. And, she reminded herself, *her time* was only months away. "Thank you again, Father Foley. God bless your work."

~

Foley and the Schmitzes talked about *it* often . . . but waited. Weeks became months; and still they waited. Waiting and praying for the *right* time. Father Foley would not impose his own wishes upon Art and Sarah Schmitz. "There will never be a right time," he insisted. "It will not get any easier for Kevin or yourselves. Please, let's the four of us get together and explain everything as best we can."

In that March conversation, Art was equally insistent. "Kevin's got enough on his mind these days. He wants to be valedictorian of his graduating class and that takes a lot of study every night." In an April conversation, Art used baseball as an excuse. By May, the delay was justified by a combination of both studies and sports.

In the months after his eighteenth birthday in February, Kevin waited, too. He waited for graduation: Graduation meant emancipation! For three years he considered his options in life. He had saved nearly three hundred dollars and believed that money, along with graduation gifts, would get him started on a college education. He did not want Art and Sarah to help him financially, although they had offered to pay for everything many times. If they paid, he stayed! That was not how he wanted it to be.

His goal was to go to the University of Minnesota in Minneapolis. He and Huddy Tusken had visited the campus the previous winter along with Denfeld Coach Monson. Huddy was being considered by the U. for a basketball scholarship. Kevin had already been offered an academic scholarship and planned to study law. Maybe the two of them could be dormitory roommates. Whatever happened, he was certain that he'd be able to find a job and somehow manage to make ends meet.

On Saturday, May 30, Kevin Schmitz graduated at the top of his 1925 Denfeld High School class. His parents had planned a graduation party for the following Sunday afternoon. "Just a small affair, some neighbors, your favorite teacher, Mr. Barker, and Father Pat, of course," Sarah told him.

"What about Uncle Tony and my cousins? And Auntie Senia. Aren't they coming down?" Kevin puzzled. The boy had received congratulatory cards and gifts of money from his Hibbing relatives earlier in the week. There must be some explanation. "I thought they'd want to be here more than anybody."

Sarah was flustered by the question that she had anticipated. "Talk to your father about that, Kevin." She skirted the issue for the moment. "He wants to talk to you about that. We both do. But, for the time being, we just want those few people I mentioned."

Art entered the kitchen and the conversation. He'd heard his wife's reference to the party. Sitting in the chair next to Kevin, he tried to explain. "I think your relatives have something already planned for you up there, son. I talked with them the other day."

"In Hibbing?" Kevin displayed some emotion for the first time. "You mean I can go up there?"

"That's the way it looks right now. It's up to you, of course. If that's something you'd really like to do. It's your summer vacation after all. What do you think about spending a couple of days up there?"

Kevin did not reply to something so obvious. He *would* be going up to Hibbing after graduation! It was in his summer plans—regardless of any graduation party or invitation from his relatives. This only made the trip much simpler. Maybe he could even find a summer job on the Range. Maybe he could work for his Uncle Tony's construction company along with his cousin Rudy. Kevin contained his excitement.

"Father Foley might be going up there with you." Art always said 'up there' as if the word Hibbing were unmentionable.

On that Sunday night *the wait* was finally over.

At the small afternoon party Sarah seemed highly agitated. Art hardly mingled at all with the guests. And even Father Pat seemed in an unseemly mood. Graduation, Kevin thought, was cause for celebration—not mourning. Kevin was at his finest, however. Always gregarious, the tall boy found time to visit with everybody there. He even took a walk with Mr. Barker and talked about his future plans. "I hope to get a job up in Hibbing this summer and save some money for college," Kevin told his former Civics teacher.

"Maybe you'll get a chance to meet Vic Power while you're up there," Barker said. "Do you remember him from class discussion?"

"How could I forget? Whenever anything about Hibbing was mentioned in class, my ears perked up, Mr. Barker."

The always pleasant dispositioned teacher knew that. In fact, there was nothing that Kevin was not interested in. Especially politics and current events. The young man was clearly his teacher's 'pet' and easily the brightest boy in class. "Kevin, you can be anything you want to be," the lanky, salt and pepper grayed teacher commented as they strolled the quiet neighborhood street. "I'd always hoped you might be a teacher; maybe even a coach. I've certainly found the profession rewarding all these years. I think being with kids keeps a person young."

Kevin smiled easily at the teacher he so admired. "There are very few people more respected than you are, Mr. Barker. I really mean that. Whatever I choose to do . . . I just hope that I can do it with the enthusiasm and dedication you've given to teaching."

Kevin's sincere compliment struck Barker. "You will, Kevin. If it's the legal profession you want to pursue, be the best darn lawyer in town. Not just good, mind you: Strive always to be the very best!"

Father Pat stayed after the last of the other guests were gone. Having had sandwiches, cake and sweets in the late afternoon, nobody was hungry for supper. "Let's all of us retire to the living room for a while," Foley suggested with a nervous edge to his voice. "Maybe we can talk about that trip up to Hibbing."

When they were all seated, Father Foley cleared his throat. "Kevin, the first thing we want to tell you tonight is . . . is how immensely proud we are of you. What you've accomplished for yourself . . ." The priest was unable to continue.

Sarah broke down sobbing. "I haven't been a very good mom to you Kevin." The stout woman blurted. "So strict . . . scolding you over dirty clothes . . . complaining about the mess in your bedroom . . ."

"And making me eat all my vegetables." Kevin laughed sensitively, trying to placate the distraught woman. Her outburst startled him. "You did just fine, Mom. I deserved a good scolding now and then." It was the first time he'd called Sarah *Mom* in years. Somehow, the feeling was a good one for him. "I love you, Mom. I haven't told you that very often, have I? I'm the one who should apologize."

Kevin's expression, however, only set his mother into a deeper bout of weeping.

Then, it was Art's turn to cry. Kevin knew his father was not a strong man, but he'd never seen him in tears before. The display of emotion was unsettling to Kevin. He'd sensed all day that his parents were out of sorts. But, this was totally unexpected. Why were they crying now?

"I'm sorry, too, son. You gave your mom and me so much to be proud of all these years and we just never told you how happy we were with you. Me especially. I should have been at every game cheering you on, and I wasn't. I should have been the one playing catch, shooting baskets . . . there were so many things. That time at the table that day when you made the varsity team and I tried to joke about gravy I'd spilt . . ." Art rubbed his eyes with the sleeve of his shirt, then cupped his narrow face in his hands. "I've got so much to apologize for, son. One thing more than anything else. I've prayed for five years now!"

Perceptive Father Foley sensed where Art was going with his remorse. "Art, Kevin and I have talked about that already."

Kevin was quick to support Father Pat, "Dad, you were a part of something horrible. Along with thousands of others. Yes, it hurt me a lot . . . but, I know it hurt you much more." Kevin got up from his chair, walked over to the sofa where his parents were sitting. He found the middle cushion between them and draped an arm over each of their shoulders. "I should have gone to you with that, dad. Instead, I went to Father Pat. I'm sorry about that because you deserved to explain your feelings to me. I deprived you of that opportunity, and I'm ashamed of myself. I know you well enough to believe you're not a hateful man."

Art could not respond to his son's apology. He turned to the priest. "Father Pat, why didn't you say something? Over all this time. Why?"

The priest cleared his throat. "I promised Kevin. That's all I can say, Art. Like almost everybody in Duluth, we both felt that nothing would be gained by talking any more about it. I'm sorry."

A long silence hung in the room. Art and Sarah got a tenuous grip on their emotions. "Will you get into the other thing now, Father?" Art said in weak voice. "I think we're ready now."

Kevin could feel the tension in Art's shoulders.

Patrick Foley began explaining the story. It was if he had rehearsed his words for eighteen years. In fact, he probably had. Barbara Chevalier was Kevin's mother. She was a beautiful woman and died tragically young, he said. Peter Moran was his father. Foley was sensitive in his portrayal of the Hibbing businessman, describing him as intelligent, ambitious but civic minded, and highly respected by those who knew him well. Senia, he said, would be able to give Kevin far more insight than he might ever be capable of doing regarding Peter. "Your father, like your mother, died under dreadful circumstances. To this day it is not certain what really happened the night your father died. We may never know. You are his heir, Kevin, and he left you an inheritance that your Aunt Senia will talk to you about." The priest was deliberately vague about the size of Moran's estate.

Kevin was not concerned about any inheritance from a father he had never known. The sober-faced boy interrupted Father Pat's discourse on only two occasions. First with a question: "I was at my father's funeral years ago, wasn't I?" Foley nodded his acknowledgment of the long-kept secret. The second was a comment directed at Art and Sarah who sat in quiet torment through the priest's lengthy explanation. "If only you had told me all this years ago—it would have made our lives so much easier."

Foley concluded by mentioning how often he thanked his God for helping him find this home for Kevin. "Whatever happens from this day on, Kevin, please remember that the two people at your side right now have been your parents all these years . . . your mom and dad."

The pieces of the puzzle that was Kevin Schmitz were finally coming together. His 'relatives' in Hibbing would help him place every piece where it belonged, and he would have the picture of himself he had always wanted. Now, Kevin would be able to answer the question on the first page of the diary he had kept for several years . . . *Who am I?*

BOOK THREE

Kevin and Angela

Home is in the Heart

Kevin said his good-byes to Art and Sarah on Monday night. The three of them talked late into the evening about good times shared and Kevin's plans for the summer before going to college in the fall. There were no tears. "I plan on getting a construction job with Uncle Tony—we talked about that this afternoon. I can make more than a hundred dollars for school. So, most of my summer will probably be spent in Hibbing. I'll get down to visit you at some time, but it'll be a few weeks," Kevin promised.

Art had taken this day off from work to help his son with his packing. The three of them went out to dinner that night. There was more closeness among the Schmitzes that day than on any other over the past several years. "Your mom and I are one hundred percent behind you, Kevin. It's going to be a great summer for you," Art smiled. "And you'll learn a lot about your father, Mr. Moran, while you're up there." Art surprised himself with his reference to Peter Moran. Maybe he was truly letting go of his son.

Sarah had a package for Kevin. "Here's something I found while rummaging through your things in the attic, Kevin." She passed him a small brown box tied with heavy string.

"A going-away present, Mom?" Kevin beamed. He always liked surprises. Shaking the box, Kevin asked, "Should I be guessing what's inside?"

"It's probably kinda silly, Kevin, but your mom wanted you to have it," Art said. "You'd never guess what it is—it's probably sixteen years old by now."

Kevin opened the box carefully. Inside was a slightly worn teddy bear with one button eye hanging loosely by a few threads. His focus narrowed upon the stuffed animal, and he shrugged his shoulders in puzzlement. "Is this mine?"

"It was from your father. He brought it over when you were a baby, Kevin. It might have some sentimental value for you. I remember how your eyes lit up when Mr. Moran gave it to you." Sarah tried to explain the unusual gift.

"You might as well take it with you, Kevin. It's about the only thing I can think of . . ." Art was careful not to spoil the emotion of the moment. He would not tell Kevin that the gift was given to the boy on the one and only occasion Peter Moran had ever seen him. "It's about the only thing we could find from . . ."

"I think it's really special. Thanks mom . . . and dad. I'll treasure it—really I will." Kevin felt an odd lump in his throat as he bounced the teddy bear in his lap. He had something from his father!

Father Pat was at the Schmitz house early on Tuesday morning. The priest would take Kevin to the depot and help him load his luggage on the train. Foley had decided not to accompany the boy to Hibbing. He believed Kevin's trip was something he needed to experience by himself. And, Foley knew, there was another passenger on the train to keep him company. At the station, Foley hugged the tall youth. "You have my phone number, Kevin. I'll expect a call every now and then." The priest swallowed hard fighting back tears. "When we talked the other night, I left out a lot of details, Kevin. I thought it best that you discover most things by yourself. Senia will help, of course. She has managed your father's estate all these years."

"She called me yesterday, Father Pat, just after Uncle Tony. It's really strange when I think about it now; they're not my *real* relatives. I'm kinda disappointed about that, Father. Anyhow, Aunt Senia and I are going to spend most of tomorrow together, I guess. She wants me to meet an attorney friend of hers." Kevin frowned. "I've never met a lawyer before. That should be really interesting."

"He's not just a lawyer, Kevin. He's Vic Power. And, yes, you'll find him to be quite interesting, I'm sure of that." The priest laughed. "You're going to learn so much these next few weeks that your head will be spinning."

"If I ever get confused, Father, I've always known who to ask for help.

Thanks for always being there for me." Kevin choked on his own emotion, offering his hand to Foley. "*Pax en Christo,* Father Pat."

During the first hour of the two hour trip, Kevin sat near the window watching the countryside whisk by. Shading his eyes against the bright eastern sun, he gazed upon the pines and poplars lining the rail bed interspersed with stands of tamarack clustered in vast bogs. Resplendent wild flowers covered the sweeping hillsides as if touched with an artist's color-filled brushstroke. Wild blue phlox, daisies, and yellow columbine waved in the gust of the speeding train. The wilderness scenery was almost mesmerizing, but he turned from the window to the diary resting in his lap. Kevin opened the book, contemplating a few lines to add to the journal.

> *Peter Moran. Father Pat described you as intelligent and ambitious, and respected by those who knew you. I intend to know you . . . and, I hope and pray respect you as well. How much am I like you? Diary, we will find out—won't we?*

Kevin closed the book on the lingering question. He had his father's intelligence—of that he was quite certain. Ambition? "I'm only eighteen," he mused to himself. "How can I know?" The trace of a smile creased his face as he closed his eyes on the rush of thoughts about his father.

"Excuse me." The familiar voice brought Kevin back from his momentary reverie. "May I join you for a while, young man?"

"Doctor Kaner!" Kevin sat up in his seat, offered his hand to the lovely lady standing in the aisle. "Please. By all means sit down, what a nice surprise."

"Tony invited me to join your party tonight, Kevin. I wouldn't miss it for the world."

"You took time off from the hospital? Gosh, that's really nice of you to do, Becca. I remember, you're only *Doctor* when you're working."

Kevin knew Becca Kaner from seeing her on several occasions. She had been to many of his ball games, sometimes with Uncle Tony, once with Father Pat, and even by herself at other times. She always took time to visit with him after a game. Although he found her to be reserved, the tall, strikingly attractive brunette was always pleasant and friendly toward him. Kevin liked Becca.

The two of them talked for nearly an hour. Soon the train was slowing for its approach into Hibbing. "You won't even recognize the town, Kevin. So many changes have happened since your last visit." Becca explained how the expanding open pit operations of the Hull-Rust-Mahoning mines were swallowing the real estate that had been North Hibbing. "A new city's being built to the south. It's been a marvelous transition, Kevin. South Hibbing has a mix of the old that's been moved these past years and the new that's being built. Your Uncle Tony has been a big part of all that's going on."

"Do they still have the baseball field where it's always been?" The ball park was one of Kevin's fondest memories of Hibbing and he hoped to play baseball on cousin Rudy's team this summer.

"That's still sitting right where you remember it. But, it won't be for long, I'm afraid. A new field is being built next to Bennett Park."

"I just want to play one time on the field where my uncle used to pitch. He was quite a player, you know." Kevin was enthusiastic whenever something sports related came into a conversation. "Maybe the best that ever pitched in Hibbing," he stated with obvious pride.

"Oh yes, I've heard about that. Not so much from your uncle as I have from the old timers who watched him play. Mr. Atkinson at the newspaper told me exactly what you just said. 'The best ever to throw a baseball in Hibbing,' Claude said of your uncle."

At the depot, Kevin was overwhelmed by the reception awaiting him. Cousin Marco held a large, homemade sign with "Welcome to your Hibbing home, Kevin!" written across the cardboard. Home? The thought was heartfelt he knew. Maybe Hibbing was the home he'd longed to find.

Looking more delightful than he could ever remember seeing her, Senia stood beside white-shirted Steven in a stylish blue chiffon dress with matching hat. Steven dwarfed a red-faced and solidly-built man in a business suit whom Kevin did not recognize.

Uncle Tony waved enthusiastically as Angela and Marco waited anxiously at his side. His younger cousins were wearing their Sunday best clothing. Kevin guessed they were uncomfortable about being dressed so fancy on a Tuesday, even if the occasion were Kevin's arrival.

Tall and handsome, cousin Rudy stood off to the side with his friend Armando Depelo. Rudy and Armando had been down to Duluth weeks before to watch him pitch a game against Central High School. "We're doing some scouting for the Hibbing team," Rudy told Kevin on that typically gray Duluth spring afternoon. (Kevin impressed the 'scouts' with a three-hit shutout. On the season, the right-hander had an 8-1 record.)

"Quite a reception, Kevin," Becca beamed as she stood clutching her overnight bag. "They are all determined to make you feel at home."

"I already feel at home, Becca. Hibbing has always had some kind of attraction for me. I can't really understand it yet, but I'm sure I will before too long."

"Maybe it's the magnetism of the iron ore, Kevin. I feel it just like you do."

The platform was washed in radiant sunshine while a cool northerly breeze softened the ninety degree heat. It felt to Kevin as if the beautiful day were 'special-ordered' for his arrival, and his spirits soared as high as the crisply flapping American flag fluttering on the flagpole above the old North Hibbing depot.

"The only thing missing is the high school band," Kevin told Becca as they made their way toward the open coach door. "I really think they're happy to have me here."

"More than you can know, Kev." Becca used the name his uncle always did. Tony had told his friend, Becca, Kevin's story. Since moving to Duluth she was seeing more of Tony than when she lived across the street in the Brooklyn neighborhood. Their relationship had flourished with a depth of conversation which was bridging the differences between them. Father Foley and Becca had spent hours talking about their respective religions while Tony and the Jewish doctor, Ambrose Hane, had become good friends. Tony was learning Jewish traditions from the aging Hibbing physician and could even speak a few lines in Yiddish. Absence had "made the heart grow fonder" for the two of them.

The party in honor of Kevin's graduation was more fun than anything Kevin could remember. It was like celebrating his birthday and Christmas together on an early June evening. Many of the guests brought their special dishes—lasagna, sarmas, pasta salads, and Swedish meatballs along with bread puddings, and a wide assortment of ethnic foods that Kevin had never tasted before. Sadie Baratto had spent days preparing the house and trimming the dining room with colorful streamers and balloons. The Sunrise Bakery had baked a variety of sweet delicacies and rich pastries.

In addition to Kevin's 'relatives,' Uncle Tony had invited several of his business friends. It was a wonderful group of people: Mr. Atkinson, the newspaper owner; Mr. Jaksa, who worked for his uncle; Mr. Udahl and his family; Mr. Dinter, another of his uncle's coworkers; Armando's parents—who had been Aunt Mary's dearest friends—the Depelos; and Doctor Hane and his wife, Ethel. Also at his party was the stout man to whom Steven had introduced him at the depot earlier in the eventful day: Victor Power himself!

At his uncle's suggestion, Kevin mingled with the guests. "You'll have plenty of time to be with your *Hibbing family* all summer," Tony said. "These folks have been waiting to meet you for some time. Enjoy them all. They're the 'salt of the earth'."

Claude had talked with Tony the day before. "I'm going to be looking for his father in the boy, Tony. I can't help doing that, you know. Can I mention Peter?"

"Absolutely, Claude. I'd appreciate if you did. Kevin's going to live with that reality the rest of his life. And, the rest of his life is beginning when he arrives tomorrow."

"I'm Kevin, Mr. Atkinson." The boy introduced himself with a self-assured smile. "I've seen your paper many times at the public library in Duluth, sir. I even used it for some research I had to do on iron ore mining for my Civics class. I'm pleased to make your acquaintance."

Claude's positive first impression was that of a young man possessed of social presence and poised beyond his years. "The pleasure is all mine, Kevin." He studied the tall youth over his spectacles while feeling the sure grip of the boy's handshake. "I knew your father quite well—all of us here tonight did. I might not be the first person to tell you that . . ." Claude paused over his next few words. "That you have Peter's good looks, lad. I'd guess you're an inch or two taller and a few pounds lighter, but there's no mistaking the resemblance."

"I'm complimented, Mr. Atkinson. I saw the first photograph of my dad this afternoon. It was a picture of Mr. Moran and my uncle when he pitched for the old Colts baseball team." The memory of his hour-long conversation with Uncle Tony was vividly etched in his thoughts. "Aunt Senia has some other pictures she's going to show me tomorrow."

"I have some myself, Kevin. And some old news stories from years ago. If ever you want to, stop by the office and we'll spend some time together. Any time!" Claude emphasized his open invitation. "I probably have the worst coffee in Hibbing, and I share it freely!"

Kevin found a few minutes to introduce himself to all of the invited guests and chat about his summer plans. "I think I'll be here all summer," he told Mr. Dinter. "I plan to go to college in the fall; probably the U in Minneapolis," he informed Mr. Udahl. "I think I'd enjoy that very much," to Mr. Jaksa, upon Lud's offer of a summer construction job. "You must be very busy with all the real estate transactions these days," he observed while talking with Mr. Dinter near a tray of sweets. "Yes, my Aunt Mary was about the most beautiful person in the world," Kevin agreed with John and Lucia Depelo. He also complimented Mrs. Depelo on the delicious lasagna she had brought to his party. "It's the very best I've ever tasted . . . ever!"

In ten minutes with Mr. Power, Kevin had difficulty getting a word in edgewise as the colorful Mayor recounted political battles as well as boasting about some land deal that he and Mr. Moran had hatched years before. "Your father was an astute businessman, Kevin. More than anyone else, he built the Old North Hibbing into the hub that it was. His hotel, my goodness—that building was beautiful beyond belief!" Kevin had heard of the hotel from other guests as well. He'd ask Senia more about it tomorrow. And, the next day he'd be visiting Vic Power in the attorney's office in the new downtown.

Cousin Marco followed Kevin around the house for nearly an hour, hanging on his tall cousin's every word. When just the two of them were together in the kitchen, Marco finally got out what he was dying to say, "Kev, we're having two parties this week. Did ya know that?" the stout, dark-haired boy asked.

"I'll bet someone's having a birthday this week."

"Do ya remember who, Kev?"

"Have I ever forgotten June sixth, Marco? Sure I remember. You're going to be a teenager on Friday, aren't you?"

Marco nodded, proud of his cousin's acknowledgment. "Yep. And I'm getting a new saxophone from my dad—I've already seen it." Marco was more enthusiastic about music than he was about sports.

At a picnic table in the large back yard, Kevin talked baseball and the Hibbing city team with Rudy and Armando. "We've got a practice on Thursday night, Kevin." Rudy said.

"We've already told Coach Bergan about you. We can sure use another pitcher," Armando Depelo added. "We've got a great bunch of guys—some of them have been playing ball since back when your uncle pitched for the Colts. Mister Bergan was the team's shortstop back then."

Angela kept her eyes on Kevin all evening. Kevin was even better looking than Armando Depelo, and that was something! She caught Kevin at the back door as he was leaving Rudy and Armando at the picnic table. "You aren't really my cousin, Kevin," she asserted in a provoking voice that reminded Kevin of his 'Aunt' Mary when she had teased him. In fact, at fourteen years old, Angela reminded Kevin of Mary in many ways. The teenager had the same long, dark tresses falling over her petite shoulders, the same dark, wide eyes and full mouth. Angela was taller than her mother, however, and had her father's straight nose. She had become quite an attractive girl since the last time he had seen her.

Kevin smiled at Angela, took her small hand in his. "You'll always be my cousin, Angie." He used the name that her father and brother always used. "And, your dad will always be my 'uncle' too. You're the only relatives I've ever known; besides, I enjoy having you as my cousin. Is that going to be okay with you?"

"No. You can keep my brother and Rudy as cousins if you'd like. They're boys after all. But not me, Kevin; I'd rather be your friend. Is that okay with you?" Angela caught the glint in his deep-set green eyes reflecting from the lamp over the doorway. "You'll want some friends in Hibbing just as much as relatives, don't you think?"

"Maybe you're right, Angie." He gave her hand a gentle squeeze. "If you want to be my *friend* I'll be more than content with that. Okay? Now, let's go inside and have a piece of Mrs. Baratto's chocolate cake."

"You'd better call her Sadie, Kevin, or she won't be one of your new friends in town. Or, you could even try calling her 'Auntie Sadie.' I'm sure she'd enjoy being called that by our special *guest* in the household." Angela's tone was intended to nettle Kevin.

Kevin did not reply to the suggestion about Sadie, but puzzled at Angela's reference to his status in the Zoretek home. What did she mean by special guest? Was she just trying to pique him? Opening the screened door for Angela, Kevin found his Uncle Tony standing in the narrow entry way. Tony gave Angela a quick frown but said nothing. Once inside the kitchen, Tony put his arm about Kevin's shoulders, "Are you having a good time, Kev?" He asked with his typical smile, making no reference to his daughter's nettling comment which he'd picked up earlier while eavesdropping on the two of them at the back door. "I sure hope you are. Would you take a minute to say good-bye to Senia and Steven? They're about to leave. I think some of the others are going as well. It's nearly eleven, and a work night for most of them."

"Sure I will, Uncle Tony. I'd like to thank them all for coming to the party and making this such a wonderful night for me. And, yes, I'm having the time of my life. Thanks to you."

Inside, Angela shifted her attention to Becca Kaner. Between Kevin and Becca, Angela had her eyes filled all night. Becca was spending most of the evening talking with Doctor Hane and his wife, while occasionally visiting with Mr. Atkinson or Senia. Doctor Kaner was pretty, Angela would have to admit, but she seemed different from other adult women Angela had met. Angela's teacher at the parochial school once commented that the Jews killed Jesus. That was unforgivable to Angela's way of thinking. And, Doctor Kaner was Jewish, so Angela drew her own unreasonable conclusions.

Her father was seeing Becca Kaner almost every other weekend. Angela had asked her father about Jewish people, and all she usually got was a history lesson with his emphasis on the fact that Jesus, Mary, and Joseph were a Jewish family. Also, from time to time, her father would mention some

Jewish holiday like Yom Kippur and try to explain what it was about. It was all very confusing to her—far more so than Catholic and Protestant differences. But, a boy in her sophomore class named Bobby Sapero went to the synagogue downtown, and he was really cute. Bobby was also a basketball player and a pretty good drummer in the high school band. It was all confusing!

Angela watched her father at the front door as Becca Kaner was about to leave. She saw him lean toward her ear and whisper a soft kiss in her hair. He was telling her something, but Angela could only guess at what he might be saying. The kiss bothered her—even if it was not on the lips. Becca smiled at her dad and gave his hands a squeeze. Then she was out the door behind the Hanes. Her father watched as Becca walked away, and Angela could tell there was an attraction—a magnetism she might not be able to do anything about.

By midnight everybody had left for home; Angela and Marco were in bed; and the overstuffed, highly exhausted graduate lay plopped on the living room couch. Joining Kevin, Tony complimented, "I was impressed by how well you mingled with all the guests, Kev. Everybody thinks you're just about the greatest young man they've met in some time. Did you enjoy yourself?" It was the third time that evening that his uncle had asked him the same question. Kevin could feel Tony's genuine affection and knew how much his uncle wanted it to be something special.

Kevin smiled at his uncle, "It was great fun! What wonderful friends you have—I honestly enjoyed each and every one of them. I can't thank you enough for the neat party." He stretched out on the sofa, resting his stockinged feet on the coffee table, relaxing with his hands behind his head. Kevin expressed his feelings of the moment. "I'm really going to enjoy being in Hibbing, Uncle Tony. Being here is like coming home from a long trip. It's hard for me to put into words."

Tony met his nephew's eyes, but didn't comment about Kevin's feelings. He believed he might be able to give the boy the same kind of opportunities that Peter Moran had given him years before. The thought was satisfying.

The two of them talked for nearly an hour about the people he'd met that evening, the job that Mr. Jaksa had offered, Bergan's baseball team, and Kevin's meeting with Senia in the morning. "Your aunt was very close to your father, Kev. I think you're well aware of that. She will fill in a lot of the blank spaces for you tomorrow."

"Uncle Tony, I'm feeling awkward about something and maybe you can help me figure out what to do."

"Anything at all."

"Well, I know that you are not *really* my uncle and the kids are not my cousins. But, I've grown up with that notion and it's always been really precious to me. Senia told me tonight that she wants me to call her 'Aunt Senia' regardless of . . . you know."

Tony pondered Kevin's concern and one of his own. "I feel the same as Senia. Being 'Uncle Tony' has always been just great with me. Let's just keep it that way."

Tony leaned back in his chair across from Kevin's, and put his own feet on the table. "I overheard what Angela told you earlier, out on the back steps. She's quite an independent thinker, as I'm sure you've realized by now. That girl has always had a mind of her own. Maybe it's all part of being an adolescent, I really don't know. Among other things, she has trouble with my seeing Becca. Always has." An unusual grimace crossed Tony's face, "I've tried to talk with her about her feelings, but she doesn't really open up to me."

Understanding Tony's concern, Kevin tried to lighten the issue. "She's fun to talk with. I like the fact that she questions things. And I can tell that she's very attached to you. More than anybody in the world." Kevin smiled at his uncle. "I think Becca's just swell. We had a wonderful talk on the train coming up to Hibbing this morning. If it's okay with you, I'll try talking with Angie about you and Becca. I have a feeling that my new *friend* might be willing to talk to me. I mean, if were not related to each other that makes things a lot easier. Don't you agree?"

Tony laughed at Kevin's good humor. "Maybe so. Let's hope."

Both men were feeling heavy eyes from a long day. "I've got one last surprise—if you want to call it that, Kev. Come along with me."

Tony had converted Mary's sewing room into a bedroom. On one wall were some cloth sports pennants—Yankees and Dodgers—along with a framed, autographed picture of Walter Johnson that Claude had given Tony on a birthday a few years ago. On the bookcase near a large dresser rested one of Tony's baseball trophies. All the room's furnishings were dark, oak, and masculine. Kevin's footlocker was in the corner and two leather pieces of luggage rested on the large bed. "I hope you like what I've done with the room. This is going to be home for you, Kevin—for as long as you want to stay with us." Tony's voice betrayed his emotion of the moment.

Kevin stepped across the space between them and gave Tony a big hug with emotion of his own. "Uncle Tony," his eyes moistened, "I've never felt more at home than I do right now."

Unpacking one of his suitcases, Kevin found what he was looking for tucked along the side of the luggage near his clean stockings. He smiled and put his treasured keepsake on the book case next to Tony's trophy. The loose button eye had fallen off the face, making the teddy bear seem as if he were winking at Kevin.

Becca was up late visiting with Ambrose Hane at the kitchen table in the doctor's new house located only a block away from the Rood Hospital in expanding South Hibbing. She was spending this night with the Hanes and planned to stay over with Senia on Wednesday. Pleasantly exhausted from the graduation party and sensing that Ambrose and Becca had things to talk about, Ethel had already retired for the evening.

"I've made up my mind, Amby." Becca smiled affectionately toward the man she respected like a father, who was sitting across the table from her. When she told Ambrose of her decision to leave her position at St. Mary's in Duluth at the end of the summer, the doctor only smiled. "You don't seem surprised at all," Becca exclaimed.

"Quite frankly, Becca, I'm not. I am absolutely delighted, however," Ambrose had a twinkle in his dark eyes. "But, probably not nearly so pleased as all your former patients will be." He reached beyond his coffee cup and took her hands in his own. "I knew it would just be a matter of time. Welcome back to Hibbing, my dear."

Becca's two years in Duluth had been bittersweet. She attended the Tifereth Israel Synagogue on occasion but did not maintain the many demanding Hebrew traditions. "I can't allow being Jewish to define me," she confided to Rabbi Lippman when they first visited. "I'll just do my best with who I am . . . and, I am my heritage—to some extent anyhow. That's why I've come to the synagogue for worship tonight. I've always been searching, Rabbi."

The Rabbi was a devout but kindly man. "As we all are, Rebecca. And always will be . . . myself as well as you."

There were several eligible men in the large Jewish community but those she dated were not what she was looking for in a potential husband. Morris Klein was handsome and owned the most successful furniture business in Duluth. But, Morris was too Jewish. Tall and slender, David Nides, was the proprietor of three fashionable clothing stores. But, David was too materialistic and too ardent in his pursuit of her affection. Neither man could ever hope to measure up to Tony Zoretek!

Becca was in love—of that she had no doubt in her mind. Tony had become more comfortable with their difficult relationship and more open about his own feelings toward her. At times they talked for hours, but he had not told her that he loved her—Not yet! Nor had she expressed those deep feelings to him. That was not, however, the only awkward thing between them. Religious issues were mostly kept hidden in the proverbial closet. Their time together, in every other respect, was just wonderful! Duluth presented so many fun places to go and interesting things to do. And, the shores of Lake Superior were a favorite place to wile away countless hours together.

"Is Tony the reason, Becca?" Ambrose interrupted her reverie, wondering where he might take his question. "He's become a good friend of mine these past few months. I know he wants to learn a much as he can about our faith and he has a thousand questions about Judaism. He even joined Ethel and me at the Zionist picnic earlier this spring. That guy has a way of getting along so well with everyone." Ambrose gave her hands a gentle squeeze. "I know he's very fond of you, Becca. I think he struggles more with his feelings about you than he does with our beliefs."

"Yes, it's Tony more than anything else." Becca let loose of his hands, rose from the table, and crossed the kitchen to the gas range for the coffee pot. Her expression was one of consternation. "I've been struggling, too. Sometimes I can't sleep at night, Amby."

"Does Tony know about your decision?"

"Not yet. Tonight just wasn't the right time to tell him. Maybe tomorrow." She remembered what Tony had told her at the door as she was leaving the party. "Tomorrow." He'd whispered with a kiss blown into her hair. "We'll go for a walk or something. I'm sorry I've been spreading myself so thin tonight. You're the person I most want to be with, and I just didn't."

Becca refilled their cups, returned the pot, and leaned over the counter to stare into the black June night. Her stomach was a knot. When she was stressed, she needed a moment to back away from her feelings. Just a minute or two would compose her.

"I have made a new friend in Duluth, Amby." Becca struggled to find the right words for her dear friend. "We visit with each other every week and talk on the phone even more often. He's a caring man, intelligent, and very insightful. He reminds me a lot of Steven Skorich," she laughed softly at the comparison.

Ambrose had no response, wondered where Becca was going with this revelation. 'A new friend?' 'A man she sees often?' He was confused but would allow Becca to explain further.

Turning back toward Ambrose seated at the table, Becca blurted, "He's a Roman Catholic priest—Father Pat Foley."

Nonplused, Ambrose only smiled. "That's understandable, Becca. I would see a priest myself if I were in your circumstance. I think Tony has visited with Rabbi Hammel once or twice. Has the priest been helpful to you?"

"Very much so, Amby."

"What are you planning to do about all this? Are you taking instructions in the Catholic faith?"

"Not yet, maybe never. I'm just feeling my way, trying to learn what I can and hoping to figure out how the two of us might be able to work things out—if it comes to that. It's all very confusing." Becca turned away, looking out the window again.

"I realize how it would be . . . confusing, Becca. Are you and Tony talking about all this—about what both of you are doing?"

"Not really. It's like that elephant in the house that you close your eyes to and don't talk about. It's my fault, I suppose. I'm afraid to bring it up when I should. I just don't want anything to come between us. I don't want issues complicating the precious hours we have together." Becca was distraught. "If only we had more time to talk . . . not dating talk, *real talk*. I'm always afraid of losing him. That makes me feel insecure—and I hate that feeling with a passion." Her long, delicate fingers covered her eyes so as to hide the pain she was feeling.

Ambrose did not want to intrude on Becca's private torments of the moment. The old physician decided to let her take the conversation where she was comfortable. Perhaps she needed a sounding board more than any advice he might be able to offer. Leaving Judaism, however, would be a difficult and uncertain step for Becca to take. He was certain about that. Watching her stare out at the tranquil night, Ambrose allowed Becca time to contemplate.

Minutes passed in silence.

When Becca turned away from her gaze at the window, tears welled in her eyes. "What would my father tell me to do? Whenever I'm troubled, I think of that dear man. Wishing . . ." Becca dabbed at her eyes with a lace handkerchief. "That's not fair—I'm sorry, Amby. But you are the one person in all the world most like my dad. I can't help but think of you as a father to me . . ."

Ambrose assured her, "I am flattered to hear you say that, Becca. At times, I've felt like a father to you—I do right now." He considered his next words carefully. "I knew your father well, Becca. He was my very dearest friend—You know that! I think, if he were here at this moment, he'd give you a hug, tell you he loved you, and that he trusted your judgment without reservation . . . and, he'd listen. I don't believe your father would want to give you any advice." Ambrose got up from the table and stepped close to Becca. The small man embraced her. "I love you, my dearest—and I think your dad would trust you to do what is right for you."

Becca sobbed. "Thanks, Amby. As always, you've done exactly what I imagine my father would do. A warm hug and willing ears . . . I love you, too."

Ambrose leaned back, placed his hands on her waist, found her eyes. "I do have one bit of advice, however. Talk with Tony! That's all. Talk without any fear of what might happen to your relationship. I think you will be surprised about how good it feels to open yourself—to be vulnerable for a change."

"You want me to 'push the river', don't you?"

A Reality to Live With

Despite years of anticipation for this very day, Senia felt woefully unprepared. She had an outline in her mind of what she wanted to say to Kevin and an agenda for their visit together on this morning. But Senia realized that patience was not one of her stronger virtues and wondered if she was expecting too much to be resolved—too fast. Kevin was going to be around for most of the summer and, at a certain level, she recognized that there was plenty of time to help him put his life together. At another level, however, she wanted him to have a grasp on everything before he left her that afternoon. She had talked with Father Foley about what the priest had told the boy about his father on the previous Sunday. She was pleased with the priest's discretion in explaining 'things,' and Senia knew that Kevin and Tony had talked the day before. She wished she knew the details of Tony's conversation. Perhaps she could ask Kevin to tell her what his uncle had to say. She wasn't quite sure.

If Senia already knew what *she* wanted to tell Kevin, she had no idea what Kevin might want to tell her. What questions would he ask? What preconceptions of Peter did he already have? Was he having difficulty with his newfound identity? How might he react to his inheritance? What plans did Kevin already have for his life? So many uncertainties raced through her thoughts. While she watched Kevin socializing with strangers at last evening's party, she was struck by his maturity, his easy confidence, and his outgoing personality. As closely connected as she had been over all these years, Kevin was still somewhat of a mystery to her.

"Relax!" Senia reminded herself as she sat near the front window looking out upon the tree-lined street. It was another gorgeous June morning with a westerly breeze rustling the stately elms between the sidewalk and her neatly trimmed front lawn. From where she watched, she could nearly see the Zoretek house below the overhanging branches only a block to the east. Kevin would be walking over to Senia's after breakfast "about eight or so," he'd told her the night before.

"Relax!" Senia repeated under her breath with a sigh. "Everything will go just fine." Casting a nervous glance at the wall clock, she realized it was already five before eight o'clock. If she hadn't taken this day off, she would already be into her typical daily routine at the bank.

Senia made a quick retreat to the kitchen for another cup of coffee. On the stove a creamy pan of hot chocolate simmered, and a pitcher of freshly squeezed orange juice waited in the ice box. "Does Kevin drink coffee?" The many things she didn't know about the boy were troubling.

When she returned to her window, she saw him sauntering down the middle of the street with his hands thrust deeply in his beige summer trousers. The morning sun at Kevin's back cast a long shadow in front of him. His eyes seemed to take in everything around him; it appeared as if he was whistling as he walked his leisurely pace. The sun highlighted his wavy auburn hair as he turned up the sidewalk.

Then he stood at the front door, knocking lightly, one hand still snug in his pocket. Escorting Kevin inside through the foyer toward the bright living room, Senia initiated an awkward range of small talk. "I love your green shirt—it accents the green in your eyes . . . What a wonderful party last night . . . Your Uncle Tony told me about your new bedroom, did you sleep well . . . Would you like cocoa or juice . . . ?"

Kevin complimented the simply furnished living room, identified some window plants, and accepted a cup of coffee with cream. "I'm developing a taste for coffee, Aunt Senia. I used it to help me stay awake late when I crammed for history and lit tests in high school."

They sat on a large pastel-flower patterned sofa in the sun-brightened room exchanging random tidbits of small talk. It was eight-twenty before Senia finally made her first overture. "I thought we might talk about your father, Kevin, before driving over to Mr. Power's office. He's expecting us at ten or so. Is that all right with you?"

"I'm looking forward to it, Auntie Senia," Kevin said sincerely. His aunt seemed unusually agitated, anxious. "I see you have some pictures." Kevin regarded the spread of photos on the coffee table. "I saw my first picture of my dad yesterday at Uncle Tony's. He said I resembled him—So did Mr. Atkinson. What do you think?"

Senia looked at Kevin levelly for a long moment. "Since the first time I laid eyes on you. Even more so as you grew older . . . I see Peter in so many of your features—your auburn hair, the broad jaw, ears—and, definitely in the way you carry yourself. Maybe it's a confident demeanor you both carried. Anyhow, you're a handsome young man, Kevin—I'm sure you've been told that many, many times." She smiled her compliment.

Senia reached to the table and picked one of the photos. There were seven she wanted to share with Kevin. Pictures, she knew, were a perfect icebreaker. "This one was taken when Peter bought his new 1908—I think it was an '08—Buick touring car, the only one in Northern Minnesota in its day. You can see he's got his arm around your Uncle Tony."

Kevin took the yellowed photo and studied the man with his uncle. Senia, he realized, used his father's name, Peter, almost affectionately. He said nothing, placing the picture back on the table with the others.

"I took this one at Peter's Independence Day garden party. Your father always enjoyed having his friends over to the house." She was expecting more reaction from Kevin. Swallowing hard, she continued, "I want to show you his beautiful Colonial house later this morning. I have so many wonderful memories of the Washington Street mansion."

Kevin took the picture. "That's Mr. Atkinson next to my father. Who is the other man?"

"That's Judge Brady. Mr. Brady was the manager of Hibbing's baseball team for many years. Peter was a big baseball fan, you know."

Kevin had heard about Tom Brady many times from his uncle. He nodded, still not making any comments. Peter Moran was a fine looking man. As Kevin returned the photo to the table, he spotted a picture of the hotel he'd heard so much about. He picked up a large color-tinted blowup. "My goodness, the building is huge!" Kevin gasped and counted the four stories with his finger. "It covers the entire block. Almost looks like something from Europe—London or Paris or maybe even Rome. I knew it was really something, but I had no idea . . ."

"It was Hibbing's landmark, that's for sure. Peter was so proud of the hotel—I can't put it into words," Senia said with a wan smile. "He called it his 'lady'."

"I've heard about the fire. What a tragedy! It must have been devastating to lose something so—" he searched for a word, " 'special.' " Tony told me it happened just before he died." Kevin sensed an opportunity to begin finding answers to some of his questions. Staring at the glossy portrait in his lap and avoiding Senia's stare, Kevin began.

"Father Pat told me three things: Mr. Moran was ambitious, intelligent, and well respected. That's not really much when you think about it—is it Auntie? And, Father Foley said you were the best person to 'fill in the blank spaces'—those were the words he used. Was Mr. Moran a good man?"

The question was unexpected . . . 'a good man?'—Senia blinked hard. "Yes, I would certainly say that about Peter. He did so much for his community. He was really civic-minded and helped so many people get started with their lives here in Hibbing—myself, Uncle Tony, Mr. Dinter, so many others it's hard to remember. Yes, I think that's what Father Foley meant by saying your father was widely respected."

Kevin looked up, regarding his aunt cooly, "I mean *good*. I know he must have had lots of money and influence, but I guess I mean something else. Father Pat is a good man—so is Uncle Tony, I really respect them. Was my father like them—good to people, caring about them, taking the time to help whenever someone needed help?"

Taken aback, Senia said with falling note, "Why, yes . . . I'd say very much so." Her mind raced for some example of Peter's *goodness*. "He gave generously to his church and to many charities in Hibbing." Senia felt a sense of defeat in her response.

"Why did he let me be placed for adoption?"

Although stung by the question, Senia had expected Kevin to ask her about those unusual circumstances. "When you were born in Duluth, your father was not informed. Not for several weeks, as I remember. He was in the middle of several major projects here in Hibbing—including the hotel. And, he was devastated by the death of your mother, too. I just don't think he felt he could do a very good job of parenting by himself at that time. And, Father Foley had already found you a place near St. James. It seemed as if the Schmitz family was the best solution at the time." Senia was struggling; *solution* sounded cold on her tongue. "I don't think Peter ever intended your adoption to be something permanent. It seemed like before he could do any—" Senia recovered her voice; choking with emotion she tried to finish the thought. "Then he died—unexpectedly. Before he had a chance to make things right."

Kevin could hear his aunt's stress as she bit off the words. His eyes had a remorseful cast, "How did Mr. Moran die?"

"That, I'm afraid, has never been determined, Kevin. His house was broken into, money was taken from his safe, and his car stolen. He was shot . . ." Senia lost her grip on composure, began lightly sobbing, "We think Peter was murdered that night. Someone passing through Hibbing—a transient, perhaps. The police recovered the automobile in a lake near Grand Rapids the following day, but . . ."

"His *murder* has never been solved, then?" Kevin winced, shrugged his shoulders. "Seventeen years . . ." He drew a sigh. "That's hard to imagine. I'd like to see the police records some day. And, maybe talk with Mr. Atkinson. Someone as important as my father—murdered!"

"The police think it might have been suicide, Kevin. I want to warn you about that. It's their convenient theory that Peter killed himself. But, I knew your father well enough to think that notion is completely wrong. Peter was a strong man—"

Kevin did not reply.

After a few moments of silence, "Do I have any relatives on my father's side?" Kevin's question moved the conversation from the unpleasant memory.

"Yes." Senia explained. She told Kevin about Peter's parents—Daly and Kathleen, a sister, and two brothers. Peter's mother had died in 1915—back in Warren, Pennsylvania. Aunt Emily was a widow still living in Warren and had three adult children. Kevin's Uncle Terrance had retired from the faculty of Villanova University in Philadelphia where he taught economics. And, Denis was probably somewhere out West. "Your Uncle Denis has not been heard from in years. He was in the timber business somewhere in Oregon before your father died. I wish I could tell you more about Denis, but . . ."

Kevin sipped at the cold coffee in his cup. He had lots of time to search his roots. Senia had told him all the important facts she remembered. He went back to where their conversation had started. "You were very fond of my father, weren't you, Auntie Senia?" His question seemed to revive her, bringing a smile to her face for the first time in nearly an hour. "You've told me that you worked for Peter." Kevin had not used his father's first name before. *Peter.* He wanted to be comfortable with the name.

"Fond? Yes, Peter was . . . he was generous and bright and truly a visionary back when people were often narrow-minded. He was always the optimist. I'd say, your father was someone who believed he could make a difference. He was a leader, and he trusted me, Kevin. He gave me my wings, so to speak—and let me fly. Yes, I had the greatest respect for Peter Moran."

"Well, that's something I hope to accomplish—respect, I mean. And, I admire optimism as well. Maybe we have something in common after all—my father and me. I hope so—I really hope so!" He slid across the sofa toward his aunt, put his arm around her slender shoulders. "I want to like my father, Auntie Senia. I want to forgive him for—"

"I know you do, Kevin—and you will. I pray you will." Senia felt closer to Kevin at that moment than she ever had before. "He'd be so proud of his son . . . if only—"

Kevin gave her a gentle squeeze, lightly kissed her forehead. "I know—if only! Let's leave things at that for now. May I have one of these pictures for myself?" Kevin spotted one of his father at the front entry of the hotel that he hadn't seen before. "This one?"

Smiling at his choice, Senia nodded her approval, regarded the wall clock, and began rising from the sofa. "I've told Mr. Power that we would stop by this morning, Kevin. I think he's expecting us any time now. Should we hop in the car? We've got so much more to talk about, but we've also got lots of time to do it." Kevin's affectionate gesture saved her morning, rejuvenating her spirits. "I'll drive by your father's house on the way there. It was the finest home in North Hibbing."

Vic Power thumbed through the thick 'Moran Estate' file on his desk, the contents of which had been audited by his associate, Robert Peterson, as of June first, and the financial paperwork was organized exactly as Senia

Arola had instructed. The prepared document had two major sections—Real Estate and Investments, with several subsections in each category. The total estate value was over $3.4 million.

When Kevin and Senia entered the room, Victor pushed away from his desk and strode across the carpeted floor to greet them. "Right on time," the lawyer smiled, offering his hand first to Kevin. "Had a wonderful time last night, young man. Tony is quite the host, that's for sure! Come on in and make yourself comfortable—I've got coffee and root beer, even some cookies around here somewhere." Greeting Senia, Victor pulled a chair from near his desk to seat her at his left elbow; the second chair was situated directly across the desk from Victor. "I understand you're going to be with us for the summer, Kevin. Wonderful! You're going to enjoy Hibbing—lots to do up here when the weather's nice. And, you're a baseball pitcher, Tony tells me. That's great, we only hope you've got some of Tony's stuff on that fastball of yours."

Kevin was amused by the attorney's energetic demeanor. Vic Power was, as he had been told, quite the talker. Kevin had not yet said a word, nor had Senia. "Do you like the outdoors, Kevin? Because, if you do, we've got the most beautiful lakes in all God's creation out of town. Steven will surely take you fishing one of these days. He knows where to get the big ones, right Senia?" Power didn't wait for an answer. "And, Bennett Park—have you seen our lovely park yet?"

"Not yet, sir." Kevin finally got three words into the conversation.

"We're building a brand new ball park over there. It should be ready for next season's games. The old North Hibbing field has seen its better days. But, the old-timers are not very enthusiastic about any new baseball stadium, regardless of how nice it's going to be. They—"

Senia interrupted politely, "Mr. Power, we'd like you to join us for lunch at the Androy after our meeting. Are you free?"

Kevin smiled pleasantly. The luncheon hadn't been mentioned before. "I'd enjoy talking baseball with you if you can . . ."

"My time is your time today, my friends. I'd imagine you're about ready to do some paperwork, Senia. I've got everything ready here on my desk. Has Mrs. Arola explained any of this estate stuff to you, Kevin?"

"No, sir."

"Well, then let's get started, Can I get either of you something—coffee or soda, perhaps?"

Both declined the offer.

Power handed Senia the thick folder. He had his own notes on a tablet in front of him. "Kevin, here's a tablet of your own—if you should want to take any notes—and a new pencil. I just got these pencils in on Monday. They've got Pete's and my name inscribed along the side—see that! Isn't it something? What will they think of next?"

"Kevin, as I've suggested, your father was an astute businessman." Senia began by casting a quick frown at Victor. "Before he passed, he left a statement requesting that I take care of his business affairs. Naturally, he left something to his close friends. But, mostly he instructed me to 'take care of your financial future'." She smiled toward Kevin. "You were basically his sole heir. For these many years I have, along with Mr. Power, been managing Mr. Moran's estate."

"When you turned eighteen last February, you became the beneficiary of your father's estate, Kevin." Power added. Sensing that Senia was not finished with what she wanted to say, the attorney swallowed his next words.

"Mr. Power and I have put together a report that we want to review with you this morning. What happens from this day on will be up to you, Kevin." Senia's voice had a slight shudder. "As you will learn, you are a very wealthy young man."

Kevin's hands were folded in his lap. He did not reply.

Opening the bulky file, Senia explained in detail the complex financial picture that was Peter Moran's estate. She reviewed the history of Peter's original property investments and enterprises. The lumber business, liquor distribution operations, and real estate investments were carefully outlined. Peter had purchased the land where much of the new South Hibbing was located back in 1908, and Senia had purchased additional acreage when the land prices were relatively low. As properties were liquidated, Senia and Victor made prudent investments in stocks and bonds. The economy had grown rapidly over the years and their investments significantly multiplied in market value.

For nearly half an hour Senia explained. Vic Power followed her discourse with a finger on his own notes, adding some small point to her descriptions from time to time. Kevin listened attentively, jotting numbers and ideas on his note pad. Senia, he could tell, was masterful with numbers and possessed remarkable insight about investment strategy. His aunt was the consummate banker.

When Senia was finished, she looked levelly at Kevin for a long moment. "Do you have some questions for me or Mr. Powers, Kevin?"

Kevin asked for a root beer, and Victor went to the small ice box in the corner of his office to retrieve a bottle for each of them. Kevin tried to collect his thoughts about information that was truly overwhelming—almost incomprehensible! He had saved nearly four hundred dollars for his college education and hoped to make another one hundred over the summer months. His savings was a source of great personal pride to him. Now? It was as if his whole life had changed dramatically in the space of an hour. He felt four eyes on him as he wriggled in his chair. Senia and Mr. Power were quietly waiting on his reaction to the news.

"Who knows about all this?" Kevin broke the silence.

"The three of us, and Mr. Peterson, my associate," Victor answered.

"And, Mr. Goldberg at my bank," Senia added. "They are pledged, of course, to keep the information confidential."

"Then, only five people in all of Hibbing have any idea?" Kevin's eyes shifted from Senia to Mr. Power. "No one else?"

"Just the five of us, Kevin," Power assured.

"Can we keep it that way?"

"We will do whatever you want us to do," Senia said firmly. "That's the purpose of this meeting. We want you to fully understand the estate you've inherited and . . ."

"And, you want some direction from me?" Kevin finished her thought.

Kevin stood from his chair and wandered over to the window looking out on busy First Avenue. From his vantage he could see the *Mesaba Ore* building up the street. He saw a shiny '23 Ford parked at the curb outside and thought about having his own car. Directly across the avenue he watched a young couple enter an electrical shop displaying new radios and phonographs in the neatly appointed window display. He thought of owning a small business in the bustling new downtown commercial district.

The world was his on this day—anything, everything! Nearly four million dollars! His imagination was staggered by the reality of it all. College was really quite unnecessary under these circumstances, a summer job meaningless. He could live like the 'King of Hibbing' on the estate's interest alone.

Kevin turned his head back toward Senia and Mr. Power, leaning against the window ledge. With the brightness of the morning sunlight behind him, the tall young man was framed in a radiant, almost surreal, posture. He forced a befuddled smile that neither of them could see with the bright backdrop. His words were carefully measured. "It's not my money. I didn't do anything to deserve any of this fortune you've told me about. It's my father's wealth—not mine. And, it's yours, too. Both of you have spent years making this estate what it's become."

After a long pause, Senia spoke. "It is yours, Kevin. That's a reality you will have to live with. It's not about earning anything. It's your father's gift to his only child and heir. He wanted to make certain that his son would have the financial security to do whatever he chose to do with his life. It's his gift to *you*—nobody else."

"Kevin, you don't have to do anything today or tomorrow for that matter. I know this must be overwhelming for you." Vic Power walked from his desk to the window, standing beside the young man. "With the gift goes a huge responsibility. It's a double-edged sword, as they say. Your inheritance has been held in a legal trust. Our job is to help you deal with that reality as best we can." Vic Power showed a different side of his personality to Kevin. "Senia and I only want to help you do what you think is right. I've taken an administrative commission over the years, so I've been fully compensated for my work. I'll continue to do the same in the future if that's your wish."

Senia noticed the time was approaching noon. "What do you gentlemen say about taking a break and having lunch together? Some time for you, Kevin, to pick Mr. Power's brains about baseball. We can talk about estate matters later on. Okay?"

"I'm starved!" Kevin rubbed his stomach. "Baseball talk can wait until I know something about Mr. Bergan's team, I think." He looked down at Mr. Power. "What I'd really like to talk about is being a lawyer, Mr. Power. That's what I'm planning to study at the U. next fall."

"It would be my pleasure to tell you about the law, Kevin. It's as fascinating to me today as it was twenty years ago when I first began to practice with my brother, Walter."

"And, I'd like to learn about local politics, too. From the Minnesota legend at that." Kevin laughed for the first time.

Vic Power regarded Kevin with obvious interest, locking eyes with the handsome young man. "I'm sure Tony has offered you a summer job with his construction outfit, but let me throw out another option for you to think about, Kevin. If you're serious about studying law, I'd like to give you a head start. Our firm could use a bright young law clerk for the summer. We're almost too busy to keep up with our files these days. Think about it. I'm not going to pay you as much as you could make with Tony, that's for sure, but . . ."

"But, that may not be an issue for me. Is that what you were going to say, Mr. Power?"

"Well, something like that." The Mayor gripped his shoulder affectionately, his round face creased with an engaging smile. "I'd love to have Peter's son working in my office. I had great respect for your father, Kevin. I think the two of us thought about things the same way—always positive and upbeat. I'd like some of Peter's stuff to rub off on his son."

Senia delighted over Victor's thoughtful remarks. She could not have said the same thing with nearly the impact. "Thanks, Victor. I'm sure Peter would appreciate what you've just said as much as we do." She spoke for Kevin as well as herself.

"If I'm going to live in Hibbing . . . maybe, I should think about claiming my birthright. Maybe I am finally ready to be *Kevin Moran*—after all these years."

Senia could feel her knees weaken. Her hand moved over her mouth to suppress her instinctive elation over what Kevin had just said. In her wildest imagination she could not have hoped for a more wonderful expression from the young man whose day had arrived. The stress of years melted away in that priceless moment. Maybe, just maybe . . . the old days could be relived in the blood of Peter's son—Kevin Moran.

During lunch at the magnificent Androy Hotel's Crystal Lounge, Kevin felt like an adult for the first time in his life. The shrimp salad was truly scrumptious, but the attention at their elegantly set table even more intoxicating. Everybody knew Victor Power. Everybody! After every bite, someone stopped by the table to offer their greeting to 'The Mayor' as he was called by everyone, and Kevin stood for the warm introductions that Mr. Power made. It was agreed upon before their arrival that it would be acceptable to mention that Kevin was Peter Moran's son. To those who might not have known his father, Kevin was introduced simply as Kevin Schmitz . . . "My new legal assistant from Duluth . . ." The Mayor would say with a tease in his voice. To others who had known Peter, Kevin was identified as Mr. Moran's son. "That'll give them something to talk about while they're eating, Kevin. None of them had any idea that Peter had a son before today."

"If they look closely, however, the resemblance is unmistakable," Senia added with a wide smile. The weight of the world seemed lifted from her shoulders, and she was truly enjoying their meal together. "Don't you agree, Victor?"

"A chip—that's what I think." Regarding Kevin, "I hope I'm not making you uncomfortable with my introductions. I like the sound of 'legal assistant.' It carries a little more punch with it. Don't you agree?"

Kevin nodded as a tall, stoop-shouldered man approached the table. The man had long, gray hair and a well-trimmed goatee. "Well, Mr. Power, I've been told this young man is Peter's son. Will you give me the privilege of an introduction?" The stranger was the only person who did not use the 'Mr. Mayor' monicker. There seemed to be a noticeable coolness in Victor's regard of the well-dressed visitor at their table.

"Elwood, this is Kevin. The young man has been attending a private academy the past many years and only visits Hibbing periodically," Victor cleverly fabricated. "Kevin, Mr. Elwood Trembart, a fellow member of the Hibbing bar, and a political activist of some reputation."

Kevin stood again, placing his napkin beside his plate. "My pleasure, Mr. Trembart." He extended his hand, offering a firm shake.

Kevin felt the intensity of the stare from the piercing gray eyes looking over spectacles only feet away. "Your father and I were old friends, Kevin." Trembart almost italicized the word 'old' in his wry comment. "Business associates of sorts back in Old Hibbing."

"I'm sure you'll see more of each other. Kevin will be spending the summer here, Mr. Trembart. Probably playing some baseball while he's here," Senia said rather sharply, dismissively.

"Nice of you to say hello, Elwood." Victor sat down to resume his meal.

Kevin stood awkwardly near his chair. The social snub was obvious. "I might be working for Mr. Power this summer so I'm sure I'll get to see more of you, Mr. Trembart."

"Going to be a law clerk, I imagine." Trembart's face seemed a permanent scowl.

"Yes, sir. A clerk."

When Trembart left, Victor commented. "Not everybody liked your father, Kevin. You've just met one of his oldest enemies. I'll have more to tell you about that situation later."

Victor's eyes followed Trembart across the room to a table where two men were awaiting his arrival. Quentin Berklich was the district's legislative representative, and Ian Roberts was Elwood's son-in-law. (The marriage of Ian Roberts and Molly Trembart Pell had been the social highlight of the past spring.) Berklich was a rising political figure on the Republican side of the Minnesota House. Their luncheon, Victor would bet, had something to do with local politics.

"Mr. Power, that was quite clever of you." Kevin interrupted the Mayor's thoughts, "The private academy thing. That might be a convenient explanation of my returning to Hibbing after all these years," Kevin grinned.

"Lawyers are good at that, Kevin. You'll learn some 'blarney' from one of the best this summer." Vic joined Kevin's laughter.

Talking outside the Androy after their meal, Kevin shook The Mayor's hand. "I'm going to talk to my uncle." The reference 'Uncle' seemed awkward on his tongue for the first time. "Mr. Zoretek, tonight. I'd like to take your job offer but I don't want to inconvenience . . ."

"You go right ahead and talk to Tony about it, Kevin. He'll warn you not to get me going on local politics, I'm sure of that. Let me know what you decide."

Power turned to Senia. "Let's the three of us plan to get together sometime next week after Kevin's had some time to think about things. How does that sound?"

Senia nodded. "Thanks for everything, Victor. You've been so very helpful. He's got lots to think about." She put her arm in Kevin's as The Mayor strolled away toward his office building five blocks down Howard Street. "Let me show you the new town on the way back to the house, Kevin. Then maybe we can have some dessert—if you've got any room left. I've baked a rhubarb pie and Steven says it's the best this side of his beloved Slovenia."

Driving away from the Androy, Senia turned her Chevrolet south on Seventh Avenue. Towering above the residential street was the incredible edifice of the Hibbing High School. The huge E-shaped building was castle-like and sprawled over four square city blocks. Senia explained the community's dedication to the education of its children as they drove slowly past. Kevin stared wide-eyed, making a mental note to visit the school the next day. He planned to get his own feeling for this new city by wandering the streets, visiting with the people who were out and about, and absorbing all the intangibles of a new environment.

Senia gestured ahead as she turned east on Portage, "Much of the land you see off to the right is owned by your father's estate, Kevin. You can see how rapidly the community is growing. Over there—" she pointed to her left—"one of your Uncle Tony's construction crews is building new homes and pouring concrete for sidewalks. He's got several projects going on between Virginia and Grand Rapids. I don't know how he keeps up with everything the way he does."

Kevin listened, absorbing everything his searching eyes beheld and carefully storing his impressions for future reference. It was exciting to be surrounded by a community still in its infancy, rising from the red earth and groping for a new identity. A new spirit was alive in the vital Mesabi mining hub.

Back on the wide artery that was Third Avenue heading north, Kevin saw expansive Bennett Park to his right and realized they were less than a mile from the remnants of the Old Hibbing he remembered from his childhood excursion with Gary Zench. How exciting that day had been for the two wayward boys! Kevin could not believe what he was seeing. Scattered houses and buildings, wide empty pockets where structures had lived only months or years before. Turning on Washington Street he saw the most beautiful house he'd ever seen. A driveway looped beyond the black steel gates toward a wide, columned porch fronting the majestic three-storied, white structure. Gardens lined the paved roadway. Well groomed trees surrounded the lush grounds. "This is it, Kevin. The Peter Moran mansion. Isn't it gorgeous?" Whenever Senia saw the house, she was tormented by her bittersweet memories of Peter. "Mr. Fred Bennett of the Oliver Mining Company lives here now, Kevin."

"How much longer will they allow the house to stay on this site?"

"That's up to the Oliver. They own all this land."

Kevin looked away from the house. Only blocks from where the car was parked on Washington Street, the voracious appetite of mining was everywhere in evidence. The air was choked with heavy red dust welling out of the gaping open pits. Long trains crawled across the landscape with their loads of ore, while huge trucks were creeping up the steep inclines of surrounding dumps like busy ants creating their little hills of dirt. Once on top of the flat dumps, the trucks would unload their cargo of overburden down the steep sides—further expanding the growing artificial mountain range. It seemed to Kevin as if the landscape had been raped and ravaged by the indomitable pace of mining activity.

"This is all pretty ugly, isn't it?" Kevin observed. "How much longer before everything up here is wiped out?"

"It might be many years, Kevin. There's still some life in the Old city. But, it's doomed. We're all aware of that fact. One day everything here will either be moved or knocked down by wrecking crews."

"I'll be back up in this neighborhood later this afternoon. Rudy and Armando are picking me up for my first baseball practice. I'm pretty excited about that." Kevin's statement hinted at the time and his plans.

"Let's get that piece of pie I promised you, Kevin." Senia gave him a light slap on his knee, shifted into first gear, and pulled away from the house. She would not speak any further about Kevin's estate on this already eventful afternoon. Senia would be patient—as painful as his orientation might have to be.

Rudy Zoretek introduced his cousin to Coach Bergan. "This is the guy we've been telling you about, coach—meet Kevin Schmitz. He's going to be around all summer and wants a shot at making the team."

Coach Bergan shook hands while giving Kevin a good looking-over.

"We can always use a pitcher, Kevin." He smiled at the youth, "I'm sure Rudy's told you that I played with your Uncle Tony. 'Zee' we used to call him . . . the Zee was for zero."

Kevin had heard the story of the nickname. "From what I've heard, I won't hold a candle to my uncle, but I'll give you the best I've got, Mr. Bergan."

And, Kevin's best that afternoon raised eyebrows. Pitching batting practice for nearly half an hour, nobody got much wood on his fastballs. Rudy couldn't get his timing on any of Kevin's pitches. "Don't you dare let me hit one, Kev. Keep throwing me the hard ones."

Of the seven batters Kevin faced, only Armando tagged one deep into the outfield. But even Armando's fly ball was in the ball park. Kevin's making the Hibbing city team seemed assured. "Practice again on Friday, game on Sunday, fellas." Bergan announced to the players. "Kevin. You're going to get some innings on Sunday so keep that right arm of yours loose. But no hard throwing, okay?"

Senia was in great spirit as she dined with Becca that evening. Having explained her day with Kevin, she concluded, "Don't you often wish you could read someone's thoughts, Becca? Kevin hardly showed any emotion when Victor and I told him his father's business affairs. But, what must have been going on his mind? I can't even imagine." In reviewing the morning conversation with Vic Power, however, Senia was very discreet about what she revealed.

"He's so incredibly bright, Senia. I'm sure that the next time the two of you get together he'll have some kind of plan for what he wants to do. I'd be surprised if he didn't."

"Wouldn't it be wonderful if he chose to take his father's surname? I probably think about that more than anything else. *Kevin Moran!* That would fulfill Peter's dream for his son," Senia said dreamily.

"Quite a slap in the face for the Schmitz family, though. Don't you think, Senia?"

Senia nodded without reply.

Becca had spent most of her Wednesday with Ambrose at the new Rood Hospital. Her news was well received by her former colleagues who were anxious to have her back on staff. "The only one who didn't seem enthusiastic about my return was Doctor Weirick, but the two of us never really got along very well. He doesn't like the idea of women doctors—never has. And, he'll never forgive me for taking a patient off some medication he'd prescribed. That was six years ago!"

While finishing up the dishes, the two friends shared their experiences of the eventful day, then retired to the living room for coffee. It was nearly nine o'clock but the sun still hung low in the western sky, casting shadows of the large elms across the beige carpeted floor. The women had no more than sat down when they heard a knock at the front door. It was Tony.

"Evening, ladies. I was just passing by and I smelled coffee . . . and, a trace of familiar perfume." Tony stepped over to Becca and leaned to sniff her dark hair. "That's it! I'd recognize the scent anywhere." He smiled and gave Becca a soft kiss on her cheek.

Senia was on her feet to get Tony a cup of coffee while he sat down next to Becca. "Your party last night was just wonderful," she said while walking toward the kitchen. "Kevin was thrilled about everything you did for him. It meant a lot, Tony."

"Can we take a walk in a few minutes, Bec? I didn't get enough time with you last night." Tony cupped his hand over the whisper in her ear, then spoke louder toward Senia. "I finally had a chance to talk with Kev before dropping over. Looks like he's going to pitch on Sunday—he's really excited about that."

Leaning toward Tony's ear, Becca whispered, "I'd love to. Just give Senia a few minutes to tell you about her day." She brushed a quick kiss on his lips, held his hands.

Returning with Tony's cup, "That's great news! It's been a wonderful day for him. What else did Kevin have to say?" Senia's curiosity was expected.

"Kevin thinks he's going to take Victor up on the law clerk thing he offered this morning. He's quite excited about that as well. I told him that Norm and Lud could use him whenever he wants to make a few extra dollars for his college."

"Victor was charming today." Senia smiled at the memory. "At lunch he introduced Kevin to half of Hibbing. And Kevin enjoyed every minute of it. Elwood Trembart even stopped by our table."

"I think Elwood's suspicious of anybody that has any connection to The Mayor. They've been adversaries for years."

The three of them talked for another half hour before Tony excused himself. "I've got a date tonight, Senia, so I've got to be leaving early."

Senia frowned. How inappropriate of Tony to say something about a date in front of Becca. His comment would surely break Becca's heart. "I'm very dis—"

Becca stood quickly, glaring at Tony. As if reading Senia's thoughts she said in a harsh tone, "I'm heartbroken!" She looked toward the floor, feigning a deep sob.

Tony shrugged his broad shoulders. "I'm sorry, Becca. Truly I am." Becca could not contain her delight at the charade and laughed out loud. "Will you take me with you, Tony? I haven't been on a 'date' in weeks—I've almost forgotten what two people do . . ."

Senia recognized the deception, joined the merriment. "You two had me going for a minute. Get out of here—both of you, this minute!"

The June evening was pleasantly cool, the sky was awash with the radiant glow of an awesome full moon, and countless stars sparkled in the dark heavens. The street was quiet except for the rustle of leaves swooshing in a gentle breeze. Tony held Becca's hand as they walked shoulders and hips touching with every step.

"I've got so many things I want to share with you, Becca. It seems as if when we're together there are all the distractions of whatever is going around about us. Not enough conversation about what's going on inside. Do you know what I'm saying?"

Becca smiled up into his face. "I could have said the same thing, Tony. As a matter of fact, I think I did when I talked with Ambrose last night. We've got a void in our communications, Mr. Zoretek."

Tony smiled inside. 'Mr. Zoretek!' That's what Mary would have said at the end of the sentence Becca had just spoken. Incredible! "I'd say 'a void'—almost like the Hull-Rust pits at times. I'm glad it's not just me."

"So, who gets the ball rolling? Not really an accurate baseball expression is it?"

"Maybe bowling." Tony laughed. Becca's good humor was becoming more endearing to him. Everything about Becca was helping him get more honestly in touch with his feelings. Mary had passed seven years ago. He was thirty-six years old. His logic, like his simple arithmetic, told him to subtract the minuses in his life and begin doing some addition. The calendar was an honest arbiter—It was time. "Becca, I'm finding that I enjoy myself much more when I'm with you than . . . than when I'm not. I mean, I miss you more than you know—more than I've been willing to admit to you, or to myself."

"So you want to see more of Becca. I like that idea. That's why I'm coming home in September. I guess I forgot to tell you that last night. I'm sorry, Tony."

"You're what? Coming home must mean Hibbing. Becca! Are you serious?"

"I'd better be, or lots of people are going to be awfully confused. I spent most of today at the Rood reacquainting myself with everything there. It felt really good."

Tony put his hands around her waist and lifted her into the air. As he let her down he held her for a moment inches from his face and gave her a deep kiss. "I can't tell you how happy I am at this moment." Setting her down on her toes, he held her close to him, feeling her full breasts against his chest. As his hands dropped over her round hips he felt his arousal in the pressure of his groin against her flat stomach. He knew that Becca was responding to his passion of the moment by her heavy breaths. He looked more deeply into her dark eyes than he had ever before and saw a sparkle that brought back memories, memories too long denied. Tony needed the softness of a woman again. He wanted the pleasurable feeling this woman could give him. His mouth had gone dry and the words did not sound the way he wanted them to. "I love you, Becca." Tony swallowed, hoping for stronger voice, "It's taken me five years to say those three words . . . but, they're finally out and I feel . . . I want to say I feel wonderful." He smiled, "But maybe *vulnerable* is the better word. Tell me you love me, too, Becca. Then I can truly feel wonderful."

Becca clung tightly onto his shirt as she felt her knees go numb beneath her. Her eyes began to spill a stream of tears down her face. "You love me . . . Tony, you said 'I love you'? Oh My God, yes. I love you—with everything that I am, I love you!"

Tony kissed away her tears. "We've taken the first step, Bec. Maybe it's the easiest step: I don't know. But we've got some big ones ahead of us."

"Tony, if we can take those steps together we will make it. I know we will . . . my dearest. I know we will!" Becca clung to her man.

The Gift of a Painting

Kevin and Rudy were already sitting at the kitchen table talking over coffee when Tony came downstairs. It was only six on this brightly awakening Thursday morning. Still feeling a glow from his walk with Becca the night before, Tony had a bounce in his step as he crossed the room to get himself some coffee. "Good morning, guys. What are you two doing up so early? Are you taking Kevin fishing, Rudy?"

"I told Lud I'd help him shoot some lines for the storm sewers over on Portage Street. You know Lud; he's up with the birds." Rudy stuffed the last of a cinnamon roll in his mouth as he glanced toward the kitchen wall clock. "I hear his truck outside already." Pushing away from the table, "Kev, I'll give you that driving lesson later this afternoon, how's that?" Catching Kevin's nod, Rudy was out the back door.

"And what about you, Kev? Trouble sleeping last night?"

"Not at all. Slept like a baby, Uncle Tony. I'm just a morning person—like Mr. Jaksa, I guess. You'll have to get used to seeing me at the table when you get up." Kevin laughed, "I'll always leave you some of Sadie's rolls, though." He regarded the plate with three remaining glazed cinnamon pastries. "Rudy ate most of them!" he said in teasing defense.

Tony pushed the plate toward Kevin, "Help yourself. I've got a breakfast meeting in half an hour, then another meeting, and a third one after that. It's a wonder that anything gets accomplished with all the meetings and conferences going on all the time. I'd rather be doing what Lud's doing out in the field than all the business stuff I'm stuck with."

"If you weren't doing the meetings, Lud wouldn't be doing the construction, I guess. From what I could see yesterday, your company is building this new city. You ought to be awfully proud of that."

"We're busy, all right. Sometimes I think we're too busy for our own good. I have trouble finding good workers these days."

Kevin regarded his uncle across the table. "I've got a favor to ask you, Uncle Tony. You've been so generous with me I almost hate to ask for something else."

"Anything, Kev."

Kevin explained his friendship with Gary Zench. Gary had dropped out of high school and was bouncing from job to job in Duluth. All Gary needed, Kevin believed, was a new start in life. "I know I could talk Gary into finishing his high school up here, and I could help him find an apartment. If you could give him a summer job, Uncle Tony . . . that might be all he needs."

"I'll do better than that, Kev. I can fix up that room in the basement, and he can stay here with us. Any friend of yours is a friend of the Zoreteks. I'll get him a train ticket and put him to work next week if he's willing to come to Hibbing. Give him a call today." Tony always felt good when he could do something for someone who needed a boost. He pulled on his pinstriped suit coat and adjusted his tie as he rose from the table. "I'm sorry I've got to run. Maybe we can play some catch in the back yard tonight. I want to see some of the stuff Rudy's been telling me about."

"I'd love to . . . and, thanks, Tony." Realizing he'd forgotten the 'Uncle,' Kevin felt an awkward moment.

"I like that. 'Tony', I mean. It puts us more on a friendship level. Let's keep it that way—okay?"

Kevin's best thinking was done while he was walking. He had a lot on his mind this morning and wanted to see the town through his own eyes. From Tony's house in Brooklyn Addition on East 16th Avenue, Kevin walked along the side of the wide avenue south to 19th Street on his way downtown. Passing some huge lumber and coal yards, he neared the site of the new municipal power plant two blocks ahead. The facility was enormous with smoke stacks taller than any he'd seen before. Turning up Seventh toward Howard Street, then west in the direction of the Androy, Kevin was amazed by all the early morning activity. Even the Mesaba Transport's electric trolley cars were filled with passengers traveling east toward Chisholm, Virginia, and Gilbert, or west to Keewatin. The Standard Oil service station with its large Red Crown Gasoline sign rising over Howard Street already had a line of three cars at the pumps. Passing the Central Laundry, garages, and shops of every variety, Kevin stopped in front of the State Theater. A new Rin-Tin-Tin movie was playing: *The Lighthouse by the Sea.* He thought of Gary Zench and his dog, Scout.

A large poster tacked to a telephone pole flapped in the light morning breeze. The advertisement was for the Lee Bros: '*4 Ring Wild Animal Show*' . . . with a newly added feature, *Cinderella in Jungleland.* A mile-long street parade was set for tomorrow with carnival performances at the Hibbing Fairgrounds throughout the weekend. Kevin crossed Howard and turned left. He wanted to see the Hibbing High School again.

Two blocks beyond the Androy, he turned south on Seventh. Reaching the high school building, Kevin climbed the series of concrete steps to the front entrance of the palatial building. Inside the school, he was struck by the enormous hand-painted murals surrounding the marbled entry foyer. The school was like an art museum. Up another flight of brass-railed stairs he peered down the wide corridors. The building was two blocks long but somehow seemed even larger. Ahead, passing inset trophy cases, Kevin strolled toward the auditorium. Once inside the opulent room, he felt as if he were in another world-a world almost beyond imagination. The auditorium seated 1800 in plush, velvet upholstered chairs. Hanging from the ornately frescoed ceilings were cut glass chandeliers that could grace the ballroom of an European castle. Sprawling across the front of the huge space was a stage large enough for a football game. Kevin had never seen anything so magnificent.

The auditorium brought his father to mind. Peter Moran's hotel must have been equally splendid. From everything he had been told, the Hotel Moran possessed an opulence beyond anything Hibbing had seen in its day. Kevin sat in one of the aisle seats to pause in his thoughts. He already knew where he was going from the school building. He knew who he wanted to talk with this morning.

If Kevin was going to learn what kind of man his father really was, that information would not come from Senia. His aunt, he already realized, had an almost unnatural affection for Peter Moran. To her, Peter had been something larger than life itself. Kevin would consider that attraction at some future point; it wasn't important to him right now. And Tony was unusually reserved in his portrayal of Peter Moran. There was something about their relationship that remained beneath the surface. In time, however, even he might be willing to talk about it. Tony was about as honest as any man might hope to be. Becca had not known his father, but if she had, Kevin believed she would be candid with him. Vic Power? Mr. Power was a business associate. No, there was someone else.

Kevin pondered where his mind was taking him this morning. Everything that had happened in the space of the past five incredible days since his graduation caused him to feel like a mouse in a maze. He needed to resolve what he would do about who he was. *He was Kevin Moran*! If he continued his life as Kevin Schmitz, he would only be denying the truth. He was heir to a fortune about which only a handful of people were aware. He was already determined that he wanted that reality kept in strictest confidence. He felt at home in this raucous mining hub. The connection with Hibbing was in his marrow. These three realities were the essence of what he'd come to grips with these past few days.

Kevin's summer would be exciting beyond any preconceived hopes he might have brought with him to Hibbing. He'd work for Vic Power and have a head start on his college pre-law classmates. He'd play baseball with his cousin Rudy, and get some pointers from Tony as well. He'd go fishing with Steven. And, hopefully, he'd spend some time with his friend, Gary. Later in the summer, he'd visit with Art and Sarah and Pat Foley about what was happening in his new life. His decisions might be hurtful to them, but . . . he had to be who he was!

Claude Atkinson was stewing over the Thursday edition of his *Ore* which would be going to press in fifteen minutes. His son, Marc, had worded the headline banner: *Insane Man Kills Eight*. Claude didn't like it. He had suggested 'Tragedy in Ohio' when he passed the news story on to Marc earlier in the morning. His son had disregarded his suggestion again. (A whacko named Lloyd Russel had murdered his mother along with his brother, sister-in-law and the couple's five children in Hamilton, Ohio.) Sadly, Claude realized, this was the kind of story that sold newspapers these days. On the *Ore's* second page was a a story depicting a local tragedy that the newspaper had carefully followed over the past month. A Chisholm youngster, only twenty, was pleading guilty to killing his father in the basement of their home. On page three was the Dumb Dora comic strip which Claude found absurd, a large ad for the coming Wild Animal Show, and smaller ads for Dollar Days at the Itasca Bazaar Department Store.

Claude flipped past the Society page and found his favorite section—Sports. Jack Dempsey would be fighting Gene Tunney this year. Hibbing's baseball team was pitching their ace, Buddy Booth, against the Zenith City nine from Duluth on Sunday. Busses would be made available for the following weekend series at International Falls. Claude chuckled to himself, "Busses for the Fall's game! What people won't do . . ." International Falls, a Canadian border city, was just across the Rainy River from legal drinking. Busses! "They'll get three hundred so-called 'fans' to ride four hours up to Falls just for some cold beer!" Rubbing his long jaw, he mused . . . "It might be kinda fun, though. Wonder if I'll sign up?"

Five Hibbing golfers from the Mesaba Country Club would be competing in the Minnesota amateur tournament at the Minneapolis Golf Club on the weekend. Club champion, Ralph Bogan, had a good chance of winning it all. Claude scratched his head, "Golf! Why God gave humanity that frustrating sport I'll never know. It's going to put me in an early grave." He had taken up the game the previous summer and was gradually becoming addicted to all the pains of making so much as a bogey. Claude had a natural slice. The course had narrow fairways fringed with deep woods. Enough said about his dilemma. "At ten cents for every new golf ball, eight dollars for my clubs, and a dollar for every round—this confounding game will be my financial ruination." Laughing at himself as he often did, Claude realized he loved the pain.

He browsed some inane comic strips on page ten, and considered spending a few minutes on the crosswords puzzle. Deciding against the waste of time, he then scanned the want ads for a good used car. Brown Motors had a Maxwell touring car. Maybe he'd check it out on Saturday. Folding the paper, Claude shouted through the open door toward Andy Zdon who was always waiting for his order at precisely ten every morning: "Roll the presses!"

"We're already pourin' ink, boss." Andy's reply was as familiar as his habit of tugging at his red beard while standing outside Claude's office. "A young man here to see ya, Mr. Atkinson. Sez yer not spectin'im."

Standing behind the print shop foreman was the tall figure of a young man Claude had met only two nights before. "Kevin. What a pleasant surprise. Come on in and pull the door shut. Your timing is perfect, I've just sent our ten thousand four hundred and twelfth issue to the press shop. I'll hope for a better newspaper tomorrow." Claude gave his traditional apology tinged with his erstwhile optimism. "Are you a coffee drinker, Kevin?"

Kevin laughed easily at Claude's comment, "It's always been a good-looking paper, sir. And, yes, I'd love a cup—black."

Claude had a small hot plate in his office and kept coffee perking all day. He poured Kevin a cup and refilled his own. "What brings you down to the *Ore* this morning? This horrible coffee I promised you or just some good, homespun conversation?" Claude knew the answer to his question before asking it. He sensed that Kevin would be searching for his sense of identity from their first meeting. "Come by anytime," he'd offered his invitation that night with the keen insight that he would be visiting with the young man before the end of the week.

"I told you I had some pictures and old news stories of your father, Kevin. I can dig those out for you, but I'd rather just talk—unless you'd rather . . ."

"Just talk, Mr. Atkinson, about my father." Kevin flashed an easy smile, then contorted his face, "This coffee—it's everything you promised, sir." Kevin had felt an immediate level of trust with this congenial gentleman and knew he had come to the right place for his answers.

"That coffee will put hair on your chest, Kevin." Claude laughed, leaned back in his chair and fingered his chin. "Let me warn you in advance—I'm an old storyteller who likes to wander with his thoughts." He leveled a serious expression across the cluttered desk. "You're going to hear some things you won't like, and maybe, some things that will make you feel pretty good about your 'old man'."

Claude closed his eyes and reminisced. "I first met Peter Moran back in '99 when I got off the train here in Hibbing. His father, Daly was . . ." Claude walked through that period's history with a comprehension of people, place, and time that was mesmerizing. Peter was the main focus of Claude's elaborate story and the center of much that was Hibbing in those days. "It was Peter Moran's town then. Nobody would argue that fact, Kevin. When his hotel opened, he was like the 'Patron Saint' of Hibbing." Pausing in his thoughts, his forehead wrinkled. "Then things began to change for Peter. His demons seemed to come after him from all sides. Business deals went sour, and old ghosts came out of the closet. Quite frankly, your father didn't handle adversity very well. His fondness for good Irish whiskey was a part of his manner of coping with setbacks, and he began to isolate himself in his mansion. You've got to see the place, Kevin, it's . . ."

Kevin cleared his throat. "I have, sir. Yesterday with Senia. I'd like to go back and meet Mr. Bennett one of these days."

Claude nodded knowingly. "Anyhow . . ." He closed his eyes and returned to the year of 1908. He told about the allegations and Peter's involvement in a subversion that resulted in a construction worker's death two years before. "The grand jury was scheduled to hear the facts—then, there was the fire!" Claude elaborated those last days of Peter's troubled life. "He was a fighter, that man. He might have cleared himself of the accusations—but I doubt . . ."

His eyes opened, locking into Kevin's stare. "Nobody knows for sure what happened the night after the hotel fire. Some believed that Peter took his own life rather than face the humiliation of the grand jury . . . or, perhaps, out of utter despair over the loss of his magnificent hotel. If I didn't know your father better, I might have sided with those who thought suicide. There was that note to Senia, of course." Claude explained the contents.

Claude continued. "If you took that letter all by itself—well, it would seem like the last words of a man who was about to take his own life. But, there were too many other facts to cloud the picture." He mentioned the dirt in the hallway that had been tracked into the house from the garden, money which apparently had been stolen from Peter's safe in the library, and the Buick missing from the garage which was recovered near Grand Rapids the following day. "Just too many pieces to the puzzle, Kevin."

"I don't know what to make of it myself, Mr. Atkinson," Kevin shrugged. "My gut feeling from what you've told me is that my father didn't... I don't think he took his own life! But who...?"

"I'm going to tread on some thin ice, Kevin. This will be just between the two of us—off the record—as some like to say."

"Fair enough, sir. You and me."

Claude told Kevin about the circumstances surrounding his childhood kidnapping. "Sam Lavalle and a woman named Brown both did time for the abduction. A third man named Ducette claimed he was involved in the plot, but Ducette was judged 'legally insane' before his trial for the arson of your father's hotel. He ended up in a hospital down near St. Peter. I think he's still there. Are you following all of this?"

"Perfectly. Are Lavalle and Brown still in prison?"

"No, they're out there somewhere. I have no idea where." Claude leaned forward, resting his elbows on the desk, dropping his long jaw into his hands. "There was a fourth man involved."

Claude explained his theory about Denis Moran, Peter's wayward brother. "There was bad blood between the two of them. Your father had Denis run out of town after an embarrassing scene during his hotel's grand opening celebration. Denis ended up in Duluth—then disappeared."

"You think he came back to Hibbing?" Kevin's stomach was in a knot. "Maybe to kill my father?"

"I told you, Kevin, I'm on thin ice with my theory. There's not a smidgeon of evidence linking your uncle to Peter's death. Nothing! The local police and the Feds have had a dead end on Denis Moran for... seventeen years it is already. He didn't go out to Warren, Pennsylvania, where your grandmother lived, and he was never seen out in Oregon where he worked with your grandfather for several years. Denis just seemed to vanish from the face of this earth."

Kevin was exhausted from the account. "My Uncle Denis?" was all he could say.

Always sensitive, Claude put his positive touch on what had been a gut-wrenching story. "Kevin. I truly liked your father. I found myself in his visions for this city. I found a kinship in his ambition to make Hibbing something of which we all could be proud. And, he always treated me with respect. We spent many hours talking about baseball, about local politics, community issues . . . everything imaginable. When his hotel opened I sat next to him in the main banquet hall. Among all the dignitaries that night, he chose me. I was flattered. When he had a party at the mansion, I always had an invitation. It was hard not to like Peter Moran. That's the honest truth!"

"But he could drive you mad at the same time, couldn't he? It must have been hard for you to see him going downhill at the end."

"Harder than anything in all my years, Kevin. And, when he died, I was devastated. Writing your father's obituary was like taking blood from my soul." Claude's eyes moistened at the memory.

"I'm going to talk with Mr. Power about having my name changed to Moran, sir. Not for my father's sake . . . for my own. It just feels right somehow."

"I can understand that, son. Despite everything else, he is your blood."

Kevin swallowed hard at his next question. "I have the greatest respect for you, Mr. Atkinson . . ." He leveled his eyes on his father's old friend. "Do you think it's a good idea?"

Claude leaned forward, splayed his long fingers on his desktop. "I'll be candid with you, Kevin. Being a Moran in Hibbing these many years after your father . . . well, it may be a blessing for you—and it may be a curse. I think that's what you're going to have to discover for yourself. But, I'd say, yes. Give it your best."

Kevin considered Claude's words: *"A blessing or a curse!"* He would meet that challenge head on. Such would be his mission in life.

"Let the clutch out slowly, Kev. You'll kill the engine every time if you let it pop up like that." Rudy was exasperated at his cousin. "Okay, back into first gear—that's right, at least you've got the gears down. Now, easy . . ."

Kevin felt the friction point in the clutch as he released. Then, easily into second . . . smoothly again—then into third. Rudy's Chevy was gliding up Third Avenue, past Bennett Park toward North Hibbing.

"That's it, Kev. Now, let's pull over to the side and start again."

On the next two tries, Kevin had no problems with his shifting. The steering and braking were easily mastered. "As easy as pitching a baseball, Rudy. Nothing to it." Kevin boasted. "Let's drive around the old town for a while." He turned around the block when reaching the Oliver Mining Company fences near Railroad Street and headed back on First Avenue. On Mahoning Street, Kevin had to sharply swerve Rudy's car to avoid chunks of blasted rock debris.

"It's getting dangerous up here with the mine blasting so close," Rudy exclaimed.

At Washington Kevin turned left, toward the east. "I want to drive by my father's old house. Have you seen it before, Rudy?"

"The mansion? Sure, everybody's seen it, Kev. We all wonder what's gonna happen to it when the mining gets another block or two in this direction. It's gotta be too big to move."

"I wonder about that. Maybe . . . maybe it could be moved. They'd have to cut it up some and put it back together. But, maybe?"

"Ask Tony about that, Kevin. He can figger out anything."

Becca called St. Mary's Hospital in Duluth and negotiated a few 'vacation days' off from her duties. She would spend the rest of the week in Hibbing. Marco's birthday was on Friday night, Kevin and Rudy played baseball on Sunday afternoon, and then there was Tony! Becca was still floating on air over Tony's revelation the night before. There was no proposal, but he'd told her . . . "Don't go out looking for a house."

So, that morning, Becca made a deposit on a spacious one-bedroom apartment at the stately Belmont on Howard Street, only a few blocks from the hospital. Leaving the Belmont, Becca did some shopping. At the music store she found an RCA phonograph, a Louie Armstrong record, and some saxophone sheet music for Marco's birthday. She'd remembered an argument between Marco and his sister over 'who could use' the living room phonograph before the party on Tuesday. With his own phonograph, some domestic issues might be resolved.

A delicate charm bracelet in Teske's Jewelry Store caught her eye, and she decided it would be a perfect little gift for Angela. Sometimes, she realized, the *other* siblings suffered through a repressed jealousy when watching a brother or sister getting all the presents and attention.

In a bookstore, she found an abridged *Blackstone Law Dictionary* that Kevin would love to have. For Rudy, she found a bottle of lilac cologne. At the Itasca Bazaar shop she found an embroidered apron for Sadie Baratto. Becca loved to shop and found pleasure in giving gifts, especially 'friendship' tokens that were unexpected. She'd find something small for the Hanes—perhaps a plant at the floral shop—and maybe, earrings for Senia. But, Tony? What might she find for the man in her life? Clothing or jewelry would be too personal and inappropriate.

While window-shopping along Howard Street, Becca spotted the old wooden sign of a quaint little art studio two doors off the main street. Inside, she browsed the landscape and wildlife paintings haphazardly covering the walls of the long narrow shop. Becca had a feeling, there was something perfect for Tony in this cluttered studio. The artist, a narrow shouldered man with long gray hair was working with his oils at an easel near the back of the shop.

"Bon jour, madame." The thickly accented French greeting startled Becca. "I am Jacque. Jacque Grojean. May I help you with something, perhaps?" The small man wore a black eye-patch and had a deep scar from the corner of his mouth across his stubble cheek. His white coat was covered with paint smearings down the front and on his sleeves.

"I'm looking for . . ." Becca shrugged. "I guess I don't have any idea what I'm looking for. A painting of some kind, but not a wild life . . ."

"For a gentleman, madame?"

"Yes. A gentleman friend of mine."

"Might I know who that is, madame? It would help me find something." Jacque offered an engaging smile. "I have lived in Hibbing for many, many years, madame. I had a small shop on Center Street in the old city. Over the years I have met most of the people here."

"Do you know Mr. Zoretek by any chance?"

"Tony? My goodness, yes. Tony a very good man and old friend. My shop was across the street from his little carpentry business years ago. Yes, Tony—a wonderful man is your friend."

"Tony's carpentry shop?" Becca's attention was piqued. That must have been years before she had come to Hibbing.

"Oh yes, madame. Just a small shop he had. That was before Tony's business got so very large." Jacque scratched his head. "I may even—yes, I have a photograph somewhere—in one of my drawers. Would you like to see the picture? I painted many old street scenes in those days from my photographs."

"Painted street scenes?"

"My goodness, yes." Jacque said emphatically. "All the streets—from different—ah, perspectives, I would say. I must have painted several old Center Street scenes. Let me check in the back room, madame."

Jacque turned abruptly, like a man with a mission. "Oh, yes . . . I know there is something," he said over his shoulder.

In ten minutes, Jacque was rushing back into the display area where Becca browsed the amazingly colorful canvases. "I told you . . ." Jacque held a large oil painting in front of him for Becca to see. "Yes, this is your friend's little shop. Can you remember it, madame?"

Becca was stunned at what she saw. In vivid color was a row of three buildings. On the left was a glass-fronted wooden structure that occupied the corner lot on the block. Across the window, in bold black lettering with golden edging was an unmistakable identification: 'Zoretek Carpentry and Construction'. Above the door was the scarcely legible, '420 Center Street' address. "That was Tony's first shop?"

"Yes, madame. As I said, right across the street from my studio. You do not remember?"

"It's a beautiful—" Becca could hardly finish the thought. What a perfect gift for Tony. "I didn't live in Hibbing back then. When did you do this work?" she asked. But before he could answer, she had another question. "Does Tony know about this painting, Mr. Grojean?"

The artist smiled, "Call me Jacque, please! No, I wouldn't think so. And, the painting has a date on the back—July, 1908."

"I'll buy it, Jacque. It's just perfect! How much do you want?" Becca was reaching into her purse.

"A gift for Tony . . . I cannot charge you for this painting," the artist said with heavy indignance in his voice. "When I moved my studio to this place, Tony took out the old walls for me, and rewired so the lighting would be better for my eye." He pointed to his good eye. "I like to think I see detail better with this than if I had vision in both eyes."

Becca was insistent. "I must pay you for this."

"Do you know what Tony charged me for the work he did? I will tell you—nothing! Not a penny did he want from me. I was outraged. You must take my money, Tony. I told him that. But no. 'Give one of your paintings to the new library, Jacque', was all he said. A good man, Tony."

Despite his protest, Becca gave him a twenty dollar bill.

"I will make you a deal, madame." Jacque shook his head. "If you insist on giving me all this money, I will frame Tony's picture in a lovely dark oak for you. I will do that this very afternoon so you can have it tomorrow."

Marco was delighted with all his birthday presents. Senia and Steven had wrapped a new fishing-tackle box with an assortment of hooks and lures inside. Marco relished his attention. One by one he opened his presents to the 'oohs' and 'ahhs' of everybody circled around his place on the floor in the center of the living room. After unwrapping the box with the phonograph, he leaped to his feet and ran over to the chair where Becca sat and gave her a hug. When the thirteen candles were blown out and birthday cake eaten, the new teenager was off to his bedroom, along with two of his neighborhood friends, to show off how he could play his new sax and to try out the fancy RCA record player.

Kevin was delighted with his book. "Becca, how could you? You gave me twenty dollars for my graduation! I'm getting much too spoiled by all of you." He gave her a kiss on the cheek and sat back paging swiftly through the thick tome.

Rudy was surprised by his small gift box and opened it at the dining room table. Sniffing the fragrance he smiled at Becca, "Do you think this will help me get a date with Colleen Grady?"

Angela's first comment at the charm bracelet was, "It's not my birthday." She followed with, "I already have a bracelet. And I don't ever wear it!"

Stung by Angela's sharp rejection, Tony was about to send Angela to her room for the evening. He felt Becca squeeze his hand under the table. "Don't, please!" Becca whispered.

"I know how you feel about bracelets, Angela." Becca smiled as best she could. "I have some, too, and I don't often wear them. But maybe we can exchange it for something else one of these days."

Realizing she had offended her father as much as she had Becca with her cruel remarks, Angela made a sarcastic attempt at reconciling "I'll keep it, *Doctor Kaner*." She bit off her words. "Maybe I will wear it to school in the fall."

The tension at the table was broken by Kevin. "Angela, Becca didn't have to get any of us anything. She only wanted to show her friendship." He reached across the table. "Can I see the bracelet?"

Angela passed it to him without comment.

"Gosh, it's beautiful, Becca. Real gold, I can tell. And the charm is a book. You must have known Angie loves to read."

Kevin's compliment of the bracelet brought a quick reaction from Angela. "You've had it long enough, Kevin. It's mine, you know."

Sadie brought coffee to the table wearing her new apron. "I just love the colors, Doctor Kaner." She smoothed the garment over her large stomach and smiled an unspoken, but well understood, thank you.

"Speaking of color, will you all excuse me for a moment? I almost forgot another package. I left it by the front door—I'll be back in a minute."

Conversation sprung to life at the table. Steven suggested a fishing excursion to Rudy and Kevin when Becca left the room. "I like to fish now and then, too, Steven." Tony gave his uncle a hurt expression. "Why not the four of us?"

Senia watched as Angela tried to attach the hasp on the bracelet under the table out of eyesight. "Let me help you, Angie. It's so delicate . . ." Angela let her fix the chain on her wrist then shot a quick frown at Kevin across the table. "Don't stare, Kevin!"

The framed Jacque Grojean painting was wrapped in old newspaper. Returning to the dining room, Becca stood at the end of the table opposite Tony, holding the bulky package behind her back. "Angela, I've got a surprise for your father. Will you step behind him and cover his eyes while I unwrap it? Please?"

"Well, I suppose." When she put her hands over her father's eyes, she whispered, "I'm sorry, daddy. I wasn't very nice again."

Tony placed his hands over his daughter's, "We'll talk later, sweetheart," he whispered back.

"Okay. You can let him see now." Becca felt a pang of apprehension. What if Tony . . ?

When Angela pulled her hands away from Tony's eyes, his jaw dropped.

A flood of memories raced through his thoughts. One of the happiest days in his life was captured on the beautiful canvas. He remembered the day when his friend, Tommy Pell, painted the inscription on the large front window. For a long minute, Tony relived the fun of cleaning his old office space with Mary working at his side. Steven and Senia were a part of the sweeping, mopping, and painting on that Saturday so many years ago. He remembered that swell of pride about owning this new little business on Center Street, and hanging all his hopes and dreams for the venture on the the fragile thread of his own self-confidence. For the moment, Tony was back in 1908, a time when he was so deeply in love that his heart ached at the sight of his beloved, Mary.

He looked up from the painting to focus his gaze upon Becca's apprehensive smile. This wonderfully thoughtful and perceptive woman who was holding a fragment of his history in her delicate grasp had captured his soul—his very essence. She was giving him a piece of himself that she knew nothing about. He was in love again—he knew it more profoundly than at any time before!

"I'm . . . speechless, Becca!" His eyes moistened as he fought with his emotions, his heart pounded in his chest. "It's the most wonderful gift I've ever been given. I mean that. Where did you—? How did . . ."

Responding to an instinct that welled inside, Tony pushed himself away from the table. Reaching Becca, he put his arms around her—almost causing her to drop the frame. "I love you!" This time, unlike the night before on the quiet street outside, everybody at the table could hear those three most intimate words a tongue can profess. He didn't care any more—their secret now belonged to all the world.

Kevin sat on his bed listening to the late August rain splashing against the window. With his diary resting in his lap, he paged through the treasured memories of the happiest summer of his young life.

Sunday: June 7.
Caught my first walleye yesterday. Steven said it was about two pounds. It was great meal last night. I didn't really embarrass myself today but pitched poorly. Three innings—two walks and a hit

given up. Tony found a flaw in where I was releasing the ball. Something to work on. We lost to Duluth by 4-2. Rudy got a single. Armando homered. Angela wore her bracelet all day. I don't think she likes me very much. She said her dad never walked anybody when he pitched.

Wednesday: June 10.
Vic Power is really a funny guy. He's always talking politics. My third day was boring though. Lots of filing papers and documents. Mr. Atkinson stopped by to visit with Mr. Power. I'm supposed to call him Claude from now on.
Having lunch with Senia tomorrow. I'll tell her to keep everything the way it is. (I want to buy a used car though.)
Tony hung his new painting in the living room. When he looks at it he remembers Aunt Mary and Becca both.
Driving lesson with Rudy went well.
It rained hard this afternoon. Angela read a book and wore her pajamas all day today. She didn't come downstairs for supper.

Tuesday: June 16.
I wonder if I really want to be a lawyer. Mostly, Mr. Power works on papers all day. I thought we would be in the court room all the time with interesting cases. Probate and deed documents are all I've seen. He will be in court next week with an auto accident case.
Claude took me up to my father's old house today and introduced me to Mr. Bennett. A nice man. Very rich. He said the house would be too expensive to move when the time came. Tony told me that it could be done. I find myself thinking about that house.
Senia will take me down to Brown's to look at a '23 Ford later in the week.
Tony was on the phone with Becca for almost an hour last night.
Still haven't been able to get ahold of Gary. He's not living at home anymore. Mr. Power called the Duluth police for me. They will let him know if they can locate Gary.

Rudy had a date with Colleen Grady—must be his cologne?
Angela taught me how to play gin rummy and I beat her.

Sunday: June 28.
I'm going to work construction two days a week with Mr. Jaksa. Mr. Power has been spending too much time finding work for me at the office. He says I'm too efficient. Good lawyers work slowly he said. He told me about my father's land deal and how Mr. Trembart was angry with dad for beating him to the property. (I called him Dad? Didn't I, diary? Sounds good enough to me.) Art and Sarah called. I guess I'm going to spend the weekend of the Fourth with them and Father Pat. I'll miss two games, the parade, and an Italian picnic. Becca will be up in Hibbing for the celebrations.
She and Tony are going to the fireworks.
Angela says she hates parades and picnics and summer in general.

Monday: July 6.
The weekend in Duluth was only OK. Too much time hanging around the house got boring. Art and Sarah were happy to see me so it was worth it to be there. Art even gave me a hug. I took a walk with Father Pat on Saturday afternoon. I wanted to ask him about my name. He says I should change it if I want to and that Art and Sarah would understand. I don't know what to do. It's like I'm just 'Kevin'—nobody uses my last name up here. I am feeling more like Moran than Schmitz. I promised to visit them all again—before school starts in the fall. Art got a promotion at work and Sarah is really active in things at St. James. They are doing fine.
Senia says she will take care of the car business for me. The Ford has a good motor and no dents. I can't wait.
I saw Becca at the depot. She was catching the train to Duluth when I was getting off at Hibbing. She said to ask Tony about 'the news' when I got home. She was happier than I've ever seen her. Now I know why. Tony proposed at the fireworks show on Saturday night. I'm really happy for both of them.

Angela told me later that her dad didn't really love Becca. I think she feels that her dad is betraying her mom.

Wednesday: July 22.
I finally got a call from Gary. He thought he was in trouble when the police came to the door of the place he was staying. He will think about coming to Hibbing and finishing high school. We talked about that time we came up here on the train. He's doing OK he says. I don't believe him. I worry about Gary a lot.
Baseball sure takes a lot of time with practice and weekend games. With Tony's help I'm getting much better at locating my pitches.
I've won four games and a no-decision in the other. Claude said he was going to call the baseball coach at the University and tell him I should get a tryout with the Gophers. Wow! I'll have to call Huddy Tusken and tell him. We are still planning to share a room in the dormitory in the fall.
I'd rather be working construction than at the law office. Mr. Power thinks I should get a degree in political science or business and not rush into law school. He's always telling me that I'm a natural politician. He used the word 'charisma' — said my dad had that.
Rudy broke his hand at work today. He's out for the rest of the baseball season. Tony is going to train him in on office stuff.
Angela says she thinks I should go to school in Hibbing and get my first two years at the junior college. I was surprised. I thought she couldn't wait to see me go.

Monday: August 3.
It's already August. Sadly, the summer is flying by too fast for me. Tony had the bad news he was expecting from Slovenia. His mother, Helen, passed at seventy-two years old. Helen was also Steven's sister. The two men went to the church to light candles and say some prayers last night. Becca was here this weekend and she went with them to the Catholic Church. I'm glad she was here for Tony. Tony told me his father, Jakob, had died some five years ago. And, that he had never returned to his home country in all the years.

We talked for a long time yesterday. Tony told me about his coming to America at my age. His story was a tragic one—like that of many immigrants back then. I enjoy the stories of the history of this area. It makes me appreciate how good I have it.

I finally got Senia to join me for Sunday Mass yesterday. Steven went along as well. Tony told me that they have been seeing more of each other this summer than they have in years. Senia has been more relaxed lately—even fun to be around.

As I feared, Gary got in with a bad crowd. He was arrested in a pool hall robbery in West Duluth last week. Victor got the news for me. He says Gary will go to the reformatory in St. Cloud.

I finally raised my batting average to over 300 with three hits on Sunday. We beat Virginia for our fifth straight.

Angela changed her mind—again. Now she thinks I'm smart to be going to Minneapolis for college. She says she'd like to see the big city some day. She was rude to Becca again this weekend. Then she apologized to her father for her bad behavior. She's a manipulator.

Monday: August 24.

My last week of summer in Hibbing lies ahead. I've put $123.00 in my savings account this summer and plan to take this week off from my two jobs. Lots of things to get done before school.

I will be having lunch with Claude and Vic tomorrow and Senia on Thursday. Senia will be sending me $25.00 every month so I can keep my savings account from going dry. I think it's too much money—even with the added expense of my car.

The guys camped overnight at Timo's Lake on Friday for our last fishing excursion. Steven, Tony, Rudy, Marco, myself—and Armando came along. We cooked our fish on the lake shore.

Angela complained that girls never 'have any fun' and wouldn't eat any of the walleye fillets we brought home. She said she wasn't going to eat fish that she didn't catch for herself from now on. She is a stubborn one. I think Angela grew three inches over the summer and looks more like her mother every day. Lucky girl.

Sunday: August 30.
We all got Becca's furniture moved this weekend. She's got a nice apartment. No wedding plans yet. Father Foley helped us load the truck down in Duluth. It was so good to see him again.
Since talking with Claude that day in June, I have wondered a lot about my dad's death. The police officer I talked with about the old files said the 'official' version was suicide. That bothers me.
Some day I will find out what really happened.
I leave for Minneapolis and the University tomorrow morning. The drive will take most of the day but I have some good directions.
Victor knows the Twin Cities very well from his many trips there.
He drew me a perfect map that will get me to my dormitory.
(Hud Tusken is already on campus for basketball training.)
Victor also redid my scholarship papers. I'm registered as Kevin Moran at the University. He is filing documents for a legal 'name change' at the courthouse next week. I talked with Art and Sarah and they were okay with it. I could tell it hurt them though.
Claude has talked with the baseball coach at the U. and I am supposed to meet him next week.
Senia will cry when she sees me off. I know that.
I wonder if Angie will. She said things won't be the same without me being around the house. She said she might write me a letter sometime if things got boring. Marco teased her that she had a crush on me and I thought she'd punch him in the mouth.
My little Ford has new tires (Senia insisted) and is all gassed and ready to go. I won't need it when I'm in school. Plan to be back here for Thanksgiving. Tony invited Art and Sarah and Father Foley to join us for the holiday.
So, the next entry will be written in my home away from home.

'... To Have Held the Bird...'

CLAUDE WAS IN HIS OFFICE when he got the call from Steven Skorich. He could hear the pain in Steven's voice. "Bad news, Claude. Very bad news, I'm afraid." Then there were deep sobs. "It's Victor."

Claude clutched his phone. "Don't tell me, Steve . . ."

On Tuesday, April 6, 1926, Victor Power died unexpectedly at his residence. Doctor Hane believed a massive heart attack had felled the forty-six year old Hibbing legend.

Thousands turned out for the funeral Mass at the Blessed Sacrament Church. Claude was asked to give an eulogy. "With his passing an era has closed on our city's history . . . an era that will remain unsurpassed for generations to come." Pausing to check his emotion his words were strained. "The Mayor's footprints are imbedded upon every street in Hibbing and his vision indelibly etched in our memory forever. Vic Power saw our tomorrows before the calendar turned them over for our eyes to see. He was always ahead of his time—always out in front of us, always giving directions at a fork in the road. As a leader he was without peer in all of Minnesota. We were richly blessed." Claude looked up from his carefully written notes. "During his time he was accused of every crime and corruption—of immorality and extravagance, and every other sin that a politician is liable to be accused of. Yet, he could smile in the face of his antagonists and could best them in every corner of the ring. 'Mr. Mayor' never backed down from a confrontation. We, all of us in this packed church, know that . . . be you his friend or his foe. This *Little Giant* who has fallen kept his focus on what was righteous. This magnificent little man will be rewarded by his

God with a place in heaven that . . ." Claude's voice strained, " . . . a place that will look very much like his place on earth. I am sure that his reward for serving us with his every fiber, until his very last breath, will be an eternity in what was his heaven while on this earth. Vic Power will forever live in Hibbing with Percy, who left us earlier to make things ready for her devoted husband."

Within hours, all of Minnesota had learned of Mayor Power's death, and mourned the loss of Mesabi's strongest voice. Thousands of letters and telegrams poured into the mining hub in the days and weeks that followed.

Outside the overcrowded church on that funereal Friday morning, Steven spoke to the hundreds who braved foul weather on the sleeted sidewalks. Claude's eulogy, spoken in purposefully measured tone, was repeated by the tall, distinguished friend of Mesabi's miners. When Claude's words were concluded, Steven spoke briefly of his own feelings. "As a mine worker of many battles, I have lost my champion. As a man of justice and righteousness, I have lost my champion. As a person who loves all people, I have lost my dearest friend."

When Kevin got the tragic news by telephone from Senia, he was out the door without packing any clothing or leaving any messages as to where he was going. He drove the nearly two hundred miles in under eight hours, arriving in Hibbing shortly before midnight. Steven and Tony were visiting in the living room when Kevin burst in the door without knocking. "Got here as fast as I could!" he exclaimed.

Steven was up from the couch and stepping across the carpet to embrace Kevin before the door closed behind him. "I knew you would be here, Kev." Steven attempted a weak smile, but his devastation was obvious. His deep-set eyes were red from crying. "We've lost a great one. I just came from Claude's house. He's, well . . . maybe, he's taking this even harder than I am."

Before Kevin could sit down and talk with the two men, Tony had a steaming cup of coffee for him. Placing the cup on the table, Tony hugged the young man. "It's always so good to see you, Kev. Too bad it's under such sad circumstances. The good ones leave us early, don't they?" Tony regarded the young man who was like a son of his own. "He'll find quite a crowd of old friends and loved ones holding open the gates of heaven—I'm sure about that."

"My dad will be one of them," Kevin added. "So will Mary."

Later that evening, the men talked about Victor, Kevin's baseball at the University, how Becca and Senia were doing, and a range of subjects until almost one in the morning. Steven and Claude were making all the arrangements and would be pallbearers for a funeral that would be like no other in Hibbing's history. By two o'clock, they were emotionally exhausted and called it a day. Steven would stay over at Tony's and begin plans for the wake and funeral with Father Dougherty in the morning.

Kevin tossed and turned all night. Vic Power had been an important mentor in his young life—much as Father Pat had been for so many years. Memories of Victor's contagious enthusiasm for everything he did, his marvelous sense of humor, his commitment to causes in the community he loved and served with an ardent passion, swam through his thoughts. Kevin often wondered how much Victor was like his own father, and had asked the Mayor that very question on more than one occasion. "Like two peas in a pod," Victor had told him. The three qualities about Peter Moran that stuck in Kevin's mind were intelligence, ambition, and community respect. Were these the same qualities that churned in his veins as well? Victor had told him, "Public service is the jewel of life's crown" and suggested, in his most sincere manner, that Kevin give some thought to a political career for himself. "Political office is the one and only endeavor your father never pursued. How many times I wished he had," Victor once shared. Kevin prayed that his dad would be one of those at heaven's gate to welcome Mr. Power.

Despite only a few hours of sleep, Kevin was up early on Wednesday morning. He hadn't been back to Hibbing since Christmas and had a lot of catching up to do. He called the university dorm and let Huddy know where he was. "Tell the coach I won't be at practice for a few days. He'll probably chew me out later, but . . . I'm where I have to be right now."

When he hung up with Hud, the phone rang. Senia had seen his car parked in the street and hoped to see him that morning. "I'm up and dressed, the coffee is on, I've taken the day off from the bank, and if you could come over for an hour or so, I'd love to visit with you."

"I'll be over in a few minutes, Senia. Everybody's still sleeping over here. We had a late night." Kevin had dropped the 'Auntie Senia' some time ago. Somehow it seemed to soften their relationship in much the same way as with Tony and his cousins.

Kevin grabbed his 'M' baseball letter jacket and headed across the street to Senia's house.

After talking about Mr. Power and all the arrangements for a few minutes, Senia mentioned, "I sent a lovely iris plant to the mortuary in your name yesterday afternoon."

Senia inquired about school, personal finances (as she always did whenever they talked), and baseball. "Will you be back in Hibbing next summer, Kevin? When I talked to you on the phone last Sunday, you thought you might have to stay in the Cities."

"If I want to continue pitching for the U., I'll have to play summer ball down there. The coach insists on it. He lines up jobs for all the guys at the breweries—Schmidt's in St. Paul or Grain Belt in Minneapolis. And, he doesn't mind if we sample the products." Kevin laughed at the fact. "I guess I'm going to keep up with the baseball, so . . ."

Senia grimaced, "If it's that important, Kevin, you'll have to do what the coach wants. Maybe some of us can come down and visit you and do some shopping in the Cities while we're there. That might be fun."

Kevin did have something he wanted to talk with Senia about. "I've thought about all that money in the estate, Senia. I still don't know what to do about it. Sometimes I wish I could give it all away to someone who needs it. I sure don't. I'll probably never be able to spend it all in a lifetime." He knew that when he expressed these sentiments, Senia became distraught. Her unspoken 'covenant' with his father seemed at the root of her purpose in life.

Kevin regarded Senia with an amused smile. She was still an attractive woman he realized, especially so when her long blonde hair was combed down over her shoulders. "You'll be pleased to know that I have an idea for spending some of the estate money."

As expected, Senia perked up.

"My dad's house, Senia. I can't really understand why, but that place has been like some kind of obsession since the first time I saw it. Anyhow, can you buy it with the estate money? Tony says it can be moved and put back together, but that it would cost a fortune. What do you think?"

Senia's deep blue eyes sparked at the idea. "That's a wonderful thought, Kevin! Fred Bennett's retired, and I know he's talked about getting away from here in the winter. Maybe . . . yes, I'm sure we can do something." Warmed by the notion of Kevin wanting to preserve the house of his father, Senia added, "This is just about the best news I've had in years. Where would you want to move the mansion?"

"You know better than I do what land is in the estate. Where do you suggest, Senia?"

She puzzled. "Would you like to have the house in town?"

"Not really. But, if there were any possible way—I have a favorite place in mind." The summer before he and Rudy had borrowed motor cycles and explored the hills south of Hibbing. There was a lovely hill off Townline Road that Rudy called Maple Hill. "Could the house go on Maple Hill? I like the idea of space and solitude."

Senia knew the area. "We don't own any land out there but I know who does. I'll look into it, Kevin." The discussion of property was something she wanted to discuss further. "Kevin, I have been investing in the market for years, and the estate has tripled with the incredible economic growth. But, I have some concerns these days." Senia explained how she believed the American economy was becoming inflated by widespread margin purchasing practices. Her bank was among the many investors who speculated by using all the loopholes in investment strategy. "Some day I think we're in for a tumble, Kevin, and, if that happens, there will be some hard times in this country."

"I don't understand stocks and bonds, Senia. I do understand land, or real estate, if that's the better terminology. More than money, I'd love to have lots of land some day. Maybe that's my dream more than anything else. Land." Kevin got up from the living room chair and paced to the window. "I'd love to have pine forests to walk through, fields to hunt in, and the sounds of waves on a lake shore to listen to. I think the Sturgeon Lakes area is simply gorgeous."

"I think the two of us think a lot alike about that. I was born in Finland and that's exactly how a Finn thinks, Kevin. Land is life itself. It's that way in Slovenia, too. Steven and Tony . . . and, thousands of men just like them came to this country with the dream of owning their own land. They came because they couldn't buy land in the old country."

"And it was land that brought the Morans to Northern Minnesota some thirty or forty years ago—Grampa Daly was a timber man, wasn't he?" Kevin was fascinated by the history of this place and the people who settled here two generations ago.

Senia nodded, and promised to follow up on their conversation. "You've made my day, Kevin." Senia hugged him at the door.

That night, Senia had invited Steven to dinner. She knew he would be out of sorts after all the funeral arrangements he and Claude had assumed responsibility for. The bond between Steven and Vic Power had always been one of trust and respect—far surpassing the mutual political interests and causes they shared. Steven was crushed with his sense of loss. Senia's heartfelt grief paled in comparison to that of her man.

Humming to herself, Senia thought about the time the two of them would share together that evening. She was beginning to view their relationship from a different perspective than had been comfortable for her over the past many years. Reflecting on how Kevin's life was flourishing these days, she found an inner contentment beyond anything she imagined or hoped for. The young man had reconciled the years between himself and his father. He was Kevin Moran! Senia believed she was ready to make some dramatic life changes herself. Toward that end, Senia managed to procure two bottles of wine from her boss. Mr. Goldberg's private stock of liquor was a poorly kept secret among his employees. Wine would be perfect for their time together.

After dinner, Senia and Steven retired to the living room where Senia had carefully set an appropriate atmosphere, with candles and a radio tuned in low volume to a music station out of Virginia. The wine was nestled in an ice bucket on the table.

Although emotionally drained, Steven's sight of the wine bottles brought a wan smile. "My goodness, dear. You've run afoul of the law! I'm delighted at the surprise . . . shall we?" He poured glasses for each of them.

"To life, Senia. *'Death slew not him, but he made death his ladder to the skies'*—that's Spencer, I think." Steven toasted to Victor's memory rather than the two of them. Before he could add a more intimate toast, Senia sipped her glass in approval of his sentiment.

"I wish I could say something to pick you up, Steven," Senia intoned. "As cold as I know it sounds, life goes on for all of us. Sometimes a tragedy like this gives us inspiration to change our lives in positive ways. I think it has with me." Senia had a shudder in her voice.

Life was short she had concluded that afternoon. The wine and candles reflected that very conviction. Peter would live through Kevin and . . . she loved Steven. Of that fact there was no longer any doubt in her mind. Now, she was struck with a reality: she wanted Steven to be the part of her life which had been so barren. Tony had come to a similar realization when he proposed to Becca. Tony was willing to trust someone to fill a hole in his life—a chasm he could not fill himself.

"You're right of course, my dear." Steven's large hand closed upon hers, taking Senia's brief reverie away. "Life will go on—with Victor keeping an eye on things, I'm sure." He found an easy laugh. "We'll all find something positive and inspiring . . . that's my prayer."

Steven's thoughts were in a different place at the moment. Senia swallowed hard at the knot in her throat. "Steven, I love you. I don't tell you that very often I know. But—"

"I know you do. And, I love you, too. But I tell you that all the time, don't I?" He smiled as he had a thousand times before.

Senia leaned close, looked into his eyes. "I mean, *really* love you. I've thought about that feeling all day, Steven. Maybe Victor's death was part of it . . . but, mostly I realized that I want to be with you. Always! I'm not happy by myself any more. It's just not the way I want to spend the rest of my life—growing old in my own private little world."

She saw confusion in Steven's face.

"What are you saying, Senia?"

"I'm saying I want to marry you, Steven." Senia began to sob softly into his shirt. "I've finally been honest with myself—after all these years."

Steven felt a pain in his heart—a constricting hurt that brought a trace of tears to his own eyes. How long he had dreamed of having this woman as his wife. How deeply he had wanted her to come to a profession of love. But . . . !

Steven had tired of waiting years before. Marriage was not something that was ever going to happen in their lives; so he had given up that hope, and settled more deeply into living his life alone. What could he say to this woman he cared for with all of his heart? This woman who had now become more his *friend* than his lover.

Steven was too honest to mislead. "Senia, my dear, I am fifty-one, going on eighty," he said as lightly as he could. "You've let me become pretty well confirmed in my bachelorhood these many years. I think that—maybe, the emotion of this time has gotten to you. One of the things I've come to admire most about you has been your independence. And, I think, that same spirit of self-reliance is something . . ." He swallowed from a dry mouth, " . . . something about my life that has kept you attracted to me."

Senia nodded without reply.

"And, I'm afraid our *family* years have passed us by, my dear." His voice was pained over that reality more than anything else. Steven would never have children of his own.

Senia was not prepared for what she was hearing from Steven. She had allowed him to drift too far away, and she realized her ship had lost its mooring. How selfish she had been. Trying to get a grip on her feelings, she backed off: " . . . the emotion of the moment . . . and, perhaps, the wine as well, Steven. As always, you see things through honest eyes. We have truly become, both of us, loners—haven't we?" She leaned away, dried her eyes with the back of her hand, and reached for her glass. "It's my turn for a profound toast, Steven. And unlike yours, I have no idea from where in literature this comes. Let me see if I can get it right . . . *'One asked of regret, And I made no reply; To have held the bird, And let it fly'* . . ." With her toast came her tears rolling down her face, and washing her soul of the regret over having loved—and lost.

Hundreds of automobiles proceeded through a driving sleet storm to the Hibbing cemetery southwest of town for the Vic Power burial rites. The small stone chapel at the cemetery site could only accommodate a small number of those who had come to offer their prayers for the soul of their beloved Mayor.

After the final cemetery blessings, a reception was held at the Memorial Building in the city, the only building that could hold the large numbers of people.

Kevin sat at a long table with Claude Atkinson. "You gave a wonderful eulogy, Mr. Atkinson. I was really moved by what you said," Kevin complimented the newsman.

Looking unusually haggard, Claude forced a smile. "Only words, I'm afraid, Kevin. I live with words and know how to make them work. But, I am always struck by their inadequacy when you want them to mean the most." Claude put his arm around the young man he regarded with such fondness. "Words can't do that man justice. He was one of those few who are beyond the realm of eulogizing. Enough! We'll have our lifetime to remember Vic and to talk about the many ways he touched us. Kevin, tell me how the season's going for you."

"Pretty well, sir." Kevin drew a sigh. "The Big Ten is tough!"

"I've picked up some reports on the wires at the office. You beat Illinois, didn't you—last weekend?"

"I was lucky, I guess. I got the win in that one, and shut out Purdue two weeks ago. But, I've got two losses as well."

The two of them talked baseball for a few more minutes before Claude had to excuse himself and mingle with some of the other folks milling in the crowded arena. When Claude left his chair, Kevin felt a tug at his shirt collar. Without looking up, he knew who was standing behind him. The scent of her perfume was alluring. Angela slid into the chair beside him. "I need a ride back to the house, Kevin. It's still miserable outside and I don't want to ruin my best dress."

"Sure, Angie. If it's okay—"

"Dad said it was fine. He's going to stay a while longer and visit more with Steven and Mr. Dinter."

In Kevin's car, Angie gave him a captivating smile. "You've been home for three days, and we haven't had any time to talk—just the two of us, I mean. Why don't you take the long way back to Brooklyn?"

Kevin felt awkward. "The long way?"

"Yes. The half-hour way to the house. You can figure something out, can't you?"

Kevin wondered where he might go as he started the engine and shifted into first. He liked the idea of being with Angela—just the two of them. Then something struck him. He'd wanted to go out to Townline Road and take a look at Maple Hill before going back to the Cities. He made a U-turn on Josephine Street and headed toward South First Avenue.

"You're wearing your hair kinda long these days, aren't you, Kevin? Is that what the college girls like?" Angie asked in a nettling voice.

Kevin ignored the question. "You look good all dressed up, Angie. Older, I guess." He looked at her from the corner of his eye as he drove down the wide avenue. He had to admit to himself that Angela had filled out nicely . Her use of rouge and eye makeup gave her a womanly aspect. In every respect she looked no different at fifteen than the older campus girls he saw every day. And, she was much prettier than most.

"Older? Is that a compliment? Maybe you're just too used to seeing college women, Kevin." She turned her eyes from him to stare out the windshield as the wipers swished at the sleet. Angie was curious. "Have you got a girlfriend yet?"

"That's the first question you asked me when I got home three days ago. I told you, no. What's the matter, don't you believe me, Angela?"

"No. And, I've told you—never call me Angela!" Persisting with her curiosity, Angela said, "Don't try to make me believe you haven't had any dates in all those months."

"Oh . . . well, I guess I've been out with a girl a couple of times. Not just me and a girl by ourselves, though." Kevin looked at Angie's profile against the curtain of gray afternoon behind her. "We've got a group that studies together sometimes before a test. There's a coffeehouse near the dorm."

Angie was quiet for a few minutes.

"My roommate, Huddy Tusken, is a crammer. He lets everything go until the night before an exam then stays up all night drinking coffee."

"What's her name?"

"Whose name? The girl in our group?"

"You know who I mean. Yes, Kevin, your girlfriend's name."

Kevin laughed. Angie was jealous. "You wouldn't know her. She's from a little town called Cambridge, outside the Cities." Enjoying their banter, he paused for effect. "Sally. Sally Olson is her name. She's in our English Lit. class along with about a hundred other freshman."

"Is she a blonde?" she asked coolly.

"Yes, she's Scandinavian."

"I'm dying my hair blond, you know. What do you think about that?" Angie blurted her question.

"Don't you dare do anything to your hair, Angela. That would be absolute foolishness. Why do you always want to provoke me?"

Kevin applied the brakes as he approached the place where he would have the best view of the aspen covered hill rising sharply in the distance to their right. "That's what I wanted to show you. It's called Maple Hill."

Kevin leaned toward the passenger window. The scent of Angela was intoxicating as his nose brushed against her dark hair. "Some day I'd like to have a house up on that hill. From up on the top you can see for miles. Rudy and I have done some exploring up there." His eyes could not help but notice the soft cleavage under Angela's loosened wool coat.

"It's a mile from town out here, Kevin." Angela sensed his closeness and imagined his thoughts. She had purposely loosened her coat. "Do you want to be a hermit or something?"

"Not at all. But, I'd love to have lots of space—wilderness all around me. I think it would be really peaceful out here." He gestured toward the west, below the hill. "And that meadow down there. Perfect for grazing."

"I want a horse some day," Angie said.

On the drive back into Hibbing, Angela was quiet.

"What's on your mind? You've got a frown on your . . . face." Kevin caught himself. He'd almost said 'pretty.'

"If my dad marries Becca next fall—and, I don't think he will—he'll come to his senses in time. But, if he makes that mistake, I'm going to move out of the house. That's what I'm thinking."

Kevin felt a rush of anger. "Don't be so damn judgmental . . ." He downshifted sharply at Portage Street. " . . . Sorry! Becca is one of the nicest people I know. And, she's perfect for your dad. You are totally unreasonable when it comes to Becca—and, to your father as well. They both deserve to be as happy as—"

"It's my mother's house, Kevin. She and dad made all the plans together. She's an intruder, that's what she is!"

"Don't you ever say that about Becca. And, furthermore, young lady, it's your father's house. I live there . . . Rudy lives there, and neither of us had anything to do with planning or building the house. Your dad made it *our* home." He swallowed hard. "Please don't ever call Becca an intruder. If she's an intruder—so am I."

"I can have my own feelings, Mr. 'Know-it-all' . . . and, I don't appreciate any lectures from you." Angela turned away, staring coldly out her window for the last few blocks of the ride.

Among the hundreds of people gathered in the cemetery that bitterly cold April afternoon stood a well-dressed, barrel-chested man, with a stylish felt hat pulled down over deep-set green eyes. His presence among so many mourners was inconspicuous although nobody there was likely to have any idea who he was under any circumstance. But, being here felt risky nonetheless. He'd read about the death of Vic Power in the *St. Paul Pioneer Press* two days before and had decided to make the drive up to Hibbing. The stranger knew who he was looking for. He had been to the Purdue baseball game two weeks before this funeral. As he watched the small crowd leaving the stone chapel, he rubbed at the narrow scar which formed a barely discernible two-inch line under the left side of his jaw. Damp weather always irritated the old wound from his days as a lumberjack so many years ago. He spied the young man walking away from the group at the chapel and heading for his car. "Bingo!" He muttered under his breath.

Danny Morgan was on the run again. When Charlie Birger joined forces with the Shelton Brothers who controlled bootlegging operations in the Southeastern states, Danny knew his days were numbered. He'd messed around with Earl Shelton's wife before the two groups combined. Leaving St. Louis before Earl could find him, Danny found himself hustling jobs in

St. Paul. He had to lay low for a while and found a bouncer job at a run-down speakeasy up on Payne Street, in the east side of the city. Figaro's seemed the safest place to be until he got some money to go back out West.

Having picked up the Duluth paper whenever he was in the area, Danny had been able to follow the footprints of Kevin Schmitz. On graduation night at Denfeld, Danny was one of the spectators standing in the back with those not having tickets. At the Duluth train depot the following Tuesday morning, Danny watched from the shadows as Kevin embraced the tall priest who had picked him up at the Schmitz house earlier in the morning. The train was departing for Hibbing, and the boy's luggage suggested a lengthy visit.

On a weekend in August the year before, Danny was hanging out in a West Duluth pool hall where he knew Art Schmitz enjoyed playing '8-ball' on Saturday nights. Danny waited, then hustled a game with the small, wiry, wispy-haired, man.

"Kids these days, they've got minds of their own, don't they?" He started the conversation. "My son just told me he was gonna work at the steel plant rather than go to college. You got any kids of yer own?" Danny offered his large hand to Art, "Name's Berducci, Dom Berducci, live over in Morgan Park."

"Art Schmitz, Dom. You're right about that. Kids can be a handful, that's for sure," he commented as he leaned over the table, called his shot, and missed badly. "My son's going to college, though. Got himself a scholarship. I'm really proud of the boy." Art smiled proudly.

"Ya don't say? Must be pretty smart—yer kid."

"Top of his class at Denfeld. He's going to the U. this fall." Art watched as the dark-haired man dropped three straight solids in the pockets. "Going to play baseball, too. He's quite a pitcher."

"Ya don't say?" In two minutes, Danny knew where Kevin was. He'd let Art win the game and head back to the Cities to pick up on the easy lead he'd cleverly wrangled from the 'proud father.'

There was no Kevin Schmitz registered at the University, however, and Danny wondered if he'd been given some bad information. But, it didn't take him long to find out that Kevin Schmitz had become Kevin Moran. A few questions here and there gave Danny some additional insights. "Kid's from Hibbing," one of the spectators told Danny at an outdoor baseball practice in early April.

It was a gut-hunch that brought Danny Morgan to Hibbing. If Kevin had taken the Moran name, it must have something to do with an inheritance. Some kind of clever stipulation that lawyers dream up to ensure they get their percentage of the estate money. He guessed that Kevin was an heir to a small fortune—maybe even a hundred grand. Peter must have left a lot of money behind. And, Danny was desperate for money these days. On the drive from St. Paul that day he'd come up with a scheme.

"I'm Art Schmitz, ma'am." Danny told the teller at the Merchants and Miners Bank. "I'd like ta make a small deposit in my son's account. He's away at school right now and couldn't come in for himself. And, I'm in town for the funeral."

The teller gave him a puzzled expression as she paged through the thick ledger behind her window. "Schmitz?"

"Oh, I'm sorry, ma'am." He checked her bank employee tag. Carolyn Johnson was the woman's name. He'd already noted that there were no rings on her fingers. Maybe . . . ? he thought to himself. His scheme had many variables.

"That would be Kevin Moran. Peter's son, if you remember his father . . ." Danny corrected. "I should have told you that."

She smiled. " . . . Here it is, sir—Mr. Schmitz. What would you like to deposit?"

"Only twenty, Carolyn." He used her first name, offering his most engaging smile before taking the risk. "Do you have an account balance?"

"Let me see . . . yes, five hundred and thirty four dollars, sir."

After closing, Danny followed Carolyn Johnson home. She lived in what appeared to be an apartment occupying the upstairs of a wood frame house on West Howard. Watching her windows for more than an hour from his car parked in the street, he saw only the silhouette of one person, Carolyn. A plan was beginning to unfold in his mind.

At about ten the following morning he observed her leaving by the side entrance of the house. Following her down Howard, he watched as she scanned the window displays. A few minutes later, Carolyn Johnson entered the Itasca Bazaar store.

"Excuse me, I'm sorry!" Danny said as he bumped into the woman browsing through a rack of inexpensive dresses. "Why, you're—Carolyn? I never forget a face . . . especially a pretty one."

Blushing at the compliment, Carolyn stammered, "Why yes, Mr. Schmitz—am I right?" A smile crossed her plain features.

"Not only pretty, but a woman with a great memory as well." Danny had a naturally seductive look about him. He was at his best with women.

"Carolyn, or should I say *Mrs.* Johnson . . . ?"

She cast her eyes downward in shy discomposure. "*Miss*. Or, I prefer just Carolyn."

"Could you help me once again, Carolyn?" Without waiting for what he knew would be a positive answer, he continued. "I haven't eaten all day. Might you be able to suggest a restaurant where I'd be likely to find a decent lunch? I don't know the town very well, I'm afraid."

"Most certainly, Mr. Schmitz . . ."

"Art, please, Carolyn. If we're going to be seeing each other every day, I think we should be on a first name basis. Don't you agree?" Danny knew when a woman had been charmed. Carolyn Johnson was an easy mark.

"There's Fay's—it's my very favorite place—when I go out to eat, I mean."

". . . May I be so forward, Carolyn? It would be a great pleasure for me if you would join me for lunch. Food is so much more agreeable when shared with pleasant company."

After lunch and a stroll in the refreshing afternoon sun, Danny Morgan made a date for that evening. "Let's go to someplace really fancy and maybe—do you like to dance, Carolyn?"

It was after midnight when they arrived at Carolyn's upstairs apartment. Danny tucked a bottle of Canadian whiskey under his topcoat when leaving his car. After a few drinks, Danny began his contrived appeal. "I'm worried about my son, Carolyn. One of my Hibbing friends told me he's been spending his inheritance money like there was no tomorrow. It's probably none of my business . . ."

"It is your bishiness, Art," Carolyn slurred.

"I don't want you to do anything that might get you in trouble at the bank but—" Danny explained the 'favor' he'd like her to do for him.

On Monday morning, Senia skipped the weekly executive staff meeting in Goldberg's conference room for the first time. She was in a depressed state and wanted to wallow in the privacy of her own office. But when she was about to put the key in her lock, she realized the door was already open. Slowly swinging the door, she startled Carolyn Johnson who was leaning over a file cabinet. "Miss Johnson! What are you doing in here?" Senia shot her question across the room. "You have no business in here—you know that."

Carolyn covered her mouth in startled fear. "I'm sorry, Miss Arola, I was just look—"

"Sit down, young lady, you've got some explaining to do." Senia hurried across the room to the file cabinet as Carolyn stood frozen. Half-pulled out from the tightly filed folders in the drawer was the estate file of Peter Moran. Senia wanted to grab the woman by the throat. "What have you been looking for? If I don't get straight answers right now, I'm calling the police."

Contrite, Carolyn Johnson explained what she was looking for—and why. "Mr. Schmitz was worried about his son, that's all. Didn't want him wasting his father's inheritance."

Senia knew something was afoul. "Describe Mr. Schmitz for me."

The description was not even close to accurate. There was an impostor in town. Someone who knew that Kevin's father had left him some money. "Tell me again—exactly!—what did this Mr. Schmitz want you to find for him?"

"He wanted to know . . . the . . . the . . . estate balance." Carolyn was sobbing uncontrollably now.

"Where in Hibbing is Mr. Schmitz staying for the week?"

Carolyn wasn't sure, but thought it was the Delvik Hotel.

Senia pushed Carolyn toward a chair. "You just sit while I sort some things out." She picked up the phone and asked the operator to connect her with the Delvik.

"No, ma'am, nobody by that name has been registered here," the desk clerk told her. "Most everybody from out of town for the funeral has gone already."

"Who's still there?"

"I don't know if I sho—"

"Would you rather I send the police?"

A Mr. Berducci from St. Paul fit the description Carolyn had given Senia. She thanked the clerk. "If Mr. Berducci leaves the building before the police arrive, follow him. Have you got that? Don't lose sight of him."

Senia's thoughts were racing. Who would be interested in Peter's estate after all these years? Could this impostor be connected to Peter's murder? (Senia would never accept the suicide theory.) Probing her memory of that painful time, only one person had the motive—and, perhaps, the opportunity. Was this stranger . . . Peter's fugitive brother?

Ten minutes later, Senia and police detective, Mike Grady, met at the Delvik front desk. Two uniformed officers were with them. They climbed the narrow staircase, then listened quietly at the door of #209. They caught the distinctive rustling of a newspaper. Waiting a few more minutes with ears to the door, they heard footsteps. The sound was coming toward them—suddenly the door swung open!

Danny Morgan jumped back, "Wha—?" Reaching into his coat pocket he pulled at the revolver—but, the barrel stuck for a second on the inside lining. Grady made a sweeping chop at the man's wrist. The dark-haired man screamed, "Wha the f— ya tryin' . . ."

The two officers squeezed through the door and grabbed the man's arms, twisting them painfully behind his back. In seconds the cuffs were locked on the stranger's wrists. Grady extracted the revolver. "You're in big trouble, mister. Whoever you are. Let's get him down to the station, fellas. We'll get to the bottom of this."

Senia strained her eyes on the arrested man. Who was he? "What's your real name, Berducci?" she shouted before the police had escorted him out of the hotel room. "None of your damned business, lady!"

"We'll find out who he is down at the station, Mrs. Arola. Don't you worry about that." He grabbed Danny Morgan by the front lapel of his coat as the two cops began to push him out into the hallway.

Senia stepped in front of the group and hurried down the stairs ahead of them. Her mind was racing. Running to the desk, she told the clerk, "When they get down here with this Berducci character, I want you to wait until they're almost out the door." She looked over her shoulder, heard the men halfway down the flight of stairs. "When they're at the door call out the name 'Denis'. Have you got that young man? 'Denis!'"

The clerk nodded and Senia hurried over to the far end of the lobby where she couldn't be seen from the front door. The cops, with the arrested man in tow, were pushing through the door . . .

"Denis!" The clerk shouted in wavering voice from behind his counter.

Senia saw the man's head begin to turn around before stopping over his left shoulder, then quickly turning back to the sidewalk in front. Senia followed them out the door. "Mr. Grady, I've got a phone call to make back at the office. I'll be down at the station within the hour. And, I'll bring Miss Johnson along with me."

At the office Senia found a phone number she hadn't called in fifteen years. "Mr. MacIntosh, please," she told the secretary who answered the phone at Jim MacIntosh's Duluth office in the Medical Arts building.

Jim MacIntosh had been Peter Moran's closest friend. Their two families grew up together, forming a tight relationship back in the days when Daly Moran was a lumber baron in these parts. Pete and Jimmy were as inseparable as twins. For many years, Mac maintained numerous business interests in Hibbing and was the owner of the bank where Senia now worked. It was Jim who arranged for Senia to get her job. Before Peter's death, however, the two men had a falling out over issues Senia never quite understood. Jim MacIntosh was one of her first calls when Peter died, and was her first thought when arranging pallbearers for the funeral.

MacIntosh's warm "hello" put a lump in Senia's throat. It had been nearly fifteen years and she remembered the voice as if it were only yesterday. "Jim, Senia Arola."

There was a long pause over the line. Then his familiar laugh. "Senia, my God, how are you?"

"Very stressed, Jim. I'll try to explain later, but I've got a big favor to ask."

On the train ride to Hibbing, Jim MacIntosh's thoughts were flooded with old memories. He hadn't been up to the 'ore capital' in years and looked forward to seeing the changes he'd heard so much about. The thought of staying overnight at the Androy made him think about his old friend's marvelous hotel and the exciting times they shared during those 'wheelin—dealin' days. But he had tired of the frequent trips to the Iron Range, and his family commitments in Duluth were Jim's first priority.

Jim contemplated Senia's unusual request and the reason for this unexpected visit to Hibbing this morning. "Would you be able to identify Denis Moran?" Senia had asked him the day before. She explained that a man named Berducci, posing as Art Schmitz, was under arrest for a concealed weapon charge, and some sort of bank conspiracy. But Senia was certain there much more to his story, and trusted her intuition.

Jim knew all the Morans better than any other living person outside the immediate family. Denis—the middle son? His last memory of Denis was back in Hibbing when Peter's brother crashed the hotel opening party. That fiasco was back in '08, almost eighteen years ago. At the time, Denis looked much as he always had—a large, swarthy, red-bearded, lumberjack. In his every appearance and demeanor, Denis looked as if he'd just come out of the woods. The man Senia described to him was nothing like the man he remembered. As he pondered Denis Moran, he scribbled on the margin of the newspaper in his lap. Denis looked more like his father, Daly, than the other two sons. He would remember Daly's green eyes and broad nose. Denis—he strained his memory—had crooked lower front teeth . . . or, was that Terrance? Now he wasn't certain. What else? Denis was large, broad-shouldered, and . . . yes, Daly's barrel chest. Jim's scribbling read:

–green eyes,
–large nostrils,
–shoulders and chest

Senia met MacIntosh at the new train depot on the dreary Tuesday morning. As the two of them walked the four blocks to the police station on Fifth, they quickly caught up on old times. Senia was delighted to see her old friend and realized the years had been kind to him. Tall and slender, with youthfully erect posture—only the traces of gray in his hair gave evidence of time passed.

"I hope I can help you with this, Senia. It's been so long."

"If you can't, Jim, I don't know who else might. Just don't be fooled by first impressions. I'm almost positive this Berducci character has had a makeover. Remember, Denis was a fugitive—still is for that matter. He had to change his appearance." Then it occurred to Senia, there were a couple of people whom Denis hung out with in Duluth. A Sam something or other, and a woman. If Jim couldn't make an identification, maybe—?

Berducci was taken to a small room at police headquarters where he was seated at a table. His hands were cuffed behind his back. Earlier that morning he had been insistent that he be allowed to brush his teeth, shave, and comb his hair. The officer in charge was accommodating of the prisoner's requests. (Danny Morgan—Denis Moran—knew his red stubble might betray his identity. Often he shaved twice a day.)

Detective Grady had been questioning Berducci for half an hour before Senia and Jim MacIntosh arrived. Carolyn Johnson had made a positive identification—insisting that Berducci was the same man who told her he was Art Schmitz. Berducci maintained she was a spurned woman. "She wanted me to run off with her, said she could get some money at the bank. I told her no, I wouldn't be caught dead with her and called her an ugly bitch . . . then, she got pissed off. Really mad! Said she'd get me."

Berducci was sticking to his story. He told Grady he was only in Hibbing for the Power funeral; said he admired the man. The revolver, he claimed, was only for his personal protection. "I've had threats on my life" was all he would tell the detective. "You guys surprised me at the door, I reacted with my instincts, that's all. I'm sorry about trying to pull the gun—ya scared the hell outta me!" Background checks were proving fruitless.

Senia introduced Jim MacIntosh to Detective Grady who offered Jim a chair opposite Berducci. "This guy wants to talk with you, Mr. Berducci," was all Grady said.

Denis sucked hard on his fear. He knew MacIntosh well and had to hide any familiarity. The person who could end his years of running was staring at him across the table. His mind raced. "Are you another detective?" Denis said in a voice unnaturally hoarse. "I've explained my situation to everybody five times already, sir. I've made a serious mistake with the gun—but, that's all I've done. I deserve to be punished for that, I know." With MacIntosh, he was careful to use his best articulation, choosing his words carefully. Denis had worked on his speech for years and could turn off the coarse patterns of his backwoods past at will.

Jim studied the face. The man had deep-set green eyes and the nose—he wondered, what was it about that nose? It was like Daly's nose, he seemed certain, but the face was narrower than that of Denis. This man had the shoulders and chest, but—he seemed too slender. Mac was confused. Berducci did not look anything like the Denis Moran he remembered from years ago. But . . . Jim searched the depths of his memory for something lingering in the corner of vague remembrance.

In the lumbering days, back in Marquette, Michigan, Denis had gained a considerable reputation as a brawler. He liked his liquor, and pushed his weight around the local taverns on more than a few occasions. In one of his fights, another drunk broke off the neck of a whiskey bottle and went after Denis. Jim remembered Denis' bandaged jaw and how Daly chewed him out for his behavior that night. Denis was probably about eighteen at the time.

Jim leaned across the table. "Will you smile, Mr. Berducci? So I can see your teeth?"

Berducci smiled widely. His white teeth were perfect.

"Will you lift your head a little, so I can see your jaw?"

Berducci had been slumped in his chair. He lifted his head slightly, turning his right jaw toward MacIntosh.

"A bit more. And, turn your head the other way, if you will please."

Berducci did as MacIntosh requested.

Jim immediately stood up from the table, and turned to Senia. "This is Peter's brother, Denis. I don't have a doubt in the world." Then, turning to the dark-haired man who sat at the table in stunned disbelief, Jim said—"It's been a long time, Denis!"

Kevin left Hibbing early on Sunday morning. On his return trip to Minneapolis he planned to swing west through St. Cloud. After registering with the reformatory officials, Kevin was led to a small meeting room where he waited for nearly twenty minutes. The middle of the long table was dissected by an iron security screen.

Much thinner than Kevin could remember, Gary Zench looked pale and haggard. "What are you doing here, Kevin?" Gary tried a weak smile as he dropped into the chair opposite his old friend. "I din't even know ya knew I was down here. Great to see ya."

After a few awkward pleasantries, Kevin asked, "How long are you in here?"

"I got a five to ten. Maybe I'll make parole in three more years. I've been doin' okay here—no trouble." Gary dabbed at his eyes. "But, it's been tough as hell, Kevin. I mean . . . the guys, they abuse me alla time—ya know what I'm sayin." He swallowed hard, "Maybe ya don't."

Kevin felt his throat constrict, "I think I do, Gary. I wish you—"

"I know. I had a good chance to get my ass outta Duluth before—"

"You can't go back there, Gary. It's a dead-end for you. The offer is still good. When you get out of this place . . . you've got to start over. Get your education finished—you know what I mean?"

"Ya. I'd do that, Kevin."

The two of them talked for the allotted twenty minutes before the door on the back wall opened and a guard stepped into the room. "You're the only real friend I got in the world, Kevin. I'm gonna need yer help."

"You can count on that, Gary. I'll keep in touch—and, stay on your best behavior. I want to pick you up when you make parole."

'FORGIVE ME'

September 1930

If Kevin had kept up with his diary over the five years he spent at the University in Minneapolis, he might, one day, look back upon his entries with mixed feelings. He had made some good decisions and some mistakes. During the chilly spring baseball practices of his junior year he developed arm problems and, subsequently, quit the Gopher team. Without baseball, Kevin had the luxury of time to focus his attention on involvements apart from baseball fields and locker rooms.

Among his new interests were his political science courses, especially those taught by Professor Prentice Garvey, the only black faculty member in the department. Kevin thoroughly enjoyed Garvey's perspectives on issues of the day and made an effort to meet the instructor one fall afternoon. Kevin was researching a paper on local government for Garvey's class. "I'd like to write about the influence of a strong mayor on the dynamics of community-building," Kevin suggested, "and I have a specific person in mind."

Garvey, a short, baldheaded man of fifty, took off his reading spectacles and regarded the young man standing in front of his desk. "Mr. Moran? I'm still trying to put names and faces together."

Kevin nodded without reply.

"Whom did you have in mind?"

"A man by the name of Victor Power . . . from Hibbing, sir."

Garvey gave Kevin a broad smile, "The 'Little Giant of the North'—

what a politician that man was. I tried to make it up for the funeral last spring, but the sleet storm around Pine City forced me to turn back to the Cities."

Kevin's eyes widened at the professor's remarks. "I was there, sir, and I remember the terrible weather. Did you know Mr. Power?"

The two of them talked for nearly an hour about the Hibbing mayor and about Kevin's plans for a major in the field of political science. From that meeting on, Kevin and Prentice Garvey had a teacher-student relationship that went beyond the classroom. The professor encouraged Kevin to write with greater passion and conviction . . . "Be true to your mentor, Mr. Power, Kevin." Garvey admonished, "Don't attempt the convenient 'middle-road' kind of analysis; form your opinions on what you believe is right—not on the popular mode of thinking. Challenge me. Don't try to impress me with your essays!"

Kevin followed his teacher's advice and found himself on the unpopular side of an argument more often than not. He began submitting articles to the University newspaper on controversial political issues of the day, and in his senior year, became an assistant editor of the *Minnesota Daily*.

Preoccupied with his studies, Kevin pushed himself to complete his degree in political science. His goal of finishing the undergraduate work in three years required summer sessions and night classes whenever he could schedule the credits he needed. Kevin Moran was getting in touch with his ambition! In April of 1928, he passed the Law School Admissions Test and enrolled in the University law program the following fall. In his obsession to achieve his Doctor of Jurisprudence degree, Kevin had little time for anything but his studies.

Trips to Hibbing or Duluth became infrequent. Aside from the Christmas holiday and Easter, Kevin could count on the fingers of one hand the number of times he had been 'home'. Tony and Becca were married in October of '26; Rudy and Colleen Grady were wed in June of the following year; Doctor Ambrose Hane's funeral was in August of '28; and 'Uncle' Steven had a stroke the previous February. These four occasions would have been entries in his diary if he'd kept at his journaling.

And, there would have been a fifth entry. Kevin was in Duluth for two days in January of '27. For the first time in his life he saw one of his *real* relatives. Denis Moran was convicted in *his own* kidnapping conspiracy of years before. Related counts of felonies committed in Hibbing were dismissed by the judge. Uncle Denis was given seven years at the Stillwater Penitentiary. No charges relating to the death of Peter Moran were ever mentioned or entered into a court of law. No evidence would ever be able to link Denis to the scene of that crime.

Pacing in his Dinkytown apartment near the campus, Kevin took a break from his studies. In two weeks he would take his Minnesota Bar Exams. He was determined to pass on his first try and, when he did, he would be returning to Hibbing. Despite his lengthy absences and the ambitious push to achieve his goals, his connection with the people and events in Hibbing remained intact. Senia called weekly. Claude regularly sent Kevin a bundle of *Mesaba Ore* issues. And, hardly a day passed without a letter from someone back home—either from Hibbing or Duluth. That day he'd received a letter from Mr. Barker, his former teacher at Denfeld. Now retired from the classroom he loved, Barker had followed Kevin's career at the University offering his encouragement and good counsel.

The letters he most treasured were from Angela. Already nineteen and taking art courses at the Hibbing Junior College, Angie's life had seen turbulent days. In his bureau drawer were several letters Kevin had saved. One of these was dated March 15, '27: more than three years ago.

Dear Kevin:

'Beware the Ides of March!' I really got myself in trouble this time. I told you once that if dad married the Doctor, I would run away from home. As you know I didn't do it then. I waited. After my birthday on Saturday (Thanks for the card and letter) I did it. I really did it. I took dad's car when they went to bed. I was going to that place on Maple Hill where no one would bother me. But I didn't quite make it. I hit a deer on Townline Road and smashed the car pretty bad. I broke my collar bone and wrist. Wouldn't you know where I ended up? Yes. At the hospital with Doctor Kaner.

She was pretty good about not really scolding me. But dad was furious. Now I'm grounded for the rest of the school year. I deserved worse. Maybe I learned something from this. Maybe Becca isn't so bad. She talked to me about my anger and said she could understand. A few years after her father died, Becca's mother remarried. I didn't know anything about her family before. Anyhow she said it is hard for someone to like the person who takes the place of a parent. I think she calmed my dad down, too. I promised not to be so foolish again.

So, how are you doing? Study, study, study. What a dull life you have, Kevin. If I lived in Minneapolis I'd find a thousand things to do. One of these days I might surprise you and come down there. I won't run away though. Maybe my dad will take me down on one of his trips. Then you could show me your apartment. Is it a messy place? Or, do you have girlfriends who come and clean up after you? Just kidding.

When you come home for Easter, maybe we can drive out to where your house is going to be. Dad says his crews will begin the moving project some time in May. The land you picked is being cleared of some trees—not too many—and a big hole has been dug already. So, if you want to take me there I'll go. It will have to be during the day because I can't leave the house at night.

Sometimes I miss you.

Angie

The house project was completed in the fall of '27. Senia had hired a landscaping firm from Duluth to restore the grounds after the site work was finished. On the south-facing slope, large gardens were established. On the pasture land on the western edge of the large property, a barn had been erected and a corral built. A property manager had been hired to oversee and maintain the house and grounds. But nobody lived in the house on Maple Hill.

Angela Zoretek was pacing in her Hibbing apartment on that same bleak September afternoon. She snubbed her cigarette in the ashtray near the tablet and empty coffee cup on the kitchen table. Her apartment was a small, cramped two-room space upstairs of a wood-frame house on West Howard Street. She shared a bathroom with a single woman named Johnson, who had a similar apartment just down the narrow hallway.

In the cluttered living room stood her easel and nearby her art supplies. Angela contemplated returning to her landscape painting or writing a letter to Kevin. Flipping her dark curls away from her face, she stared at the canvas she'd started days before. But her indecision of the moment was just another in a series of torments. Nineteen year old Angela was prone to becoming consumed with unhappiness and self-pity. What did she have to tell Kevin? Her letters were always so dull. Why did he even bother to answer them? "Dull!" Angela said to no one in the room. "Dull. That's me . . . that's my letters, that's my painting. Dull."

Flopping on her worn sofa and throwing her legs over the armrest, Angela lit another cigarette as she lay back to do another self-inventory. She had no one to blame but herself for what she was doing with her life. Her father would build her a house tomorrow if she wanted one. Senia had offered her a well-paying job at the bank if she ever decided to start a career. Becca had proven to be the only one in her world that tried to understand her rebellion without giving her 'good advice'—"Find yourself," Becca told her. "Nothing else matters more than that. You'll discover a person of beauty—inside as well as out." And Becca confided about her own early days of making lots of mistakes. "I learned more from doing things the wrong way than I ever learned from doing things right. Maybe you're going about things just like I did."

Angela had her own history of doing things the 'wrong way'. Her running away at sixteen, and crashing her father's car seemed to put her young life in the wrong direction. When she struck the deer that night, Angie was lucky to escape with minor injuries and a bad bump on the head. Later, her grades in school dropped from excellent to average, she estranged herself from her girlfriends by shunning all of the school activities, and became a loner in high school as well as at home. After graduation, Angela enrolled in art and literature classes at the junior college, but had little motivation to go beyond the minimal requirements. Her only goals in life at that time were to have her own apartment and to live by herself.

But, her life would change. Angela regarded the easel standing in the center of the room and remembered that transforming day about a year ago. Becca had introduced her to an old friend of her father's.

Jacque Grojean gave Angela an inspiration to create . . . "Worlds of your own to live in. Places where you can escape and explore. From within yourself you'll discover a capacity to bring beauty to those who can see things as only your eyes have imagined them." Jacque's little studio soon became Angela's favorite refuge from a world she refused to come to terms with. But the one-eyed artist who brought a spark to her life was also a harsh critic of her early efforts at expressing what was inside. "Angie, mon cherie, where are your feelings? I see only lines and shapes and colors . . . I must see spirit and heart and soul!"

Angela watched her mentor boldly stroke the canvas with a flair of broad brushings, refine the obscure images with touches so delicate only a trained eye could detect them, and conjure vivid colors on a pallet smeared with oils that would create a collage of pigmentation beyond imagination. "Voila!" Jacque would literally shout when his creation pleased his senses.

Angela took a canvas home from the studio one evening and spent an entire weekend opening her soul onto the white surface. The spirit of her focus was a horse running freely into an abstract golden dawn. The images flowed from her brush as if unleashed in a torrent of pent emotion. She could actually feel the power transfer from herself to the blue-gray stallion charging into the unknown advent of the day. Her imagery of freedom and confidence found exhilarating expression before her dark, sparkling eyes.

"Magnifique, Angie . . . tres bien, mon cherie!" Jacque embraced her affectionately when she showed him her creation. "You are an artiste! Finalement!" The small man beamed his satisfaction. "This one will hang in my shop for all to see."

Angela realized she was smiling as she left her comfortable reverie on the sofa. The project on her easel was a painting she wanted to give Kevin. It had to be perfect. She knew how Kevin loved "his little mountain"—as he sometimes called Maple Hill. Angela would capture the spirit of that special place fusing its own essence with that of himself. It would be her gift when Kevin passed the bar exams he was studying for.

She pictured him in his apartment at this very minute, poring over tomes of legal documents, his strong fingers running through his hair as he concentrated. When did she fall in love with Kevin? She wondered if it was that night of his graduation party while she watched him move among the adults at her house as if he were one of them. She remembered eyeing him from the back doorway as he talked with Rudy and Armando. How handsome he was. It was that night when she told him that she didn't want to be his cousin anymore.

Or, was it when they drove out to Maple Hill that sleety afternoon after the funeral? They teased and argued that day. She remembered his closeness while looking over her shoulder at the distant hill. His eyes, she could feel, were fantasizing over the warmth of her scarcely exposed breasts—his nose drinking in the perfumed fragrance of her hair.

No. There was no specific time or place. Angela had fallen in love with Kevin when he was nowhere near to her. Kevin touched her mind and her soul from the distances. She could feel him now.

Maybe it was as Becca had told Angela about herself and dad. "Angie, when I lived across the street from your father, I was infatuated with him. Then, when I moved away and he wasn't anywhere close—I fell in love. Sometimes space can conjure the most powerful feelings."

Angie pondered Becca and her timely wisdom. After their miserable start, the two of them had become very close. "I'll never be your mother, Angie—I'll never even come close to that. But, I will love your father . . . and, his children as if they were my own. Each of you . . . as best as I know how."

Becca became someone Angela could always talk with, confide her emotions with. She was the only person in the world who knew the depth of her feelings for Kevin. Angela remembered something Becca had said only days before: "Don't push the river . . . it flows by itself!"

Returning to the kitchen, Angela began a short letter to Kevin. Her feeling of being 'dull' had passed as it usually did. She was more at peace with herself and would write some uplifting words for a change. As she wrote she wondered if she would have the courage to sign . . . 'with love, Angie.'

When she finished the letter she realized she couldn't say what she wanted to say. Not yet.

Senia was feeling depressed this afternoon. Steven's recovery from a stroke six months ago was progressing more slowly than she had hoped. His right side motor dexterity—arm and hand—was noticeably impaired and he walked with an exaggerated limp. Steven's speech, although improving over time, was still slurred and made him self-conscious. Doctor Becca Zoretek proved a marvelous caretaker for Steven and kept his spirit of optimism alive. The daily care of Steven was a responsibility that Senia lovingly assumed. When released from the hospital, she took Steven into her Brooklyn neighborhood home. Although a burden on her time and energy, Senia patiently doted on her man. Her life's priority became Steven's rapid and complete recovery. Caregiving gave her a different sense of fulfillment than marriage might have, but having Steven to herself brought Senia pleasant consolation.

Senia's mild depression of the moment, however, was not related to Steven's daily rehabilitation. The Peter Moran estate had suffered a significant loss in the stock market crash the previous October. Although she had seen some signs of trouble long before the bottom fell out, Senia had failed to divest of several stocks in time. The losses were close to one million dollars. Senia was very critical of herself for failing to protect the estate in its entirety. Noticing it was five o'clock, she decided to make her weekly call to Kevin to see how he was doing with his studies.

Senia's initial question brought a laugh. "Senia, let me tell you the truth. If somebody brought me a bottle of whiskey this afternoon, I'd be tempted to get illegally and absolutely drunk!"

Senia could visualize his smile from two hundred miles away. "You know better than to do something like that," she responded affectionately. "... Sometimes I feel as if I'm talking to your father."

"He would understand how I feel right now."

"So, what's getting you down?"

"Mostly, 'due process of law.' Thank God, Mr. Garvey's only a phone call away. He's prepped me pretty well on the kinds of questions asked on the bar exam."

They talked for another fifteen minutes about Steven, Tony, and Becca, and things in Hibbing before Kevin began getting antsy to continue outlining the main points in his stack of law books. Before saying his good-bye, Kevin added a final thought. "I don't thank you enough for all the things you do for me, Auntie Senia. Sometimes I think you worry too much about all the estate stuff." Kevin knew that Senia's oversight of his affairs stole hours from her every week and that her personal involvement was more stressful than it ought to be. "We've come through the worst of this market business in really good shape. I can really appreciate why my dad trusted you more than anyone else in the world."

Kevin's remark came like a touch of spring-fresh air to Senia's lagging spirits of the moment.

Everybody felt the impact of a ruptured national economy. Tony Zoretek was philosophical. "I've made more money than I could ever spend, Becca." Evenings were their special time to talk about all the things going on in their busy lives. "We've got everything, don't we, sweetheart? Sometimes I feel guilty about that."

Smiling at her husband, Becca put her book aside on the sofa and took Tony's hand in hers. "We've been blessed . . ." Becca wanted to say that they had earned what they had through their own hard work. But she had come to know Tony too well to offer that consolation. Her husband's guilt was something felt deeply in the fabric of who he was. Tony's generous contributions to the church were given with the stipulation that they be used to help community families in need. Despite the dramatic slowdown in construction activity, he kept his crews employed doing maintenance projects on homes where the breadwinner was out of work. The mines had been seriously impacted as the economy stalled and unemployment rates in Hibbing approached all time highs.

Becca nestled her head on Tony's chest. "What more can you do, honey? I know you'd like to take care of every soul in Hibbing. But—"

"We'll figure something out." He smiled and softly kissed her hair. Tony was happy in their relationship. Next month would be the fourth anniversary of their marriage—four comfortable and fulfilling years. The woman at his side was his best friend, companion, and lover. Becca was a remarkable woman and her work at the hospital, as well as within the community, had earned her a reputation as the 'good doctor.' And, she had made personal sacrifices for both him and his family. Without any encouragement from him, Becca had converted to Catholicism before their wedding. Father Foley came to Hibbing for her baptism. Since joining his church, Becca became involved in parish activities and made certain the entire family attended Mass on Sunday.

Sensitive to her Jewish heritage, however, the Zoretek family maintained a connection with the traditions of her former faith as well their own. At times their contrasting religious observances seemed awkward, but they never failed to find a measure of respect and humor about how they practiced their different patterns of belief.

"I've talked with the people at the Remington coal yards about this winter. A few of us at the Chamber of Commerce are going to do our best to see that nobody goes without fuel," Tony said. "That's a start in the right direction. Hopefully, things will turn around next spring, and we won't have that ugly Depression that some people are talking about."

Becca steered her husband's attention away from the heavy thoughts of difficult economic forecasts and toward more pleasant family matters. "The newlyweds want us over for dinner on Sunday. Colleen called earlier and wants me to make some *baklava* for Rudy."

"For Rudy? What about me, Becca?"

"I have something even better for you, my dear." Becca ran her fingers along his thigh. "Let's go to bed."

Claude Atkinson opened the envelope from Kevin. His young friend was dabbling at journalism and the editor was delighted. Every couple of weeks Kevin mailed him the clippings of articles he'd written for the *Minnesota Daily*—the University's campus newspaper. Claude was impressed with Kevin's candid appraisal of issues, but, at the same time recognized there was a 'generation gap' between the two of them. Over the years, Claude's philosophy had tended toward conservatism.

"What bee hives has Kevin stirred with this batch of editorials?" Claude mumbled to himself as he found himself laughing about the controversies he'd come to expect from the aspiring journalist.

Claude reflected on one of Kevin's early commentaries on the '28 presidential campaign. Kevin was a staunch Al Smith supporter at the time. Governor Al Smith of New York was the first Roman Catholic ever to seek the American Presidency. "A vote for Hoover is a vote against Catholics!" Kevin had boldly stated. "The issues that Al Smith has raised are being deliberately ignored by Hoover and his cronies. The Republicans are simply playing the religion card because it's their ace. 'If a Catholic becomes president, the United States will be controlled by the Pope in Rome!' is all they want to say. What is even more ludicrous than that Republican balderdash is that voters are believing it."

As Claude mused over Kevin's letter and enclosures, he was reminded of his dear old friend, Victor. The Mayor would be as proud as Claude was over Kevin's political bent and of his plans to follow in the Power footsteps toward the practice of law. Kevin Moran, Claude was realizing more than ever before, was Peter's son. And, part of Claude's concern was whether Kevin would do a better job with his life than his father before him had done. Along with that thought was his hope that the 'Good Lord' would give Claude enough years to be a vigilant mentor as Kevin's career in Hibbing unfolded.

Kevin put aside his books and tablets. He'd been outlining court cases for nearly five hours, and the lamps outside were glowing in the early fall night. It was a Friday night before a Gopher football game, and students were milling in the streets, looking for parties along the row of frat houses just down the block from his apartment. Despite prohibition, college drinking was rampant. Kevin learned as a freshman that to fit into the social circles on campus, drinking was almost a requisite behavior. Most of the athletes, however, kept their distance from the ribald college party scene.

As he watched the revelry on the street corner below his second story window, he saw a couple kissing in the shadows beyond a lamppost.

He thought of Angela. Imagined kissing her, fondling her, making love to her. He tried to push the thoughts out of his mind but couldn't. One day . . . maybe?

A group of college men clustered across the street, passing a flask among themselves. Another memory pained his awareness of the moment.

It was a party down by the river in the spring of his junior year. Kevin and Huddy were a part of the scene that night. "What the hell, Kevin," Hud said. "Everybody else is drinking."

Sometime after midnight one of the girls near the bonfire screamed, "Police!" Everybody scattered, some even leaping into the freezing currents of the Mississippi River only twenty feet from where they all had gathered. Kevin and Hud, both feeling the effects of too much gin, panicked at the warning. About twenty cops were coming down the steep hill to the river bank, closing off the best means of escape. Following a group of kids who seemed to know where they were going, Kevin darted south through some thick brush with Hud close on his heels.

"Kkk-eee-vvv-!..."

Kevin looked over his shoulder and saw his friend had slipped on the muddy bank and was hanging onto some tree roots. Hud was up to his arm pits in the frothy water. Kevin turned back, arriving at the scene of Hud's dilemma at the same time as two police officers.

In his five years at the University, Kevin had one blemish on his otherwise distinguished record. Kevin Moran's fingerprints were on file with the Minneapolis police department where he had spent a night in jail. The following day, Professor Garvey posted bail for the two young men. Fortunately for Hud Tusken, his basketball season was over. His conviction would have cost him his athletic scholarship. Fortunately for Kevin Moran, Prentice Garvey was able to negotiate a misdemeanor fine with the Hennepin County court where the Judge was a former student of his. Although his name was listed along with nine others in the *Star Tribune,* his misadventure was something the people back home might never know about. Garvey's further interventions kept Kevin from being dropped from the law school program.

Kevin remembered the incident of eighteen months before as if it were yesterday. He was lucky! Consumption of liquor was a felony under the Volstead Act.

At twenty-three, Kevin already had a wide range of *real world* experiences which were integrated with his law school studies. In addition to his short stint as Mayor Power's law clerk five years ago and his Hennepin conviction, Kevin had been a courtroom observer of the Denis Moran trial in Duluth. He'd been to the St. Cloud Reformatory on several occasions to visit his friend, Gary Zench. And, twice he'd driven over to the river city of Stillwater to visit with his Uncle Denis at the state penitentiary.

On his first trip to the enormous, intimidating, granite-walled prison, Kevin didn't know what to expect from the man who had tried to kidnap him when he was little more than an infant.

Uncle Denis had been incarcerated for nearly a year and looked quite different from the-dark haired man at the trial when Kevin arrived for the visit. Denis now wore a full red beard and had put on several pounds. Beyond the hardened exterior, Kevin hoped to find something decent within the soul of this man he had every reason to despise. In this regard, however, Kevin came away with only frustration and disappointment. Denis Moran was everything his own value system found abhorrent. His uncle had not expected the visit and began with—"What the hell do ya wanna see me for? I ain't no good, ya otta know that by now."

Kevin's only reply was, "You're my uncle—my father's brother. I never knew my father, he died when I was . . . I guess you know about that."

"Whatta ya mean, 'I know about that?'" Denis growled, narrowing his eyes at the young man.

"That my father, your brother, died. Suicide is what the police records say. That's what I mean." Kevin would not be bullied by the obnoxious man behind the screen. "I was at the trial, Uncle Denis. You know that. You looked in my direction several times."

Denis nodded at the memory, a cool expression fixed in his eyes.

"Let's try to get this conversation going in the right direction. I just wanted to meet you. That's all. I've got lots of questions. I'm still trying to learn about who I am." Kevin gave Denis a level look.

Both men were on edge, needing to relax before continuing their dialogue. "Mostly I'm here to listen. If you'll tell me about yourself and your life, it might help me to understand mine. Right now we're like two strangers who happen to be related to each other." Kevin smiled, "Where can we go from here, Uncle Denis?"

"I know a lot more 'bout you, Kevin, than you know about me." From that unexpected revelation, Denis began an explanation of his years on the run. He softened his guard, even gave a hint of remorse, as he told about his life as a fugitive. Kevin puzzled when the tones of expression changed. From time to time, his uncle spoke in clear, almost precise, language. Whenever he talked about Danny Morgan, both his voice and words were measured, articulate. *Danny* was taking his nephew into worlds of criminal vice and corruption the young law student had only read about in newspapers. *Denis* brought Kevin back to the reality of a convicted felon who had messed up his life.

"Despite my criminal activities, I tried to keep track of your life in Duluth—at Denfeld. Strange as it may seem, I needed to be connected to what you were doing."

Kevin wondered at the acknowledgment. Who was saying that? Was it Denis or Danny?

Time ran out on their first conversation, but Kevin promised to visit again. His sometimes schizophrenic uncle was a bad man in either personality—but, strangely alluring in both. Could he discover something of his father in the bizarre brother whose life was almost beyond fiction?

The second visit was only two months ago, in late July. This time Kevin was determined to find out more about his family: mostly, he wanted to learn about the issues between his father and his father's brother, Denis, which Senia had alluded to in previous conversations.

His uncle was more Denis, and less Danny Morgan, on this day.

"At the trial you admitted to hating your brother—my father. You blamed him for the death of Grampa Daly out in Oregon. I didn't understand that." Kevin got their conversation focused on what he wanted to know.

Denis rambled, coughing frequently as he responded to Kevin's inquiries. "I'll never forget that day, back in Hibbing it was, when yer dad told Daly to get outta town. 'This is my town' he told pa."

But, when Kevin probed his uncle's memory, some obvious contradictions surfaced from the original story. "Ya. Me and Pa wanted to give our lumbering business one last shot. Me and Pa, not Peter! He, your dad, offered to buy us both out of the Hibbing operations. Pete called it a 'square deal'." From there, Denis told how the Morans didn't do as well as they expected in Oregon. "Then, Daly got really sick—pneumonia. We buried him out there, Kevin. Your pa never came to the funeral. Too busy he was with all his business stuff back in Minnesota." Denis spoke through compressed lips of pent anger, often covering his mouth against his coughs. "Too busy to come out for the funeral. I ain't never gonna forgive him fer that."

Kevin believed that Denis' hatreds were largely contrived. Peter was a convenient scapegoat for his own failures. Denis squandered his share of the Hibbing business money, married badly, and had trouble with liquor. "No. I can't blame yer dad for what I did with my own life out there. Yer right about that." Denis tried to define his frustrations more clearly. "I think more than anythin else, Pete broke my dad's heart. He did, ya know. Peter was always Daly's favrit growing up. I never got the attention from pa that I shoulda. Maybe that's what made me so damn mad all'a time. I wasn't as smart as Peter . . . I wasn't ambitious like Peter, I wasn't someone who dressed so fancy in clothes like Peter." Denis self-deprecated—it was Daly's favor of Peter that was at the root of Denis' deep-seeded frustration. Perspiring, Denis turned his head away and coughed again.

"Are you all right . . ."

"Damn naggin cold, ain't been able to shake it," Denis said. In the last few minutes, Denis recalled how Peter had him beaten up and run out of town. "I was awful drunk that night at his fancy new hotel but I don't think I shoulda—" Denis grimaced, "His cops broke my ribs."

"And that was the last time you saw my father?"

Denis squinted his eyes at Kevin, hesitated noticeably. "Ya, like I said, never laid my eyes on him again."

Kevin left the second visit with new insights on how the brothers became divided by their ambitious father's affection. He could understand the feelings of alienation Denis imagined. Kevin also concluded that Peter's treatment of Denis at the grand opening of the new hotel was mean-spirited. If Denis' story was to be believed, Peter had a nasty temper and some deep-seeded hatreds of his own. He would visit his uncle again and try to learn more about his father's relationship with Daly Moran. And . . . he might ask Denis where he was when Peter died in August of 1908.

Denis Moran did not leave his cell that September afternoon for the half-hour walk outside the prison building. He had been coughing throughout the night before and felt weak and feverish all day. Denis was scared.

Two days before, another cellmate had been admitted to the prison infirmary with symptoms similar to those he was experiencing. Despite his questions to the security guard about his friend's condition, Denis was unable to get any answers. Some of the prisoners across the block were mumbling about tuberculosis!

"O'Malley!" Denis called in a weak voice down the corridor for the ward officer on duty. "O'Malley! I need some help."

About five minutes later, O'Malley was standing outside the barred door. Denis was sweating profusely. "I gotta get to the infirmary, O"Malley. Feel like I'm gonna die . . . never been so damn sick in my life."

Quarantined in the isolation room of the prison hospital, Denis' appeal to contact his nephew was denied. "You can't have any visitors, Mr. Moran. What you've got is contagious."

"What's contagious?" Denis had a shudder in his voice. "Tell me the truth, damn it! I got TB?"

The nurse nodded in reply.

Nurse Beverly Staples wrote his letter while sitting at his bedside.

"I done somethin really terrible years ago." The words of Denis Moran were hardly audible from his dry mouth. "I gotta tell my nephew so he knows the truth, d'ya understand, nurse? This letter's gotta get to him."

Nurse Staples nodded. "Just tell me what to write."

"It don't make no difference anymore, ya see. I ain't gonna live to have no more trials." He coughed yellow bile into the sleeve of his white gown. "Gonna get it all offa my chest."

That afternoon Nurse Staples dutifully transcribed the last words Denis Moran would share with another human being. As he spoke in halting sentences, she reworked his words so they made better sense. Her patient was drifting from lucid thoughts to delusions—and back again. She understood, however, exactly what he was trying to say. In the hour it took to write his short letter, Nurse Staples winced many times.

Dear Kevin.

We won't be talking again. I don't want to leave this world with something on my conscience. You know your uncle has been a bad man most of his life. I even wanted to steal your money from you. I'm sorry for that. I'm sorry for lots of things I've done. I'm going to burn in hell.

Kevin, I've been a liar. Even with you, I lied. I don't know if any good can come of telling the truth before I die. I hope it will. I killed your father that night. I wish I didn't do what I did. I wish he would have stopped me. I wish we could have forgiven each other.

More than anything I wish you will be a better man than any of us were. I think you will be, Kevin. Please try to find it in your heart to forgive me. Forgive your father too. I would ask you to pray for me but it won't do any good.

Thank you for visiting me in the prison. You were the only person in the world that did.

Sincerely,
Uncle Denis

Kevin had three letters to open on this bright September Monday. The first was from Angie.

Dear Kevin:

I am in a good mood this afternoon. I think it's because I chose to be happy. Does that make any sense? I will have a surprise for you when you come home next month.

I know you are busy studying for your big test. You will do very well because you are so smart. Sometimes, I wish I had used my intelligence in school. I wasted so many opportunities . . . I think I lamed school for things that weren't going the way I wanted them to in my distressing life.

I was thinking about that today and let it get me down for a while. I was in what I call a 'dull' mood. But, I'm over it now. I don't count my blessings often enough. Do you get in moods like I do, Kevin? Times when you think you're not doing what you're supposed to be doing, when you're going down the dead-end streets of life? If you do, think of me. Think positive thoughts like I'm learning to do. Jacque told me that 'life is our own painting—we have the canvas before us, the brush in our hand, and many colors to choose.' I believe that with all my heart. Do you? As I read what I've written this afternoon, I wonder if this is a stupid letter. Forgive me, but I just had to write something to you—maybe I just wanted to let you know that I was thinking about you.

Your friend,
Angie

p.s. You don't have to answer this letter.

Kevin smiled to himself. It was a beautiful expression of her thoughts. He would answer Angela's letter in very few words. *'I've been thinking about you, too.'*

The second letter was from Father Pat Foley. It began . . .

Dear Kevin:
Forgive me for not writing in several weeks . . .

Foley's letter went on to tell of the priest's recent promotion to Monsignor in the Duluth Catholic Diocese.

After reading the third letter, Kevin cried. Something profound touched him. Each of his letters that day used a common word to express one sentiment in three very different ways . . . *forgive!*

GIFTS OF LOVE

THE EARLY OCTOBER AFTERNOON SUN emblazoned the western slope of Maple Hill. The trees were beginning their splendid autumnal transformation, and Kevin's breath was taken away by the beauty he beheld. Along the lower hillside, fringing the meadow, clusters of birch stood like yellow torches against a background of dark pines. Further up, the majestic maples and oaks were awash in amber and red-orange hues so stunning he wanted to capture the collage of color in his memory forever. No place on earth could match the beauty he beheld at this moment. He pulled over to the side of Townline Road to soak up the sensual splendor spread out like an endless blanket of nature's finest painting. This was *his* land! The feeling of ownership was emotionally overwhelming.

Down below on the tawny field surrounded by wood-railed fencing grazed the horse he had been told about only the week before. The black thoroughbred Arabian would be his surprise gift for Angela, but he would wait until the weekend to take her out to the barn to see him. Stepping out onto the road, Kevin walked to the front of his car, and sat contentedly on the fender, allowing his eyes their survey over the tranquil property stretching toward the western horizon. About fifty yards ahead of his line of sight an opening in the tree line revealed a new gravel driveway winding up toward the mansion atop the hill. Off in the distance, a spiral of smoke wafted above the the red tile roof of his house. One day he would live here. That day, however deep in his future, would come when he married. Kevin had vowed to himself not to live in this majestic house alone—as his father had done a generation before him.

Returning to his car, Kevin decided to wait until tomorrow to visit the house and meet with Leon Gunther, the caretaker who had overseen the property these past three years. Mr. Gunther, nearly seventy, but as hardy as the old trees surrounding him, had been Peter Moran's gardener at the old Washington Street address. Kevin held Mr. Gunther in the highest regard and communicated with him nearly every month since the moving project commenced. And it was Mr. Gunther who found the gelding that Kevin wanted to buy for Angela. "His name is 'Flare,' Mr. Moran, and he's got all the spirit you said you wanted in a horse. I'm sure you and the lady will be happy with him," Gunther informed.

It was approaching six and Kevin had been driving most of the day from Minneapolis. Tony was expecting him for a late dinner and had promised that his room at the house would be ready. It had been six months since Kevin had been back to Hibbing, and he was excited. This time he was *home* for good!

Kevin's homecomings were always like a family reunion. Tony liked celebration, and the occasion of Kevin's passing the Minnesota bar exams was something to be shared with all those who cared about the young man's future. When he pulled up to the Zoretek house, Kevin realized he was going to be feted with another graduation party. Several automobiles lined the Brooklyn street but a conspicuous opening had been left in front of the house for him to park his car.

Tony, now showing slight traces of gray in his hair, was the first to greet him at the front door with his typical bear-like hug. His 'uncle' was still a powerful man at forty-one, and looked every bit the strapping athlete of his younger years. At Tony's shoulder stood Becca, looking as radiant as ever. "Welcome home, Kev!" Their words came in almost rehearsed unison, and their affection felt as warm as the sun on his back.

Kevin embraced Senia, then Steven, leaning on his cane at her side. Rudy and Colleen were the third couple in the line at the foyer, and then eighteen year-old Marco, who was nearly as tall as Kevin. Hugs and kisses and handshakes. Claude had been invited over along with Lud Jaksa, Norman Dinter, and Robert Peterson. Their wives stood in the background of the living room waiting their turn to welcome Kevin back to Hibbing. Mr. Peterson had been Vic Power's associate and was going to be Kevin's mentor at the law office.

Greeting everybody with his warmest regards, Kevin searched for the one face he wanted most to see. Where was Angela? Rather than let his disappointment remain inside, Kevin pulled Tony aside by the elbow. "Where is your lovely daughter, Tony?"

Tony was about to answer when Becca stepped between the two men. "She's in the back yard, Kevin. I think she wanted to . . . say hello, without all the people around. Angie's waiting her turn . . ."

Tony smiled an interruption of his wife's words, "You're excused for a few minutes, Kev." Placing his arm around Kevin's shoulder, Tony gave a quick wink. "You've got her father's permission to give her a kiss on the cheek. I think she's waited a long time for that."

"Both of you have—am I right about that?" Becca asked in a teasing voice.

Kevin blushed. "I guess . . . I mean, are you sure Angie . . . ?"

"I'm sure, Kevin." Becca steered Kevin through the crowd gathering in the kitchen where Sadie had trays of hors d'oeuvres spread on the table and counter tops. At the back door, Becca gave him a light kiss on his cheek, "Take your time, Kevin. We'll all be here when the two of you come in."

Outside, Kevin saw her sitting at the picnic table. He stood at the door for a moment quietly taking in her beauty. It was like seeing his Aunt Mary as he remembered her from his childhood. Mary was the loveliest woman he had ever seen—until that moment! Angie turned her face in his direction, stood and smiled the most exquisite smile Kevin's eyes had ever beheld.

Stepping toward her, Kevin was at a loss for words. He tried a smile of his own, but it felt as awkward and weak as the legs he walked on. The only two words that he could stammer at the moment were . . . "Hi, Angie."

Angela sensed his self-consciousness at the apparent arrangement for their meeting outside—by themselves. "You look great, Kevin. Good to have you home." She took two steps toward him, held her hands out for him to take in his.

"You look . . . just wonderful, yourself." Kevin's words were sticking in his throat. "I mean, beautiful."

Angela smiled at his compliment. She did look beautiful and she knew it. She had the look of a woman in love and it radiated like a sunbeam in the shadowed yard. "You can kiss me if you want to, Kevin," she said in the halting voice of uncertainty.

Both of them had saved their first kiss for each other and for this moment—not knowing when, or if, it might ever happen. Kevin took her hands and placed them behind him, arching her so that her face was just beneath his own. His eyes became lost in the dark enchantment of her eyes, his lips found her soft full mouth, and his body pressed against her firm breasts. The feeling rendered him lightheaded for a long moment. Then, letting go of her hands, he wrapped his arms around her and parted his lips from their kiss. "You feel better than . . . I ever imagined, Angie." He wanted to say "I love you", but held those words inside. The vulnerability of telling Angie he loved her was too scary for him right now. He could wait he realized—but not for too much longer.

Angie felt the heat of his embrace when she opened her mouth to his first kiss. Every fiber of her body seemed unloosed as he held her in his arms. She wanted to tell Kevin she loved him in her first breath, but decided her profession could wait. "I saved my first kiss for you," Angela said with a shutter in her voice. "It was worth waiting for . . ."

Flushed, Kevin cradled her soft face in his strong hands, locked into her sparking brown eyes. "I always hoped you would save that kiss for me, Angie." He swallowed hard on his emotions, "I waited for this, too."

Both seemed to realize that one kiss was enough for the moment, and found each other's hands. "Let's take a walk down the street before going inside," Angie suggested. "I think I need to cool down."

"I think we both do," Kevin admitted. "I'm going to ask your father if I can date you on Saturday. There's something I'm dying to show you, Angie."

"Dad's permission won't be necessary, Kevin. I'm on my own these days—you know that. And, even if it were up to him, you'd have yourself a date on Saturday." She smiled up into his face as they strolled along the street side holding hands. "I've got a little surprise for you too."

Kevin's Thursday morning was structured with appointments. Before lunch with Claude, he would pay a visit to the new office of his soon-to-be legal associate, Robert Peterson. Then, across the street, he'd meet with Senia at the Merchants and Miners bank. And, he'd promised Tony he'd stop by the Zoretek Construction Company warehouse building to discuss *something* Tony wanted to talk about.

As Kevin approached the address of the law office on the corner of East Fourth and Howard Street, he noticed a large strip of brown paper taped across the front window bordering the wide sidewalk. Kevin squelched his first thought as to what the paper covered. "Don't let your ego get away from you," he muttered under his breath.

Inside he was welcomed by Mr. Peterson and his associate, Albert Raukar. Kevin was introduced to Mr. Raukar, a round-faced man of fifty, and the two secretaries, Louise Sillman and Martha Reiter. The room was spacious, one wall lined with bookshelves, another with file cabinets. In the corner, behind newly installed oak railings, was a large mahogany desk with an engraved nameplate—'Kevin Moran, L.L.D.'

Gesturing toward the desk, Robert Peterson said, "I think you'll find the chair fits, Mr. Moran. Are we in agreement about starting your new job next Monday morning?" The slender, baldheaded, senior attorney offered his hand. "A handshake will make a binding contract between us, Kevin. What do you say?"

"Yes, sir. Monday morning it will be." He gave Peterson a firm handshake. "An oral contract, with three credible witnesses, Mr. Peterson," he grinned.

Peterson gave Kevin a superficial tour of the office complex. There were two separate offices, one for each of the senior partners. The arrangement was fine with Kevin. From his desk he could see everything going on and have the benefit of a fine view of the street outside.

Peterson smiled, "Let's step out on the sidewalk for a minute; I'm sure you noticed the front window has been under repair." The lanky attorney put his hand on Kevin's shoulder before pulling the brown sheet from the window pane. "Oh, and I'm 'Pete' among my friends—especially when they're my partners. Welcome on board, Kevin!"

In newly painted black script across the window read 'Peterson, Raukar, and Moran.'

Senia had coffee waiting in her office. Through the open door she saw Kevin shaking hands with Mr. Goldberg and chatting about something that brought an easy laugh between them. As she watched, Senia was struck once more by how much Kevin had come to look like his father. His face had filled out and he combed his auburn hair in much the same manner as Peter had styled his. She remembered Tony making the same observation the night before—and Claude agreed, "I thought it was Peter himself coming through the front door." Claude mentioned his aside to Norm Dinter within earshot of Senia.

Kevin was wearing a stylish navy blue pinstriped suit, starched white shirt, and a colorful paisley tie that was coordinated perfectly. His sideburns were trimmed down to his jaw line, and he wore his hair longer than was customary among most professionals in the Hibbing business community.

"Good morning, Senia." Kevin stepped toward her and gave her a quick hug. As his eyes scanned her office, he noticed the yellowed photograph of his father and Senia standing in front of the former hotel resting on the file cabinet near her desk. A smaller picture of Steven was set beside Peter's, along with three photos of himself. "I'll have to get you a better picture than those, Senia." Kevin smiled at the old shot of when he was wearing his Denfeld baseball uniform. "Mr. Peterson wants me to get a portrait for his office. I'll order a few extra for you and Tony, and—"

"Angela." Senia finished his sentence and returned his smile.

Kevin nodded without reply.

"Sit down and have some coffee, Kevin. As you might imagine, I've got some things to go over with you this morning. And, I know you've got a busy schedule, so it won't take us long." Senia poured two cups, sat down, and withdrew a tablet from her desk drawer.

Her management of the estate funds was meticulous. Senia reviewed the costs of the house—moving, excavation, renovation, and the ongoing maintenance costs. "Mr. Gunther was a marvelous choice for the caretaker position, Kevin. You can't imagine what lovely gardens he kept at your father's mansion. Absolutely gorgeous."

"I'm planning to go out to Maple Hill later this afternoon. I've heard he's done a great job with the grounds up there as well. It's too bad I didn't get to see his gardens while they were in bloom last summer."

"When are you planning to move out to the house, Kevin? Everything is ready. We even found some of your father's furnishings—the library is almost exactly as it was back in Peter's . . ."

"Not for a while," Kevin interrupted. "I'm going to get an apartment in town for now." Senia had told him about Peter's library before, and he had plans to completely redecorate the huge room. From what he had learned, the library was a place of isolation for his father.

Senia looked puzzled. "You're going to live in town after everything we've—?"

"For the time being. I'll go out there from time to time, just to get away from town. But, I'm not ready to live in the house by myself yet." Sensing the disappointment in Senia's expression, Kevin reached across the table and put his hand upon hers. "Let's you and me go out there one of these days. You could tell me some of the history."

Smiling easily, Senia felt his affection in the unexpected invitation. "I'd like that very much. It's been a dream of mine for the two of us to see the house together."

Senia checked her emotion by regarding the table before her. One word stared out at her from the page—Androy. "Let me give you something to think about, Kevin. It's just an idea mind you, but—" She explained that the Androy Hotel was quietly for sale. Only a few, Harvey Goldberg included, were aware of the hotel's availability. A price of $800,000.00 had been mentioned to a few reputable bankers and realtors. The Peter Moran estate balance remained close to three million dollars.

"It's a great building," Kevin agreed. The thought of buying the hotel was something that had wandered through his private thoughts on several occasions. Nothing would connect him with his father's legacy more perfectly than owning the most exquisite hotel in Northern Minnesota. The notion was intriguing, but . . . "I've got a lot of settling in to do right now; maybe we can think more about that later."

Senia was satisfied with his deferral. The seed of her idea had been planted and Kevin would think about it. "That's fine with me," she said.

It was nearly ten-thirty when Kevin pushed his chair from the desk.

"I can certainly understand your feelings, Kevin, but the hotel wouldn't be something that you'd have to be involved with on a day-to-day basis. You could hire a manager to take care of the operations," Senia said. Realizing Kevin was anxious to get over to Tony's office, she stood up herself. "Kevin, please stop over to the house and visit Steven when you get a few minutes. He'd so love your companionship. He doesn't get out much these days."

"No need to mention that, Senia. I've made plans to take Steven fishing on Sunday morning. We talked about that last night. Fall fishing is the greatest according to Steven, and he's really excited about wetting his line again in Timo's Lake."

Tony and Lud Jaksa were visiting over coffee when Kevin arrived. The three of them talked for a few minutes about the Maple Hill project before Lud—who had supervised the move of the Moran house three years earlier—excused himself, leaving Tony and Kevin to have some time together.

"I didn't even ask you last night when you were moving out to the house, Kev," Tony said.

Kevin explained his plans in much the same way as he had with Senia an hour before.

"I understand your feelings. It's a lot of house for one person." Tony nodded his agreement. "After you get married, though—"

Kevin smiled knowingly. "Hopefully that won't be too far in the future." But, neither of them mentioned Angela.

Tony wanted to let Kevin know that he was going to transfer his company's legal affairs to Bob Peterson's firm with the understanding that Kevin take care of them in the future. "We've already talked about it. It's not much, but it's a little start for your practice. Mostly contracts, titles, deeds and a ton of paper work I'm afraid."

"I know. Those are the kind of things lawyers call their 'bread and butter'. Tony, I'm grateful."

More than anything else, Tony wanted to help Kevin become integrated into all the things going on in Hibbing during these troublesome times. He explained how the mining slowdowns and growing rates of unemployment presented the community with some difficult challenges. "I'm working with a lot of businessmen in the Chamber about developing some type of strategy for taking care of our people if things get even worse than they are right now. Food and fuel are our major concerns, of course, and winter's right around the corner."

"I'd like to be involved in what you're doing," Kevin said. "And, I'd like to join the Chamber of Commerce. Mr. Peterson is pretty active in the organization from what I understand."

"Pete's a goodhearted man. A lot of Vic Power rubbed off on him through the years the two of them practiced law together. And, Al Raukar's a prince of a guy, too. You couldn't be with a better firm."

Kevin looked at Tony levelly for a long moment. He didn't think that his 'uncle' knew very much about the fortune that had accumulated in his trust estate. He was torn between keeping his affairs confidential and sharing this circumstance with Tony. There was a compromise, however. "I can help with any emergency contingencies your group is planning." Kevin chose his words carefully. "My father left me a considerable inheritance, Tony. As I'm sure Senia told you, some of that money was used to cover the costs of moving the house and buying the property. But—"

"I'm aware of that, Kev. Whatever Peter left you is your own affair." Tony reflected a moment. "Your father's will, if you'd call it that, was something I'll never forget. He instructed Senia to pay off the note on my little business at the time. He touched a lot of people in his own unique way—your dad." He let the thought end where it started.

"What we're talking about at the Chamber, however, is each of our business members pledging ten percent of their net toward what we're calling the 'H.C.C.F.'—the Hibbing Community Contingency Fund." Tony smiled at the acronym which had been contrived, "Sounds kinda fancy and dramatic, don't you think?"

"I think it's great. I'll want to do what others are doing, and more."

They talked about the sagging local economy and the implications of shrinking national demand for steel. The Hibbing economy was almost totally dependent on the Eastern plants that processed Mesabi's rich iron ore. The entire Iron Range was already feeling the effects of a predicted depression—long before the rest of the country. The giant Oliver Iron Mining Company, so critical to Hibbing's fortunes, was operating at less than fifty percent of its previous capacity. "It's probably going to get worse before it gets better up here." Tony's frown evidenced his certainty in that dire prediction. "Construction this year has been so far below our expectations that I've got my crews doing charity work. Frankly, I worry about how much longer I can go without some layoffs. It's frightening."

From the heavy dialogue of difficult times, the two men drifted into lighter family conversation. "I can't believe the transformation," Tony said about Becca's relationship with his daughter. "Angie and Becca have become like sisters while you've been away, Kevin. I can't tell you how much happier that has made my life."

They talked about Marco's popular jazz combo and what a remarkable musician the young man had become. "What that boy can do with his saxophone is almost magical," Tony bragged of the son who was so unlike himself. Marco never had any interest in sports, but was a top student and among the best liked boys in his Hibbing High School graduating class last summer.

Tony got up from his chair, moved over to where Kevin was sitting, and placed his hands affectionately on Kevin's shoulders. "You know, I couldn't be happier. I've got an artistic daughter, a musician son—and, now I've got my athlete as well!" His voice strained. "I don't have to tell you, Kev, over all these years you've been like my own son. Seeing you come in the door last night . . . well, it was like one of my own kids coming home. I'm so proud of what you've done . . ."

Kevin's eyes moistened as he felt Tony's grip on his shoulders. He stood up, turned, and met Tony's eyes. "You've made me feel like a son. And, any pride you might feel toward me—well, double it! Then you'll have some idea about how I feel about you, Tony. Both Rudy and I are like your sons." Kevin sought to ease the emotion of the moment. "Speaking of, I've never seen Rudy so happy."

Tony nodded at the observation. "He and Colleen are about as content as two people can be with each other." Tony's smile faded for a moment. "Just between us, Kevin—they just went through a pretty tough episode. Colleen miscarried back in July. They were heartbroken!"

"Did Colleen come out of it okay? I mean, can they . . ."

"Oh yes. They'll keep trying. We're all praying—" Tony was a devout Christian and prayer centered his life. "Becca can't wait for grandchildren. She's going to be more thrilled than any of us when that time comes."

The last few minutes of their conversation drifted to their shared love of baseball and the World Series which had started the week before. Tony was a Philadelphia Athletics (and Lefty Grove) fan of many years, and his beloved A's were up three games to two on the St. Louis Cardinals.

∼

Arriving a few minutes early, Kevin found the table Claude had reserved in the Androy dining room. He remembered his only previous luncheon in the splendid, ornately appointed room, with Mayor Power and Senia. How quickly those five years had passed: passed from his being a kid just out of high school sitting beside one of Minnesota's most esteemed lawyers, to sitting at a table this afternoon with a law degree of his own. Kevin allowed himself a moment of self-pride.

Claude was showing his fifty-seven years in wrinkles and gray hair. But those remarkable blue eyes still had the keen sparkle of a much younger, vibrant, and engaging newsman. If Kevin would never know a grandfather, Claude was as close as any human might be to filling that special role in his life. Kevin had been blessed with mentors throughout the years: Father Pat Foley when he was a boy, Mr. Barker during the Denfeld years, and Prentice Garvey while he was at the U. But Claude Atkinson enjoyed a special place in new life and was the veritable *soul* of this place Kevin now called home.

As Claude made his way to the table, the newsman stopped often to chat with other diners in the crowded room. There was not a person in Hibbing whom Claude did not know in some way or another. Through the years, his *Ore* had become a chronicle of the Hibbing family.

"Kevin, my boy!" Claude extended his long and narrow hand. "Permit an old man that reference. It carries a ton of affection."

Kevin smiled and stood. "Hello Claude. I'm flattered."

The two of them relaxed at their table, catching up on the six months since their last visit. Naturally, the World Series entered their conversation early, and both predicted an Athletics win in game six.

Kevin ordered a chicken salad, Claude a bowl of clam chowder with a popover dinner roll "with lots of butter and jam on the side."

Claude measured Kevin with his intelligent eyes. "I've enjoyed your clippings these past two years. You have a knack for taking on the tough issues, and I like that, even when I don't agree with you."

"Which was most of the time." Grinning, Kevin took the bait.

"Only some of the time." Claude pulled at his ear lobe. "I liked Al Smith—or, was it that I disliked Hoover? Anyhow, we both agreed about who should have won that election. Hoover's got us in a pickle these days. Not that it's his fault, mind you, but he's at a loss about what to do about it. He's going to be a one-termer, Kevin, that's almost for certain."

Politics was a bond between the two men. Politics at every level. From national issues, their conversation moved to Governor Christianson's administration in St. Paul. "Floyd Olson's going to win next month's election, Kevin. I'm not inclined to vote for many Democrats, but this guy's got the fire of our old friend, Victor. I've got to believe that the Republicans are in for a beating here in Minnesota. And, whoever runs for President as a Democrat is going to win in '32. I wouldn't be surprised if it's Governor Roosevelt of New York. Anyone who can run that state can manage this country just as well."

Local politics was where Kevin wanted Claude to take their discussion. "So, what about Mayor Weirick? I haven't followed things up here as closely as I should. He goes back a lot of years, doesn't he?"

The mention of Doc Weirick touched a fuse in Claude. "Sometimes I can't understand Hibbing voters. They elected this guy back in '07 and now he's back again twenty years later. He was no good then and he's even worse now." Claude leaned forward in his chair. "There was bad blood between Weirick and Victor for years."

Claude was an astute political observer, and local elections were his greatest passion. "Most of the *real* politics up here goes on behind the scenes, Kevin. It's always been that way. Insiders with money and connections are the power brokers. There's a guy—I think you might have met him once—by the name of Elwood Trembart. He pulls Weirick's strings, just as he did John Gannon's before John decided not to run for mayor again a couple of years back. Elwood runs the Republican machine from the background of his law office."

"I remember him, Claude. Victor introduced me to Trembart in this very room five years ago. Vic said Trembart and my father were enemies—I think that's the word he used: *Enemies!*"

"They were. And, like I said, Trembart despised Mayor Power, too."

Lost in a thought for a moment, Kevin made no reply. In his mind he visualized Elwood Trembart and recalled the stoop-shouldered man's piercing gray eyes, his cold stare over spectacles riding low on the bridge of his nose.

Claude picked up the thread of his political commentary. "The Democrats in this town are so divided and disorganized these days! It's no wonder Trembart gets his people elected, not only in Hibbing, but in the sixtieth legislative district as well."

"I had no idea politics up here were so manipulated."

"A good choice of words—manipulated! In a lot of ways, Victor did the same things, I'll admit. But, he never put his own interests above those of the people." Claude dabbed at his mouth after a last spoonful of chowder, pushed his bowl to the side of the table. "Let me tell you something else. "Elwood's daughter, Molly, married a mine superintendent by the name of Ian Roberts a few years ago. I think Roberts has political ambitions, and Molly—well, she's always been the force behind him."

"I don't know the name."

"You will. Roberts is a bigwig at the Algonquin Club. That's where Hibbing's elitist nabobs hang out. It's a men's only social club. A lot of the same people who belong to the Mesaba Country Club like to carry their socializing to the Algonquin. Sometimes, I think more local decisions are made by these folks than by the city council."

"Do you belong, Claude?"

"I golf at the Club in the summer—God knows I'll never master that miserable sport—but, the Algonquin Club? Nope. Not my cup of tea, Kevin. I'm just a common man with no pretensions to be anything more." Claude smiled inwardly at his admission. Aside from a decent golf score, he had few aspirations remaining in life. "I'm going to get you out on the golf course next summer, Kevin. It's a good place to meet some of the local folks." He paused and grinned. "And it would be a good place for me to see how you deal with frustration!"

Kevin had an amused smile. "I'd like that very much." In his thoughts of the moment, however, he wished he'd grown up in Hibbing and knew more about the people who formed this diverse local population, as well as their relationships, and the organizations—each of which would tell him much about the fabric of his chosen community. He would have a lot of catching up to do in the months ahead. "This is all very interesting to me, Claude. How would I go about getting . . . involved in all this? Politically, I'm more in tune with Democrats. Like yourself, I think Floyd Olson and Franklin Roosevelt are people of the future."

"I get carried away by all this, Kevin. And, maybe I'm putting my own bias into your thinking. I don't want to do that. Perhaps we should have talked baseball instead of politics."

"Oh, no. We both got hooked on all this local politics through our mutual friend, Mayor Power, I'm afraid. God rest his soul."

The time was slipping beyond one o'clock. "Kevin, I might have mentioned this to you before, but there's really only one person in this town who could turn things around." Claude paused for effect, "One person who has a vision like our man Victor Power had. But, unfortunately, that man doesn't have an ounce of political ambition."

Kevin remembered, and finished Claude's thought. "Tony."

That afternoon, Kevin drove out to the house on Maple Hill to visit with Mr. Gunther. The two of them walked the lush property for nearly an hour, ending up at the stable below the hill. "He's an absolute beauty!" Kevin said while regarding the Arabian gelding. Flare had white blaze from his forehead down his face to the nose, white fetlocks on his lower front legs, and the largest brown eyes Kevin had ever seen. "Tell me about the horse, Mr. Gunther. Where is he from? Is he easy to ride?"

"I wouldn't worry, sir. Once Flare's saddled, his disposition is pretty mild. Gets along fine with your mares most of the time." Leon Gunther explained that he had found the horse on a ranch near Aitkin weeks before. Mentioning he had all the thoroughbred's papers back at the house along with the sales documents, Leon continued. "I bought three others as you asked me to do, Mr. Moran. Found them through a friend of mine in Brainerd. They're all standard breeds—but, really great stock as you'll see for yourself."

"Where are they?"

Leon Gunther led Kevin through the back door of the barn and swung it open toward the western pasture. Grazing together were the two chocolate brown mares. In a double-fenced paddock some distance off to his left was a slate gray stallion.

"Does the stallion have a name?"

"He's been called 'Stony,' sir. Kinda fits with his color. I've made a special area for him away from the mares. Stony's not a gelding and we gotta be careful." Kevin gave Leon a pat on the back. "I've always wanted to have some riding horses of my own and you've found me some really good stock to start with." Then he remembered another detail, "Oh, were you able to find some saddles, Leon?"

"A pair of them, sir. They're both in the tack room. They've been used some, but I'd guess they're better than new from the wear they got."

Back at the house, Kevin wandered around the many spacious, well-furnished rooms. It was truly a mansion in its every aspect. Upstairs were five bedrooms and a sewing room. Downstairs, a huge oak paneled dining room, a remodeled kitchen with new white ceramic-tiled flooring, a living room with large windows opening toward the slope to the southwest, and the dark mahogany walled library with a north-facing window.

"Tomorrow I'd like to do some work in here," Kevin told Mr. Gunther. "Aside from the bookshelves . . ." Kevin dropped the thought, realizing the changes he wanted to make were hard to visualize. Angie might be able to help him redecorate. The only thing of which he was certain was that he did not want this space to haunt him with any vague memories of the man who once took refuge here. "Maybe we can just move everything out and store it in the attic for the time being."

"Yes, sir, Mr. Moran. Happy to do that for you."

"We'll work on it together, Leon." Kevin smiled at the smaller man, offering his hand. "I want to thank you for everything you've done with this place. Outside, as well as inside—it's just about perfect."

"I'm glad you're pleased, sir. It's been a labor of love. I've been a part of this place for nearly thirty years. I should thank you for saving it from being demolished. Nobody was going to move this house when the mining came up to the front yard on Washington Street." His smile was a roadmap of wrinkles. "No sir. Nobody but Mr. Moran's son cared enough about this great house. It's me that otta be grateful, sir."

Kevin put his hand on Leon's slight shoulder. "This place's got a few more generations left in it." He wandered over to the large desk off to his left, near the corner of the large library. His father sat at this desk—died at this very desk! "I'll be back tomorrow morning, Leon. Maybe I can talk Rudy into helping us out with our project."

Before leaving, Kevin returned to the living room, plunked down on the dark green velvet sofa, and placed a call to the St. Cloud Reformatory.

He would leave a message with the prison officials and wait for Gary Zench to return his call. Gary's behavior, Kevin was certain, would earn his friend parole next spring. He would make a trip to St. Cloud when that time came and present an endorsement for the parole hearing. Gary had already told Kevin that he'd come up to Hibbing and finish his schooling after his prison time was completed.

While he waited for Gary's call, Kevin absorbed himself in the pleasant scene outside the windows. The four horses pranced playfully in the afternoon sun as Kevin allowed his imagination to wander into the coming Saturday when he and Angela would be out there where the horses ranged the meadow's wide acreage. Afterwards, they might lounge on this very sofa and—maybe? Their kiss of the night before still lingered in his thoughts. In her kiss he sensed the promise of a deeper intimacy. What might he do if the two of them were here, on this sofa, alone in the house? Along the north wall of the living room was a large fireplace with a neat stack of split birch logs. How late might she stay? He would bring out some steaks when he came to the house tomorrow . . .

The ringing phone snapped Kevin from his reverie. The operator connected Gary's call. "Hey, Kevin. What're ya doing calling me on a Thursday? Is something the matter?" (Kevin's calls were almost always on Sunday evenings.)

"Not at all, Gary. Everything's just great up here." Kevin explained he called to let Gary know that he was not living in Minneapolis any more. "I start my new job on Monday. Can you believe it? Your West Duluth buddy a lawyer up in Hibbing."

"Ya, I can believe it, Kevin. Remember that day we hitched the train up there? Ya told me then you was gonna live in Hibbing some day. I'll never forget ya tellin' me that."

The two of them talked for the allotted ten minutes before Gary would have to get off the line. "I've been promoted to the laundry room, Kevin. That's about the best job to have in this place. And, I been readin' in the library when I get a chance."

"You're keeping your record clean, Gary?" Kevin prayed that his friend would not do anything to jeopardize his parole chances . . .

"I ain't gettin in nobody's way. Just doing what I'm s'posed to. I want outta this here place soon as I can. Don't worry about that, buddy."

Kevin heard the guard's voice in the background. "Time's up, Zench."

"Yessir . . . gotta run, Kevin. Keep in touch."

Angela awoke on Thursday morning with red eyes and a headache following a nearly sleepless night.

Kevin had kissed her.

While tossing and turning for hours, she tried to replay what happened in her mind but couldn't sort out the details. From that first awkward moment of meeting in the yard, everything was blurred in her memory. Kevin had told her that she looked "beautiful" . . . that much she remembered clearly. After Kevin said that—Angie puzzled to recall—did she say . . . "You can kiss me, if you want to." But, she wondered, who actually initiated the embrace that led to that kiss? Kevin had reached for her hands . . . or, had she? Did he pull her close to him . . . or, did she lean into his chest?

Sitting at her bedroom bureau, combing her long dark hair that morning, Angie regarded herself in the mirror. Every feature was given a critical appraisal—her eyes, nose, full mouth. Together, everything seemed to fit attractively. But, when taken separately, Angie found faults. Her ovaline eyes seemed too far apart from each other; her nose had a slight tilt (she had her father's nose) and her mouth seemed pouty in its fullness. She had her mother's eyes and mouth she knew, and Mary was beautiful beyond any comparison she would ever make. "Kevin thinks I'm attractive," she said dreamily to herself. Angie drew a deep sigh, "That's all that really matters." Then, she remembered the heat she felt when he held her so tightly to himself. That heat was scary. Kevin, she knew from his closeness, felt a heat of his own.

Angela had two classes at the junior college that morning. She was not prepared for Western Art History. Her assignment, a report on the contrasting color schemes of impressionist Edouard Manet's, *Luncheon on the*

Grass, would be superficial. In English Lit, her class was studying more of Charles Dickens' works. Angela loved to read, but poetry was her greatest passion. Elizabeth Barrett Browning's poems struck her emotions far more than the great novels of Dickens would ever do.

That afternoon, Angie spent a few hours in Jacque Grojean's studio.

"What are you doing, mon cherie!" Jacque called from his work bench. "Just sitting there . . . staring off into some remote place with the look of a lost puppy on your lovely face."

Angie smiled with a hint of weariness. "I've been this way all day, Jacque. Like I *am* in some far away place—trying to find myself."

"That is good, Angela. Put that 'far away' place on your canvas. If that place is already in your mind's eye—then, start with some colors." Jacque found an easy laugh. "I will hope in my heart that your place has some yellow, and blue—happy colors!" Then, the mentor went about his own tasks of the moment, becoming absorbed in a drawing of an autumn landscape that was coming to life in his tranquil imagination of the moment. Color drove the artist's imagination more than details.

Arriving back at the Zoretek house that evening, Kevin smelled the roast beef from the kitchen as soon as he opened the front door. Sadie had remembered his favorite meal.

The dinner table that night, however, was unusually quiet. Tony had a dinner meeting and Becca relayed his apologies. Marco would be late in arriving from a city band practice. All the food was on the table and Sadie busied herself at the sink. Noting the empty chairs, Kevin said something he'd always wanted to say. "Sadie, put the pans aside for a few minutes. Come over here and sit next to me in Mr. Zoretek's chair."

Obviously embarrassed and confused by the invitation, Sadie looked to Becca for some idea of what to do.

"Sadie, the man of the table has spoken. Please do join us." Becca smiled and gestured for her to sit with the family. "Kevin isn't the only one who appreciates your excellent cooking. We all do!"

When Sadie was seated, he gave her hand a squeeze, "Everything looks just delicious," he complimented. Then Kevin bowed his head and led them in saying grace. "Bless us, Oh Lord, in these thy gifts . . ."

Angela was still possessed of her memories of the evening before, and felt uncomfortable in Kevin's presence. Did he believe that she had saved her first kiss for him? Had she been too forward? Could Kevin have been thinking about her all day as she had thought about him? Was he embarrassed by what happened? As all these questions raced through her thoughts, Angela avoided his eyes and remained unusually quiet.

Becca sensed a strain in the silence following grace. She noticed Angie's eyes were downcast and Kevin's expression puzzled. Angie had told her, when the the two of them were together for a minute last night, about their kiss. And, she knew from experience the pain of first love. Her empathy was with both Kevin and Angie in this confusing time. Realizing that someone had to say something pretty soon, Becca assumed the role as catalyst for a light dinnertime conversation.

"I'm sure you'd all enjoy hearing about my day," Becca smiled with a hint of amusement in her voice. The doctor whimsically shared her busy day at the hospital—a cesarean section baby girl early that morning, a report that strep throat was going around town, and, more emphatically, that the high school quarterback had been carried into her office from football practice with a broken ankle. Becca had become an avid sports fan and treated the assorted injuries for most of the athletes. "Hibbing plays Chisholm tomorrow night and without Sammy Karich, I don't think we can beat the Bluestreaks." Finding little reaction to her comments, Becca tossed Kevin the ball. "So, Mr. Moran, what did you do all day?"

Kevin's eyes had been locked on Angela sitting across the table from him while Becca was speaking. "Lots of running around," he stammered weakly. "I had a meeting with Mr. Peterson . . ." Kevin summarized his visit with Peterson, his stop by Senia's office, his talk with Tony down at the warehouse, and lunch with Claude Atkinson. When he shared his conversation with Claude, Kevin became more noticeably animated. "We talked a lot about politics. I've really got a lot to learn about Hibbing, especially people's names and relationships. I told Claude that I wished I'd grown up in Hibbing."

"Anybody we can help you with, Kevin? Claude, of course, knows everybody who lives and breathes in this town," Becca offered.

"Well, there's Elwood Trembart, and a guy named Roberts—Ian Roberts.

He's a mine superintendent, Claude said, and he's married to Trembart's daughter." Kevin's reference inspired cool stares from both Becca and Angie. "Do you know either of them?"

Becca picked up his question. "Oh yes. I guess if you and Claude were talking about local politics, Elwood's name would come up. And Mayor Weirick's, too. Our mayor happens to be the chief of staff at the Rood Hospital. I've known him for years, and let me put it this way, I've never voted for him. He's tried to make my life miserable—and failed at that as completely as he's failed at running our city." Becca was not usually so outspokenly critical of people. "I'm sorry, but I don't like the man."

Angela broke her silence with a wry smile and cool observation of her own. "And we all know Molly, Trembart's sumptuous daughter. Maybe you should ask Tony about these folks when he gets home." As soon as the remark left her mouth, Angie wished she hadn't said what she had. She would never purposely offend Becca's feelings.

Becca, however, was unruffled by the reference. She had a tough side to her nature and jealousy was not something she bothered with. "Molly had eyes for Tony after Mary passed, Kevin. Years ago."

Angie found an opportunity to offer a genuine smile. "But, the best woman won the contest for my father." Turning her gaze from Kevin to Becca, she added, " . . . the river flowed by itself."

The strange analogy brought a furrow to Kevin's forehead, but Becca laughed immediately.

"What's that all about?" Kevin caught their mutual smile.

Her spirit enlivened, Angie said, "I'll tell you about *the river* later. We'll have all day on Saturday, won't we Kevin?"

Finally, Kevin saw the smile on her lips that he had been waiting for all evening. The thought of those soft lips on his made Saturday seem too far away. "The whole day. Just you and me, Angie." The ice had been broken.

Saturday dawned with continued sunshine and unseasonable warmth. The azure skies were cloudless, and the crisp winds of the past few days were pushed toward Canada by a warm front sitting in the south. It was like an August day that Mother Nature slipped into early October.

When Kevin picked up Angela at her West Howard Street apartment, she had a large package string-wrapped in old issues of the *Mesaba Ore* newspaper. Her mood was in perfect harmony with the late morning radiance. Angie was dressed for the outdoors as Kevin had suggested. Wearing slacks—which were becoming popular with younger women—and a loose yellow cotton blouse under her cardigan sweater, she looked marvelous. "Have I ever told you that you're beautiful, Angie?"

"Yes, I think you did, once! But, I'd be pleased to hear it as often as you like." She smiled at Kevin's flattery.

Taking her hand in his, he said, "It's going to be a great day. I can't wait to get out in the country." Then, watching Angie put the package in the back seat, he gave her a puzzled look. "Wha—?"

"Oh, it's something for you, Kevin. A little surprise I've been hanging on to for a few months. You'll have to wait, though, I'm saving it for later—much later! I won't be easy to get rid of today." Angie cuddled in the corner of the seat across from Kevin as he pulled from the street. "Just you and me. I think it's going to be a wonderful time."

"You think? Let me guarantee it. I've got a surprise . . . I can't wait, Angie.

The day before Kevin and Rudy had spent several hours at the Maple Hill property. They moved the library furniture in the morning and went horseback riding in the afternoon. Kevin rode Flare to get a feeling for the gelding's gait and temperament. Although spirited, Flare reined easily and seemed comfortable with the saddle Angie would be using. Kevin had not been on a horse since high school when he and Huddy Tusken rode in the hills of West Duluth a few times.

Before leaving, Kevin gave Leon a twenty dollar bill and the weekend off. "Take the missus out to dinner at the Androy if you'd like, and there's a new Gary Cooper movie playing at the State," Kevin told Mr. Gunther.

Gunther was appreciative of the gesture. "I'll feed the horses in the morning and put them out to pasture for you, sir. If you spend the weekend, you'll find everything in good order, I'm sure."

Pulling to a stop at the end of the long gravel driveway, Kevin turned off the ignition and took Angela's hand. "Before anything else today . . . I want to tell you something that I just couldn't get out of my mouth the other night."

He looked into her face for a long moment, hoping her eyes would give him the courage to finally open his heart to his feelings. Angela's smile lit her expectant eyes. "Angie, I want this to be our house some day." He swallowed hard on his next words, "I love you, Angie."

Fighting her tears, Angie leaned across the seat and kissed him lightly on the lips. "Was it hard to say, Kevin?"

Kevin cupped her delicate chin in his hand and gave her a kiss. "When you've got these feelings inside for so long . . . sometimes it's hard to get them out, Angie." With his admission, he felt a pang of vulnerability unlike anything he'd ever experienced. A voice in the back of his head screamed, "Say something, Angie! Tell me that—"

"Kevin, at this moment . . . my life has found meaning. I love you, I've loved you . . ." Angela's composure melted into soft sobs. "Oh how much I love you. My Kevin . . . my dream." She caught her breath, "Tell me again, Kevin. Tell me one more time—a hundred more times!"

Through the lump in his throat, Kevin said "I love you, Angie. I want to tell you that every day of my life—a hundred times every day of my life!" He kissed her again. This time their tongues touched and their breath came with a sudden gasps.

Hand in hand, Kevin led Angela down the hillside trail winding along a ridge of pines toward the barn. "Kevin, you never told me you had horses out here," Angela said excitedly as they approached the corral.

"I've got three of them, Angie."

Angie puzzled, then smiled up at him. "What, they don't teach counting at law school?"

"I've only got three. The two browns, and Stony—he's the gray stallion over there in his own paddock," he gestured.

Angie's eyes had been riveted on the black Arabian from the moment they approached the barn. "The black one?"

"The black horse isn't mine."

Almost as if on cue, Flare trotted over to the railing near where the two of them stood. "Nope. He belongs to . . . he belongs to the most beautiful woman in the world. Angie, the Arabian's name is Flare. He's your horse."

Wide-eyed, Angie leaped into Kevin's arms, wrapping her long legs about his waist. "My God, Kevin! That's the horse—" She lost all ability to express the surreal experience she was feeling. "It is *my horse*! He's been in my imagination, my dreams . . . he's on my canvas."

Kevin could feel her quiver of excitement.

"I painted him—Flare!" Angie was almost speechless. "How could you know, Kevin?"

"Maybe there's always been something uncanny between us, Angie. Something we're just now getting in touch with."

"I can believe that. But . . . there's even more. You've been inside my creative thoughts without even knowing it. This horse inspired my imagination long before this morning. It's unreal!"

"How would you like to take your horse for a little ride this morning?"

Angie have him a stern look. "How can you ask such a question, Mr. Kevin Moran? Flare and I go back in time—we've both been waiting to ride into the sunrise." She looked up at the yellow ball in the eastern sky as she spoke. "Let's saddle up, Kevin."

"Have you done much riding?"

"There are still a lot of things you don't know about me. I skipped school more than once to go riding with a girlfriend who had horses over in Mahoning Location. That was during my rebellion days, as I call them. Yes, Kevin, I can ride. It's you I'm worried about."

Kevin laughed at Angie's candid humor. "I guess I did know that you were a rebel a few years back. Didn't you hit a tree . . . ?"

"Enough, Kevin." She laughed as she took his hand and led him toward the barn.

When Kevin and Rudy had explored the area the previous afternoon, they came upon a small pond hidden from the sight of the hilltop. The pond was fed by a narrow, winding stream that bordered his property's southwestern corner. "There's a neat little place I want to show you, Angie." Kevin turned Stony toward the break in the tree line. He and Angie had been riding a wide loop to the north for nearly an hour.

When they arrived at the pond, Kevin dismounted and tied his horse to an overhanging pine branch close enough to the water while Angie did the same with Flare. She grabbed the blanket tied to the back of her saddle and spread it across a soft cushion of pine needles below the tree. "What a perfect place, what a perfect day." Angie's words muffled against the background gurgle of the creek's current dancing across a small rock outcropping.

Their race across the meadow under the harsh sun left them both uncomfortably warm. Rubbing a trickle of perspiration from his brow, Kevin unbuttoned his shirt to cool off. Hoping to relax for a while in the inviting shade, he removed his heavy western boots. With her back to Kevin, Angie spread a wool plaid blanket across a pineneedle matted patch of ground. Her slacks outlined her round bottom and Kevin could not avoid staring, imagining. Angie's sumptuous body inspired sudden lustful thoughts.

Kneeling at her side, Kevin helped to smooth the blanket. "What a ride! I don't know about you, but I could take a nap right here." His suggestion brought a quick smile from Angie.

"Let's do just that, Kevin." Angie sat comfortably, removing her own boots. "The smell of pine trees, the sound of gurgling water, the cool shade—and my man beside me. What more could I ever want?"

Kevin lay down resting his head on her lap gazing up at her beautiful face outlined by the sun hanging in its zenith above. The rays highlighted her brown curls in a halo of brilliance. "You are so beautiful, Angie. And, to think you love me!"

Angie bent over and kissed him, her lips parting for his warm tongue. "I do," was all she could say as she felt a rush of incredible warmth even stronger than the experience of several nights ago.

Kevin lifted his head and gently pulled Angie down beside him. No words could express his feelings of the moment, but no words were necessary. He kissed the front of her neck, drinking in her scent as his face moved to the cleavage of her bosom. Angie's light wool sweater was open, exposing part of her soft flesh. Her skin felt warm, damp and inviting on his mouth. He felt her tongue on his neck and the tingle of her hands moving under his loosened shirt. Delicate fingers moved over his bare shoulders, fondling his chest, then moving lower under his belt. Awkwardly, Kevin loosened the buckle, unbuttoned the top of his pants, placing a hand upon Angie's as she stroked his abdomen.

Passion flooded over their bodies as their hands explored each other.

Their kisses probed more deeply, their bodies melted together. The fire of their passion consumed heart, mind, body, soul. Angie's wide open sweater exposed her lush breasts to Kevin's pleasure, her thighs spread to offer herself completely to the man she would possess. The pleasure of their lovemaking went beyond measure of time, intensity, or satisfaction.

After a wondrous hour lost in passionate ecstasy, the two lovers dressed each other, returned to their horses, and rode back up a trail leading toward the house on Maple Hill. Kevin slowed his mount, sidling next to Angie's Flare near a wooden fence. Leaning across to kiss her after their silent ride back to the house, Kevin brushed a kiss on her mouth. "I love you, Angie," he said in a voice still quivering from their experience. "I will never forget our first time . . ."

Angie's smile said more than her words, "Our first in . . . a lifetime of loving each other, Kevin."

After hitching their horses, Angie retrieved her package from the back seat of the car before joining Kevin at the doorway. Inside, Kevin took her hand and escorted her on a tour of the mansion, delaying Angie in every room for a kiss. In the empty library, Kevin told her about his father's tragic death and how that memory needed to be exorcised. Emotion cracked in his voice, "I'll want your ideas, Angie. It's got to be brightened up somehow. I want to work in this room someday without feeling . . ."

Sensing Kevin's deep feelings over the stories he'd heard of Peter Moran's death, Angie put her arm around his waist. Rather than dwell on what had happened in this room long before, Angie offered a brighter perspective. "Color is what inspires me more than anything, Kevin. We'll make this library a happy retreat for you. I promise." Then she remembered the gift she'd left in the side foyer. "Let me leave you alone for a minute."

When she returned, she had the package. "Maybe we have a good start on this room."

Kevin opened her gift slowly, gradually exposing the painting from top to bottom. His eyes were wide as he recognized the bright sky rolling in waves of blues and silvers above the mansion. The hill, with its apron of meadows below, spread before his eyes in green and yellow tones that struck his senses. Angela had captured the very essence of this place in a burst of colors that would flow into a room if not for the frame that kept them in perspective.

Kevin stared in stunned disbelief. "Angie . . . I don't have the words! It's beautiful." His memory flashed back to when Becca gave Tony his painting of the old carpentry shop. "This is the finest gift I've ever been given!"

Angela kissed him lightly. "If you remember, it was a painting that won my father's heart years ago." She swallowed her emotion, "I thought it might work a second time."

"You read my thoughts, Angie. Thank you for this—it's my treasure."

"I'm your treasure, Kevin. I'll never let you forget that."

Angie prepared steaks on the outside stone fireplace as it was getting dark, and they both had their first meal together in the kitchen where they shared their dream of having many children around their table.

"Tell me about *the river,* Angie. It's been on my mind for three days. Or, is it something between only you and Becca?"

Angie smiled. "It's a philosophy of life. Hers and mine . . . and, I'll pray—ours as well."

TOGETHER

A FRESH LAYER OF SNOW had fallen overnight and Maple Hill wore winter's pristine white blanket like a princess in a kingdom of silence. No place on earth possessed the quietude of this wilderness retreat in Minnesota's northern forest. Winter's manifestation of stark and austere severity was exhilarating to Kevin. The weekend before, he and Angie had gone tobogganing on the steep hillside with bright moonbeams lighting the slope while casting long shadows from the tree lines bordering their run. Once they went ice-skating on the pond nearly a mile from the house. Sometimes the evening chill would sting their faces and numb their hands, but afterwards the warmth of the fireplace and hot chocolate awaited to give them a pleasurable revival. Often they would make love on the living room floor before retiring to their bedroom upstairs.

From his library window, Kevin watched the morning birds at the feeders hanging from the trees only several paces from the mansion. Leon had familiarized him with the various species that wintered in this wooded sanctuary. The caretaker always purchased black oil sunflower seeds and mixed them with red millet, favorites of the black-capped chickadees and white-breasted nuthatches. Suet balls also attracted feathered visitors from all parts of the woodland. Of all the birds, however, Kevin was most fascinated with the majestic blue jays that frequented the trees in the early mornings and late afternoons. Four jays crowded at the feeders this morning. Although each season brought a unique panorama to the varied acreage of their property, both he and Angela found the winter months the most awe inspiring.

Kevin rubbed the Saturday morning sleep from his eyes as he glanced at the calendar on his desk. February twenty-first.

Angie would sleep late this morning as the two of them had been talking most of the previous night. Kevin didn't really fall asleep at all. His thoughts were a tumult of happiness, expectancy, fulfillment . . . and anxiety. Angela was certain of her pregnancy. She had missed three periods and was feeling sickly—especially in the mornings. She would see Becca next week.

Kevin was elated over the prospect of having a child—their child. The two of them had talked often of a late-summer wedding, and Kevin had the diamond engagement ring in the drawer of his desk. He was planning to surprise Angela with the ring on her birthday next month—only three weeks from this Saturday morning. All of their plans, however, would have to change. He would call Father Foley on Monday, but already imagined what his priest friend would tell him. Father Pat would certainly be disappointed. Kevin was also certain that the Catholic Church would not allow them a sacramental wedding.

Kevin walked to the kitchen for a cup of fresh coffee perking noisily on the stove, turned down the burner, and wandered into the living room to gaze down the hillside toward the distant pasture. In the field he spied a large doe, with a fawn at her side, nibbling tufts of alfalfa that had not been covered with the snow. Two weeks before he had seen a wide-antlered moose in the same area. Outside the window a covey of grouse stirred beneath a cluster of pines near the southwestern corner of the house.

Angela watched Kevin from the living room entry way. She couldn't sleep through her morning sickness and came quietly down the stairs to be with him. "What was he thinking?" she wondered as she contemplated her man seemingly absorbed in the wintery scene outside. She knew his excitement about the child was honestly felt, but . . . the timing? "We'll get married as fast as we possibly can, Angie," Kevin had promised the night before. "Then we can live here, in our own home, forever . . . Mr. and Mrs. Moran—and little—" They'd talked about a boy, then a girl—then names for the child. They were giddy in their happiness last night. But, this was the next day. Kevin was surely contemplating that reality as he stared absently while sipping his coffee. Was he having second thoughts, doubts, apprehensions? Before telling him her 'news,' Kevin had been talking about his frustration over the law practice routine and how restless he was feeling. "I'm not happy, Angie." He told her about the boring travails of deeds and abstracts and legal paperwork which failed to challenge either his training or imagination.

Angie so loved this complex man. Over the past months he opened his heart and soul to her when they had talked at great length about their lives and dreams. Kevin was trying to understand the ambitions that churned inside him and allowed her to help him put them in better focus. He always asked what she thought about what was going on in his mind. Often they talked about his father, the estate, and what to do with all the money. Every corner of their separate lives was opened and shared through their hours of intimate conversation. If something bothered Kevin, it became a weight on her mind as well. The depth of their relationship, however, had been something kept mostly to themselves—their weekends at the mansion a secret.

Then, Angie thought of complications their new *situation* would bring them. Her dream of a big wedding in the magnificent Blessed Sacrament Church was probably never going to happen. Both her reputation and that of Kevin would be tarnished in the community. How might her unmarried pregnancy affect Kevin's job and the political aspirations he'd talked often to her about? What would her father think? Becca? Had she made a mess of their lives? Angie's eyes moistened as the dark side slipped into perspective. What they had been doing these past months had been sinful, but that reality had never interfered with the intimacy that centered their relationship. There could no longer be any secrets.

Kevin could always feel her presence in a room. While standing before the window, he wondered what Angela was thinking as he imagined her watching him sip at his tepid coffee Was she feeling disappointment? Guilt? Did she think that this pregnancy would change things between them? Was his promise of getting married as soon as possible something Angie felt she had forced upon him? A church wedding? He must reassure her that everything could be worked out—that everything was going to be even more wonderful between them. Angie needed to be more secure about his love for her and told of his feelings frequently, openly, and honestly. Together they could face any obstacle that might come before them. Kevin and

Angie—together, they were invincible, he believed. He would share his own confidence with Angie and find inspiration in the strength of her character. Together.

Kevin thought of Tony and Becca and Senia. His 'family' would be disappointed with behavior they would consider both immoral and irresponsible. Yet, their support was something he had no doubts about. They must be the very first to know. Tomorrow. He'd talk with Angie about how they would go about telling everybody. Then, he would make a difficult phone call to Father Foley in Duluth.

Art and Sarah briefly crossed his thoughts. How estranged his adoptive parents had become. Only a phone call away, the Schmitzes might have lived in Florida. Kevin resolved to visit them in Duluth soon.

But, there were other misgivings, along with a sense of confusion, running in his thoughts this morning. He could not help thinking about the reaction of Pete and Albert at the firm. And, Claude. Perhaps, more than anybody in Kevin's world, Claude had become the person with whom he felt the strongest connection. Claude had inspired his political involvements and ambitions. Claude had hopes and dreams for him. What might Claude think?

Before turning from the window, Kevin spoke in a soft voice. "I know you're there, Angie. What's on your mind this morning?" Then, he turned his smile on her. Angie began to sob lightly, and Kevin moved quickly to hold her and comfort the worries behind the tears. "You're not feeling well, are you? And, it's more than that morning sickness of yours, isn't it?"

"I'm feeling terrible!" Angela's sob became more intense. "What have I done? Kevin, I've ruined everything for us. People are going to talk behind our backs . . . nothing will ever be the same."

Kevin kissed away the tears on Angie's cheeks, kissed her damp forehead, her full mouth. "Don't ever say anything like that again, Angela Zoretek! Nothing is ruined." He held her at arm's length, "And who cares what other people think?"

"You do, Kevin. Be honest about that. Please!" Her voice was strained. "You care a lot about what people think of you. You have to. One day you'll want their support—we've both talked about politics a hundred times, Kevin. Now . . . now, maybe they will have doubts about you—about your character. And, it's my fault!"

Kevin would not get into any arguments about fault, nor would he allow Angie to take any sense of blame for what the two of them had done. "We're in this together, Angie. We're going to do everything right from here on. No apologies to anyone are necessary. We're in love and we're going to get married. That's all that really matters. This child is going to be blessed with the best two parents in the world and the happiest home in God's creation to grow up in. We both know that."

Angie put her head on Kevin's chest. "I know," she said in a weak voice. "I have to believe that, Kevin. That everything will work out—that we can always be happy. I would die if this . . ." She sobbed heavily now. "I would die if we didn't get through this. Together. I need you, Kevin. Don't let me get down, because I can go to the bottom. I'm not as strong as you think."

Kevin kissed her hair as he held her close. He imagined the tiny person inside Angela's stomach, under her cotton robe, as she pressed against him. His child was touching him at this moment and the thought was overwhelming. "I can't live without you, Angie. I feel closer to you right now than I've ever felt before. Honest to God, I do. What you have given me is like a dream come true. We will have a baby, Angie! Just think of the miracle we've made. It's wonderful beyond belief."

Angie insisted that they talk to her father first. That afternoon, together. For the first time, Angie told Kevin about the *voices* of her childhood, and how her father comforted her, helped her cope with the pains of her mother's memory. "He's always been there for me, Kevin. Always—and, I've given him some gray hairs over the years." She tried to laugh. "He's got to know before anybody else."

Tony paced the floor as Angie and Kevin sat holding hands on the living room sofa. For several minutes he said nothing. His demeanor seemed to betray his feelings of remorse about what Angie had told him. He knew his daughter and Kevin were planning to be married in the fall and had no doubts about the love between them. But, this was not right. Was it even possible for them to be married in a Catholic Church?

Becca, sitting across from the couple, listened without trace of emotion. She could feel her husband's pain as she watched him walk from one end of the room to the other, wringing his hands and avoiding their eyes. She noticed Kevin's squeeze of Angie's hand in his lap. Someone had to break the silent tension engulfing the room. What could she say? Was it her place to say anything? For the first time in her memory, Becca felt like an outsider in her family's crisis.

Kevin cleared his throat. "Tony . . ." Somehow the name of the man he so respected and loved felt awkward on his tongue. He wanted to say 'Dad' in the worst way. But in this situation, Tony was Angie's dad and not his own. Kevin tried to pick up the thread of what he'd started to say. "Tony, I'm sorry about this. It may seem like we've made a big mistake. I'm sure there will be people who will chastise us for this . . . but, please don't you be one of them. We need you more than anybody." Kevin's voice was clear and he spoke in resolute tone. "Tony, I love your daughter. More than any words can say. And, our child will be your child—nothing will ever change that. I pledge to you that—"

Turning from his stare out the front window, Tony met Kevin's eyes levelly. They had come to him with their burden hoping for support, not judgment. They were his children—Kevin as much as Angela—and they needed him now. They had confided in him before anybody else and if he failed to show them an unconditional love—who else would? "Kevin . . . Angie—come here, both of you." He stepped toward the sofa with his arms outstretched. "We're . . . all of us, we're together." Tony hugged them both warmly, fighting his tears. "Becca, this baby belongs to all of us—you and me and the kids. Come here . . . we need you."

Becca joined them in the center of the room. She was of this family after all! Kissing Tony on the mouth, she hugged her husband, "Thank you for needing me," was all she could say. The four of them had crossed a bridge together.

They all went to Sunday Mass together, but Kevin and Angie did not go up to the communion rail with the family. Angie could almost feel the cool stare of many eyes. Were members of the congregation wondering why they sat? Catholics, she believed, were too judgmental. When Angie began to show her condition, it would only get worse.

That afternoon, they visited Senia and Steven. Steven was especially delighted to see them both and talked self-consciously through his slur of familiar words. In recent months, Tony's uncle had been spending a few hours each day on matters relating to his faltering miners' investment fund business. These days, the word *depression* was a widely spoken reality touching every life in Hibbing in one way or another. Steven was involved in the administration of the local Chamber's HCCF (Hibbing Community Contingency Fund) activities, but explained how far short of their initial goals their effort had reached. "Our hearts are in the right place, but we can't help everybody who needs help. If it weren't for the gardens that almost everybody has, it would be a hungry winter."

Senia had baked an apple pie that morning, and the aroma wafted from the kitchen into the living room where the two men were talking about the difficult times. The two women made small talk of their own over the dining table, while Angie topped the slices of pie with scoops of ice cream and helped Senia serve the dessert and coffee.

When they were all seated at the dining room table, Senia smiled toward Kevin. "I'd guess things are pretty slow at the law office—like at the bank and everywhere else—aren't they Kevin?"

Kevin nodded as he finished the bite of pie in his mouth. "Very slow, I'm afraid." He frowned, "And, boring. Sometimes I wonder what I'm doing there. It's like we're shuffling papers between us—from Pete's desk, to Albert's, then to mine. Next week I've got a property dispute to file with the court. That's all." He wanted to go more deeply into his growing frustration but decided not to.

He felt Angie's hand clasp his under the table and gave her a smile. It was her signal to get into the purpose of their visit. Both had agreed beforehand that Kevin would share their news. He gave Angie a knowing smile. "Auntie Senia . . . and Steven—" He moved his eyes from one to the other. "Angie and I are getting married."

Senia smiled, she had expected the two of them would be making their announcement one of these days and she couldn't be happier. "Have you picked a date yet?"

"We're thinking . . . maybe, next weekend, Senia."

He noticed Senia's eyes widen.

"And, we're thinking of being married in Duluth." Kevin would get all the information out before any other questions came. "It will be a small affair at the courthouse. I'm hoping that Father Foley will be with us and give us his blessing. I'll call him tomorrow." He leaned forward on his elbows, "We're going to have a baby. Probably sometime in August, Angie's going to see Becca tomorrow for an exam."

Senia's smile became twisted. She dabbed at her mouth with the linen napkin and looked from Kevin to Angie, then to Steven. She was at a loss for words. Her first reaction, however, was apparent by her silence.

Steven recognized Senia's disappointment immediately. "We will be there," Steven promised, "wearing our happiest smiles, I might add. That's wonderful news."

Steven saved the moment.

"Of course . . . I mean, yes we're happy for you, Kevin—and Angie. It's just that, well . . . I guess you caught me off-guard. I thought—" What struck her more sharply than anything else was Kevin's reputation. The Moran name she held in such esteem would be tarnished.

"It's going to work out fine, Auntie Senia." Kevin found her hand on the table. "I know it comes as a shock to you, but we're both excited. We've talked with Tony and Becca already and they're excited, too. So we'll be moving out to my dad's place in a couple of weeks." Kevin caught a glimpse of spark in Senia's blue eyes. "You know that room that used to be your office when you lived at the mansion? Well, that's going to be the baby's room. Angie's going to make it just perfect."

"Maybe you and Becca can help me decorate, Senia." Angie smiled.

"I'd really like that."

The thought of Peter's grandchild coming into this world and being in her special room of the mansion brought goose bumps to Senia's skin. "Oh yes. I'd love to help, Angela. That would be great fun."

After talking for another hour about all the details of having a 'hurry up' wedding, making the move out to the Maple Hill house, and whether the child would be a boy or a girl, Kevin asked Steven if he'd excuse himself and Senia for a few minutes. "And leave me with my great niece . . . I was going to ask the two of you to give us some time together. By all means, Angie let's go off by ourselves in the living room."

"Senia." Kevin usually dropped the 'auntie' when they talked business. "Senia, I'm going to want to talk with you more about the Androy Hotel. I mentioned earlier that my job is not what I'd hoped. I think Vic Power told me that this might happen years ago when I clerked for him."

Senia nodded at the memories.

"With the economy being what it is these days, maybe it's a good time to make an offer. What do you think?"

Senia had mentioned the idea months before and hoped Kevin would consider the purchase. In her mind, Kevin's ownership of the luxury hotel might be the ultimate testimony to his father's memory. "I think it's a wonderful idea."

Kevin could almost see wheels turning behind Senia's intelligent eyes. "Would you check things out for me, behind the scenes, of course? If *we* did make an offer (when discussing estate affairs, Kevin often used 'we' rather than 'I')—I'd want my involvement to stay out of the forefront. Do you know what I mean?"

Senia wrinkled her nose. "No, I don't Kevin. You want to front your ownership?"

"I think that's the word—front, isn't it? I don't think it's a good time for Kevin Moran to be buying a million dollar hotel. I've managed to keep the estate pretty quiet over all these years and want to keep it that way."

Senia understood. "We'll talk more about this. Do you have any ideas about whom you might get to front a transaction?"

"I'll give it more thought, Senia." With that, Kevin had opened a door and would let her do what she could. Senia was a genius when it came to financial matters.

Kevin left the law office earlier than usual on Monday afternoon. He'd called Claude at the *Ore* and asked him to meet at the Crystal Lounge in the Androy for a beer. "It's on me this time," he promised. A city council meeting was coming up the next night. "I think we're going to be in public disagreement, Claude. Maybe we need draw some lines before the battle," he teased.

The city council was going to debate a proposal to allow a major department store to purchase one of the city's largest downtown buildings which was owned by Hibbing's new economic development board. The sale had stirred considerable controversy. Marshall Wells owned one of Duluth's largest department stores and was seeking the council's authority to locate a branch on Hibbing's Howard Street. Local merchants were banded in rigid opposition to the proposal. Their major argument was that the new competition would seriously undermine what was already a very shaky ground for the Hibbing business community. The volume buyer would offer lower prices on appliances, hardware, and clothing. "They will cause us to go bankrupt!" . . . "We can't match their prices." . . . "We'll have to lay off employees." Their litany of objections made sense to many on the council. Aldermen Rufus Isaackson and Karl Wright were the most adamant opponents, and Claude was inclined to agree with both men. Small businesses were his newspaper's major advertisers, and they were pressuring him to publicly denounce the sale.

Seated at a table away from the bar, Kevin and Claude talked over their mugs of Grain Belt beer. "Claude, it would send a negative message to any out of town businessmen who might want to locate here in the future. We've got to be progressive thinking about this. Denying Marshall Well's purchase is shortsighted, and we'll all regret it once this depression is behind us. In the last analysis, consumers benefit from lower prices."

Claude sighed with a hint of weariness. Kevin was right, but his own sympathies were torn. "Your friend, Armando Depelo, has a hardware store that is just barely eking through these bad times. He'd go under, that's for certain. Neal Dorsher's electronics business would be history. There's no way he can sell radios and appliances at the prices Marshall Wells can. And, Chet Grant's furniture store? These folks, and twenty just like them, need our help. They have been here through the years and contributed to making our community what it is. We'd be opening the doors to outsiders."

"Is it all about loyalty, Claude? Be honest with me, are you getting some pressure?"

"I've lived with pressure from various interest groups all my adult life, Kevin."

"And, you've always listened to your conscience. It's always been a matter of what's right—not what's popular!"

"I know." Claude took a long swallow. "But, loyalty is right. Would you abandon someone who needed your help so easily?"

Kevin thought for a moment. "I won't ever argue loyalty with you, Claude." He couldn't help but think of Angie and himself. Was there a parallel in this issue? "I don't know where loyalty ends and greed takes over. I wonder if some of the merchants don't hide their selfish ambitions behind the rhetoric of 'unfair competition'. I just don't know."

"For the sake of argument, Kevin, let's just focus on Armando's situation. There's not an ounce of selfishness or ambition or greed in his body. You know that better than most. I'd rather save his neck than get a new washing machine for five dollars less than Armando can sell me one."

"So would I, Claude. So would most people in Hibbing. If it's a matter of loyalty, maybe small businesses like Armando's won't be that badly impacted."

"That, my son, is an awfully big "maybe," these days anyhow. Five bucks is a lot of groceries for most folks."

Kevin nodded his agreement. Arguing with Claude always challenged him to bring his thinking to a personal level. Claude would often admit to being a people person and share his insight: "Philosophy is for scholars, not for pragmatic newsmen. People's day-to-day lives are far more important than great ideas and theories to me."

"What are you going to say at the council meeting, Claude?"

Claude smiled wearily. "I think I'll let my son Marc do most of the talking. This is one of the few things we seem to be in agreement about these days." Claude had gradually been giving the reins of his beloved paper to his son. "By the end of the year, Marc will be running most things at the office and the old man will be watching from the sidelines."

Kevin and Marc Atkinson had never been close. Claude's thirty-nine year old son seemed aloof and rarely offered more than a perfunctory "Hello" when Kevin visited Claude's office.

In most respects, the two friends agreed to disagree on the issue that began their conversation. The main reason for asking Claude to join him this afternoon, however, was to share the news about him and Angie. Somehow, this would be harder than it had been with either Tony or Senia. "I've got something—*personal,* Claude." Kevin swallowed on the word, personal. " . . . that I want to tell you about." He made his best effort to explain his present circumstance in his most positive voice. As he explained the upcoming marriage, Kevin noticed a sadness in Claude's eyes. " . . . And, we're both very happy about everything."

Claude did not comment on Kevin's disclosure for a long minute. He would be candid with the young man he had such high hopes for. "I'm happy that the two of you are happy, Kevin." He offered some weak humor to lighten the stress he sensed Kevin was feeling. "What a child that will be. Moran and Zoretek blood—you two might have a governor there: be it a boy or a girl." But, Claude's smile was strained.

"Maybe you're right about that."

Claude looked at Kevin with the intelligent eyes of experience. "It will change your life in ways you can't imagine, Kevin. Most of them positive, for certain . . . but, there is a downside as well. We live in a small town, a town with big ears and loose tongues. Folks here, bless their hearts, live on gossip. If the incident appears to be something immoral or indecent to their way of thinking and judging . . . it becomes all the more damning."

"We both know that. Angie is far more sensitive than I am about what people think."

Claude would give Kevin the best advice he could, and hoped he would take the suggestion in the good spirit it was rendered. "If you're serious about seeking political office in this town, and I'm certain from our many conversations that you are—there's only one thing to do, Kevin. Leave Hibbing for a while. Get married, of course, but . . . give yourselves a year or so away from the local small talk."

Kevin leaned back in his chair. What Claude was suggesting had never entered his mind. Go where? Do what? Certainly money was not an issue for them, but—? "Can you give me any specific ideas, Claude? Go where? We've both been looking forward to living out on Maple Hill—all of our friends are here in Hibbing."

As Claude pondered the potentials behind Kevin's logical question of where to relocate, an idea began to take shape in his thoughts. The mayor of St. Paul, a popular Democrat by the name of Brandon Brady, was the nephew of an old Hibbing pioneer—Judge Thomas Brady. Claude knew Mayor Brady well enough to ask the mayor for a favor. "The mayor of St.

Paul is a dear old friend of mine and was one of Vic Power's closest allies back in the early twenties. He runs that city like a maestro, Kevin."

"Are you suggesting—?"

"Yes, Kevin, I am. It would be a marvelous experience for you, and St. Paul is far enough away . . ." Claude imagined the insights Kevin might gain from a year in the state capitol. Governor Floyd Olson was there, the state legislature, Ramsey County—St. Paul was unquestionably the political hub of everything in the state. "I think I could get you an administrative position with Mayor Brady. I'm sure of it."

Kevin's mind was racing over the possibilities as well. He might be able to take some graduate classes at the University. Maybe in business. Then, the doubts cropped into his thinking. Was moving away selfish? Was he thinking only of his own ambitions? What would Angie think about leaving a place where she had lived all her life?

"I'll talk with Angie tonight, Claude. I'd appreciate if you could get in touch with Mayor Brady and see if he'd give me an interview." Kevin breathed a sigh of relief. "This might be the answer to everything. I'll let Pete and Al know I'm thinking about a leave of absence to do some graduate work in the Cities. The underlying reasons are probably best left unsaid, don't you think, Claude?"

~

Kevin dabbed at the perspiration on his forehead as he waited through the pause in his conversation with Father Foley. He imagined his priest friend saying a prayer of forgiveness under his breath. After the initial pleasantries, Kevin had explained everything as best he could. "The Church has what are called the 'Six Instructions,' Kevin. In that you are both adults, a Catholic wedding can be arranged once the instructions are completed." Foley went on to explain that he would ask the Bishop about 'cutting some corners' and get back to him that evening.

"Let's pray that Father Foley can help us out, Kevin. It's important to everybody, especially dad, that our marriage is blessed."

Kevin agreed. "If we can get the instructions done in one day with Father Pat, then he can marry us down in Duluth."

Then Kevin explained his conversation with Claude.

Although reluctant at first, Angela agreed to Kevin's suggestion that they move 'temporarily' to St. Paul. Her gut feeling was that they were running away and hiding from a reality that should be dealt with more respectably. "I feel like a coward, Kevin," Angie told him. But, Kevin's enthusiasm won her over. "Look at moving like an adventure in the big city, Angie. You'll love it there—shopping, theater, museums—the capitol's got everything. Besides, we can come home any time we want after the baby is born. Our house will be waiting for us."

Angie's greatest fear was that Kevin would become so involved in the political scene that she would take a back seat to his career. Kevin's ambitions, which were becoming more evident to her, were something she held misgivings about. Would he ever be content with the simple life of going to work and returning to his family every night? Political life was demanding of time and energy and required a great deal of commitment.

Kevin Moran and Angela Zoretek were married by Father Patrick Foley in the chapel of Sacred Heart Church in Duluth on Saturday, March 14, 1931— two days after Angela's twentieth birthday. Tony and Becca were joined by Art and Sarah Schmitz for the small ceremony.

The following Monday, Mr. and Mrs. Kevin Moran signed a rental lease on a spacious and well-furnished, three bedroom upstairs apartment on stately East Summit Avenue in St. Paul. The St. Paul Basilica was within walking distance, and the Minnesota Capitol Building towered above the hill to the east of the majestic church. The shops of Grand Avenue were only blocks away, and downtown St. Paul a short trolley ride.

Claude Atkinson had two wedding surprises for Kevin before the couple moved quietly to St. Paul. Kevin's position with Mayor Brady would be that of assistant liaison with the Governor's Office on city affairs, a job that would allow Kevin to spend much of his time lobbying Governor Floyd Olson on behalf of St. Paul. "It's a plum, Kevin. The best of both worlds— city government and state politics," Claude said.

The second surprise was even more exciting to Kevin. Claude would run a weekly article in the *Mesaba Ore* under Kevin's own byline. The column *(Moran's Milieu)* would inform Hibbing's readers of state issues and allow Kevin to do his own analysis. "That will keep you connected with folks back home. Plus, the locals will believe that your move was career driven."

Back in Hibbing, Senia was working on the Androy Hotel purchase. Kevin had made an arrangement with his friend, Armando Depelo, to be the financial backer and the 'front man' in the transaction. Armando would keep the manager and staff, and keep both Senia and Kevin apprised of operations. In early April, the sale was finalized. Kevin Moran now owned the most prestigious hotel in Northern Minnesota.

Angie's reservations about living in St. Paul proved accurate. Kevin was working long hours and coming home late—exhausted. On Tuesday and Thursday nights, Kevin was taking Business Economics at the University, and on weekends he caught up on his studying. "It's only for a year," he reminded Angie. "Then we can live a normal life." Angie would bite her tongue. Kevin's promise, however well-intended, was painful.

Kevin became fascinated with the populist governor who had forged the successful Farmer-Labor coalition, and he found himself spending more of his time at the capitol than at the mayor's office. The political philosophy of Floyd B. Olson was almost revolutionary and excited Kevin's imagination. Olson's advocacy of unemployment insurance, minimum wages, old age pensions, and the right to collective bargaining were attracting the national attention of people like Franklin Roosevelt.

As Kevin learned more about the state issues, his weekly columns for the *Mesaba Ore* became more provocative. He often published quotations from the Governor that had not found their way into the big city papers. Kevin Moran was becoming an insider with legitimate access to the Governor's office. From Olson's strategies, Kevin came to believe that disparate elements of the Iron Range Democrats could also be brought together.

In one of his articles, Kevin sought to explain the charges of those critics who suggested that Olson was . . . "too liberal for the good of Minnesota's population." Kevin used a comment that Olson would later use at a Farmer Labor convention. "I am not a liberal at all. I am what I want to be—I am a radical. I am a radical in the sense that I want a definite change in the system. I am not satisfied with tinkering with things or patching them up." Kevin added a dictionary meaning of the word radical. "It means in substance one who endeavors to get to the root of evils and their causes." Kevin went on to compare Olson to Thomas Jefferson.

In the late morning of August 18, Angela's water broke while she was mopping up some flour that had spilled onto the floor as she baked Kevin's favorite sugar cookies. She panicked. Kevin was at City Hall and had told her before leaving for work that today was going to be a busy one. "I'll call later in the afternoon to check on you, but I expect to get home late again."

Kevin was going over the final details of the city's financial agenda for Governor Olson's budget. He would be going to the Governor's office for a meeting that might last for hours. Mayor Brady's secretary interrupted their meeting with a message that Kevin must call home immediately. Minutes later, Kevin rushed into the Mayor's office. He was breathless, "I've got to get home to my wife, sir. She's going to have our baby. Her water's—"

Brady cast him a stern look. "I need you right now, Kevin. I'll send a doctor and ambulance to your place immediately. She'll be in good hands. You can join her at the hospital afterwards." The Mayor was not making a suggestion, Kevin realized. Brady was giving him an order. "Women have babies a thousand times a day, Kevin. Our budget requests come once a year."

Kevin was frustrated, torn. Realizing his political career hung in the balance of his decision, he told the Mayor. "I'm truly sorry, sir. I can't let my wife go through this alone. I'm going home, Mr. Brady. I'll get in touch with you as soon as I possibly can."

"That won't be necessary, Mr. Moran. If you aren't at our meeting with the Governor this afternoon, you can consider your position on my staff terminated."

Patrick Anthony Claude Moran was born at eight forty-two that Tuesday night. Angie had difficulty with hemorrhaging after the birth but by the next morning was in highest spirits and regaining some of her strength. "Thanks for being with me through all this, Kevin. I really needed to know that I was more important to you than anything else." Kevin smiled at his exhausted wife, "Thank you for our son. The two of you are what's most important in my life. It's always going to be that way. You have my word, Angie." Kevin did not tell Angie about the price he had paid to be with her that day. He never would. Within the next few days, he planned on sending a letter of apology to Mayor Brady, thanking him for the wonderful opportunity and tendering his resignation. The following week, Kevin got a three-month appointment to Governor Olson's staff. The Governor's main speech-writer was taking a short sabbatical at Harvard's School of Political Science, and Kevin would serve in that capacity until after Thanksgiving.

When Angie got home from the hospital on Saturday afternoon, she found a reception awaiting her. Kevin had sent word of their son's arrival immediately to Hibbing and Duluth. Everybody took the train down to St. Paul to see the new parents and their baby. The Hibbing contingency included Tony and Becca, Senia and Steven, Rudy and Colleen, Armando and Estelle Depelo, Claude Atkinson, and Marco. From Duluth, Art and Sarah traveled with Father Pat Foley and Tony's old friend Hud Tusken.

Of all the visitors, Becca was probably the most elated. Angie had given Becca her first child. She moved her chair to the bassinet so that she could watch every breath from the small pink mouth. "He's adorable!" Becca commented at least twenty times in the first hour. Looking at young Pat's tiny hands, Tony bragged, "We'll have a pitcher in this little fella. I can already tell." For Senia, to behold the son of Peter's son marked another milestone in her life. Rudy and Colleen had mixed feelings as they were still trying to have a child of their own.

To most everyone's surprise and delight, Art and Sarah displayed more emotion than ever before at a social gathering of Kevin's Hibbing 'family.' Cradling the boy in his arms, Art announced with obvious pride, "Don't be offended, Angie, but this boy of yours is the spitting image of his father when Kevin was a baby." Sarah readily agreed.

Father Foley commented on what he considered to be a perfect name for the boy. "St. Patrick is the patron saint of the Irish. I'll pray that he becomes a priest." Everybody laughed.

Claude agreed with the pastor, but had his own observation. "I knew a man with three names once—Adam, Almore, and John. Wouldn't you know, everybody ended up calling him, 'Johnny'." Claude's reference brought more laughter to the room. "Claude Moran sounds pretty good to me," he added.

Dismissing the physical weakness she felt, Angie passed the baby around the room and visited with everyone as her son's features were discussed. Tony, of course, was adamant that young Patrick had Angie's eyes and mouth. "I'll never forget when you were born, sweetheart. Your mom and I could see ourselves in every little detail. And, we predicted you'd have Mary's eyes and mouth with my nose in the middle of your lovely face."

Becca laughed at her husband's observation. Mary, she knew, was a beautiful woman. "Angie, I think your father's got a good point. I see your eyes and mouth, too. And, the nose, that's going to be Kevin's."

Standing nearby, Kevin turned to a mirror on a closet door, and ran his finger down the profile of his nose. "If you two are right about that, the boy will be blessed."

Angie gave him a punch in the ribs. "What's wrong with my nose, Kevin?"

Kevin had arranged for a smorgasbord of foods, along with a chocolate sheet cake and assorted beverages catered to the Summit Avenue apartment. Everybody found a place to sit and enjoy the food and each other's company. Marco had mastered the guitar—along with several other instruments—and played some popular music which had everybody singing along.

Weary from the long trip, Steven spent much of the afternoon taking a nap in the guest bedroom. Hud Tusken left the party early to run over to the U. and visit with some of his old friends from basketball days.

The Depelos had relatives in St. Paul, so they also left early.

Father Foley was staying at the rectory of the Cathedral of St. Paul and excused himself after eating. All of the others had rooms at the St. Paul Hotel. By eight o'clock, everyone was ready to leave for the day. It was agreed that after Sunday Mass, Foley would perform Patrick's Baptism, and following the sacramental ceremony, all of them would get together for a family picnic at Como Park.

In addition to Kevin's popular column in Claude's newspaper, he made several visits to Hibbing throughout the fall months. Governor Olson was very popular on the Mesabi Iron Range, and everybody wanted an inside scoop on his ambitious programs. While on the Range, Kevin spoke to several local organizations in Virginia, Ely, and Grand Rapids as well as in Hibbing. He visited with members of the Kiwanis and Rotary Clubs, the League of Women Voters, and student assemblies at the various high schools. The more public appearances he made, the better he became at his oratory. By the advent of national election year 1932, the name of Kevin Moran was as well-known across the Iron Range as it was in his home town.

While in Hibbing, Kevin met with Senia and Harvey Goldberg at the bank as well as with Armando Depelo. Armando was doing a wonderful job running the Androy Hotel. When he visited, Kevin stayed at the mansion, keeping in close touch with caretaker Leon Gunther.

∼

Keeping a close watch on the activities of good-looking and well-spoken Kevin Moran was Elwood Trembart. The Hibbing attorney was not among the many admirers of Governor Floyd B. Olson. And, his animosity toward Kevin's father had been kept alive by the very sight of the increasingly popular son. What was Moran up to, Trembart wondered as he read the weekly column in Atkinson's newspaper? "I'm getting damn tired of all his Olson bullshit he writes about," Elwood said to his son-in-law sitting across from him in the lawyer's office.

Ian Roberts nodded without reply.

"Did I ever tell you about how Pete Moran stole some property from me years ago, Ian? He was a cutthroat, son-of-a-bitch, that guy." Elwood went on to explain how the elder Moran had purchased 120 acres of prime land south of what was now called North Hibbing. "Moran knew I was a day away from closing the deal for myself, and then he stabbed me in the back and got clean title. That damnable Vic Power helped him pull it off."

"Power was no good, Dad. I remember how he stuck it to the mining companies whenever he could," Roberts said to his father-in-law.

"We're going to have our revenge, Ian. Just wait."

∼

Kevin and Angela quietly celebrated the new year in their St. Paul apartment. Four and a half month old Patrick welcomed in 1932 at Angie's breast. Kevin had finished his assignment with Governor Olson, would be taking the final exam in his college coursework next week, and was anxious to go home.

"This is going to be our greatest year, Angie," Kevin kissed her as she nursed. "I can't wait to get back to our house."

Angie had tired of apartment living months before. "Kevin, this has been the longest year of my life. But, it's been wonderful, too. In a strange way." She had made few friends and spent long days by herself before Patrick came into their life. Since August, however, Kevin had been with her much of the time. His job with the Governor was not nearly so time consuming as his work for the mayor. But his frequent trips to Hibbing meant time by herself. Angie chose not to travel with the baby. She had not been back home since last March.

"I know it's been hard on you, sweetheart. Everything's revolved around me these past months, and I'm sorry about that. Truly. Things are going to be different for both of us from now on."

"You still don't know what you want to do when we get back, Kevin. Things are awfully slow in Hibbing these days. You're not excited about going back to the law office routines, and the . . ." Angie had not been enthusiastic about the hotel transaction. She had hoped that Kevin would go into business with her father. Tony could use an attorney with his real estate affairs and had offered Kevin a job—any time he wanted.

". . . The hotel. Is that what you were going to say?" Kevin gave her a smile. "I'm not going to get involved in the hotel operations, Angie. That's kind of like *your river* . . . it's going to flow by itself." Kevin leaned over and kissed his son on the forehead, then ran his fingers through Angie's thick dark, hair. "I know you aren't too crazy about the Androy, but it's only an investment. One day it's going to pay off for us—when the economy gets better. You'll see."

"I don't worry about that, Kevin. We're fortunate that we don't have to worry about money like most everyone else. I thank God for that every day."

"Are you worried that I'll just get fat and lazy?" Kevin's grin always lifted Angie's spirits.

"Don't you dare, Kevin Moran. I'll have Mr. Gunther put you to work splitting wood and cleaning the barn."

Kevin knew what he was going to do when they got back to Hibbing. He'd given the matter lots of thought. He had a political agenda and kept Claude apprised of what he wanted to do in that regard. Both he and Claude were anxious to get that started. "Angie, what do you think about being a mayor's wife, or, maybe, the wife of a state representative?"

Angie turned, pulling her nipple away from the baby's mouth causing a quick cry. "What? I know we've talked about politics, but I thought you wanted to work for campaigns, not be a candidate yourself."

"I want to do both, honey. The Democrats on the Range are so divided—"

"I think you've been talking with Claude too much. Is he putting these ideas in your head?"

"No, not at all. He's been more like a sounding board." Kevin scratched his head. "Well, maybe more than that, but it's what I want to do more than anything else."

What Kevin was saying was no surprise to Angie. They'd talked about it many times before. Politics was behind their moving to St. Paul in the first place. "Do you mean you'll working full time on running your own campaign? Will it take all your time?" Angie did not want to be a widow to politics.

"We'd both be together in whatever I do, Angie. It will take a lot of involvement on your part as well as mine. I can't do anything without you beside me."

Angie could not warm to the idea. It might be something the two of them could do together, but—? She saw the trace of a frown on her husband's face. "You know I'll be behind you—whatever you do. But won't you have a job of some kind?"

Kevin had kept a surprise up his sleeve. "Sure I plan to have a job. I talked with your dad about that very thing. I'm going to buy my way into his construction business." He laughed at his recall of that conversation only days before with his 'father-in-law' (and at how awkward that relationship sounded to him). Tony told Kevin that he could use a partner. "I'll want you to invest in company ownership, though." Tony suggested the investment would have to be five dollars.

Angela's New Year's Eve was her greatest ever. They were going home with their new son, Kevin would be working with her father, and their relationship would flourish with more time spent together.

Before leaving St. Paul, Kevin had lunch with Mayor Brady to mend fences with his former employer. The two of them left McGuire's after a long conversation about politics and a warm handshake. "You're a bright young man, Kevin. If I can be of any help to you along the way, just let me know. One thing I've learned in my many years of public service is that you've got to have thick skin. And, if you can't forget about yesterday's setbacks, your tomorrows can be pretty miserable."

A visit at the Governor's residence established a bond that would last over the next four years. The two men shared a concern about 'dog eat dog' capitalism that could wreak havoc on labor and small businessmen and women. Both advocated a program of unemployment insurance, progressive taxes, and environmental conservation. "The mining companies up there are going to be held accountable for reclaiming the lands they've ravaged, Kevin. However unpopular that might be with the power structure, that's a fight we're going to have to wage," Olson told him. "And beware of the chain-store people who will surely undermine the base of entrepreneurship. Small businesses need to be protected from gigantism." Kevin told Governor Olson that he would work on Olson's reelection campaign across the Range. "I'll make sure you get eighty percent of the vote, sir."

After their meeting, Kevin sent a quick letter to Claude. "You were right about small businesses, my friend." Claude would surely remember their conversation on that issue at the Androy nearly a year ago.

(Governor Olson would get nearly eighty-five percent in both sweeping victories—1932 and 1934. Floyd Bjerstjerne Olson, like Kevin's old political mentor, Victor Power, however, would die a young man. Olson was only forty-four when he died of cancer at the Mayo Clinic in Rochester on August 22, 1936.)

A Blessing or a Curse

ON TUESDAY, MARCH 1, 1932, the Moran family moved into the Maple Hill mansion. The late winter morning winds swept across the hilltop, causing the thick snow cover to drift into hard ridges across the entry driveway.

"Mother Nature's giving us quite a homecoming, Angie," Kevin said as he pulled his Ford up next to the side entry door. Mr. Gunther had already shoveled a path to the house. "You get Patrick inside, sweetheart, while I unload the car."

Angie pulled the blanket over the baby's face and raced across the wind chilled fifty feet to where Leon waited with the door held open. Once inside, Angie drew a deep sigh, "Mr. Gunther, it's so wonderful to be home." Scanning the kitchen and peering down the hallway to the living room, Angie could see that Leon had everything in readiness for their arrival. She could smell the rich aroma of birch logs from the fireplace.

"Welcome back to Hibbing, Mrs. Moran," Leon said politely and then opened the blanket covering the baby's face. He smiled widely at the sleeping boy. "Can I hold young Patrick, ma'am? I've been waiting to meet him for months."

Kevin and Angie spent the rest of the day by themselves, settling in and enjoying the feeling of their home. They planned to have everybody over for dinner on Sunday. So just a quick phone call to let their family know they were safely back in Hibbing was sufficient for the present. Today would belong to the three of them. Alone.

Talking late into the night, Angie explained the projects she was planning for the baby's room. "Becca and Senia are coming over on Saturday morning to help me with some wallpapering, and I found the perfect material for curtains at a shop on Grand Avenue. It's packed in one of the boxes we shipped up here last week, and I'll find it in the morning." Angie's excitement over being in her own house brought a spark to her eyes. "When I wake up tomorrow, it will be the beginning of a new life."

Kevin nodded, the fatigue of the long drive settling over him like a heavy drape. Angie had already made plans for the weekend. Seeking to revive his waning attention to her words, he commented in slow speech, "That leaves Tony and Steven for some plans of my own on Saturday. Maybe the guys would like to do some ice-fishing."

Kevin lifted his head, explaining what he wanted to accomplish before the weekend with all the enthusiasm he could muster. "I'll be in town for a couple of hours tomorrow morning, but I'll keep the rest of the day free to help you out around here." Being early risers, Kevin and Claude were planning an early breakfast at Fay's; then Kevin would visit with Mr. Peterson at the law office to discuss working on a part-time basis with the firm.

"I hope Patrick lets me sleep late. You just take your time," Angie smiled. "I'm going to be looking for a nanny in the newspaper ads. I'd like to be free enough to be involved in some of the charity and church work in Hibbing. And, maybe, finding a class at the college worth taking or spending some time with Jacque at his studio." Angela was anxious to pick up the thread of her former life and accomplish some of her own goals. "It's so good to be back in my familiar world, Kevin. To have you, and Patrick, and our home. I'm the happiest woman in the world tonight." Angie gave him her peculiar, suggestive smile. "I'm going to show how truly happy I am . . . let's go to bed before you fall asleep on me."

Stopping by the *Ore* building to pick up his friend at seven on this blustery Wednesday morning, Kevin was surprised to find Marc Atkinson standing in Claude's office doorway. "Well, if it isn't 'Mr. Minnesota Politics' in the flesh," Marc said sarcastically. The new editor offered a limp handshake, "Dad's in the office over there," he gestured to a corner across the wide room. "I thought you knew."

Kevin smiled coolly, "Congratulations, Marc. I knew your dad was stepping aside, but I didn't know he'd given up his office."

"The office goes with the job, Mr. Moran."

"I know you'll do well, Marc. You've had the best newspaper mentor in the business."

"I won't argue that. But, I will be my own man, and I'm planning some changes." Marc's smile was twisted. "Now that you're back in Hibbing after all these months; nearly a year—hasn't it been?"

"Almost exactly. It's great to be back." Despite Marc's obvious derision, Kevin would try to be pleasant. For a long time he sensed that Marc was resentful of Claude's affection for him. Marc's jealousy, however, would not become Kevin's problem.

"You've been married and had a kid since you left." Marc's eyebrows raised at the statement which he deliberately phrased as a question. "You move pretty fast."

Before Kevin could respond to the innuendo, a shout pierced the air.

"Something big coming in on the wires!" One of the reporters was pulling the tape from the telegraph machine. "Lindbergh's baby! Kidnapped! Last night in New Jersey!" The news had everybody rushing to see the printout. "A ladder was up against the house by the nursery window sill. It says more details to follow." The collective gasps were audible above the newsroom murmur.

"Gotta get on this right away." Marc Atkinson left Kevin standing by himself.

Hearing the announcement, Claude stepped out of his small office, spotting Kevin on the other side of the room. He waved, "Let me get my jacket. This place is going to be a madhouse for the next few hours," Claude called above the growing din. "I'll catch up on the Lindbergh story when I get back."

The two men walked east on Howard Street toward Fay's with a sharp wind billowing their slacks from behind. March in Northern Minnesota had come in like a lion this year.

In a corner booth away from the crowd, the two men ordered coffee and toast, deciding to wait on anything heavier for a while. After several minutes of catching up on small talk, Kevin steered the conversation where it needed to go. "I'm anxious to get involved, Claude. For almost a year we've talked about what's going to happen when I get back to Hibbing. But, before I say anything about any ideas of my own, I'd like to get your thoughts out in front of me. I never learn anything when I'm talking, you know." Kevin borrowed one of Claude's favorite sayings.

Claude's intelligent eyes sparked above the spectacles situated low on the crown of his narrow nose. Nobody knew the local political scene better than the veteran newsman.

"What are the options, Claude?"

Claude explained that Doc Weirick was not seeking reelection as mayor. "He'd never win anyhow. Things are pretty bad around here and Weirick hasn't done anything to make it any better. He's a glad-hander. If he ever had an original idea . . . well, you'd probably hear it rattle in that empty head of his. Sorry, that was pretty mean to say, but—"

Kevin laughed at what he already knew to be true. "You're forgiven, Claude." Then Kevin inquired about his strongest concern. "How about Berklich? I've read that he's not going to run either." Quentin Berklich had served the district in the Minnesota House of Representatives for ten years. It was common knowledge that he was giving it up.

"You're right. He's stepping aside, Kevin—and, thank God for that." Claude suggested that conservative Republican Berklich probably wouldn't be reelected anyhow—despite the fact that district Democrats were still alarmingly disorganized.

"He wasn't very highly regarded by his peers in St. Paul," Kevin added. "And Governor Olson believed the Range had a very weak voice on the issues that affected miners up here the most. He told me to get the Democrats organized—beginning with the mineworkers and their families. Then, small business owners who haven't had any tax breaks in years."

Claude measured the two opportunities in his mind. Kevin was seeking his best advice and insight. Both positions would be highly contested and a few names had already surfaced. "Weirick will endorse Frank Molinaro for mayor. Molinaro's well-liked and connected." Claude considered the Italian postmaster. He respected Frank and considered him a viable candidate.

"Frank hasn't got an enemy in town. He served on the school board without getting in any trouble, he's active in numerous community affairs, and he's an officer in the VFW post. Add to that, he's on the parish council at your church, Kevin."

"I've never met the man, Claude," Kevin admitted. As he often had, Kevin wished he had deeper Hibbing roots. "Would you vote for him?"

Claude considered the question. "He's better than any other person whose name has been tossed around. A hell of a lot better than what we've had since . . . maybe, since Vic. Yes, I'd support Frank."

"He'd be tough to beat?"

"Very tough." As much as Claude loved this young man across the table from him, there were some political realities that Kevin needed to know. "We've got to take an inventory, Kevin. Let's consider your assets and liabilities for a few minutes."

Kevin sensed a concern in Claude's words. Liabilities? "Be candid with me, Claude. I've always respected your opinions more than those of anybody else. Where do we start?"

Claude measured his words. "Let's start with some assets." He would be objective and, at the same time, realistic. "You've got some mighty fine things going for you, Kevin. Intelligence, good looks, and some money to campaign with. The Moran name is still familiar, and Hibbing people read your weekly column." Claude laughed at his next observation. "Plus, the baseball fans will remember that you were a pretty fair pitcher for the locals a few years back."

Kevin offered a wry smile. "But—?"

"There are some 'buts,' for sure." Claude did not believe Kevin could win an election for mayor. Local voters were highly sensitive about roots. Molinaro was a second generation Hibbingite, and his parents were widely known in the Italian community. Frank's reputation was impeccable, and his wife, Viola, was active in both ethnic and Catholic activities. The couple's six children were another asset. Their oldest son, Lucas, was a popular high school athlete. Kevin, on the other hand, was not a Hibbing native. "Forget about the mayor position for now, Kevin. It would be an uphill fight you'd probably never win anyhow. Not even with your three strongest assets."

Kevin puzzled, "... Three strongest assets?"

"Kevin, you've been fortunate to have a respected Hibbing 'family' without having any *real* roots of your own. Tony Zoretek would beat our Mr. Molinaro without even campaigning. I'd bet on that. He's done more for this town than any three people put together. And, Becca, she's delivered more babies, set more broken bones, and doctored more sicknesses than any Doc in the Rood Hospital. To say that she's a beloved lady is putting it mildly." Claude let the thought drop for a moment as he remembered that Rebecca Kaner came to Hibbing as a total stranger years ago. A single female, a doctor, and a Jew. She worked a modern-day miracle by surviving her incredible liabilities.

"You said three, Claude?" Kevin wondered at who a third person might be.

"You're probably too young to realize it, Kevin, but Steven Skorich is like a saint to many of the old timers—especially the miners." Claude gave Kevin a quick history of the difficult times which faced labor organizers over the years, and Steven's heroic efforts during the '07 and '16 Mesabi mineworker strikes. "And when Chisholm had their terrible fire back in '08, Steven saved many lives at the risk of losing his own. As I'm sure you know, Kevin, Steven was pretty badly burned—almost didn't make it."

The story was a familiar one to Kevin, but he enjoyed Claude's reminiscence anyhow. He had planned to talk with Steven later.

"What about the state representative race, Claude?"

"That's a different matter entirely." Claude explained that Hibbing roots were not nearly so important, and that Chisholm was a major factor in the Sixtieth District. Kevin's experience in St. Paul and his connection with the popular Governor Olson might be huge advantages in running for representative. That race would also be more expensive, but Kevin could easily match the opposition's spending. Kevin had confided in Claude months ago that he had money from his father's estate without giving the newsman much in the manner of detail. "I'm not suggesting it would be easy by any means."

"Who's going to run for Berklich's position? Have you heard any names, Claude?"

The newsman gave Kevin a smile of amusement. "I know who's running! That's what makes it rather interesting." Claude, picked up his menu and signaled the waitress without further comment. "I'm getting hungry, Kevin, how about you? Fay's makes marvelous wheat cakes."

"I'll have whatever you're having, Claude. What's so interesting, anyhow. I know by that grin of yours—"

"How much have I told you about Elwood Trembart?"

"Quite a bit, Claude." Kevin recalled earlier conversations and began to put the puzzle together for himself. "Ian Roberts?"

"I knew you could figure that out without my telling you."

Saying "good-bye" to Claude at the intersection, Kevin crossed Howard and turned into the wind. When he got to the law office, he paused to gaze at the names on the sidewalk-facing window, 'Peterson, Raukar, and Moran.' He felt good about that. Inside, Kevin was warmly greeted by his partners and soon found another cup of coffee in his hands. Before getting into business matters, however, all three of them talked about the Lindbergh kidnapping tragedy. "Lindbergh's a Minnesota boy," Pete mentioned, "from Little Falls—down by St. Cloud." The lawyer informed Kevin of America's favorite son and world famous transatlantic pilot.

Pete and Kevin had talked often on the phone about his return to the firm. Both had agreed to a part-time arrangement without going into specific details. Business was slow these days, but Kevin still had some clients from the previous year to keep him busy. It was mutually agreed that Kevin would work between fifteen and twenty hours a week. He would come in for three hours on Monday mornings, when staff meetings were a standard office routine, and set his own schedule for the remainder of the week.

Sitting at his own desk for the first time in a year, Kevin telephoned Angela to hear how she was settling in at the house. It was nearly eleven. Angie had talked again with Becca and Senia about their Saturday project and both were almost as excited as she was. Sadie Baratto wanted to be included, too. Leon was helping her rearrange some furniture in the living and dining rooms as she spoke. "I've been busy, Kevin, and Patrick has been a little doll. I think he likes his new home."

Kevin amused over his wife's excitement. "Do you need me at home for anything, sweetheart?"

"Not at all. Why don't you give dad a call and see if the two of you can have lunch together? I wouldn't give you anything more than sandwiches if you did come home. But, I'll have a pot roast for supper."

Tony shared his chicken sandwiches with Kevin while the two men sat in the contractor's office talking about the Lindbergh episode. Eventually, conversation drifted into business matters. Construction activity had slowed to nearly a standstill. "I'm not going to complain about things. March is always slow, and I'm sure this economy is going to turn around one of these days, Kev."

Kevin always admired Tony's optimism. "What do you think of Roosevelt, and the 'New Deal' he's been talking about?"

"He's a good-thinking man. I believe we've all had enough of Hoover's stumbling along."

Kevin would pick Tony's thoughts. "What do you think of Frank Molinaro, Tony? Claude says he's going to run for mayor."

Tony smiled. "Have you and Claude been talking politics already this morning? Well, what does the 'sage' think of Frank?"

"He likes him a lot."

"So do I. Frank's been on many of the same committees I have over the years. He cares about people." Tony went on to explain about the latest community project that both he and Frank were working on. The 'Hibbing Provide a Job' campaign had already raised over $100,000 for employing the large numbers of out of work residents. The American Legion Post and Central Labor Assembly were sponsoring the drive and all the civic clubs, churches, along with the B'nai B'rith, were getting pledges from businessmen and homeowners. A massive public improvements program would be initiated next spring. Tony offered to provide materials at cost in addition to his sizable pledge of five thousand dollars.

"Can I get involved in the program, Tony? I'd love to help out in any way I can."

"We'd certainly welcome you with open arms, Kev."

Kevin wanted to do more than go to meetings. He had never told Tony much more about his inheritance than that it was sizable. "I'm going to see Senia about my estate later and . . . I'd like to make a contribution to the fund."

"That's great. We're hoping to double what we've raised so far."

Kevin would tell Senia to contribute $25,000 and suggest to Armando Depelo that the Androy give that same amount. Moving their conversation back to where they started, Kevin inquired. "So, what kind of job do you have for your ambitious son-in-law, Dad?" Kevin had already insisted that he'd do any legal work *pro bono* and wondered if he could apprentice with the carpenters during some of his free time. "I want to learn how to build things, Tony. It would really come in handy out at the house. I'm sure your daughter will have a hundred projects for me to do over the years."

Tony could relate to Kevin's desire for physical activity. "I'll tell you what. Me and Lars Udahl will teach you some of the basics. We've both got too much time on our hands these days." The idea of spending a few hours each week with Lars and Kevin brought an easy grin.

"I'd learn from masters of the craft," Kevin complimented.

"I loved carpentry, Kev. You know, your dad got me started, and I'll always be grateful for the opportunity. I still enjoy working with my hands." Tony smiled at a thought that cropped into his mind. He still had the set of tools that Peter Moran had given him so many years ago. "Excuse me a minute, Kevin, there's something I've been meaning to pass along to you. I think I know exactly where to find . . ." Pushing his root beer bottle to the side, Tony got to his feet and left the room.

When he returned, Tony had a wide smile on his face. Holding a red wooden box toward Kevin, he said, "Your dad gave me these tools years ago. They're old, but as good as anything you could buy at the hardware store."

Wide-eyed, Kevin regarded the tool box in his hands as if it were a veritable treasure. "Did my dad ever use any of these himself?"

"You bet he did, Kev. You know the railings on the south porch of your house? Well, me and your dad did that project together one weekend. He was pretty good."

"I've got an idea for my first project, Tony: a fish house." From that suggestion, plans to talk with Steven and Rudy about a Saturday ice-fishing excursion unfolded.

~

Marc Atkinson spoke with Elwood Trembart from his office telephone. The Lindbergh story was already headlined on the afternoon issue, and he had a few minutes to pass along some information. "You told me to let you know when Kevin Moran was in town, Mr. Trembart. He stopped by here this morning to pick up my dad. The two of them went to Fay's for breakfast. They must have been gone for two hours."

Marc was a new member of the Algonquin Club (which he could hardly afford), and, through that elite organization, made his way into Trembart's 'circle of influence.' Elwood liked the idea of having someone from the press in his pocket, but Marc was too naive to realize he was being used. Rubbing shoulders with Trembart's associates gave him feelings of power and importance. "I was going to tell Moran that his stupid column was going to be canceled, but then the Lindbergh story came on the wires."

Trembart was more concerned about Kevin Moran than Charles Lindberg. "Marc, do you know any people down at the University? People connected with that liberal rag the students publish?"

"The *Minnesota Daily*, yes—I know a journalism professor at the U. He has something to do with the paper. Why?"

"Moran was some kind of editor there while he was in college. I'd like you to do some research for me, Marc." Trembart wanted to locate back issues of every Daily that contained an article written by Kevin Moran. "Can you do that for me, Marc?"

Marc promised to give the matter his priority attention. "When do you need the issues, Mr. Trembart?"

"I'm having a meeting of the 'guys'—you know who I mean—sometime next week. We're going to talk about the mayor's election and do some planning for Ian's campaign. It would be great if you could get a hold of something in the next few days."

Marc promised he would get the issues, "Even if I have to drive down to Minneapolis."

Although unaware of it on the following Tuesday morning, two cars headed south of Hibbing within fifteen minutes of each other. They would be within a few miles of each other until the Ford turned west on Highway 23 toward St. Cloud. Kevin had been summoned to Gary's parole hearing at the reformatory. He was excited for two very good reasons. First, the warden was optimistic that Gary would be traveling back to Hibbing with him, and, secondly, Kevin's old friend, Prentice Garvey, was in St. Cloud for some meetings that day. Kevin hoped that the three of them might be able to have a late luncheon together to celebrate what he expected to be great news.

The lead car continued on past the west turn and continued on toward Minneapolis. Marc Atkinson was going to visit an old professor at the *Minnesota Daily* office and would be taking some old *Daily* issues back to Hibbing. What was it about Kevin Moran that so intrigued Trembart? Marc would readily admit he could not hold a candle to his father when it came to having a political nose.

The parole hearing was relatively brief. The warden made a positive recommendation to the five member panel, and Kevin explained his own role in Gary's future plans. Kevin informed the board that Gary would live with his father-in-law in Hibbing, finish his high school training, and be employed part-time at the Androy Hotel. It was the first time Kevin really felt like an attorney, and he presented his testimonial in an eloquent and convincing manner.

The panel voted 5-0 to grant Gary Zench his parole.

After packing Gary's suitcase with his few belongings and attending to all the paper work, Kevin and Gary met Doctor Prentice Garvey at a place called Brickies for a celebratory lunch. Gary was animated and impressed the professor with some of the books he had read while at the reformatory. "I read *A Tale of Two Cities* and understood it," Gary stated with no small measure of pride. Prentice informed Gary that, if he did well in school, he would help find a scholarship, or financial aid, at the University. The possibility of going to college inspired Gary. His life had been a trail of disappointments up until now. For the first time Gary could remember, he had a fresh start in a new place and some goals to focus upon. "I'll keep up my end of the bargain," Gary promised, "And I'll keep in touch with you about how well I'm doing, Dr. Garvey."

Gary looked from the professor to his friend, Kevin. "I've found my 'guardian angel,' sir, and I ain't gonna make any more mistakes." He caught himself, laughed, "Ain't gonna make any . . . ! I just made a big mistake, didn't I? Let me say that over again the way I should have in the first place. 'I will not make another mistake!' How's that?"

Both Kevin and Prentice laughed at Gary's sincere optimism and ability to laugh at himself without self-consciousness.

Elwood Trembart ruffled through the stack of old *Daily* issues, using his scissors to cut out any articles written by Kevin Moran. He smiled as he scanned some of the 1928 Presidential campaign editorials. "Our Mr. Moran was quite the young liberal," Trembart said to himself. "I think we've got enough rope here to hang him if it ever comes down to that."

It was late Friday afternoon and the members of Elwood's little group would be arriving at his office, one at a time. Ian Roberts was an hour early and had a brandy with his father-in-law before the others arrived.

Mayor Weirick was followed by Representative Berklich—both of whom were finishing their last terms in office.

Alphonse Gerard, reputedly the wealthiest man in Hibbing, was the next to arrive. Watching from his window, Elwood was quickly at the door to welcome his influential friend. The retired Oliver Mining Company official once owned much of the hematite-rich property between Hibbing and Chisholm. The real estate broker turned a few hundred thousand into nearly three million dollars. Gerard bankrolled the Trembart political machine and had much to say about who would be elected to what position. His influence went far beyond Hibbing, but he managed to always stay well into the background of political activity.

When Gerard entered the room, everybody stood respectfully.

The final members of Trembart's little group were Harvey Goldberg from the Merchants and Miners Bank, and Marc Atkinson from the *Mesaba Ore* newspaper.

Elwood cleared his throat after mixing drinks at the sideboard, and exchanging theories about the Lindbergh kidnapping. "Gentlemen. I'm sure that Mr. Gerard has a busy schedule, so we'd better get down to business." Elwood smiled deferentially toward the large, wide-jowled, and impeccably dressed mining official seated to his right in the most comfortable chair in the room.

Gerard nodded at his recognition.

"Let's start with the Mayor's election. Doc, first we all want to congratulate you on the fine job you've been doing and express our regrets that you've decided to retire." Elwood acknowledged the Mayor with a wan smile. The compliment was a courtesy. Most of the men in the room realized that Weirick had not been an effective leader.

"Thanks, Elwood. We all have a pretty good idea what's going on to succeed me as mayor." Weirick said in a tone of self-importance, "Frank Molinaro is a 'shoe-in.' I've already told Frank that he can count on my endorsement." Weirick looked from face to face for consensus.

"Your point is well-taken, Doc," Trembart agreed. "It's a matter of what we have to do about that reality. As much as we all like Frank, we've got to make the candidate beholden to our little group—someone who will seek our counsel before going out and making a mess of things." Elwood's smile was devious. "I think you all know what I mean. We've got to create some good competition for Frank and make it appear like he might just be in a really tight race. Then, when he gets a little nervous about his prospects, we come in with some money for his campaign." Elwood had used the very same strategy many times before.

"I can talk Vince Saccoman from the council into running. He'd take some of the Italian vote away. And, what about Mike Matthews on the school board? Mike's been active in the 'Jobs Program' that Zoretek and his do-gooders are all promoting," Weirick suggested.

"What about Ian?" Harv Goldberg asked.

Claude was quick to respond. "Ian's got some other ideas—we'll get to that in a few minutes."

It was agreed that at least two opponents needed to be recruited and convinced to file papers for the mayor's race. The group would discretely give each candidate some 'seed money' and their promise of support.

Elwood made some notes, then turned to Quentin Berklich. "Quent, we're going to miss you—St. Paul is going to miss you."

Everybody gave the representative a round of warm applause.

"Time has come to step aside, fellas. With that radical Olson stuffing his wild ideas down the throat of the legislature, I just got fed up with it all. If it weren't for the guy who's gonna be taking my place, I'd probably give it one more term." Berklich's smile shifted from Elwood to Ian Roberts.

Quentin Berklich had been a foreman at the Sellars Mine before being asked to run for the legislature ten years ago. The mine worker was someone the company officials could easily manipulate. Over his decade in St. Paul, Berklich consistently did what was economically beneficial for the mining companies. On social issues, the Trembart group gave Berklich his needed direction. The Chisholmite was a perfect puppet.

Ian Roberts took his cue from Elwood. "Gentlemen, friends . . . I'm honored to be your choice to seek the office of state representative from our Sixtieth District." He patted Quent, sitting next to him in the circle of men, on the shoulder. "I hope I can do as well as you did down there."

Elwood cut short what might have been an intended speech by his son-in-law. Ian would have plenty of time to say his 'thank yous' and assure the group of his good intentions later. "The only opponent that we know about at this time is a guy from Chisholm by the name of Melvin Alto. His father was one of those agitators from the union."

"We've got a pretty good book on Martin Alto, this guy's father. I've already looked through it down at the Oliver office. He and Skorich were big-time mine organizers during the '07 and '16 strikes. Both of them were blacklisted," Ian said in the mocking tone of one feeling a sense of self-importance and credibility. "The kid, Melvin, runs a dairy operation over in Balkan Township."

"Damn good milk, too. He ought to stick with his cows and stay out of politics." Weirick laughed at his own weak humor.

"He'll have the Finnish vote in his pocket, and that's no laughing matter," Elwood said in cool reprimand. "And, his milk bottles are all over Hibbing. Alto's Dairy Company has a damn good reputation around here. Let's not get overconfident. Ian's going to have to do his homework."

"But, he's not going to have enough money to do an effective job advertising," Goldberg said. "We've got his account at the bank, and I can assure you he's not well-fixed. He puts everything back into his business and has very little in the way of fluid capital."

Elwood appreciated the banker's insight. It was good to have someone with Harvey Goldberg's background and financial knowledge in his group. "We need to come up with another candidate. Someone from Chisholm would be ideal. Folks over there would vote for a jackass if he was from Chisholm." Trembart knew that Hibbing candidates never got much of their neighboring city's vote.

"I'll bet I could get my brother to run. He's out of work these days," Berklich offered.

Elwood gave the idea some thought. Berklich was an Austrian name, and he might be able to capture the Slovenian, Croatian, and Serbian bloc of voters. He was also a mine worker and lived in Chisholm. "Talk to him, Quent. He might be able to help us out."

Only Marc Atkinson and Alphonse Gerard had not contributed to the conversation. Elwood would keep his Kevin Moran concerns to himself for the moment. "It would be nice if you could do some stories on Ian's involvement in the community, Marc. We'd like to see his name in the paper as much as possible over the next few weeks."

Mark nodded with a befuddled smile. It would be hard to make Ian Roberts into some kind of community booster. "I'll talk with Ian later, sir. We can put together some kind of profile."

Gerard shifted his bulk in the leather chair. "What kind of money are we going to need, Ian? Have you worked out any kind of budget?"

Elwood answered for his handsome, but less articulate, son-in-law. He didn't want Ian to put his foot in his mouth, especially with Mr. Gerard. "We'll have something drafted for our next meeting, Al. Ian's going to file a week before the deadline—let me see, that's coming up next month—April 19th. We should be just fine until then."

The group talked national politics for another fifteen minutes. Most concurred that Hoover was unelectable and the 'ultraliberal' New York Governor, Franklin Roosevelt, was going to walk away with everything in November—including a majority in both houses of Congress.

To their collective dismay, Floyd Olson also appeared unbeatable.

∼

Several days after the closed door meeting in Trembart's office, another political meeting took place. This smaller confab met in the Zoretek Construction Company office on North First Avenue. Three men drinking cups of coffee sat around a table cluttered with blueprints. The door was open and no hushed tones were in evidence.

Steven Skorich laughed when Kevin mentioned the name of Ian Roberts. "Elwood's son-in-law? I guess we all saw that coming the day he married Molly." But, the humor was lost in a reality that would pain Steven's soul, a pain born of the fact that his dearest friend's son was also an announced candidate for the Minnesota House. Martin Alto and Steven were like brothers.

Tony, however, wasn't laughing at the mention of Ian Roberts. The thought of Kevin's political ambition was deeply troubling. Why? Kevin had everything a young man might ever dream of having. Tony had a justifiable contempt for local politics, and Kevin's announcement settled uncomfortably in his stomach. He'd seen too many good people get hurt by the character assassination that surfaced in every campaign. Iron Range politics was a brutal business—people here played for keeps! If there were any skeletons in someone's closet they were certain to get dragged out through the mud, and Kevin had a skeleton of his own. When that fact found the light of day, as it certainly might—it would hurt Tony deeply. The public revelation of Angela's pre-marriage pregnancy would tarnish both his daughter's and Kevin's reputation in the community he loved and served with a passion. And reputations, once blemished, were hard to cleanse.

Also, there was the matter of Kevin's surname. A lot of old dirt might rub off on the young man. Did Kevin have some idealized perception of the unscrupulous businessman who was his father? Peter Moran had made enemies over the years and, in Hibbing, memories were long-lived.

"I'm going to need lots of help," Kevin admitted, breaking the long moments of silence hanging over the room. "Claude thinks—" He went on to explain his previous conversations with his political mentor.

Steven's voice betrayed his reluctance. "Of course, Kevin, I'll help you out if I can. But I'm an old-timer, and I haven't done anything political in years. Most people will probably scratch their heads and wonder 'Who is this Steven Skorich'?"

Claude had already explained the connection between Steven and Martin Alto to Kevin. "His loyalties are going to be divided," Claude had warned. "He may want to ride the fence until after the primary election."

"The Finnish vote is solid, Kevin. You won't scratch it in the primary. And, then, there's Chisholm—Melvin will be tough to beat there, too." Steven reflected, "I still have a some good friends in Chisholm . . ." Then, he let the thought drop. He felt like he was in the middle of a river without a rope to grab on to. How could he possibly do this? When Melvin was born, Steven was the first to get a call from Martin announcing the good news. Steven was at the boy's Baptism and numerous birthday parties after that. It would be so much easier if Kevin were to consider running for Mayor, but that was a race he could never hope to win.

Kevin sensed Tony's discomfort as well as Steven's. "I would do a good job for Hibbing . . . and the whole district, if the voters will send me to St. Paul. I know that for a fact. That's why I want to run."

"That's not the issue, Kevin. Not at all. Both Steven and I know you would do well down there. You've had some good experience, and you've got a perfect personality for the job." Wringing his large hands, Tony tried to smile and failed miserably. "It's the price you'll have to pay. And, I'm not talking dollars . . ."

"Nothing worth having comes easily, Tony. You know that better than anybody. I'll give it everything I've got and take my chances. But, I can't do this alone," Kevin appealed.

"What does Angie think about all this?" Tony focused on Kevin's eyes.

"She's lukewarm on the idea right now. I'll be honest about that. She doesn't like the idea of my being away . . . but, she's willing to do anything to help. We are committed to being in everything together. If she ever told me she didn't want me to do something—it would end right there."

"It's hard on a family. Separation . . ." Tony's words held traces of pain. He knew how much Angie loved this man. And, so did he. Kevin was like a son to him. Why was he making Kevin feel like this was an inquisition? Kevin deserved his unreserved support and confidence. "Kevin, I will do everything I can to help. I'd be dishonest if I said I'm totally in favor of what you're planning to do. In fact, I'm somewhat troubled by it." Tony's eyes moistened. "But, if you want this, I'll help you get it. If it means moving a mountain, let's roll up our sleeves, young man."

Steven regarded Tony with melancholy eyes. His nephew was a decent and loyal man. Tony personified what the America dream was all about. Steven's loyalty had to be with his blood. "I'm behind you, Kevin. We'll figure out what has to be done and do it." He would pray that Martin and Melvin would understand what he had to do.

"Do you think Norm Dinter and Lud Jaksa will help me out, Tony? I'm going to have put a lot of good heads together in the next few days," Kevin said. "And, Claude will do what he can."

"Claude, bless his heart, will stay in the background, Kevin. We all know that. Even with Vic Power, Claude was always behind the scenes. And his son pretty much runs the paper these days. Marc Atkinson will be doing the editorials. How do you get along with Marc?" Tony asked.

"Not too well."

"I'm sure Claude has told you enough about Elwood Trembart, but let me add . . . that man is a scorpion. He will do anything—I repeat—anything, to get Ian Roberts elected!"

"I know that, Tony." Kevin swallowed hard. "And I know he despised my father. But so did a lot of other people, I've learned. Claude once told me that my name might be *a blessing* . . . and it might be *a curse*. I made the decision to take my chances with being a Moran years ago. It's been working pretty well so far."

AN ULTIMATE IRONY?

ANGELA MORAN HAD A RECURRING NIGHTMARE. In her dream she saw an open upstairs window with a ladder leaning against the house—a fear inspired by the Lindbergh baby's kidnapping only weeks before. The tragic story had monopolized the front pages and radio news like nothing in her memory. Their house on Maple Hill was far more isolated than the Lindbergh mansion, and in that reality, Angela felt vulnerable. Kevin's political campaign increasingly brought the Moran name to public attention, and there were enough crazy people desperate for money in these difficult times.

Mr. Gunther installed a heavy metal gate at the driveway entrance and fencing around the perimeters of the house, but Angela did not feel any added sense of security. So, Gunther installed large flood lights on the roof of the house to illuminate the wide space between the yard and tree line, along with adding dead-bolt locks on all the entry doors.

"I'm sorry, honey. But I can't be home before dark every night. I've got meetings . . . and, more meetings. What do you want me to do?" Kevin asked his wife.

"I don't know, Kevin. You and Mr. Gunther have probably done everything possible . . . but I worry about Patrick whenever you're not here."

"Would you rather live in town for a while, Angie? Dad and Becca would love to have us stay with them."

Angela did not want to leave their home. "Don't think I'm too paranoid, Kevin, but there is something I need to ask." Her idea was almost frightening. "I want a gun, Kevin. Something small that I can learn to shoot."

Kevin had never owned a pistol, and the thought of a firearm in the house was disturbing. But, if it would allay Angie's fears, he would find something for her. "I'll get you a handgun today, Angie. And, I don't think you're paranoid at all. It's probably a good idea. I can put the pistol in a safe place—maybe in the library. We can both learn to use it together and, maybe, even do some target-practicing this weekend."

Kevin regarded his lovely wife. Angie's life had been painfully impacted by his political activities these past few weeks. Since his announcement in mid-April, he had been working long hours trying to build a coalition among diverse Democrats. Organizing required numerous evening meetings at the labor assemblies and ethnic halls, as well as with the Chambers of Commerce—he would speak to any group willing to listen to his views on the issues he was raising.

"Angie, I'm sorry about all this—the politics, I mean. It's been harder on you than either of us imagined it might be. I didn't expect—" He swallowed hard on what he had to say. "It's selfish—my ambition. I've been putting what I want ahead of you and my family responsibilities, aren't I, sweetheart? I can quit—get out before I've made too many commitments."

Angie looked at her husband across the breakfast table. He meant what he was saying. Smiling at the temptation to take him up on his offer, she reached for his hand. "Kevin, if it were me and there were something I believed in so strongly that I needed you to make some sacrifices for me . . ." She met his eyes, "I wouldn't even have to ask for your support, would I?"

By July, local Democrats were feeling the euphoria of Franklin Roosevelt's sweeping popularity. FDR's proposed 'New Deal' for America became as widely discussed in Hibbing as it was across the country. And, at the state level, Governor Floyd Olson's innovative proposals were making him more popular than ever before. Taking every advantage of a groundswell of enthusiasm about easing the terrible clutches of the Depression, Kevin worked tirelessly at organizing what might become his political base. His efforts were rewarded by gaining endorsements from both the miners and building trades local unions. Steven worked on promoting Kevin's candidacy among his friends in Chisholm, while Tony met frequently with small business owners. Even Becca did some politicking at the Rood Hospital.

Claude, mostly a behind-the-scenes advisor, continued to provide Kevin with insight and direction. "I'm certain you've caught Elwood's attention, Kevin. The endorsements that Quentin Berklich and Mayor Weirick gave to Ian Roberts are Trembart's doing. I can smell a skunk ten miles away. Pretty soon Elwood's money, along with any dirt he's uncovered, will begin to come out. He's not going to stop at anything, I'll assure you of that . . . anything! to get his 'all smiles and no brains' son-in-law elected.

The 'circle,' as they called themselves, met at Elwood's plush Alexander Street house on a pleasant Friday evening in late June. The regulars were all seated at an oak table in the host's spacious study. The critical primary election was ten weeks away.

Trembart brought the meeting to order by clearing his throat, "Gentlemen, we've got our work cut out for us." His eyes passed from Ian Roberts at his right to Harvey Goldberg, Quentin and John Berklich, Alphonse Gerard (at the other end of the table), Doc Weirick, and Marc Atkinson. An obviously nervous Frank Molinaro sat at Trembart's left elbow. "You all know Frank. I've asked him to join us for a few minutes before we get on with our regular meeting." Everybody nodded in the direction of their guest. "Frank has agreed to stay neutral in the Representative race. Ian would like his support, but it's probably best for everybody if Frank stays in the middle of the road through the primary. Right, Frank?"

Molinaro nodded. "Elwood, gentlemen, I appreciate your generous contribution to my campaign. As you know, I've got my hands full with some very respectable opponents. I'm more than happy to let Ian fight his own battles. With your support, I'm confident he'll do just fine."

The circle talked about the mayor's race for fifteen minutes, gave Molinaro their best wishes, and watched as Elwood led the candidate to the door. Molinaro would win his race despite the credible opponents their group had lined up to run against him. Trembart had also given the other candidates some money to use against Molinaro.

"Now, let's get down to business," Trembart said, giving his friends a twisted smile. "We're going to have to sink that little ship that Kevin Moran is sailing in, and I think we've got all the ammunition we need."

Trembart detailed his strategy of character assassination. On his note pad he had outlined the timetable for Kevin Moran's political destruction.

Elwood's 'bombshells,' as he called them, would begin exploding after the Fourth of July celebrations. "Let him enjoy his Fairground's fireworks show for the moment. Then we can enjoy ours." Elwood was amused by his holiday analogy. "Our good friend, Marc Atkinson, will be very important in the plans Ian and I have laid out. We've done our homework, gentlemen."

Marc smiled at the recognition without reply.

The public attacks would be carefully staggered in Marc's newspaper. Quotations they had uncovered from Moran's 'radical' political views expressed years before in the *Minnesota Daily* articles would open the barrage. In addition, Kevin would be portrayed as having a youthful drinking problem which put him afoul with the law. Records of his arrest had been obtained from the Minneapolis police department.

Then, on the anniversary of the Hotel Moran fire, Peter Moran would be vilified as a "coward who took his own life rather than face a grand jury on charges of conspiracy to commit murder..."

"I'm only getting started, gentlemen. Even Marc here doesn't know about the the stories I'm saving until the end of August. If Moran's still around by then." Elwood enjoyed the feeling of power he had in his circle. The opportunity to stab Kevin's father in the back one more time was especially satisfying.

Trembart turned toward Goldberg, "Thanks for getting us this information, Harvey. That lady at the bank, what's her name? . . . Arola? Well, she'll shit her pants when she sees the estate numbers in the paper."

Harvey Goldberg had provided the circle with information on Kevin Moran's "incredible wealth." Goldberg was a reluctant participant in Trembart's scheming. But, the respected banker had a well-hidden gambling problem and owed Elwood a considerable sum of money. When Elwood demanded the confidential Moran estate information, Goldberg had little choice but to cooperate.

Goldberg cursed his high-stakes poker addiction under his breath. Senia would be furious. She would identify the source of the 'leak' immediately. His gambling debts would cost him a friendship he had cherished for years. "I'd be lying if I told you I liked this idea, Elwood. The confidentiality of my bank is going to be compromised."

Elwood gave the banker a condescending look. "Consider it a public service, Harvey."

Marc felt a pang of empathy for the banker. Perhaps, he was not the only one at the table feeling a sense of guilt.

"I've got a few more 'bombs' to drop as we get closer to the primary," Trembart promised. "Harvey's given me a scoop that might surprise all of you. Kevin Moran actually owns the Androy—his friend Depelo is only the front man. Now, why didn't we figure that out for ourselves, gentlemen? Marc's going to put something together on that little known fact next month."

For a brief moment, Marc Atkinson basked in the warmth of peer respect. His inclusion in this powerful circle gave him a feeling of self-importance. But his father would be enraged by his complicity. Claude had always been a man of the highest ethics—the family newspaper a chronicle of truth. Marc rationalized that what he was doing, however despicable, was factual. Maybe his reporting would be heralded as what Trembart deemed "a public service." Maybe his father would realize that he'd been taken in by Moran's smooth talking charm. Maybe . . . ?

Alphonse Gerard promised to write another check for the Roberts' campaign. "I've left the amount blank, Ian. Just don't bankrupt me!" Everybody laughed at the impossibility. Gerard had already given Ian more than ten thousand dollars.

John Berklich had filed for the office on the last day. It was hoped that the Representative's younger brother would split the primary vote by cutting into the Slovene and Croatian support that Moran's friend, Steven Skorich, was building. "Skorich has a following in Chisholm, but Johnny here will cut into that. Who knows, maybe he can even beat Alto over there," Elwood speculated.

All of the circle members agreed, however, that Melvin Alto was showing surprising strength throughout the district. "People like their Finlander milkman," Ian Roberts insighted sarcastically.

Elwood frowned at his son-in-law, wishing he'd keep his ears open and mouth shut. "Never underestimate, Ian!" he cautioned.

∼

At Kevin's invitation, Governor Olson would be in Hibbing for the community's Independence Day celebrations. As a personal favor, Olson scheduled a rally at the Fairgrounds on the Sunday night prior to the annual Fourth of July parade the following morning. The Governor's appearance had been widely publicized on the radio, and thousands of posters and leaflets were distributed throughout the Sixtieth District. The *Mesaba Ore* gave the prestigious occasion no more than a small acknowledgement in a front page corner article under the small banner, *'Governor To Speak Sunday'*. But, the Labor Assembly purchased numerous advertisements so that the event had been given sufficient advance publicity.

The Saturday evening was star-filled and pleasantly warm. Kevin sat in the chair next to Governor Olson on the makeshift stage erected in front of the large grandstand. Steven, Tony, Claude, and Norm Dinter joined the dignitaries near the podium at the center of the stage. Neal Dorsher of the Chamber and George Jackola of the Iron Miners' local organization were also seated along with the Governor's delegation from St. Paul.

Claude Atkinson reluctantly agreed to serve as master of ceremonies for the rally. Stepping up to the podium, the newsman made the appropriate introductions—asking each dignitary to stand when acknowledged. Tony Zoretek thanked everybody for joining the "finest showing of unified Democrats in years!" Several hundred hands clapped at Tony's timely political observation. After making a few more comments, Tony asked Steven Skorich to join him at the podium. "This man needs no introduction to any Mesabi iron miner!" Steven's presence brought a standing ovation.

Tony whispered in Steven's ear as the roar rose from the crowded grandstand. "You've got to say a few words, Steven. They love you."

"My dear friends and fellow mine workers," Steven strained to enunciate his words clearly. "I haven't got much of a voice these days . . . and I don't speak very well, either." Feeling self-conscious, Steven continued his speech. "But I want you to know why I'm on this stage tonight. There's a fine young man sitting beside me. A man who I'm proud to call my friend." Steven turned his gaze toward Kevin sitting behind him. "Give them a wave, Kevin," he said. Kevin got a warm applause, but nothing comparable to that of either Tony or Steven.

Steven continued, "Kevin Moran will be asking for your vote in the

September primary election. As you all know, the primary is critical. Only two candidates will be chosen to go on to the general election." Steven paused over his final words. "I want to be as honest with each of you tonight as I've been when we were shoulder-to-shoulder during the strikes. Melvin Alto, one of Kevin's opponents, is a good man—like his father. But, in these difficult times, we need to go beyond past friendships. We need to look at the kind of experience that will help us the most in getting back to work. Kevin Moran has that kind of experience. I think our Governor will speak words to that effect as well." Steven was feeling tired from only a few minutes standing at the podium, and his bad leg ached. "Thank you, my friends, you will vote as your conscience dictates—I know that. I will do the same. And I will vote for Kevin Moran in September."

Kevin's speech was brief. He knew that the crowd wanted to hear the eloquent Governor of Minnesota. Olson's endorsement, along with Steven's few but well-chosen words, were far more important than anything he might have to say. Over the previous two months, his focus had been on the goals and issues of small business owners, laborers, and women alike. Kevin had not campaigned against Melvin Alto or Representative Quentin Berklich's brother, Joe Berklich. His major focus was Republican Ian Roberts, whom he characterized as being "another puppet of the mining interests."

"As the Governor will attest in his remarks, our district has not been represented in St. Paul in nearly a decade. The only voice in your behalf has been that of the mining companies. I will change that." Kevin paused at the scattered applause, caught the smiles of Angie, Becca, and Senia in the front row. "I will listen to you . . . I will speak for you . . . I will fight for what is right for the working man on the Iron Range." Borrowing from Olson's political philosophy, Kevin emphasized, "We are the *real producers* in this mineral-based economy. The big corporations are the parasites of our labors, and with the capital we earn for them, they seek only to get richer at our expense. That must change, my friends. And, with your support, I will bring your fight to St. Paul."

Raising his arms to the applause his words inspired, Kevin thanked the crowd. Clapping along with the crowd, Governor Olson stepped behind him. The others stood as well, clasping hands together in a circle behind

Kevin to show their support and unity. The newly-forged Democratic 'team' Kevin was building in Hibbing got a standing ovation.

Governor Olson did not disappoint. Hitting on his favorite themes, Olson's fiery rhetoric incited many outbursts of applause, along with excited hoots and whistles. "You've been cheated, Iron Rangers! Your representation in the legislature has been pathetic! As your Governor, I implore you to change all that. Give my friend, and yours—Kevin Moran—your vote." The raucous noise from the Fairground's rally could be heard as far away as Alexander Street, nearly a mile away.

Elwood Trembart and his group listened to the speeches on the local station broadcasting the event from the fairgrounds. "Moran's just had his finest hour, gentlemen. Beginning next week his so-called 'coalition' of Democrats will begin to learn more about their ambitious young hero. Right, Marc?" Elwood's sneer made the journalist uncomfortable. Marc had been having serious doubts about his role in the ruthless destruction of his father's close friend.

At the office, Marc kept his door closed, avoiding his father as best he could. He came to work early, left late. His guilt had kept him sleepless at night and despondent during the day. Claude was on the stage with Kevin at that very minute, he knew. But, Marc was already in this conspiracy too deeply, and the defaming newspaper articles were already drafted. Marc Atkinson was a Judas!

"Where did the *Ore* get all this?" Kevin asked Angie as he read the front page newspaper story on events from his college days. Under the auspices of a *'Meet the Candidates'* series, Marc Atkinson chose to focus on Kevin's past *Minnesota Daily* articles rather than on the current issues he was raising in the campaign. Previously, Marc had done a wonderful profile on Melvin Alto, and an exaggerated "community activist" piece on Ian Roberts. Both articles had a positive slant. This was malicious!

> Moran was clearly anti-Protestant when he wrote about the 1928 presidential campaign, " . . . A vote for Hoover is a vote against Catholics" . . . One might be led to question whether Moran's religious prejudices are tolerable in a Christian community which in-

cludes Lutherans, Methodists, Presbyterians and other non-Catholic denominations.

Later, the article suggested.

In a May, 1930, article Moran compared radical Floyd Olson to our esteemed President, Thomas Jefferson. Perhaps, the young 'Daily' editor was still feeling the effects of a wild 'Gopher' weekend when he wrote that absurdity. In fact, Kevin Moran was arrested for illegal consumption while partying at the U. Hennepin County court records indicate he was charged only with a misdemeanor for the felony offense. It would seem that our young lawyer had already mastered an ability to pull the right strings so as to avoid the consequences of his crime. Some may consider that manipulating behavior an asset for an aspiring public servant. Most, however, have higher standards for elected officials.

Marc Atkinson detailed several other 'out of context' commentaries that Kevin had written over his years with the *Daily*. Kevin was portrayed as being everything from a *"communist sympathizer"* to an *"opponent of the American free enterprise system."* The only positive perspective in the entire article was a reference to his sizable contribution to the 'Hibbing Provide a Job' campaign. Even that reference, however, was couched in blatant negativity.

"Moran's significant donation from his family fortune put the 'Jobs' campaign over the top last spring."

"I can't believe it!" Kevin voiced his exasperation. "I know Marc doesn't care much for me, but this is almost libelous."

"Is any of it true? I don't really understand the political stuff—but, were you really arrested, Kevin?" Angie frowned.

"I did one foolish thing in five years at the University. One! Yes, I was arrested and spent a night in jail for drinking. I was lucky, I guess, Prentice Garvey helped me out in the court proceedings."

Angela was troubled. "Is this the kind of thing we can expect over the next few weeks? Innuendoes and personal attacks in the newspaper? What else haven't you told me about, Kevin? Your life will be an open book before this is over."

Kevin failed in his attempt at smiling. "Nothing, sweetheart. Honestly. I never expected anything like this to ever come up."

"I believe you, Kevin." Angie reached across the table and found his hand. "But, what will people think about this? What will Bob Peterson and Al Raukar at the law office think about your criminal record?"

"I'll just have to be honest with them and everybody else." Kevin realized that Angie was right. His life would be an 'open book' and the Ian Roberts group would exploit every nook and cranny. He remembered Tony's concern regarding "skeletons in the closet" and about the dirty politics that would bring them out. Was there anything in his life that he had not shared with Angie? As Kevin searched his memory, only one secret remained. The truth of his father's death, however, was something that no other living person needed to know about. Not even Senia.

In early August, the *Ore* ran an historical piece under the banner, *'Remembering Our Past.'* The article focused on the tragic Hotel Moran fire on this date in 1908. In the last paragraph, Marc Atkinson stated:

> *Devastated by the loss of the majestic hotel, and facing the possibility of a grand jury indictment for 'conspiracy to commit murder,' Peter Moran took his life at the mansion where he resided. The local entrepreneur was only thirty-three. The hotel was never rebuilt. Peter Moran's mansion, however, was purchased by his heir, Kevin Moran, and moved at considerable expense to Maple Hill where the Moran estate had purchased eighty acres of prime land.*

The following day, the *Ore* ran an Ian Roberts' full-page political ad. It was an 'open letter to the voters of the Sixtieth Legislative District':

> *Voters, I am saddened by yesterday's story on the Hotel Moran fire of twenty-four years ago. The reference to Peter Moran's suicide was completely unnecessary in the otherwise well-written historical piece.*

What concerns me even more is the fact that my opponent in this campaign for state representative has enough money to actually buy the election. I know these are difficult financial times for most of us, but I feel compelled to ask each of you make a one dollar contribution to my campaign. It will help my efforts to offset the millions of dollars in the Moran trust account. As I have promised all of you throughout this campaign, your dollar will be an investment in my program to restore your employment in the mines of our great Mesabi area. As a mining company official, I have the necessary influence and experience to make our economy work again so all of you can get back to work.

I thank you for your anticipated financial support, but even more importantly, your vote in the important September primary.

Sincerely, Ian Roberts

'A Vote For Roberts is a Vote For Jobs.'
(Paid for by the candidate on his own behalf.)

Incensed by the advertisement, Kevin asked his team of advisors for an assessment of damages when they met in Tony's construction company office the following day.

"My son and I are not on speaking terms these days," Claude said. "In all my days I've never seen a smear campaign like this one, and I'm saddened that my newspaper has been an instrument in Kevin's character assassination," he told the group. "It's mean spirited journalism at its worst. I'm truly sorry, Kevin."

"Can you think of anything you've done to Marc that's made him so strongly opposed to your campaign?" Tony asked Kevin.

Kevin shrugged his shoulders. "Nothing I can think of, Tony."

"He's just a tool. Trembart's behind what he's printing in the paper. Since Marc joined the high-rollers at the Algonquin Club, he's been a different person," Claude defended. "He's not doing anything illegal—he's smart enough to stay away from that—but his ethics are in the toilet."

"From what I'm hearing, the article about your father's . . . *death,* has stirred up a lot of old memories," Norm Dinter added. "And Roberts wants to characterize you as a millionaire. That's not going to help us."

"What do you think about the money issue that Roberts raised in that disgraceful ad yesterday, Claude?" Kevin would be candid with his friends. "I want you all to know that my father left me a lot of money. I guess I am a millionaire . . . but, I intend to do as much good as I can with my inheritance."

"Common folks resent the rich—always have," Claude observed. "I think Harvey Goldberg is a part of Trembart's group. If I'm right about that, Harvey's given them all your financial records. However unethical, they will play the 'rich kid' card whenever they can."

"It's none of our business, Kevin, but is there anything else about your money that might come up?" Dinter asked.

If Goldberg was in the enemy camp, Kevin could imagine another matter that could be embarrassing. "I put up the money for Armando Depelo. I own the Androy Hotel." He looked toward Steven who sat across from him at the table. "Senia suggested it would be a good investment to make . . . I've stayed in the background from the beginning."

Nobody had any other comments or questions about Kevin's estate.

"The stuff on your college days—being arrested and all—was laughable, though. Everybody's broken the prohibition laws at some time or another." Lud Jaksa made light of the early accusations. That's not going to hurt you, Kevin. Almost makes you more of a 'regular guy.'

"But the Catholics against Protestants thing hurt you, Kev." Tony shook his head. "That was really misconstrued, but effective, nevertheless. Religion is a sensitive matter, especially with women voters."

Kevin's confidence was becoming deflated. "All Roberts has done is smile and kiss babies and promise he'll get people back to work. There's no way in hell he can do that. How can anybody believe him?"

Steven finally spoke. "Unemployed people want to believe it. Promise a hungry man food, and he'll follow you to hell and back again. It's human nature."

"But, do the people you're talking with actually think Roberts can get them back to work, Steven?" Kevin asked.

"Most miners are pretty smart, especially the old-timers. But, the younger guys are impatient. Yes, I'd have to say that there are quite a few who don't see through Roberts. I'm working on that."

Tony wriggled uncomfortably in his chair. The allegations and innuendos in the press so far were disturbing, but he was convinced there was more dirt coming. Angela's pre-marriage pregnancy and the 'rushed wedding' in Duluth would surface at some point. He kept these concerns in his private thoughts for the moment. "Let's try to focus on something positive, guys. The Chamber folks, at least most of them, are still squarely behind Kevin. His position on reducing the tax burden on small businesses is the one issue they're most concerned about."

Steven scratched his head. "Melvin Alto is a small businessman himself, Tony. He's saying the same things that Kevin is on that issue. And, even Ian Roberts wants to keep their taxes down."

"We've got the union endorsements," Dinter said. "That's the most critical voting group in the District."

Claude smiled at his friend. "If they vote in the primary, Norm. They'll all go to the polls in November, but . . . turnout for the primary is usually less than fifty percent."

"And, there's the possibility that the mineworkers' wives will cancel out their husbands' votes. Hibbing women are an independent sort. They're not going to vote the way their husbands want them to vote. They might say they will . . . but, when the curtain is pulled behind them . . ." Lud Jaksa's observation brought knowing nods at the table.

"How are things going in Chisholm, Steven?" Kevin sensed his friend was troubled by the conversation. "I don't expect to run well over there, but I wonder if Berklich will split Melvin Alto's vote?"

Steven would be candid. "I wish I could be more helpful over there, Kevin. If I were running . . . well, several close friends have told me they would vote for me in a heartbeat. They don't know you, Kevin. To most of them you are a Hibbing attorney with lots of money. They don't trust that." Brushing the stubble on his chin with his long fingers, Steven met Kevin's eyes. "But, they really like Melvin Alto over there. Berklich, on the other hand, will probably get one vote in four at best."

"Trembart is a master at running candidates. I've seen him working behind the scenes for thirty years. The only reason Berklich is running is to siphon off Steven's influence in the Slovenian community—in Chisholm as well as in Hibbing. He's just a Trembart pawn." Claude offered a political veteran's observation. "Even one vote in five or six for Berklich is going to hurt us, fellas."

Although discouraged, Kevin pushed himself in the final two weeks of August. He walked up and down Lake Street in Chisholm twice a week and greeted people at the Hibbing post office almost every morning. Whenever there was a meeting in either community, Kevin made an appearance. Angela was at his side much of the time. His lovely wife joined the League of Women Voters, attended Slovenian Lodge meetings, became involved with the Carmelites at their church. She didn't enjoy any of these activities, but wanted to help her husband in any way she could. Angie enjoyed being at home with Patrick, riding Flare in the afternoons, and keeping up the house. She disliked politics. Secretly, she carried guilt. Most of the time, Angie Moran hoped that Kevin would lose.

Elwood Trembart saved his final 'bombshells' for the last two weeks before the primary. Meeting with Ian Roberts and Marc Atkinson, Elwood puffed on his Cuban cigar. "Marc, we're going for the throat. I've been saving the best for last." Trembart had employed some business and legal connections in Duluth to do some digging for him. Richard McKanna worked as a clerk in the 'Public Records Division' at the St. Louis County courthouse. The adoption transcripts of Kevin Schmitz (a male born of Barbara Chevalier—5502 Wadena Street in West Duluth and Peter Moran—402 Washington Street in Hibbing—on February 13, 1907) was a lucky stroke. The mother had died during the 'illegitimate' birth of her son, and a priest by the name of Patrick Foley at St. James' parish had initiated the adoption proceedings that McKanna uncovered.

Records of the name change—from Schmitz to Moran—filed by attorney Victor Power on August 18, 1925, were later discovered, and passed along. Elwood Trembart pushed his court house contact for even more information, telling him he was willing to pay an extra thousand dollars for marriage records.

"Here's what I want in the Sunday paper, Marc." Trembart narrowed his eyes on the newsman. "I've even got an idea for the banner—'Who is He?'" Elwood spread the papers on the table in front of him. "Our Kevin Moran is actually a bastard." He explained the birth to adoption to name change scenario. "It cost our group some money, but it's dynamite stuff, don't you think?" Elwood gave the two men a twisted smile. "And bastards beget bastards. That son-of-a-bitch, Moran, had to get married. Zoretek's lovely daughter was as pregnant as this information's going to be when people read about it."

Marc Atkinson had a sinking feeling. What Trembart was suggesting knotted his stomach. The editor had already besmirched his own, and his newspaper's reputation, and ruined the relationship between him and his father. Marc's conscience would not allow this annihilation of Kevin Moran's reputation to continue any further. "I'm sorry, Mr. Trembart. I won't have anything to do with that information. It's the dirtiest smear tactic I've ever heard of. No, sir."

Elwood's jaw dropped. "Did I hear you correctly? Listen, you son-of-a-bitch, you're already over your head in this campaign. This has been a 'team' effort from the start . . . there's no bailing out two weeks before the primary. Do you understand that?" Elwood's compsosure drained. "I asked you a question, don't just sit there staring at me!"

Marc searched deeply for a courage he hoped might be inside him. Through compressed lips, he bit off his next several words, "Not only am I 'bailing out', Trembart, I'm going to do my best to retract some of the crap I've already printed." Surprised at what he'd just said, he completed the thought, "I'll ask my father to help me get out of this mess before it's too late." Marc pushed away from the table and left the room. Tears streaked his face as he stepped out into the evening drizzle. "God forgive me . . . Dad forgive me . . ." Marc prayed for the courage to undo the damage he'd already done.

For nearly two hours, Marc walked through the chilly night. Soaking wet, he found himself at his father's front door. The light from Claude's study shown through the window. Marc rehearsed his confession under his breath. Before knocking, he heaved a sigh of relief. His father was a forgiving man, a loving man . . . It was not too late.

Undeterred by the Atkinson rebuff, Ian Roberts ran several ads in the competing newspaper. The first ad was indeed titled, 'Who is He?' and suggested that voters support "one of their own . . ." while citing that Kevin (Schmitz) Moran was a 'Duluthian'—not an Iron Ranger.

The second political ad was openly addressed to the voters of the Sixtieth Legislative District.

> *Friends and voters. My opponent has claimed that my candidacy has been devoid of meaningful issues. That charge has been raised despite my pledge to return our unemployed workers to their jobs, and my promise to protect small business owners from tax increases, and my firm position against the radical socialism of Governor Olson. This so-called 'Democrat' calls me a "person without vision and a man of shallow character." Perhaps there is an issue of greater import than any of the others that have been raised in this campaign. We must always hold our leaders to the highest moral standards. In that regard, I believe that MORALITY is a legitimate political concern for all of us.*
>
> *It is with the deepest regret, however, that I share another shameful episode in the well-guarded personal life of my opponent. Mr. Moran, and his expecting 'girlfriend' were secretly married on March 14 of last year in Duluth. Why is everything about my opponent shrouded in mystery? One week ago we didn't even know his real name. One week ago we didn't even know that my opponent was actually a transplanted Duluthian. And, to this day, we wonder why his ownership of the Androy Hotel has not been disclosed to the voters of our district. Once again, Mr. Moran does not want us to know the truth.*
>
> *Please, Mr. Moran, let the voters know who they are voting for in the primary. We deserve honesty and integrity and morality.*
>
>   *'A Vote for Ian Roberts is a Vote for Morality.'*
>   *(Paid for by the friends of Ian Roberts Committee.)*

Angela was devastated. "How can I ever walk down the street in Hibbing without feeling that everybody is talking behind my back? Our reputation has been ruined, Kevin. Absolutely ruined!" She sobbed uncontrollably. "And, my father's good name is . . ."

Kevin was at a loss for any words of comfort. He would call Marc Atkinson later that morning and announce his withdrawal from the race. The latest smear had pushed him over the edge. He had believed that he'd lived a good life, worked hard, given to those in need. Now, he believed differently. Perhaps, his money was the 'root of all evil'—but, he didn't *love* money. More than anything, he had hurt the people he loved most. Could he ever repair the damage to his relationship with Angie, to his cherished freindships? Kevin thought of his father's depression in the final hours of his life. Was there an ultimate irony in every man's life? *He remembered the .38 caliber Smith & Wesson hidden in the desk drawer.* Tormented, Kevin momentarily shifted his tearing eyes toward the library door only several feet away.

"I got us into this mess, sweetheart, and somehow, I'll make things right again. I promise." His moist eyes betrayed the depth of his emotion. Could he really change what had happened and make everything right again? Kevin wondered from the depths of his soul. "I'm so very sorry, Angie. What else can I say? I'm going to quit the campaign. Then I'm going to take the three of us away from here for a while." Kevin's troubled words tumbled out as he tried to get a hold on his emotions.

"What? Run away again? No, Kevin, this is our home and these are our people. I'm tough enough to deal with the gossip. I thought you were, too. Running is cowardice, Kevin."

Their kitchen table conversation was interrupted by Patrick's crying from the nursery at the top of the stairs. When Angie left to get the baby, Kevin slipped into his library, closed the door, and picked up the telephone. Before he did anything else, he would make this call.

"Marc Atkinson, please." Kevin told the secretary at the *Ore* office.

"Hello, Marc, here."

"Marc, Kevin Moran." His voice was strained.

There was a silence on the line.

"Marc? Are you there?"

"Yes." Marc swallowed hard. He had not talked to Kevin Moran in weeks, nor had he seen Kevin visit his father at the office. Feeling terrible about what he had done, Marc wanted to apologize. "Kevin, I'm truly sorry about all this—"

Kevin interrupted, "Well, your father warned me about the politics up here." He tried to be light, to disguise the pain of the moment. "I've got something newsworthy to share with you, Marc. I'm sure it will make you happy."

"Nothing about this election could make me happy."

"I'm done, Marc! I've had enough! I'd appreciate it if you would front-page an article on my withdrawal from the race. Would you do that for me?"

Marc bit at his lip. "You can't do that, Kevin."

"What do you mean? I've been pretty well beaten up, Marc. I made a mistake and I'm willing to admit it. It's still going to be a good race between Melvin and Ian Roberts," Kevin rationalized in his grief.

"You didn't make a mistake, Kevin. You're the best candidate in the field. I believe that. I'm the one who made the mistake, and I'm going to do everything I can to repair it. I've already talked to Dad and he's going to help me." In careful detail, Marc explained everything that had been going on behind Trembart's closed doors. "I got taken in with being in his 'circle,' Kevin. My weak ego, I guess. Anyhow, I'm terribly sorry about what I did, and if you'll allow me, I'm going to let everybody in Hibbing know what's been happening. It's not too late!"

Kevin contemplated Marc's words. Was it already too late? "I've got to talk with my wife and with Tony. Let me call you back later this morning. And, Marc, thanks for telling me."

Still sobbing, Angela was nursing Patrick at the table. In the few minutes since Kevin had left the kitchen, she had time to sort her troubled thoughts. She could hear the low tones of his voice from the library. Kevin was on the phone with someone. If running was cowardly, she realized—so was quitting this campaign. The Morans would have to handle their adversities. Together.

As she saw Kevin approaching, Angie could feel his pain as if it were her own. "Kevin, you can't quit," she said in a clear, confident voice. "I won't stand for it. Dropping out now would only make things more difficult for us. We're going to show this town what we are made of."

Pulling a chair next to his wife and son, Kevin leaned over and kissed her full on the mouth. "I love you, Angie. Regardless of anything that might happen, I love you."

Trying to smile, Angela asked, "Will you change your mind, Kevin?"

"I don't know if I can. I've disappointed so many people . . . it breaks my heart." For the first time in his life, Kevin Moran believed that the name of his father was truly *a curse*. "I'm going to spend a few minutes thinking about it. Praying about it."

Kevin left Angie sitting at the table and wandered back to the privacy of his library.

~

Claude and Marc Atkinson worked together that morning on a front page editorial entitled, *'We are Ashamed!'*

> *I am sitting beside my father as I write this heartfelt apology. I should have respected my dad's integrity and the integrity of his newspaper—but, I have failed to do so. Instead, I allowed myself to become involved in the character assassination of a decent young man. Allowing the good reputation of the 'Mesaba Ore' to be compromised and manipulated by an unnamed political faction in our community, I participated in a scheme to undermine the candidacy of Kevin Moran. For that terrible mistake, I am compelled to make amends to our readers. Over the next several days the Mesaba Ore will feature a profile on the life of Kevin Moran, his contributions to our community in the short time he has lived among us, and his views on the 'real' issues facing our district. In addition, we will attempt to provide you with a more sensitive perspective on Kevin's maligned father. It is my hope that Angela Zoretek Moran will share her insights on courage and loyalty and sacrifice with our readers.*
>
> *Having expressed my apology, I yield the family 'Adler' to my beloved father.*

> *Friends, I am reminded of a favorite passage from the Bible. 'Let those amongst us who are without sin, cast the first stone.' My son, Marc made some mistakes. My friend, Kevin made some mistakes. I*

have made some mistakes. Allow me a few lines to express my own indiscretions. From his first day in Hibbing, I became a friend and mentor of then eighteen year old, Kevin Moran. I told him about a father he had never known. I encouraged him to take a clerk job with my friend, Vic Power, and to go into the legal profession. I even gave him tips on how to be a better baseball pitcher for our local team than he had been at Duluth Denfeld, where he graduated at the top of his class.

It was Claude Atkinson who suggested that he get married to his lovely wife Angela as soon as possible and then found him a job in St. Paul where he worked with Mayor Brady and our Governor Olson before returning to our community with his son, Patrick Anthony Claude Moran. (How honored I am to have my name given to that precious boy.) And, it was me who prodded Kevin into filing for the office of state representative.

Everything I have done I would do over again. There is only one thing I would do differently, if given the chance. If I could go back to that first day of Kevin's campaign and start over again, I would walk every mile that he has walked through our Range communities. I would walk proudly at his side. I would openly encourage every person I know to vote for the best candidate for public office we have had since the days of Victor Power.

Instead, I failed my friend by staying on the sidelines and letting him do everything for himself. In doing that, I failed others who believed in him—Tony Zoretek, Steven Skorich, Angela Moran, and young 'Claude.' Kevin, it's not too late, and if you'll forgive an old man for his failures, I want to walk the last few miles of this campaign at your side. I'd be honored to do that.

THE END

PAT MCGAULEY is a former Hibbing High School teacher and worked for both the Erie and Hanna Mining Companies. He served as an historian for IRONWORLD in Chisholm before becoming the Commissioner of Iron Range Resources under Governor Al Quie. McGauley was born in Duluth, received his masters degree from the University of Minnesota, and has lived in Hibbing for the past thirty eight years. McGauley's first novel, *To Bless or To Blame,* was published in 2002.

To order Pat McGauley's books

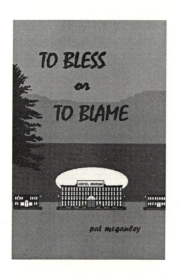

TO BLESS or TO BLAME
$22.50
(price includes Minnesota Sales Tax and shipping and handling)

A BLESSING or A CURSE
$25.00
(price includes Minnesota Sales Tax and shipping and handling)

Send check or money orders only to:
Pat McGauley Publishing
2808 Fifth Ave. West
Hibbing, MN 55746